P9-APC-199

Julia Duckworth Stephen

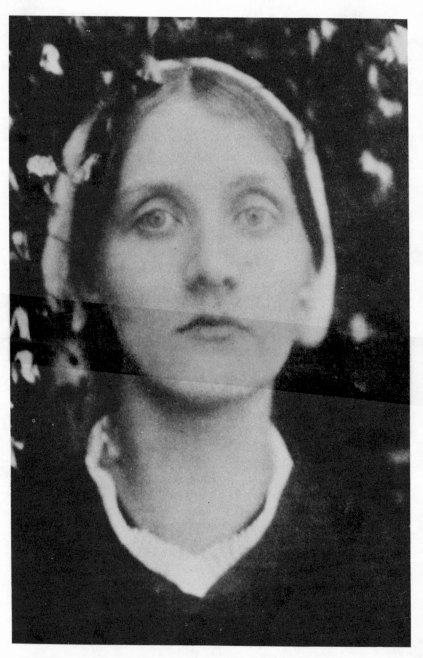

JULIA MARGARET CAMERON. *Julia Jackson.* 1867. Permission of the National Portrait Gallery, London.

Julia Duckworth Stephen

STORIES FOR CHILDREN, ESSAYS FOR ADULTS

Edited by

DIANE F. GILLESPIE

ELIZABETH STEELE

SYRACUSE UNIVERSITY PRESS

Copyright © 1987, by Diane F. Gillespie and Elizabeth Steele
     © 1987, by Washington State University: ["Agnostic Women"], "The Black Cat or the Grey Parrot,"
"Cat's Meat," ["Dinner at Baron Bruin's"], ["Domestic Arrangements of the Ordinary English Home"], "The
Duke's Coal Cellar," "Emlycaunt," "The Monkey on the Moor," "The Mysterious Voice," "Tommy and His
Neighbours," ["The Servant Question"], and "The Wandering Pigs"; six photographs of Vanessa Bell's water-
color illustrations from the Bloomsbury Collection at Washington State University Libraries, Pullman, Wash-
ington; and thirteen photographs of Leslie Stephen's drawings from the Woolf Library at Washington State
University Libraries, Pullman, Washington.

First published 1987 by SYRACUSE UNIVERSITY PRESS, Syracuse, New York 13244-5160

FIRST EDITION

All Rights Reserved

92 91 90 89 88 87   6 5 4 3 2 1

The paper used in this publication meets the minimum requirements of American National Standard for Information Sciences—Permanence of Paper for Printed Library Materials, ANSI Z39.48-1984. ∞™

Library of Congress Cataloging-in-Publication Data

Stephen, Julia Duckworth, 1846–1895.
    [Selections. 1987]
    Julia Duckworth Stephen : stories for children, essays for adults
/ edited by Diane F. Gillespie, Elizabeth Steele. — 1st ed.
       p. cm.
    Bibliography: p.
    Includes index.
    Summary: An illustrated critical edition of the stories and essays
of Julia Stephen, the mother of the novelist Virginia Woolf.
Includes biographical information, notes, and some drawings by her
husband.
    ISBN 0-8156-0217-0 (alk. paper) :
    1. Children's stories, English. [1. Short stories. 2. Essays.]
I. Gillespie, Diane F. II. Steele, Elizabeth. III. Title.
PR5473.S44A6 1987
823'.8—dc19   87-16009
                                                      CIP
                                                       AC

Manufactured in the United States of America

To Dick and Art

who believed in this book

DIANE F. GILLESPIE, Associate Professor of English at Washington State University, has just completed *The Sisters' Arts: The Writing and Painting of Virginia Woolf and Vanessa Bell*. She has published articles on Virginia Woolf, guest-edited the *Virginia Woolf Miscellany*, and presented papers on Woolf at Modern Language Association (MLA) national conventions.

ELIZABETH STEELE, Professor Emerita of English at the University of Toledo, has completed two books on the essays of Virginia Woolf—*Virginia Woolf's Literary Sources and Allusions* and *Virginia Woolf's Rediscovered Essays*—and she has also published articles on Virginia Woolf and children's literature in America. Dr. Steele has also chaired sessions on Virginia Woolf for MLA and on children's literature for the Popular Culture Association.

CONTENTS

ILLUSTRATIONS

ACKNOWLEDGMENTS

For permission to publish the stories and essays by Julia Stephen we wish to thank Professor Quentin Bell, Trekkie Parsons, Anne Synge, Angelica Garnett, Janet Henderson, and the other heirs of Nigel Henderson. We are also indebted to John Guido, Head of Manuscripts, Archives, and Special Collections, Washington State University Libraries, where the manuscripts are located.

We gratefully acknowledge those who helped us obtain and granted us permission to reproduce the visual materials in this book: John Guido, Head of Manuscripts, Archives, and Special Collections, Washington State University Libraries; Roger Sheppard, David Chandler, and Terence Pepper of the National Portrait Gallery, London; Philippe Garner of Sotheby's, London; Lola Szladits of the Berg Collection, New York Public Library; Cathy Henderson and staff, Harry Ransom Humanities Research Center at the University of Texas at Austin; Philip Vainker of the Royal Pavilion Art Gallery, Brighton; C. M. Perry of the Walker Art Gallery, National Museums and Galleries on Merseyside; and Beth Laidlaw, formerly of Davis and Langdale Company, New York, as well as Melinda Kahn Tally, currently of that gallery.

We thank Professor Thomas Faulkner, Rhonda Blair, and Hongbo Tan of the Humanities Research Center, Department of English, Washington State University, as well as Gary Allen, research assistant, for help in producing the text of the stories and essays.

For providing useful information, suggestions, and encouragement, we are grateful to Professors Alex Zwerdling, Virginia Leland, Evelyn Haller, and S. P. Rosenbaum. We especially wish to thank Professor John Bicknell for the time he graciously spent and the important details he provided. Any flaws that remain are our responsibility, not theirs. Also of assistance at various stages were Roberta Armstrong, Angelica Garnett, Barbara Britsch, Terry

Smith, Richard Shone of the *Burlington Magazine*, and Robin Vousden of the Anthony d'Offay Gallery in London. Leila Luedeking, Library Assistant in Manuscripts, Archives and Special Collections, Washington State University Libraries, has helped us with this edition from inception to completion.

EDITORIAL NOTE

THE MANUSCRIPTS OF Julia Stephen's unpublished essays and stories were discovered by Martine Stemerick in 1979 when they were in the possession of Quentin Bell. He subsequently sold them, and they are now in Manuscripts, Archives, and Special Collections, Holland Library, Washington State University, Pullman, Washington. References to the essays and stories in the scholarship of Dr. Stemerick as well as Professors Jane Marcus, Alex Zwerdling, and others, have generated both interest in Julia Stephen's unpublished work and demands that it be accessible to more readers. This edition also includes her *Dictionary of National Biography* entry on her aunt, Julia Margaret Cameron, and, because of its relationships to the essays and stories, Julia Stephen's one longer printed work, *Notes from Sick Rooms*.[1] We provide sufficient background information in our introductory essays and chronology to place Julia Stephen's published and unpublished work in its biographical, historical, and critical contexts for general as well as more informed readers. Several recent and forthcoming articles and books listed in our notes and bibliography complement ours. Slowly the details begin to fill in the outlines of Julia Stephen's portrait.

Julia Stephen's unpublished essay manuscripts are especially difficult to decipher. They must have been written rapidly, judging from the quality of the handwriting; the number of words, lines, and paragraphs crossed out; and the number of emendations between lines and in the margins. Yet these revisions also suggest that Julia Stephen wrote her essays thoughtfully although she did not edit them closely for publication. Punctuation is sometimes inconsistent or nonexistent, often with dashes of varying lengths instead of commas and periods, and paragraph divisions are frequently uncertain. A number of shorthand-like symbols and abbreviations appear. Julia even used the back page of one essay for account keeping and some light drawings of flowers. For these reasons, as we discovered, each of several readers will produce somewhat different transcriptions. The story manuscripts are much more legible, with fewer deletions, substitutions, and abbreviations, more punctuation, and clearer paragraph divisions. Probably recopied, their condition supports the speculation that they were being readied for possible publication.

Having in mind general, educated readers with a variety of backgrounds and interests, we have made the punctuation, capitalization, spelling, and paragraphing regular and consistent, as indeed they are in *Notes from Sick Rooms*. We have retained, however, "eat" as the past tense of the verb "to eat," according to Julia Stephen's custom and that of her time, but we have replaced abbreviations and symbols with the words for which they stand. We have not transcribed deletions except when they aid in understanding; in those rare instances in the essays, notes explain the procedure. Uncancelled comments written between lines or in margins are incorporated into the text. Very infrequently, we have divided an extremely long sentence or used ellipses to indicate the omission of a word that Julia Stephen herself seems to have neglected to cancel. When the handwriting remained impenetrable, we have enclosed a speculation followed by a question mark, or simply the word *illegible*, in square brackets. The titles for the essays, originally untitled, are also enclosed in brackets and derive from the topics announced in the first paragraphs. Titles for the stories are those used by Julia Stephen, except "Dinner at Baron Bruin's," whose first page is missing. We have omitted an uncompleted story along with alternate versions or portions of the stories and essays. Since it is impossible to decide, in some instances, the chronology of the alternatives or which one Julia Stephen preferred, we present in our text those where the sequence of pages is greatest.

We selected the visual reproductions for this book from a wealth of possible materials. Using some of Leslie Stephen's animal drawings seemed a natural decision. In an essay on her father, Virginia Woolf remembers how he drew "beast after beast—an art that he practised almost unconsciously as he read, so that the fly-leaves of his books swarm with owls and donkeys as if to illustrate the 'Oh, you ass!' or 'Conceited dunce,' that he was wont to scribble impatiently in the margin." Or she describes the great "dexterity with his fingers" which he used to "twist a sheet of paper beneath a pair of scissors and out would drop an elephant, a stag, or a monkey with trunks, horns, and tails delicately and exactly formed."[2] Leslie also drew animals to amuse his children "as fast as we could demand them" until they were old enough for him to read aloud to them.[3] Leslie Stephen's drawings, therefore, are visual parallels to his wife's stories. In fact, he wrote on the first manuscript page of Julia Stephen's "The Monkey on the Moor," "I had made some drawings according to a queer trick of mine & Julia thought that they would do for illustrations of some children's stories—alas!"[4] Her death is probably responsible for the verbal sigh at the end of his sentence. What drawings Leslie had in mind we do not know, but we have chosen, from the many, often droll sketches in his books, ones appropriate for particular stories.

Decades later, Vanessa Bell illustrated some of her sister's stories and one of her mother's as well. She did thirty-three drawings for "Emlycaunt" and stitched them into the appropriate places in a typescript of the story. Angelica Garnett remembers that, when she was in her teens, the Hogarth Press thought of publishing both story and illustrations but, for reasons unknown, never did.[5] We have selected several of the most striking and representative of Vanessa's pencil and ink sketches, many of which are touched up with water colors. Like most of her book designs, these have a spontaneity and freshness that make them delightful complements to her mother's least moralizing story.

We chose the other visual materials in this edition for a variety of reasons. The photographs of the young Julia by her aunt, Julia Margaret Cameron, and the one attributed to Oscar Gustav Rejlander reveal the serene beauty praised so effusively by many admirers.[6] Vanessa Bell's painting of her mother,[7] done much later from a Cameron photograph, complements these.

The Burne-Jones "Annunciation," in which Julia Stephen appears as the Virgin, traces her beauty into her second marriage. Watts perhaps suggested her as Burne-Jones' model for this painting, conceived in 1876 and completed for the Grosvenor Gallery Exhibition in the summer of 1879, a few months after Julia gave birth to Vanessa, the first child born to her and Leslie.[8] Those aware of Julia's agnosticism, remarriage, and early pregnancy can read the painting as a commentary not upon sacred but upon secular maternity. With her hand upon her "'poor dead heart,'"[9] Julia's face and gesture express incredulity at its gradual reawakening.

Other later drawings and photographs show a beauty more austere; Julia is thinner, more worn. William Rothenstein, who became acquainted with the Stephens after their marriage, drew both of them. Not the sketch of Leslie, also reproduced here, but the drawing of Julia, done in about 1890, caused controversy. Rothenstein recalls a visit to 22 Hyde Park Gate during which he "had the temerity" to draw her.

> When the drawing was done she looked at it, then handed it in silence to her daughter. The others came up and looked over her shoulder; finally it reached Leslie Stephen. The consternation was general. I was already looked on with suspicion, for in those days Whistler, whose disciple I was known to be, was anathema in Burne-Jones' and Watts' circles. The alarm must have spread upstairs; for a message came down from old Mrs. Jackson, . . . and

the drawing was taken up for her to see. A confirmed invalid, Mrs. Jackson had not for long come down from her room, but on seeing the drawing she rang for a stick, like the Baron calling for his boots, and prepared to give me a piece of her mind. I can still hear the thump of her stick as she came heavily downstairs, and the piece of her mind which she gave me was a solid one. I went away discomfited, well punished for my rashness.[10]

Virginia Woolf punished him more gently in 1929 when she wrote to him about the drawing: "I admit that I think, perhaps with the partiality of a daughter, that my mother was more beautiful than you show her."[11]

Nevertheless, Rothenstein's drawing of Julia with her bent back and tired eyes reinforces Woolf's comments on her mother's exhausting efforts on behalf of others. The drawing resembles several photographs of the older Julia included in a small album belonging to Stella Duckworth, Julia's daughter from her first marriage.[12] Virginia's age in the often reproduced snapshot of her watching her parents reading indicates that it was taken in the early 1890s, about the same time that Rothenstein drew Julia. The three photographs we selected from the album, like some of the earlier photographs, indicate Julia's life-long commitment both to reading everything from poetry and fiction to essays in periodicals, and to writing not only letters but also stories and essays of her own. In a life full of caring for her large family and nursing others, however, creative or reflective moments like these were rare and, captured on film, are especially significant.

CHRONOLOGY

1832	Nov. 28	Leslie Stephen is born.
1833	May 19	Herbert Duckworth is born.
1846	Feb. 7	Julia Prinsep Jackson is born in India, third daughter of John Jackson, a medical doctor at Calcutta, and Maria Pattle Jackson.
1848		Maria Jackson returns to England with Julia. The other children, Adeline and Mary, are already there with Maria Jackson's sister, Sarah, and her husband, Henry Thoby Prinsep. From 1851 to 1855 Maria and her daughters live in various places including Well Walk, Hampstead.
1854		Leslie Stephen completes his mathematics degree at Trinity Hall College, Cambridge.
1855		Dr. Jackson rejoins his family.
		Herbert Duckworth completes his degree at Trinity College, Cambridge, and joins the Northern Circuit as a barrister.
		Leslie Stephen is ordained a deacon in order to obtain a fellowship and tutorship at Trinity Hall College, Cambridge.
1855–66		The Jacksons live at Brent Lodge, Hendon. During these and later years, they visit the Prinseps at Little Holland House, a gathering place for well-known politicians, writers, and visual artists. Over the years,

		Julia is painted or drawn by Burne-Jones, Watts, and others and photographed frequently by her aunt, Julia Margaret Cameron, another of Maria Jackson's sisters, who lived at Putney and then at Freshwater.
1856		Mrs. Jackson begins to suffer from rheumatism.
1862		Leslie Stephen resigns his tutorship at Cambridge because of loss of faith.

Both of Julia's sisters now being married (Adeline to Henry Halford Vaughan in 1856 and Mary to Herbert Fisher in 1862), she becomes her mother's chief nurse and companion on trips in search of better health.

While visiting her sister, Mary Fisher, and her new husband in Venice, Julia meets her brother-in-law's friend, Herbert Duckworth, who is vacationing; they meet elsewhere, including Switzerland, on their travels.

1863		Leslie Stephen visits the United States, where he and James Russell Lowell become friends.
	Dec.	James Fitzjames Stephen's "Women and Scepticism" appears in *Fraser's Magazine*.
1864		Leslie Stephen comes to London to be a writer; he lives with his mother and sister at 19 Porchester Square. Through mutual friends he meets Anne Isabella (Anny) and Harriet Marian (Minny) Thackeray, the daughters of William Makepeace Thackeray.

Julia Jackson rejects offers of marriage around this time from Holman Hunt, the painter, and Thomas Woolner, the sculptor.

1866		The Jacksons move to Saxonbury, a country house in Frant, near Tunbridge Wells.

Leslie Stephen's first memory of Julia, standing on the green at a picnic, wearing a white dress and a hat with blue flowers.

	Dec. 4	Leslie Stephen and Minny Thackeray are engaged.
1867	Feb. 1	Julia Jackson and Herbert Duckworth are engaged.
	May 4	Julia Jackson and Herbert Duckworth are married. Julia is twenty-one.

	June 19	Leslie Stephen and Minny Thackeray are married. They live with Anny at 16 Onslow Gardens.
1868	March 5	George Herbert Duckworth is born.
1869	May 30	Stella Duckworth is born.
1870	Sept. 19	On a visit to the Vaughans, Herbert Duckworth dies of an undiagnosed abscess which bursts as he reaches up to pick a fig.
	Oct. 29	Gerald de l'Etang Duckworth is born six weeks after his father's death; his mother is twenty-four.

Julia Duckworth subsequently spends a considerable amount of time at Freshwater, the Camerons' home on the Isle of Wight, where her aunt often photographs her. She devotes herself to the care of her children and of others in need. She loses her faith and sympathizes with the liberal views on religion that Leslie Stephen is expressing in his articles.

	Dec. 7	Laura Makepeace Stephen is born.
1871	March	Leslie Stephen becomes editor of *Cornhill Magazine*.
1873		Leslie Stephen's *Essays on Freethinking and Plainspeaking* is published.

Sometime after her own daughter dies, Julia Margaret Cameron tries to persuade Julia to marry the widower Charles Norman. She resists without damaging her friendship with him.

1874		Among their many publications during these years are Leslie Stephen's "Housekeeping" and Anne Thackeray Ritchie's "Maids-of-all-Work and Blue Books" in *Cornhill Magazine*.
1875	Nov. 28	On Leslie Stephen's forty-third birthday, Minny Stephen dies after a convulsion the night before. Julia visits the Stephens just a few hours before Minny's seizure. She subsequently helps Leslie and Anny to move into 11 Hyde Park Gate South (later 20 Hyde Park Gate) near the house into which she had recently moved (13 Hyde Park Gate South), then spends the summer with Mary and Herbert Fisher.

1876		Leslie Stephen's *History of English Thought in the Eighteenth Century* and "An Agnostic's Apology" are published.
1877	Jan.	Leslie Stephen discovers he is in love with Julia. He declares his love on February 5 and they agree to be close friends but, because she does not want to remarry, nothing closer. They correspond constantly. Slowly Julia changes her mind about marriage.
	Jan.	Anny Thackeray becomes engaged to Richmond Ritchie against practically everyone's wishes, including Leslie Stephen's. Julia, however, intervenes in the crisis and defends Anny's decision to Leslie.
	Aug. 2	Anny Thackeray and Richmond Ritchie are married.
1878	Jan. 5	Julia Jackson Duckworth and Leslie Stephen are engaged. Julia is nurse to her dying uncle, Henry Thoby Prinsep, until her marriage.
	March 26	Julia Jackson Duckworth and Leslie Stephen are married. Leslie is forty-six; Julia is thirty-two. After several weeks at Eastnor Castle near Ledbury, they settle at 13 Hyde Park Gate South, Julia's house (which becomes 22 Hyde Park Gate in 1884), with their children: George, Stella, Gerald, and Laura.
1879		Leslie, along with F. Pollock, begins to lead a group of "Sunday Tramps" on walks. Julia's "at homes" are on alternate Sundays.
		Burne-Jones paints Julia Stephen, then in early pregnancy, as the Virgin in his "Annunciation."
		Mrs. Clifford whose husband, W. K. Clifford, had just died, becomes a close friend of Julia's.
		Caroline E. Stephen's "Mistress and Servants" appears in *Nineteenth Century.*
	May 30	Vanessa Stephen is born.
	Oct. 4	Julia writes to the *Pall Mall Gazette* about encroachments of the temperance movement at St. George's Workhouse.
	Nov./Dec.	Julia nurses her mother at Eastnor Castle, where she was visiting when taken ill with rheumatic fever.
1880	July	James Russell Lowell arrives in London as U.S. Am-

| | | bassador to the Court of St. James. A friend of Leslie's since the 1860s, he now becomes a close friend and admirer of Julia as well. |

Sept. 8   Julian Thoby Stephen is born.

Julia Stephen writes "Agnostic Women" in response to an essay by Mrs. Lathbury in *Nineteenth Century*. Between 1880 and 1884, Julia Stephen writes her children's stories.

1881   April   Julia goes to Upton Castle to nurse her sister Adeline Vaughan, who dies on April 14.

      Sept.   Leslie Stephen leases Talland House, St. Ives; from 1882–94 the family spends summers there, often with visitors.

1882   Jan. 25   Adeline Virginia Stephen is born. Lowell is her godfather.

      Nov.   Leslie Stephen begins editing the *Dictionary of National Biography*. Julia Stephen contributes the entry on her aunt, Julia Margaret Cameron.

Leslie and Julia Stephen are increasingly concerned about Laura's "backwardness."

1883   Oct. 27   Adrian Leslie Stephen is born.

Julia Stephen's *Notes from Sick Rooms* is published in London by Smith, Elder, & Co.

1884   Jan.   Julia nurses her friend, Mrs. Lushington, in her final illness. After her death, Julia befriends the Lushington daughters.

1885   Julia and Leslie Stephen negotiate unsuccessfully with Routledge about publishing her children's stories with his drawings.

Henry Vaughan dies and Julia increasingly befriends her late sister Adeline's children.

Julia successfully matchmakes between her niece, Florence Fisher, and F. W. Maitland.

1887   March 31   Dr. Jackson, Julia's father, dies. Julia, who had nursed her father, now nurses her invalid mother at Brighton and, from this time on, is continually concerned with her health and nursing. Mrs. Jackson stays frequently with the Stephens until her death.

1888–89		Leslie Stephen has a breakdown, after three years of headaches and sleepless nights, from his work on the *DNB*.
1889	June	The signatures of "Mrs. Leslie Stephen" and approximately one hundred other women support "An Appeal Against Female Suffrage" published in *Nineteenth Century*.
	June 13	George Meredith writes to Julia reproaching her for "irrational obstructiveness."
	August	Twenty-seven pages of additional signatures appear in *Nineteenth Century*.
1891		Laura Stephen is placed in an asylum after having been cared for in a separate part of the house as well as in a "Home."
		Virginia and Vanessa Stephen record the life of their large household in the *Hyde Park Gate News*.
		Leslie Stephen finally gives up his grueling work on the *DNB*.
	Aug. 12	James Russell Lowell dies.
1892	April 2	Maria Jackson, Julia's mother, dies. Julia and Leslie stay for about a month at Chenies so Julia can recover from her loss.
1893		At Julia's request, Leslie Stephen writes a letter to the *Times* proposing a tribute to James Russell Lowell.
	June 7	Leslie Stephen gives the dedicatory speech for a memorial window erected in the Westminster Chapter House in honor of Lowell.
		Julia Stephen writes "The Servant Question" and "Domestic Arrangements of an Ordinary English Home" in response to articles in *Nineteenth Century*.
		Leslie Stephen's *An Agnostic's Apology and Other Essays* appears.
1895	May 5	Julia Stephen dies of rheumatic fever after several bouts with influenza. She is forty-nine.
		Leslie Stephen begins his "Mausoleum Book."
1903		Leslie Stephen completes his "Mausoleum Book."
1904	Feb. 22	Leslie Stephen dies of cancer at seventy-two.

Julia Duckworth Stephen

The Elusive Julia Stephen

DIANE F. GILLESPIE

I N *A Room of One's Own,* Virginia Woolf expresses her frustration about the lack of information on women's education, accomplishments, living conditions, and maternity prior to the eighteenth century. About the two centuries preceding ours, certainly we know more facts. Still, it is difficult to form them into coherent pictures. Is there a portrait, for instance, of the "Victorian woman"? Her legal and political status is clear, but when we glance at the individual faces and lives of wives and mothers of several different social classes, not to mention unmarried dependents, actresses and novelists, nurses and governesses, prostitutes, domestic servants, factory workers, and seamstresses, we see infinite variety.[1] A look at any one of these women reveals further complexities.

We know some facts about Julia Stephen's life, largely because of her family. She was the second wife of a prominent Victorian intellectual, Leslie Stephen, and the mother of Virginia Woolf, the well-known novelist. Another daughter was the increasingly respected painter, Vanessa Bell. Yet, as Woolf's Lily Briscoe says in *To the Lighthouse* of Mrs. Ramsay, for whom Julia Stephen provided the inspiration, "One wanted fifty pairs of eyes to see with. . . . Fifty pairs of eyes were not enough to get round that one woman with."[2]

Julia Duckworth Stephen: Stories for Children, Essays for Adults presents "that one woman" from several, but by no means all possible vantage points. Compared to her mother, Virginia Woolf is accessible in all her complexity because we have the published diaries, letters, essays, and memoirs in addition to her short stories and novels. In contrast, Julia Stephen published little dur-

1

ing her forty-nine years: an entry on her aunt, Julia Margaret Cameron, in
the *Dictionary of National Biography* under her husband's editorship and *Notes
from Sick Rooms* (1883), both reprinted here.[3] While she wrote stories and drafted
lengthy responses to articles she read in various periodicals, these have never
before been printed.[4] Nor have her letters although Leslie Stephen quotes
some in *The Mausoleum Book*, his posthumous, idealized tribute to her.[5] These
reminiscences provide essential facts, but often expose his character more than
they reveal his wife's. Virginia Woolf also tried to recreate her mother, once
in a short biography of her sister, Vanessa, written in 1907–8; once in a memoir written near the end of her life (1939–40); and once, fictionalized as Mrs.
Ramsay, in *To the Lighthouse* (1927).[6] "Until I was in the forties . . . ," she wrote
in the memoir, "the presence of my mother obsessed me. I could hear her
voice, see her, imagine what she would do or say as I went about my day's
doings" (MOB 80). Writing *To the Lighthouse*, however, freed her from the ob-
session: "I no longer hear her voice; I do not see her" (MOB 81; D III 208).
We can see her, however, in surviving family snapshots, Julia Cameron's more
professional photographs, and paintings and drawings for which Julia Stephen
served as model (MB 31–32). We also know some of the books that once belonged to her mother because Virginia Woolf inherited them from her father.[7]
Beyond these, we have only a few references in the letters and memoirs of
contemporaries who knew her and the attempts of biographers and critics
to outline her life and assess her character, mainly as it influenced the lives
of more famous family members.[8]

When Virginia Woolf notes in *A Room of One's Own* that "we think
back through our mothers if we are women," she is talking about published
women writers.[9] Yet, as the biographical and critical commentaries increasingly observe, Woolf thought back through her biological mother too.[10] Leslie Stephen, according to many accounts, was the parent with whom Virginia
identified.[11] Vanessa recalls a childhood discussion in which she said her
mother was her favorite parent while Virginia "went on to explain why she,
on the whole, preferred my father."[12] While Julia Stephen died when Virginia
was thirteen, Leslie Stephen lived nine years more. He was the writer in the
family and the one who encouraged Virginia to write. Yet, although he wrote
about it, Leslie did not write fiction. Like her husband, Julia wrote essays,
but more frequently she told her children stories. How many mothers not
only invent their own tales as Julia did but also write them down, then re-
work them? The influence of such a parent is difficult to document and difficult to recognize even for the gifted child involved. Woolf remembers her
mother "writing at her table in London" (MOB 84), and she has Mrs. Ramsay, who has wrapped her shawl around a boar's skull, help her frightened
child to see in it "a mountain, a bird's nest, a garden, . . . and little antelopes"

(TTL 172). But Woolf does not have Mrs. Ramsay tell James one of her own stories, although in an earlier draft she does put the children to sleep with a tale about bears;[13] instead she reads "The Fisherman and His Wife," one of Grimm's. "For my wife, good Ilsabil," complains the fisherman, "Wills not as I'd have her will" (TTL 87). Grimm's story, both an ironic and an appropriate commentary on the Ramsays' marriage, suits Woolf's artistic purposes better.

Whether we look at the facts of her life, the memoirs and letters of others, or her own published and unpublished writing, it is difficult to see Julia Stephen apart from her relationships with other people. She amuses and teaches them, creates environments conducive to mental and physical health and labor, and intervenes on behalf of those less able to defend themselves. Virginia Woolf remembers her mother at forty as "central," as someone who "was keeping what I call in my shorthand the panoply of life—that which we all lived in common—in being." She had seven lively children ranging in age from infancy to maturity; another, a stepchild, who was "an idiot"; an "elder, difficult, exacting, dependent" husband; and everyone's friends visiting the houses in London or in St. Ives where they spent their summers after 1881. Virginia recreates Julia as surrounded, continually interrupted, incapable of focusing her attention on any individual for more than a moment, yet concerned with them all (MOB 83; L VI 32). Even when she wrote her essays and stories, she did so to pose solutions to problems, to point morals to audiences, young and old, who needed her instruction. No wonder Virginia tried to imagine in *To the Lighthouse* what Mrs. Ramsay was like when she could sink into herself, free from the demands so constantly made upon her by children, husband, guests, the poor, and the ill:

> For now she need not think about anybody. She could be herself, by herself. And that was what now she often felt the need of—to think; well, not even to think. To be silent; to be alone. All the being and the doing, expansive, glittering, vocal, evaporated; and one shrunk, with a sense of solemnity, to being oneself, a wedge-shaped core of darkness, something invisible to others (TTL 95).

How did Julia Stephen assume this centrality in the lives of so many? More to the point, out of what context did her stories and essays emerge? We know that her father was John Jackson, a doctor with few distinguishing characteristics other than his successful practice at Calcutta. Her mother, Maria

1. OSCAR GUSTAV REJLANDER (attributed to). *Julia Jackson.* c. 1860. Permission of Sotheby's, London.

Jackson, was one of seven Pattle sisters, many of them remarkable for their beauty and talent. Mrs. Jackson and her three children, Adeline, Mary, and Julia, returned from India in the late 1840s; Dr. Jackson rejoined them in 1855. The family frequently visited the homes of Maria's sisters, especially Little Holland House where Sarah and her husband, Henry Thoby Prinsep, lived, as well as Putney and, after 1860, Freshwater where Julia Margaret and Charles Hay Cameron established themselves. Well-known statesmen, writers, painters, and sculptors, among them Gladstone and Disraeli; Tennyson and Thackeray; G. F. Watts, Holman Hunt, and Edward Burne-Jones, frequented these houses. In this environment Julia grew up, loved and admired, proposed to, painted, and photographed. Leslie Stephen first met and admired her at Little Holland House.

In *To the Lighthouse* Woolf has Mr. Ramsay exaggerate his wife's "ignorance, her simplicity, for he liked to think that she was not clever, not booklearned at all" (TTL 182). Julia Stephen probably was educated by governesses who taught her at least French and music. Yet Virginia Woolf remembers her mother's "keen" although untrained mind and her "strong" instinct where books were concerned. Julia's favorites were De Quincey's *Opium Eater* and the novels of Walter Scott (MOB 32, 86). Her mother, Mrs. Jackson, did not reinforce "the aesthetic and intellectual interests of Little Holland House," however. Reading the many letters she wrote to Julia, Quentin Bell says,

> one feels as though one were struggling through a wilderness of treacle. Mrs. Jackson was as good as gold; but there is not one original thought, very little commonsense and not the slightest dexterity in the use of language in all her hundreds and hundreds of letters.
>
> Mrs. Jackson's letters display the dull side of the Pattles; their silliness, their gush, their cloying sweetness, their continual demands for affection and with it a mawkish vein, a kind of tender gloating over disease and death.[14]

Youngest of the three daughters, Julia was closest to her mother. When her sisters, Adeline and Mary, became the wives of Henry Vaughan and Herbert Fisher, Julia accompanied Mrs. Jackson on trips and served as both companion and nurse to a woman suffering ailments ranging from rheumatism to headaches. On a trip to the Continent in 1862 in search of health, Mrs. Jackson and Julia visited Mary Fisher in Venice. There Julia met her brother-in-law's friend, a young barrister with a degree from Trinity College, Cambridge. Although Julia presumably had offers of marriage from Holman Hunt, the painter, and Thomas Woolner, the sculptor, she chose Herbert Duckworth. And "the atmosphere of her home . . . cast over the figure of her bridegroom all the golden enchantments of Tennysonian sentiment," Virginia Woolf says. She wonders that her mother did not see Duckworth as "her inferior in all ways" (MOB 32). To Woolf, Julia Stephen's first husband represented "the pink of propriety" as Leslie Stephen, her father, represented "the pink of intellectuality." Yet she admired her mother's complexity which could encompass two such different spouses (MOB 85). Duckworth was, according to Leslie Stephen, "a thorough gentleman in the best sense of the phrase":

2. Unknown photographer. *Julia Jackson and her mother, Maria Jackson* (formerly described as Julia and her aunt, Julia Margaret Cameron, and recently retitled by the National Portrait Gallery). c. 1860. Permission of the National Portrait Gallery, London.

A man of honour, of fair accomplishments and interest in books, he was fitted to take his place in any society, without being the least of a dandy or a fop: simple, straightforward and manly. But, besides this, he was, as everyone could perceive who knew him, a singularly modest and sweet-tempered man (MB 35).

Married in 1867 when Julia was twenty-one, the Duckworths seem to have been virtually inseparable and very happy. But not for long. They had two children and a third on the way when Herbert Duckworth died unexpectedly in 1870 of an undiagnosed abscess which suddenly burst. Julia, bereft, gave birth to her third child six weeks later and subsequently devoted herself to her children and any others who needed her. Having lost her faith as a result of her experience, she was receptive to the liberal religious views Leslie Stephen was expressing in print although she was shy of him. "How could any Lord have made this world?" Woolf has Mrs. Ramsay ask. "With her mind she had always seized the fact that there is no reason, order, justice. . . . There was no treachery too base for the world to commit; she knew that. No happiness lasted; she knew that" (TTL 98). At twenty-four, Leslie Stephen reports, Julia described her life as

> "a shipwreck, and I knew that I had to live on and on, and the only thing to be done was to be as cheerful as I could and do as much as I could and think as little. And so I got deadened. I had all along felt that if it had been possible for me to be myself, it would have been better for me individually; and that I could have got more real life out of the wreck if I had broken down more. But there was Baby to be thought of and everyone around me urging me to keep up, and I could never be alone which sometimes was such torture. So that by degrees I felt that though I was more cheerful and content than most people, I was more changed" (MB 40).

Anne Thackeray was a good friend to Julia during this time. She "'helped me into some sort of shelter and made things more real to me again,'" Julia said. Anny tried to keep Julia interested in events and people. Julia also helped Anny, a writer like her more famous father, keep her manuscripts in order; sometimes she did copy work for her friend (MB 42). It is not surprising, therefore, to find among Virginia Woolf's books the volume of *Five Old Friends and a Young Prince* (1876) that Anny inscribed and gave to Julia. A conversation about the reasons why the old fairy tales remain popular, as well as modern versions of five of them, Anny's book would have appealed to a woman with small children to instruct and entertain, especially one who would soon begin to devise her own stories.[15] Virginia also inherited Anne Thackeray's *Miss Angel*, a book about the painter Angelica Kauffmann's life, dedicated "To Mrs. Herbert Duckworth." The dedication continues, "Will you take what is mine to dedicate to you in this little book, of which so much is yours already." Anny is imprecise, but here she suggests collaboration with Julia that went beyond mere arranging and copying.[16]

This friendship also kept Julia involved with Anny's sister, Minny, and with Leslie Stephen, whom Minny had married in 1867. Julia visited her, in fact, shortly before her fatal convulsion in 1876, then helped the widower and Anny to move into a house near hers. The domestic alliance between Leslie and Anny was unsatisfactory. As Winifred Gérin puts it, Anny "was crushed by his pedantic intellect, and he was irritated by her 'ignorance'" although he credited her with "'real genius and originality.'"[17] Two years later, Julia had to intervene to defend her friend's decision to marry Richmond Ritchie when everyone, including Leslie, opposed it on the grounds that Ritchie was sixteen years younger, still a year away from his college degree, and without sufficient funds. With Julia's help, Anny and Richmond were married in 1877. In attendance, a witness reported, were "'poor Leslie, who looked very deplorable, and Julia Duckworth, who wore the thickest black velvet dress and heavy black veil, and gave the gloomiest, most tragic aspect to her side of the chancel.'"[18]

Julia helped Anny bear the loss of her sister, Minny Stephen, as Anny had helped Julia recover from Herbert Duckworth's death. Her sympathy began to extend to Leslie. Early in 1877 he declared his love for her, but, because she did not think she could ever marry again, they agreed to remain the closest of friends. Corresponding constantly whenever apart, however, they examined their situation. Julia's refusals to marry were, somewhat morbidly, encouraging:

> "If I could be quite close to you, and feel you holding me, I should be so content to die. Knowing what I am, it is no temptation to me to marry you from the thought that I should make your life happier or brighter—I don't think I should. So if you want an answer, I can only say that as I am now it would be wrong for me to marry. . . . All this sounds cold and horrid—but you know I do love you with my whole heart—only it seems such a poor dead heart" (MB 52–53).

Finally, after they had discussed the matter once more without seeming to have made any progress, Julia suddenly agreed to the marriage: "'I will be your wife and will do my best to be a good wife to you,'" she said as he was leaving

3. VANESSA BELL. *The Artist's Mother* (from a photograph by Julia Margaret Cameron). Courtesy of the Royal Pavilion Art Gallery, Brighton.

(MB 57). Mrs. Cameron, Julia's aunt, and Mrs. Jackson had concluded by that time that Leslie was not devoid of emotion. Anny Thackeray was pleased with the engagement, and the Stephens and Ritchies maintained cordial relationships after Julia's and Leslie's marriage in 1878.

Anne Thackeray was not the only one who tried to comfort Julia during the eight years between Herbert Duckworth's death and her remarriage to Leslie Stephen, although she was probably the most successful. Julia's parents, especially her mother, seem to have tried, in part by giving her books expressing conventional sentiments about woman's role and religion. "Nothing was more striking about Mrs. Jackson," Leslie Stephen said, "than the high strain of moral feeling which she transmitted to Julia" (MB 71) although she could not revive her daughter's religious faith. Mrs. Jackson gave Julia Sir Aubrey DeVere's *St. Thomas of Canterbury* (1876), for example, after Dr. Jackson had given her *Mary Tudor* (1875) by the same author. The latter volume contains not only a historical drama, but also sentimental sonnets like "The Family Picture" depicting a mother smiling down upon her "rosy boy," "timid girl," and "chubby urchin" while their thankful owner looks on: "And he, the happy man! to whom belong / These treasures."[19] Isa Blagdon's *Poems*, inscribed "J. D. from Mother April 1874," has an introduction by Alfred Austin that describes the poet as a Christian "in her steady and cheerful exercise of the virtues it especially inculcates. Inexhaustible patience and resignation to her own sufferings, inexhaustible sympathy and help for the afflictions of others, boundless toleration for their weaknesses and boundless forgiveness for their sins."[20] The poems are generally sentimental, conventional in both thought and style. In "To Georges [*sic*] Sand: On Her Interview with Elizabeth Barrett Browning," for instance, an angel of womanliness, Browning, redeems her tormented, deviant colleague:

> Thy genius to her stainless genius knelt,
> And with pathetic reverential awe
> The holiness of womanhood was felt
> Deep in thy soul; to thee, she was a shrine
> Of sanctuary—inexorable law—
> The earthly human won to God's divine![21]

Three months after her marriage to Leslie Stephen, Julia received from her mother a book by Coventry Patmore: *Amelia, Tamerton Church-Tower, etc. with Prefatory Study on English Metrical Law* (1878). In it are poems like "The Girl of All Periods: An Idyll" which begins, "'And even our women,' lastly grumbles Ben, / 'Leaving their nature, dress and talk like men!'" and ends with Ben perceiving, like the narrator of the poem, that the New Woman's behavior is just another ploy to catch a man:

> This aping man is crafty Love's devising
> To make the woman's difference more surprising;
> And, as for feeling wroth at such rebelling,
> Who'd scold the child for now and then repelling
> Lures with "I won't!" or for a moment's straying
> In its sure growth towards more full obeying?[22]

Julia already owned the fourth edition of *The Angel in the House* (1866) inscribed to "Julia Jackson with the kind regard of Coventry Patmore." She received his books, from his hands and from her mother's, because Patmore and Mrs. Jackson were good friends. Upon her death, as Frederick Maitland reports, Patmore said, "'To me she was always as tender as to a real son.'"[23]

Leslie Stephen, however, did not share his mother-in-law's regard for Patmore. "I never liked him, nor he, me," he noted in *The Mausoleum Book* (MB 102). Judging from a letter of apology he wrote to Mrs. Jackson in 1877, he must have told her so. He said he was sorry for offending her, for speaking "rather roughly" and sarcastically, but he did not withdraw his criticisms:

> I do think C. P. effeminate[.] Every man ought to be feminine, i.e., to have quick and delicate feelings; but no man ought to be effeminate, i.e., to let his feelings get the better of his intellect and produce a cowardly view of life and the world. . . .
>
> Thus the sentiment of the poem about his boy seems to me still effeminate as well as commonplace. It is one of those pretty, proper little reflections that one meets in tracts and hears in sermons, and which one knows to be hollow. It won't do out of church. A poet ought to live in the open air, not inside a chapel with incense and painted windows.[24]

When Virginia Woolf spoke in "Professions for Women" of the need for the woman writer to kill "the angel in the house" who would have her reinforce men's views of themselves and the world, she had her mother's volumes of Patmore at hand. Perhaps she also had heard of her grandmother's and father's conflicting reactions to his sentiments.[25]

What Julia's specific responses to all of these books were, we do not know. Certainly she held many traditional notions about woman's role and education, an issue I will discuss further in my introduction to her essays. Leslie, his reservations about Patmore notwithstanding, saw her as the angel in his house, although "saint" is the word he preferred. The picture he paints of her in The Mausoleum Book is as sentimental or, as Alan Bell puts it, "emotionally self-indulgent" (MB x), as any in the books Mrs. Jackson gave her daughter. Courting Julia, Leslie said that he felt "'reverence as well as love. . . . You see I have not got any Saints and you must not be angry if I put you in the place where my Saints ought to be'" (MB 53). After her death, he repeated, "She is still my saint" (MB 54). James Russell Lowell, Leslie's friend who also became one of Julia's, canonizes her more playfully in a letter:

> The Abbey looks across over the red roofs into my window and seems to say, "Why are you not at church today?" and I answer fallaciously, "Because like yourself I have gone out of the business, and, moreover, I am writing to a certain saint of my own canonization who looks amazingly as your St. Hilda must have looked (as I fancy her), and the thought of whom has both prayers and praise in it."[26]

Although they exchanged gifts and affectionate letters, and although Lowell thought that Virginia, his god-daughter, would wonder someday "how her mother ever could have loved so dull a fellow,"[27] he was twenty-seven years Julia's senior, and she was the only one of three attractive and devoted female friends he had in England with whom London gossip did not link him.[28] She was "Her Super Excellency," and to her "his Ex-Excellency" inscribed his volume of essays, My Study Windows (1882).[29]

Julia Stephen's beauty no doubt played a part in her canonization by some of the men in her life. "Did I ever tell you how handsome—how beautiful—a person Leslie Stephen's new wife is?" Henry James wrote to a friend in 1879. "She has, literally, a beautiful face and head—but this is, I think, to the outside world, her main interest."[30] To his sister he marvelled that such a "charming woman" had "consented to become, matrimonially, the receptacle" of Leslie Stephen's "ineffable and impossible taciturnity and dreariness."[31] Leslie thought that his wife's "exquisite delicacy of line and form" was captured best in Julia Margaret Cameron's photographs (MB 32). Still, he goes on, her physical beauty was in "perfect balance" with her "beauty of soul, refinement, nobility and tenderness of character." This ideal harmony made Stephen think of Greek sculpture. To him Julia was "the complete reconciliation and fulfillment of all conditions of feminine beauty" (MB 32–33).

Lowell, in a poem to his god-daughter, writes that he wishes Virginia

4. JULIA MARGARET CAMERON. *Julia Jackson as Stella.* 1867. Permission of the Gernsheim Collection, Harry Ransom Humanities Research Center, University of Texas at Austin.

> Her mother's beauty—nay, but two
> So fair at once would never do.
> Then let her but the half possess,
> Troy was besieged ten years for less.[32]

Nevertheless, Virginia Woolf questions whether or not, as a child, she was even conscious of her mother's appearance as a quality separate from her maternal "calling," although she is sure she knew and was proud of her mother's reputation as a "very beautiful woman" (MOB 82). While her appearance is an important part of the characterization of Mrs. Ramsay in *To the Lighthouse*, William Bankes thinks that "'she's no more aware of her beauty than a child'" and that always

> there was something incongruous to be worked into the harmony of her face. She clapped a deer-stalker's hat on her head; she ran across the lawn in galoshes to snatch a child from mischief. So that if it was her beauty merely that one thought of, one must remember the quivering thing, the living thing . . . and work it into a picture; or if one thought of her simply as a woman, one must endow her with some freak of idiosyncrasy—she did not like admiration—or suppose some latent desire to doff her royalty of form as if her beauty bored her and all that men say of beauty, and she wanted only to be like other people, insignificant. He did not know (TTL 47–48).

William Bankes is wrong, however; Mrs. Ramsay is aware of her effect on others. She knows that she carries "the torch of her beauty . . . erect into any room that she enters; and after all, veil it as she might, and shrink from the monotony of bearing that it imposed on her, her beauty was apparent. She had been admired. She had been loved" (TTL 64–65). To Mr. Ramsay she is "astonishingly beautiful" (TTL 182), and, when she knows that he is thinking as much, "she felt herself very beautiful" (TTL 185).

If Leslie Stephen, James Russell Lowell, Henry James, and some of the characters in *To the Lighthouse* put Julia Stephen on a pedestal, George Meredith did not, at least not consistently. He did write to Leslie Stephen that he never "'reverenced a woman more'" (MB 74). He also wrote to Vanessa after Leslie's death, "He was the one man in my knowledge worthy of being mated with your mother. I could not say more of any man's nobility."[33] Yet while she lived, Julia received several reproaches from Meredith for what he considered her conventional notions about women. When he sent her a copy of *Diana of the Crossways* (1885) he wrote in it, "An Emma might this Julia have been, / To love, at least forgive, the heroine."[34] Clearly Meredith anticipated Julia's initial discomfort with his "new woman" and her greater approval of Emma, Diana's more traditional friend. While working on the novel, in fact, he wrote to Julia on August 23, 1884, that he would like to be with them at St. Ives to witness their four-year-old son, Thoby's,

> first recreancy!—before his father has taught him that he must act the superior, and you have schooled the little maids to accept the fact supposed: —for it is largely (I expect you to dissent) a matter of training. Courage is proper to women, if it is trained; as with the infant man. —My *Diana* still holds me; only by the last chapter; but the coupling of such a woman and her man is a delicate business. She is no puppet-pliancy.[35]

The chapter is entitled "Nuptial Chapter; and of how a barely willing woman was led to bloom with the nuptial sentiment." From calling marriage "slavery" and "banality," Diana begins to see it as both "sovereignty" and "submission" to a man at once friend, lover, and servant.

In 1889 Julia Stephen signed "An Appeal Against Female Suffrage," published in *Nineteenth Century*, because she thought, as Virginia Woolf recalled it, "that women had enough to do in their own homes without a vote" (MOB 120). George Meredith wrote to her that Leslie Stephen must have "a double," a "False Leslie" whose wife endorsed such a statement:

> For it would be to accuse you of the fatuousness of a Liberal Unionist, to charge the true Mrs. Leslie with this irrational obstructiveness. The case with women resembles that of the Irish. We have played fast and loose with them, until now they are encouraged to demand what they know not how to use, but have a just right to claim.

Had they had access to the professions and "learnt the business of the world," then they could help to govern, Meredith says. But, he adds, they have had no such opportunities. They will get the vote, and what follows will be "a horrible time. But better that than present sights." Meredith then relates a report that Julia has said, "'Enough for me that my Leslie should vote, should think.' Beautiful posture of the Britannic wife!" Meredith exclaims. "But the world is a moving one and will pass her by."[36]

Mrs. Ramsay's daughters suspect as much in *To the Lighthouse*. Mrs. Ramsay feels that she has

> the whole of the other sex under her protection; for reasons she could not explain, for their chivalry and valour, for the fact that they negotiated treaties,

5. JULIA MARGARET CAMERON. *Julia Jackson.* 1867. Permission of the Gernsheim Collection, Harry Ransom Humanities Research Center, University of Texas at Austin.

ruled India, controlled finance; finally for an attitude towards herself which no woman could fail to feel or to find agreeable, something trustful, child-like, reverential; which an old woman could take from a young man with-out loss of dignity, and woe betide the girl—pray Heaven it was none of her daughters!—who did not feel the worth of it, and all that it implied to the marrow of her bones! (TTL 13)

But Mrs. Ramsay's daughters do have "infidel ideas . . . of a life different from hers . . . not always taking care of some man or other." They silently question "deference and chivalry" even while they admire their mother's "strange se-verity, her extreme courtesy" (TTL 14). As Susan Squier observes, Virginia's early "tea-table training" limited her but also taught her indirect ways to criti-cize society sometimes more effective than direct attacks.[37]

When the Stephens married, they moved into Julia's house, renumbered 22 Hyde Park Gate in 1884. Quentin Bell imagines what it was like:

The decorations would have been sober—dark crimson curtains relieved by dusky bronze, black shiny furniture picked out with a narrow gold line. In a draped alcove a marble bust by Marochetti, Watts quoting from Titian in a heavy gilt and stucco frame, a large photograph of the Ansidei Ma-donna on a bed of purple velvet, glazed and framed in gilt and darkly ja-panned wood, a great many small photographs of gentlemen wearing reso-lute expressions and a lot of hair, ladies with fine eyes and bare shoulders and everywhere books, books treated with respect and clothed in leather or at the very least in cloth.[38]

Living with them were Laura, Leslie's daughter, as well as George, Stella, and Gerald, Julia's three children. Leslie admits to some discomfort in his early relations with his wife's children (MB 65). An added difficulty was his slow acknowledgment after his marriage that Laura was mentally deficient. He speaks of her "waywardness and inarticulate ways of thinking and speaking," her illnesses, and problems with her schooling as a "trouble" he inflicted upon Julia (MB 91–92). Within the next five years, the Stephens produced four more children: Vanessa, Thoby, Virginia, and Adrian. By the time she was thirty-seven, then, Julia had borne seven children, three in three years, four in five years, with an eight-year respite in between. Her life, therefore, after her re-marriage, was filled with family concerns. She taught the children "Latin,

6. EDWARD BURNE-JONES. *The Annunciation*. 1879. Courtesy of the National Museums and Galleries on Merseyside (Lady Lever Art Gallery).

French, and history—not very well," Vanessa recalls, "and I am sure most mistakenly, both on her own account and on ours."[39] Virginia remembers her "mother's finger with the opal ring I loved" guiding them through "French and Latin grammars" (MOB 117). Leslie taught them mathematics. Both parents were impatient, ineffective teachers, however, and the children learned little about these subjects from them.[40] Fortunately, in addition to the stories Julia told, Leslie read novels and history to his "ragamice" and drew amusing animals in the margins, fronts, and backs of books. Fortunately, too, Leslie considered the education of his daughters more important than Julia did.[41]

Just as Julia Stephen lost her faith in her mother's Divine Patriarch, so Virginia and Vanessa lost theirs in earthly ones. In this oft-quoted passage, Woolf portrays Mrs. Ramsay reverencing her husband and giving him abundant sympathy when his ego requires it:

> Mrs. Ramsay . . . seemed to raise herself with an effort, and at once to pour erect into the air a rain of energy, a column of spray, looking at the same time animated and alive as if all her energies were being fused into force, burning and illuminating . . . , and into this delicious fecundity, this fountain and spray of life, the fatal sterility of the male plunged itself, like a beak of brass, barren and bare. He wanted sympathy. He was a failure, he said (TTL 58).

Leslie Stephen admits that he professed "a rather exaggerated self-deprecation in order to extort some of her delicious compliments" (MB 93). Nevertheless, "the pure joy" in their relationship, Woolf has Mrs. Ramsay recognize, is diminished by Mr. Ramsay's public exhibitions of emotional dependence on her and by his inability to face everyday facts, like the cost of a greenhouse roof (TTL 62). He, in turn, is aggravated by what he considers his wife's irrationality, her tendency to exaggerate. The marriage, Lily Briscoe recalls, "was no monotony of bliss—she with her impulses and quicknesses; he with his shudders and glooms." There were tensions and flare-ups, the bedroom door slamming, his plate sent whizzing out of the window, followed by slow reconciliations (TTL 296). In The Mausoleum Book Leslie acknowledges his "'skinless': over-sensitive and nervously irritable" as well as absent-minded and often unsociable nature; he admits the trials these characteristics were at times for Julia. Stress from overwork on the Dictionary of National Biography caused sleeplessness, fits of "the horrors," and nervous collapses in 1888 and 1890. Through these Julia nursed her husband often at the expense of her own sleep and health (MB 88–89). She also managed their money so he would not worry over his solvency. Still he could not banish his cares entirely, and they, he realizes, were "reflected upon her" (MB 90).

With all the satisfactions as well as the challenges and responsibilities in her second marriage, Julia was no longer "deadened," but her former sorrow left its traces upon her facial expressions and general manner (MB 60). Woolf remembers her mother as sometimes "Severe; with a background of knowledge that made her sad. She had her own sorrow waiting behind her to dip into privately" (MOB 82). She had concluded that "sorrow is our lot, and at best we can but face it bravely" (MOB 32). In *To the Lighthouse* Woolf imagines Julia Stephen's view of the world when she has Mrs. Ramsay realize that her husband, "with all his gloom and desperation," is far more optimistic than she:

> He had always his work to fall back on. Not that she was "pessimistic," as he accused her of being. . . . but for the most part, oddly enough, she must admit that she felt this thing called life terrible, hostile, and quick to pounce on you if you gave it a chance. There were the eternal problems: suffering; death; the poor. There was always a woman dying of cancer even here. And yet she had said to all these children, You shall go through it all. . . . And then she said to herself, brandishing her sword at life, Nonsense. They will be perfectly happy (TTL 91–92).

Mrs. Ramsay escapes from her sober view of life in part by encouraging people to marry and to have children, just as Leslie Stephen recalls Julia Stephen having done (MB 75).

Julia also worked hard to alleviate the inevitable suffering she saw around her. In this way, like her husband, she did have her work to fall back upon. This work, Virginia Woolf concludes, was no "mischievous philanthropy" like that practiced "so complacently" by others. Julia's services to the poor and the dying were based upon breadth of experience, "great clearness of insight, sound judgement, humour, and a power of grasping very quickly the real nature of someone's circumstances, and so arranging that the matter . . . fell into its true proportions at once" (MOB 34–35). Yet her "natural impetuosity" led her to solve problems "like some commanding Empress" (MOB 34–35). So Lily Briscoe in *To the Lighthouse* sees Mrs. Ramsay "presiding with immutable calm over destinies which she completely failed to understand" (TTL 78).

In London, Julia Stephen made her "immense rounds—shopping, calling, visiting hospitals and work houses,—in omnibuses," Virginia Woolf recalls. No domestic nun hovering around the sacred hearth, Julia moved confidently throughout London. An "expert on schedules and connections," she

returned home filled with stories of people with whom she had talked or
of others she had merely observed (MOB 121). At St. Ives, as Constance
Hunting notes, while her children enjoyed the seaside, Julia "progressed from
unpaid 'angel' to more professional but still unpaid practitioner" as she made
her rounds among the poor and ill. The Julia Prinsep Stephen Nursing
Association of St. Ives was one result.[42] Another was the concern with nursing evident in some of the stories and essays in this book. A third was *Notes
from Sick Rooms* (1883). Although she introduces this pamphlet by apologizing
for her relatively limited experience and for saying too much that is obvious
and too little that is important, still she establishes her authority. She mentions how carefully she has observed what relieves or irritates a patient and
what professional nurses with a great range of skills have done under similar
circumstances. She writes so that others will benefit from her experience
(NFSR vi).

Wondering why people associate nursing the sick with virtue, Julia
Stephen observes that it is often "easier and pleasanter" to deal with the ill
than with the well (NFSR 1). Jane Marcus suggests that some Victorian wom-
en's relationships with patients, as well as with servants, allowed them to exercise power denied them in relationships with husbands.[43] This explanation
is consistent with Mrs. Ramsay's suspicion in *To the Lighthouse* that her service to others may be only selfishness and vanity. It is not, however, Julia's
explanation here. We get along better with the ill and the dying, not because
we can give them orders but, she says, because the proximity of death allows us to overlook idiosyncrasies in the patient that would otherwise irritate
us (NFSR 1–2). When Julia has Poppy in "The Black Cat or the Grey Parrot"
tell Nurse Dove that she wants to be a nurse because she feels "'so sorry for
sick people,'" the dove approves. "'A great many people tell me they want to
be nurses, but I find out it is only because they are sorry for themselves, which
is quite a different thing,'" she says. Julia Stephen may have begun her nursing in self-pity, but there is every reason to believe she had more professional
motivations.

The work can be satisfying, she says, if the nurse considers it an "*art.*"
That means loving "the 'case' and not . . . the individual patient" and therefore treating strangers as tenderly and effectively as intimates (NFSR 3). It
means vigilance about details. The humor with which Woolf credited her
mother as well as the ability to invest even ordinary events and activities with
importance (MOB 36) is evident here. She "never belittled her own works,"
Woolf says, "thinking them, if properly discharged, of equal, though other,
importance with her husband's" (MOB 37). Two and a half pages, then, on
banishing the tiny, animated crumbs that "lurk" in sheets and clothing fol-

lowed by an even more detailed description of how to make up a sick bed properly are part of Julia Stephen's professional commitment and art. So are instructions on everything from bedpans and enemas to ventilation and diet.

In *Notes from Sick Rooms* and in "The Black Cat or the Grey Parrot," Julia Stephen notes some of the difficulties ill-tempered and nervous patients pose. "To be nursed by her, I know it alas! was a luxury even in the midst of suffering," exclaimed Leslie Stephen, probably one of the most ill-tempered and nervous of all her charges (MB 40). Julia may have been the angel in his house, but she certainly was no incorporeal one. Elizabeth Robins, Woolf recalls, described Julia as "a mixture of the Madonna and a woman of the world" (MOB 90; D III 183). Thoroughly substantial and practical, capable of confronting and dealing calmly with every manner of unpleasantness and catastrophe, she communicates in *Notes from Sick Rooms* a dedication to her task far beyond that of the ethereal lady with the lamp or the amateur trying to do her Christian duty. So committed was Julia to nursing that Leslie notes how much she was in demand: "Most of our few separations were caused by her attendance upon some sufferer," whether relative or friend (MB 61). Julia's story, "Cat's Meat," perhaps reveals some guilt, but it is also an attempt to reconcile her children to their mother's absences. When the children in the story decide they must run away and become poor in order to get attention from their philanthropic mother, she does not conclude that she is neglecting them; rather, they learn to appreciate the advantages they have.

In *To the Lighthouse* Woolf creates a Mrs. Ramsay who not only attends to the sick and dying but thinks about other social problems as well. Early in the novel she considers the gap between "rich and poor" as she "visited this widow, or that struggling wife in person with a bag on her arm." As she makes her visits, she systematically writes down "spendings, employment and unemployment, in the hope that thus she would cease to be a private woman whose charity was half a sop to her own indignation, half a relief to her own curiosity, and become what with her untrained mind she greatly admired, an investigator, elucidating the social problem," however "insoluble" the questions (TTL 17–18). Later in the novel, we discover that Mrs. Ramsay feels "passionately" about "hospitals and drains and the dairy" and would like "to take people by the scruff of their necks and make them see" the need for a hospital on the island and for sanitation laws to regulate the dairy in London. While she does not regret her eight children, they leave her no time for such causes (TTL 89). Still, she speaks "with warmth and eloquence" at the dinner table about "the iniquity of the English dairy system, and in what state milk was delivered at the door, and was about to prove her charges, for she had gone into the matter," when she is stopped by the laughter of her children. They do not take her proclamations seriously. If the scene in the novel is based on fact, it is small wonder that Julia Stephen's opinions on social issues remained, even when written down, unpublished.

With all of her seriousness, Julia Stephen had another side. Virginia Woolf credits her mother with the kind of wit and vitality that could make family life proceed "merrily." Her wit apparently involved the ability to "stamp people with characters at once" and then draw out from them "such sparks of character as they have never shown to anyone since" (MOB 35). Whether at home, at St. Ives, or merely standing on a railway platform, her caricatures "in a phrase or two" could keep her companions "laughing till the train went" (MOB 36). One of Virginia Woolf's early memories is her mother's laugh ending in "three diminishing ahs . . . 'Ah–ah–ah . . .'" (MOB 40, 81). Some of Julia Stephen's sense of the funny side of people and situations, an attitude her daughter certainly inherited, appears in her essays and stories but not so much, perhaps, as we would like. The essays represent her more serious side except for a mocking comment on women and fashion, an amusing anecdote about a little girl who sees her future as an endless series of baths, and a couple of droll comparisons between poets and pigs, bishops and butlers. Her stories, in spite of the lessons they teach, contain more of the amusement she obviously derived from the naivete of children and the antics of animals with human characteristics.

The essays and stories were parts of Julia Stephen's efforts to give of herself to those who needed her. Near the end of *To the Lighthouse*, Lily Briscoe thinks of love: "And the roar and the crackle repelled her with fear and disgust, as if while she saw its splendour and power she saw too how it fed on the treasure of the house, greedily, disgustingly, and she loathed it" (TTL 261). Desperate to save money, desperate to save time as the "duties and desires" increased, Julia Stephen, Woolf says, "sank, like an exhausted swimmer, deeper and deeper in the water" (MOB 39). Henry James mentions influenza in the Stephen family in March of 1895, "Mrs. Stephen having had it severely, but having looked so intensely beautiful on her sofa in her longish convalescence that one felt it to be a sort of blessing in disguise."[44] Her illness was no blessing. "No doubt her unsparing labours for us and for others had produced that weakness of the heart," Leslie wrote, that rendered her incapable of recovery (MB 96). No doubt any nursing she received did not meet her own ideal of freeing the patient's mind from disturbances. To the end she

7. WILLIAM ROTHENSTEIN. *Mrs. Leslie Stephen.* c. 1890. Permission of the National Portrait Gallery, London.

helped and instructed others. "'Hold yourself straight, my little Goat,'" Virginia remembers as her mother's last words to her (MOB 84). Julia Stephen died on the morning of May 5, 1895.

"I leant out of the nursery window the morning she died," Woolf wrote in 1939–40:

> It was about six, I suppose. I saw Dr Seton walk away up the street with his hands clasped behind his back. I saw the pigeons floating and settling. I got a feeling of calm, sadness, and finality. It was a beautiful blue spring morning, and very still. That brings back the feeling that everything had come to an end (MOB 84).

Woolf had recorded a variation on this scene in her diary on the twenty-ninth anniversary of her mother's death and another on the forty-second (D II 300; V 85). The scene remained with her for life and, although she did not grieve as self-indulgently as her father, she could comprehend his loss: "[Mr. Ramsay, stumbling along a passage one dark morning, stretched his arms out, but Mrs. Ramsay having died rather suddenly the night before, his arms, though stretched out, remained empty.]" (TTL 194).

In a lecture entitled "Forgotten Benefactors," Leslie described his wife's impact: "'the good done by a noble life and character may last far beyond any horizon which can be realised by our imaginations,'" he said (D III 164, n. 8). In *To the Lighthouse* Mrs. Ramsay lives on in the memories of her survivors as, according to her daughter, she knew she would. "Children never forget," Mrs. Ramsay knows (TTL 95). She knows too that Paul Rayley and Minta Doyle who, with her encouragement, got engaged, will always remember her: "It flattered her, where she was most susceptible of flattery, to think how, wound about in their hearts, however long they lived she would be woven" (TTL 170). As concerned in her way about her reputation as Mr. Ramsay is about his, her influence on people's lives is a kind of immortality. Lily Briscoe especially feels her influence. Mrs. Ramsay's ability, using people as her medium, to make "'Life stand still here'" is Lily's goal as a painter (TTL 241) and ultimately Virginia Woolf's as a writer.

But her mother was a writer too. Julia Stephen is not among the previously neglected or undiscovered great women writers, but she is a far more interesting, complex, and talented person than most people realize. Her history, what we know of it, is one of the many women's stories of the kind that Virginia Woolf says in *A Room of One's Own* should be told. Julia Stephen combined the traditional ideal, for women, of service to others with the kind of professionalism and independence of mind we associate with less

8. WILLIAM ROTHENSTEIN. *Sir Leslie Stephen.* c. 1903. Permission of the National Portrait Gallery, London.

conventional women. Neither clingingly dependent nor feminist, she valued the activities assigned to women. Their work is noble if it is done properly, even, at its best, creatively. Since this life is all we have, she concluded, women's time is too precious to waste in idleness or self-indulgence.

This edition of Julia Stephen's writing makes accessible documents that can help Virginia Woolf scholars better understand her childhood, family background, and even her writing abilities. For students of the Victorian era, Julia Stephen's writings provide insight into the role and concerns of the women of her social class. The book also is for readers interested in the history of children's literature, book illustration, and the visual arts of the nineteenth century in general. With Julia Stephen's own work at the center, the edition is a compendium of information about her and her work; indirectly, it illuminates the literary genres through which she chose to express her ideas and the era in which she lived and wrote.

Stories for Children

ELIZABETH STEELE

*J*ULIA WAS BORN IN 1846 and would thus have had the benefit of the Brothers Grimm[1] and Hans Christian Andersen[2] in her own youthful reading, as well as England's Harriet Martineau, with her "Playfellow" series,[3] and Frederick Marryat for adventure stories.[4] But there is little question that Lewis Carroll, whose Alice books came out when Julia was in her twenties, had the most lasting influence on nineteenth-century British writing for children—if not on all children's literature from that day to this.[5]

Many qualities can be found in Julia's writings that are present also in Carroll's.[6] Aside from the parallels between features of English culture, there are the deadpan humor, the regard for "propriety," and the strong sense of social class, its obligations and weaknesses. When, as a finale to "Dinner at Baron Bruin's," Mrs. Pig's family decides "never to eat with the aristocracy [the Bear family] again," Julia Stephen aims a glancing blow at British aristocracy, as well as tells us something of general middle-class attitudes—upper middle class, to be sure (like the Stephens themselves); for "Dinner at Baron Bruin's" is pure satire.

Humor and fancy did not fail Julia either. The well-plotted "Tommy and His Neighbours," like "Dinner at Baron Bruin's," is a funny story: not side-splitting perhaps (neither are the Alice books), but worth a hearty laugh. In fact, one finds oneself smiling often in the course of reading nearly all of her stories.[7]

Absurdities of situation abound—and what can be more "absurd" in the modern sense than falling down a rabbit hole with shelves built along the sides, or melting through a mirror to confront a chess-board landscape? But here we must make a distinction: though Carroll's landscapes are pure fantasy, Julia Stephen's are not. While it is unusual, even ludicrous, for a middle-class boy like Tommy Jones to climb up on his neighbors' roofs and throw

29

stones down their chimneys, the author provides a perfectly natural way for
him to get up there (a position regularly attained anyway by nineteenth-century
London chimney sweeps).

On the other hand, when Jack in "The Black Cat or the Grey Parrot" follows the house cat, Zulu, out onto the roofs, the story's atmosphere
is distinctly eerie; and we soon find him descending, at an unspecified point,
in the opposite direction down to a sort of Hell, which Julia Stephen takes
care not to place geographically.

When Jack "comes to," he is back in bed, without explanation or
obvious transportation. Yet there is no doubt that he has been away. His cousin
Poppy mourns for him in the next room, and his aunt, Poppy's mother, agrees
that he has been gone. Only the children's Nurse, critical though she nor-
mally is of Jack, shows herself willing to believe what he insists: that black
Zulu led him astray—a role filled by the white rabbit in the first Alice book.

In fact, "The Black Cat or the Grey Parrot" can be considered a double Carrollian adventure, insofar as Poppy is led by the grey parrot in another, more profitable, direction while Jack and Zulu take their horrible journey. In neither case, though, is the child allowed to wake up as Alice does
at the end of *Wonderland*, brushing leaves off herself and wondering if the
experience, good or bad (and Poppy too has some frightening moments), was
just a dream.

The only place in Julia Stephen's stories where a lapse of clock-time
is not accounted for in realistic terms occurs in "Emlycaunt." Here the reader
is bound to feel that Tommy (Julia Stephen did not mind repeating names)
has dreamed, or been in a trance, during his entire adventure with the rocking horse. The author closes off all avenues whereby Tommy might confirm
his own sense of what happened. Instead, he is back home, without undue
loss of time. No rational explanation is offered for what he thinks occurred.
With him, the reader is encouraged to believe that perhaps it did not. And
correspondingly few lessons are learned along the way.

Whereas Lewis Carroll, college don and bachelor, mocked the lesson-
giving propensities of nineteenth-century children's literature, Julia Stephen,
wife and mother, found this harder to do and perhaps undesirable. Lessons
in her stories, though not really didactic, deal usually with one of two things:
(1) fostering home relationships, and (2) being kind to animals, wild as well
as domestic. There are "lessons" sometimes for parents also. In "Cat's Meat,"
for instance, criticism is implied of crusading parents who leave their children at home in the sole care of servants, while they themselves visit "the
poor" and try to better conditions elsewhere than on home ground.

As stated in the Introduction to the present volume, Julia Stephen
herself was charged with similar behavior by her doting husband. One of

Dickens' characters, Mrs. Jellyby in *Bleak House,* is probably the all-time proto-type of such a mode of living. So it may be that Julia wrote this particular story in a self-critical mood. On the other hand, the children in the story do not get off scot-free either. The son, Bob, particularly feels guilty as ring-leader of the overnight expedition made by him and his sister without telling their parents; and both children learn to appreciate, through fair means and foul, that appearances, whether at home or abroad, can be deceiving.

Maggie, the daughter in this story, is an anomaly. She is more sub-servient to her brother than the little girls in other Stephen stories, perhaps because in "Cat's Meat" there are only two children; but she is also more clever than Bob. She solves an arithmetic problem that temporarily stumps him. "Cleverness" in girls is unusual in these stories; for if there is any fault in Julia Stephen's characters, it lies in her portrayal of small girls (not of women, whose abilities are allowed a wider range). Their tenderness of heart and anxiety to please lead regularly to floods of tears and contorted manners which make the reader wish that Elsie Dinsmore and her ilk had never been created be-fore Julia Stephen began to write.[8] It is hard to believe that she, the youngest of three daughters and no sons, could have been like that herself, even in childhood.

Certainly her own daughters Vanessa and Virginia were not. About Stella Duckworth, the daughter of her first marriage, it is harder to say. Apparently impressionable and easier to manage than Leslie Stephen's four off-spring, she may have served as her mother's fictional model. Yet these stories were written when Stella was grown, and the little female eyes that watched Julia as she wrote and read aloud (we assume) her own tales, contained an expression of a very different sort, fostered partly by their father in his dis-cussions with them of more sophisticated literature: an expression mocking and analytical, albeit admiring. Was it to tame this attitude, which she may have feared would serve them ill in adolescence and nubile young-womanhood, that Julia wrote of little girls who wake their brothers and male cousins with a kiss in the mornings and drag out chairs for the lordly young males to sit on at mealtimes?

Wisely, Carroll does not place his Alice in like circumstances. Sur-rounded as she is by "creatures" and such contorted human figures as the Ugly Duchess, she is seldom obliged to be subservient; and home life is only a far-distant background. Besides, Carroll, despite his penchant for little girls, really understood little boys better, whether he wanted to or not, and a study might well be made of Alice as a disguised young male. In any case, however, more pertness like hers would be a welcome change in Julia Stephen's girl children.

Still, Maggie with her sum-solving is a relief. So too, in "The Mysterious Voice," is Helen, who enjoys hearing about football games. On the whole, though, we would have to say that similarities between Julia Stephen's heroines and Lewis Carroll's do not serve to ally the lesser artist with the greater. The strongest links between them are their humor and mutual use of the natural world.

The latter element in Julia Stephen's stories needs more explanation.

The greatest age – at least the most prolific – of "children's literature," or writing for children, was yet to come when Julia Stephen took pen in the early 1880s to amuse and educate her own young ones and perhaps sell the results to publishers. Rudyard Kipling, Kenneth Grahame, Beatrix Potter, and Hugh Lofting (for "Dr. Doolittle") were still, though shortly, to emerge.[9] But two relevant women artists had appeared on the scene just shortly before: the English "Mrs. Molesworth" (b. Mary Louise Stewart), whose dates,[10] if Julia had lived a full lifetime, would have almost exactly coincided with hers; and the American Anna Sewell, whose one classic, *Black Beauty* (1877), had an influence that belied the lack of prolixity in its author.

Domestic life in Great Britain during the last quarter of the nineteenth century is well illustrated in Julia Stephen's stories for children, as also in her essays for adults. Mrs. Molesworth, who began writing in the 1870s, practiced just the sort of realism Julia liked: stories set against a solid home background which, if her young characters did not always stay near, they gladly returned to – as in the case of the near-ragamuffin, Jimmy, in Julia's "The Duke's Coal Cellar"; and stories allowing for the characteristic faults and virtues of most children, but with an underlying moral lesson. Among the Julia Stephen stories, only the irrepressible Tommy, in "Tommy and His Neighbours," is allowed to escape censure in the end. Neither he nor his weak parents finally "learn anything"; and one has the impression that Tommy will turn up again and again all his life, doing mischief, like a young Till Eulenspiegel except that he will never face the gallows. A kind of tribute to Julia's sneaking admiration for devilish ingenuity, especially as practiced by small boys, Tommy would have had no place in Mrs. Molesworth's pantheon.

Meanwhile, however, Anna Sewell's *Black Beauty* invited emulation in a complementary but quite different area. Its message became the rallying cry of the newly-formed Society for the Prevention of Cruelty to Animals, in both America and England: not to harm one's helpless fellow-creatures, the so-called "dumb beasts."

Few of Julia Stephen's stories are without animals many of which talk in an anthropomorphic way, though some do not. Two of the London pieces ("Tommy and His Neighbours" and "The Duke's Coal Cellar") lack them completely; but otherwise animals, including birds and fish, play a large part in Julia Stephen's portrayal of the world.

For this there are several reasons. It was an attitude shared by the whole family. The Editorial Note to this volume quotes from Virginia Woolf, telling how her father cut out and drew animals easily, prolifically. He valued them, apparently, for their satirical value, their wordless commentary on human interactions. It is also well to remember that Virginia and her sister and brothers delighted in assigning animal nicknames to each other. Thus the seemingly placid, ever-confident Vanessa became "Dolphin" to the family, who chose in turn to dub the skittish, somewhat awkward young Virginia "Goat." Even her mother called her that: "Hold yourself straight, my little Goat" were the last words Julia addressed, from her deathbed, to her youngest daughter.

Close friends shared in this zoological custom willy-nilly, especially female ones. Thus Virginia had a whole list of pet epithets from the animal world to connect her with sororal companions like Violet Dickinson (wallaby), her cousin-in-law Emma Vaughan (toad), and Vita Sackville-West (sheepdog). Such Stephen-bred allusions ranged the field of natural fauna, by no means limited to creatures whose usual habitat was Great Britain or even western Europe. After all, one had London menageries and zoos—especially the Zoo at Regent's Park—to choose among and fuel one's imagination.

Julia too reflects this catholicity. In one story, for example, "Dinner at Baron Bruin's," she mentions both marmottes and marmosets. To the lay reader this might seem an overlap in terms, perhaps a spelling error. But one species is a rodent, the other a primate, and it is clear she knew which was which and what their characteristics were.

She and, one suspects, the whole family were also aware of the comings and goings of exotic creatures to British shores. In "The Black Cat or the Grey Parrot" Julia speaks of the rarity of opossum mice (small phalangers, flying rodents, from Australia), newly arrived in Britain. The same story also makes use of topical animals like "Boreas, the dancing bear" from Russia; while "dear old Jumbo," a feature of the London scene for many years, plays an important part in "Emlycaunt."[11]

Julia Stephen's knowledge of and interest in animals extends to some of their less familiar appellations. Most of us know "Bruin" as a name for "bear," but how many realize its origin in the Old French beast-epic (fourteenth century) *Reynard the Fox*? A nice touch, also in "Dinner at Baron Bruin's," is Col. Isegrim, the wolf. In *Reynard the Fox* Isegrim was Reynard's "uncle." Julia Stephen, though, when she wants to name a fox, in "The Black Cat or the Grey Parrot," uses not Reynard, but "Mr. Reinecke," a label that takes us back even farther, to the German beast-epic *Reinecke Fuchs*, current among Frankish tribes as early as the Middle Ages. A clever innovation of Julia's: in the French *Reynard*, the fox blinds Isegrim's children, while in "The Black Cat or the Grey Parrot" he meets his comeuppance. She has "Mr. Reinecke" languishing in the animal hospital after a bad operation on his eyes.

Monkeys abound in Julia's stories, as in her husband's drawings. Not only were monkeys popular pets in the 1800s, but no thinking person born in or near mid-century could have been unaware, after Darwin, of the psychological and religious challenge monkeys and apes appeared to provide to the hegemony of mankind. In her stories, however, monkeys receive no more nor less credit than other animals, of whom both "bad" and "good" examples are provided.

Meanwhile, Julia's natural kindness of heart and nursing experience put her in tune with the message of *Black Beauty*. Thus we hear, echoing through her pages, exhortations not to kill, not to hunt, not to harm, not to deprive members of the animal kingdom. No vegetarian, however, she found it necessary sometimes to take a pragmatic view. Not only do many animals eat one another to have food, but most people eat animals also in her stories; and in "The Wandering Pigs" the probable future of the main characters, three bonny porkers, is admitted to be in the shape of bacon. But she slips the message in gently. According to Curly, one of the pigs, "'It is well to be useful when one is dead, and bacon has a savoury sound.'" In the same story she balances the scale between fauna and flora, identifying the pains of trampled thistles and the distress of pulled-up turnips. The longest of the stories, "The Wandering Pigs" is also, in many ways, the most complex.

Despite the enormous amount of publicity surrounding Virginia Woolf in the past few decades, no mention of Julia Stephen's writings for children occurred until a catalogue from Sotheby's listed the manuscripts for sale in July of 1980. Analyses of her handwriting, ink and/or the kinds of paper used, have failed so far to establish a pattern for the order in which she wrote them. Even the fact that three manuscripts—"The Monkey on the Moor," "Tommy and His Neighbours," and "The Wandering Pigs"—have her name and address written on the back is probably not a clue to chronology. Critics and historians have located two letters from Leslie Stephen to his wife, dated 1885, which speak of sending at least some of the stories (no hint as to which) to Routledge for publication as a book illustrated by Leslie himself.[12] But nothing came of it, though Julia, as an alternative, may have considered dispatching one or more to children's magazines flourishing at the time.[13] This would account for her name and address on the back of individual works. That such data are absent from the other manuscripts may or may not be significant, since in some cases the final words of the story are also missing (intuited and supplied here, by the editor, in brackets as the ones most likely to have been used).

Lacking chronological indications, then, the stories stand as follows: seven pieces dealing more or less with animals, flanked on each end by a story solely about people. An effort has been made to alternate settings, from city to country and back again, as well as moods. Only the individual reader, of course, can ultimately spell out "mood." But attributing words like "buoyant" to some stories, "Gothic" to others, and "sociable" to a third group, might be at least a beginning.[14]

Tommy and His Neighbours

IN A ROW OF HOUSES all of which looked just the same, each with a little strip of garden at the back, lived Mr. and Mrs. Jones and their son, Tommy. Tommy was the only child Mr. and Mrs. Jones ever had, and they thought that no one ever had seen such a wonderful child. Tommy was rather wonderful, I think, but I don't think Mr. and Mrs. Jones would have agreed with me in thinking that it would have been better if Tommy had been a little less wonderful. The servants said Tommy kept them in hot water. One day he really did keep them in hot water, for he turned on the tap of the kitchen boiler, flooded the kitchen and burst the boiler, before anyone found out that Master Tommy had been at work. Even then, Mr. and Mrs. Jones excused him and thought that Tommy must have his fun.

I have said that all the houses were alike in the row, but all the gardens were not. One garden was all turf, which means, in London, something that is green for three weeks and dirty brown the rest of the year. Other gardens had beds in which geraniums were put in the summer—but Mrs. Jones was the only one who had a rockery. She thought she would like to have something quite new so she made a rockery. Have you ever seen a London "rockery"? The rocks are cinders burnt red and purple. A few badly baked bricks are put in between, and Mrs. Jones had put some earth and some ferns in the crevices; and every now and then, when she went to the seaside, she would get a bit of shining granite or crystal and place them where they would show most. Mr. Jones had an office in the city and used to be away all day. In the evening he and Mrs. Jones and Tommy would sit in the garden. Tommy didn't sit much but generally found some mischief to do and Mrs. Jones would water her ferns with pride. One evening, Mr. Jones had been reading an account of a great fire and how the people whose house was burnt escaped by a ladder onto the roof. "I think, my dear," he said, "we should have such a ladder. There is a parapet outside our house and if we had a fire, we could all escape easily to the top of our own roof and then walk onto our neighbour's."

"A very good idea," said Mrs. Jones. "I will send for Jenkins tomorrow." Jenkins was the carpenter, builder, plumber, glazier, who did all the

odd bits of work for Mr. Jones. Tommy was delighted to think that
Jenkins would come.

He was able to do lots of mischief when a workman was in the
house. There were all the tools about and Tommy was able to knock holes in
the furniture and to make noises and messes of every description.

The idea of the steps too was a pleasant one to him. He would not
wait for a fire to get onto the neighbours' roofs! No. The very first time he
could do so, without his mother's knowing it, he would get onto the roof.
He knew he must not do it when his mother was near, for though Mrs.
Jones would let him hurt anything else, she was very angry if he ever hurt
himself. The carpenter came and went—the steps were put up, and Mr. and
Mrs. Jones both said they felt they could sleep much better in their beds
now they knew they could escape onto the roof if there were a fire.

One day, Mrs. Jones told Tommy that she was going out for the
afternoon to pay some visits and that she would not take him with her as
she did not think it would amuse him. The truth was, that she was going to
see her maiden aunt at Clapham who always put poor Mrs. Jones in a state
by asking Tommy how he got on with his Latin grammar and making little
jokes about sums. She would also ask him questions out of English history
and as Tommy never answered right, and generally made dreadful faces, the
old lady used to say to Mrs. Jones that she thought it high time the boy
should go to school—and that she was sure he would end his days in prison.

Tommy was very glad when he heard that his mother was going
out, for he thought he would be able to have a fine afternoon on the roofs.
As soon as his mother was well off, Tommy ran up to the top attic, which he
knew he should find empty, and climbing out of the window by the help of
the ladder, he was soon on the roof. He was rather frightened at first, but he
soon found that there was no one looking and that as the roofs were very
flat, it was not difficult to walk from one to the other. However, even being
on a roof becomes dull. If Tommy could have looked down the chimneys
and frightened someone, that would have been fun; but as it was, he only
frightened a big black cat, and got his clothes, face and hands very dirty. At
last a bright idea struck him. He would get some stones and throw them
down the chimneys. It was unlucky he should not be able to see all the mess
and fright that the stones would cause but he might hear something of it
and, at all events, he could imagine it. The first thing was to get the stones,
for there were none on the roof. So he climbed off the roof, which was not
so easy as climbing up, especially as it was getting dusk; however, down he
got, without being seen and now where were the stones? These are not so
plentiful in London as might be supposed, and Tommy was beginning to fear

that his delightful plan would have to be given up, at all events for that day, when another bright idea struck him, which was that he would get some of the bricks and stones from his mother's rockwork. Off he went and soon had pulled down some cinders and the bits of white crystal and granite which his mother had placed among her ferns with such care, and then he went off again to the top attic.

Getting up the ladder with his arms full of rough bits of stone and brick was neither easy nor pleasant, but once on the roof, Tommy laid down his little heap and with a couple of bits in each hand, went to see which was the best chimney to begin on. He went quite to the end of the row, which was rather a long one; and down the last chimney, which he supposed was the kitchen chimney from its size and the smoke that came from it, he dropped a big bit of brick.

Tommy could not see down the chimney but I can, so I will tell you what happened. The chimney did belong to a kitchen, and the kitchen was a very busy one for there was a dinner party that evening. The cook was standing by the fire, stirring some white soup. She had a jug in her hand and was pouring in drop by drop some rich cream, stirring all the time. On the fire, in an open frying pan, some lard was sizzling and bubbling, all ready for the fish which were lying on the kitchen table. On the hotplate by the cook's side, a stew pan full of fruit was sending forth a delicious scent. All was well ahead and the cook, though hot and tired, looked well pleased with all the good things she was preparing. "The white soup has never looked so well, Bessie," said Cook to a girl who had come in to help, "and the roast will be done to a turn. I do hope the company will be punctual and then I have no fear. . . ." Poor Cook, she had hardly said these words when splash — plump, came something, she did not know what, into the midst of the beautiful white soup! The cream jug dropped out of Cook's hands. The soup splashed up onto her hands, scalding them.

The kitchen maid, whose back was turned, only saw Cook's face of horror and burst out laughing, on which the cook, with the ladle still hot and dripping in her hand, turned on the girl in such fury that she rushed out of the kitchen, screaming, "Mercies, murder, fire, — Cook's gone mad." The mistress of the house, who was trying on her dress, rushed down in terror. The master, who was decanting wine in the back dining room, instantly seized the dinner bell and rang it loudly. It was the first thing that came to hand and on the whole less trouble than running to see what was the matter.

The poor cook, meantime, had recovered herself, and as her mistress came into the kitchen, had managed to get the unlucky bit of brick out of its new home. The soup could only be thrown away. What was to be done? "What *are* you about, Cook? Are you mad?" said Mrs. Grey, really frightened as she saw the cook pouring away the excellent soup. At this moment the dinner bell rang and the poor cook did indeed seem as if she had gone mad; but Mrs. Grey at once knew that it was her husband, and running to the stairs begged him to come down and leave the bell alone. Neither Mr. nor Mrs. Grey could make the soup nor could they guess how a stone could have fallen down their chimney. However, they decided to have the sweeps tomorrow and to send the kitchen maid off to the confectioner for some soup at once.

Though we know all the mischief done by Tommy's first throw, he did not or he might perhaps have been satisfied. As it was, though he could hear a certain amount of noise going on below, he had no idea of what success he had really had, and he went on to the next row of chimneys. He lay still by them for some time, as he feared someone might come up from Mrs. Grey's. However, as we know, all were much too busy about the dinner to think of examining the roof, so Tommy was undisturbed.

The next chimney he wished to attack, belonged to the house of an old maid, Miss Perkins by name. Tommy had a particular dislike to Miss Perkins, who in return looked on him as a "terrible boy." Miss Perkins had a little niece living with her, Clara Mason by name, and Tommy often wished to entrap this child into joining his mischievous plans. But Clara was too well looked after ever to be able to join in any bits of wickedness, even if she had wished to. She was a gentle bright girl who led rather a dull life, as Miss Perkins, though kind, was rather too fond of teaching, and Clara seemed to be always at lessons. Tommy chose the bright sharp bit of white crystal, which he had stolen from his mother's rockery, to throw down Miss Perkins' chimney. He hoped that if not Miss Perkins, he might at least hit her favourite cat with it, and he chose a chimney which he felt sure was not the kitchen. The old lady was seated by the fire and was reading aloud to her niece a book on geology—a most interesting study, she told Clara; and as poor Clara did not seem to agree, Miss Perkins was beginning to get rather angry and declared that *she* had studied geology when she was Clara's age and now there was no stone she could see, that she did not know where it came from. At this moment a curious rattle was heard and leaping down through the flame onto the bright steel fender near to Miss Perkins' feet came the crystal, rather blackened by its journey through the chimney, but still showing some whiteness and brightness. Clara gave a little scream, which Miss Perkins quickly repressed; and though she had started herself at the noise, she was far too anxious to show Clara how excellent a thing calmness is, even to touch the odd lump at her feet. Suddenly her face brightened. She seized the bright steel poker and gave the stone a gentle but decided tap. In doing so, some of the soot shook off and the stone, catching the light of the fire, gave forth a slight sparkle.

"A most remarkable and fortunate occurrence, my dear Clara," said Miss Perkins. "Just as I was reading to you about the earth's formation, the primaeval ages and all those interesting periods rightly called the stone ages, this most interesting specimen has descended on us. I see at a glance that the specimen before me is volcanic. There is evidently some disturbance going on in the elements and one of those remarkable meteoric stones of which we have read has penetrated even to my hearth." Miss Perkins had, by this time, taken the stone in her hand and was carefully removing the dust and soot. She then applied her thin and pointed nose to the crystal. "From the sulphurous smell and latent heat which I can detect, there is no doubt as to where this stone came from. You, yourself, will be able to perceive both, Clara."

Clara touched and smelt the stone rather doubtfully. "Would not the heat and smoke of the chimney through which it came, cause both, Aunt?" she said, seeing that an answer was expected.

"Nonsense, child," said Miss Perkins, impatiently, "have you any theory as to where the stone did come from then, as you don't believe me?"

"I thought it might be part of the chimney falling in," said Clara shyly, for Miss Perkins looked angry.

"Have you ever seen crystals put into London walls?" said Miss Perkins with a snort. "If I had not seen the descent of this stone, I should have believed it to be a bit of Derbyshire spar; but as it is, I do not doubt that I have in my possession a most precious aerolite, and as I am going to dine with the Greys tonight, I will take it with me. It will no doubt provoke a scientific discussion." Clara said no more, but at the words "Derbyshire spar," a light broke on her.

She remembered Mrs. Jones' rockwork and the pride with which Mrs. Jones had pointed out her one piece of white crystal: "Brought, my dear, on my lap the whole way from Matlock," and she felt sure that the aerolite was a bit of Master Tommy's mischief.

Tommy had felt a little uncomfortable as he sent down the pretty bit of crystal. He knew his mother was fond of the bit of stone and when he was not taken up with his mischievous pranks, he was fond of his mother. However, it was gone now and he little thought that it was to be raised to the dignity of an aerolite. In fact, he would not have known any more than you or I do, what an aerolite is. He had still one more bit of stone which he thought he would like to throw down. It was a sharp-pointed bit of granite and he threw it down the chimney of the last house next to their own. The owner of this house was an old gentleman, very bald, somewhat nervous and very cross. He was sitting by his fire, reading his paper, when he fell asleep, a thing he hated doing. His spectacles slid off his nose and in their fall, woke him with a start. Nothing would have been easier than for him to ring the bell and his attentive man servant would have found them in a minute; but then he would have had to confess first that he had been to sleep and secondly that he was too blind to find them himself; and Mr. Gregory did not wish to confess, so he groped about with his blind eyes, the heat of the fire striking on his bald head and making him feel doubly irritable. He thought he felt the slender end of his spectacles when suddenly a sharp blow was dealt him and he felt a warm stream of blood trickling down the side of his cheek. He jumped up in a fury, treading on his spectacles as he did so. "Who has dared to strike me?" he cried. But no one answered. The small bit of granite lay at his feet but he could not see it, and even if he had been able, he would not have known how it came there.

However much he disliked doing so, there was no help for it now. He *must* ring the bell and submit to having his wound plastered. The very quiet man who looked after Mr. Gregory answered the bell in a moment. He was much surprised to see his master's state. "You seem to have given yourself a scratch, Sir," he said very respectfully and quietly.

"A scratch!–Given myself," spluttered Mr. Gregory. "You must be mad, Roberts. Have you ever known me [to] scratch myself? Some unseen burglar must have dealt me this blow. I felt a sharp missile striking me as I stooped." Here Mr. Gregory got very red. He did not like to say what he had been stooping for. "Where are my spectacles?" he asked crossly.

"Dear, dear, Sir, you have broken your spectacles," said Roberts, who saw fragments of the crystal on the floor.

"Broken my spectacles, impossible!" said Mr. Gregory; but sure enough they were broken and by the side of them lay the little bit of granite.

"Here is a bit of stone, Sir," said Roberts. "It may have cut your head."

"It *must* have cut my head," said Mr. Gregory. "I told you something had struck me. I heard nothing."

"The shutters are all shut, Sir," said Roberts as he looked round the room. Nothing could look more cosy and peaceful than Mr. Gregory's study. The thick red curtains were closely drawn, four wax candles were lighted in shining silver candlesticks, a bunch of yellow roses stood on the table on which were numbers of books, papers, ivory paper knives and all the things that an old gentle[man] fond of ease and comfort would have collected round him. It was a picture of comfort, all disturbed by Tommy's little bit of granite. Poor Mr. Gregory, with troubled face and two little black patches carefully arranged over the scratch, did not [look] like the same old gentleman to whom Roberts had taken his cup of tea and hot muffin an hour before!

Mr. Gregory was not only disturbed about his cut but what had caused it, though that was unaccountable. Nor did the loss of his spectacles make him seriously unhappy, for he had other pairs; but what he thought of was his dinner! Mr. Gregory was very particular about his meals. He did not like hastily prepared dinners and he was expecting to spend a pleasant evening with his neighbour, Mrs. Grey, whose dinners were always good, and where he expected to meet Miss Perkins, with whom he disagreed on every subject and therefore always had a lively talk. All these pleasant thoughts were at an end. He could never show himself at a dinner party with a black patch. No, he must write and tell Mrs. Grey that he could not come, and with a sigh, poor Mr. Gregory wrote his note and ordered Roberts to see [if] dinner could be got ready.

We must now see what Tommy was doing with himself. He had come to the end of all his stones and it was getting quite dark, so he clambered carefully down the side of the roof. Having done this, an unexpected difficulty met him. The housemaid had been up to the spare attic to put away some clothes, and finding to her surprise that the window was wide open, she shut it down and locked it. Now Tommy was in a great fix. He knew that the servants did not often come into the attic; and now that the window was shut, there was no chance that anyone would come there. When his mother came home, she would be certain to ask for him as soon as she came home; but the servants would say he had gone out, and they would all be too glad of the quiet to make any search for him till very late. Tommy called as loudly as he could and rattled at the window; but no one heard him or if they did, they were too well accustomed to Tommy's cries to take any notice of them. At last, Tommy, who was not very patient, had to make up his mind to breaking the window and opening it. He did not mind the breaking of the window but he did mind cutting his hand, and he was afraid that he would be found out. However, there was nothing else for it, and he dashed his hand through the pane, unlocked the window and then got in. His hand was a good deal cut but he went as quietly as he could to his own room and put a handkerchief round it, hoping the bleeding would soon cease. Cuts with glass are not so easily cured and Tommy felt that the blood had not stopped flowing and that little bits of the glass were still cutting him; so he was forced to go to his old nurse and ask her to bind it up properly. "What on earth have you been about, Master Tommy?" she cried. "You must have been up to some mischief, you have been so quiet. Have you been out? What have you been doing to cut your hand like this?" Tommy muttered something about having been out, and having met with an accident, but old Nurse knew that he had been up to some mischief; and as she also knew that there was no use in questioning Tommy, she wisely left off doing so.

When Mrs. Jones came home, she was in a great state at seeing Tommy's hand. It never occurred to her that Tommy himself had caused it and as she was home late and was dining out, she had to hurry off to dress for dinner.

Mr. and Mrs. Grey were full of anxieties about their dinner party. They had never given so large a one and as they were very particular about their cooking, they felt very much afraid that this dinner, half of which had had to come from the pastry cook, would not do them any credit. They did not like to tell their guests what had happened, though they felt sure that their cook would never send up any of the food properly. Mr. and Mrs. Jones, Miss Perkins and her niece and two or three gentlemen were all assembled, when the bell rang. Mr. and Mrs. Grey looked nervously at each other. Some new misfortune! The maid brought a note. "Dear me! From our neighbour Mr. Gregory," said Mrs. Grey, reading the letter: "Dear Madam, an unprecedented accident has occurred and I fear I cannot fulfill the engagement which I had such pleasure in making and that I must forgo the happiness I had promised myself this evening. While sitting by my fire this evening, a missile suddenly darted through the air and struck me so severely that I could not venture to present myself to your company. I am yours faithfully, Josiah Gregory."

Mrs. Grey was not able to finish reading the letter aloud, for Miss Perkins, forgetting her usual good manners, screamed out, "Another. I told you so, Clara." Everyone started. Was Miss Perkins going mad?

Mr. Grey, who was very good-natured, said, "Poor old gentleman, what can have happened? I had better go and fetch him over. He will have no dinner ready at home."

"Yes," said Miss Perkins. "And I will go too." The surprise of everyone was now very great. It had been thought by some that Miss Perkins would not mind becoming Mrs. Gregory, but no one expected her to become so excited at hearing of Mr. Gregory's accident.

"Soothe yourself, dear Madame; I daresay it is nothing," said Mr. Grey. "I will bring him back."

"Nothing?" said Miss Perkins. "Doesn't he say a missile? Tell him to bring it with him. I have mine in my pocket!" Mrs. Grey, now really alarmed lest Miss Perkins should be going out of her mind, beckoned to Clara and asked her if she had perceived anything odd with her aunt.

"No!" said Clara, "I think the stone that fell just before we came excited her."

"Stone!" said Mrs. Grey. "How very odd!" But she could ask no more for the door opened, and Mr. Grey appeared with Mr. Gregory. Mr. Gregory had been very pleased to come, but he was a little ashamed when he remembered how he had described the severe cuts received. The two little patches did not show much now.

"It is most kind of you to have come," said Mrs. Grey as they went into the dining room.

"The kindness is on your side," said Mr. Gregory politely. "The accident was really a trifling one, and now that I am here I hardly regret it. I should have had to have recourse to the pastry cook had I remained at home; and if there is one thing I hate, it is soup from the pastry cook's." Mrs. Grey gave a little gasp. If Mr. Gregory only knew that he *was* eating soup from the pastry cook! She looked anxiously at her husband and was only too glad when Miss Perkins seized on Mr. Gregory and took up all his attention. Dinner had never seemed so long and weary to Mrs. Grey.

At last it was getting done and the dessert, which could have come to no harm, was appearing when Miss Perkins' voice was heard in loud tones. "Aerolite, of that there is no doubt. My dear Sir, have you got it?— Don't deny it. I have got mine." "No such thing, Ma'am," answered Mr. Gregory, looking red and angry. The dinner had not been as good as he expected and this woman had been pestering him the whole time to know how and where this stone had struck him. "Got the stone here? I should think not. A common flint, which jumped out of the fire, or a bit of stone which gave way from the chimney."

"Say rather a meteoric stone swiftly hurled by the elements which descended on you. Perhaps you had fallen asleep, Mr. Gregory, so may not have noticed its descent as *I* did. I saw the stone, swift as a flash, strike the floor and at once exclaimed to Clara, 'A meteoric stone.' I see now it was a meteoric shower."

"Meteoric fiddlesticks," said Mr. Gregory, now thoroughly out of temper, and he turned to Mr. Grey; but Mrs. Grey, now that the anxiety of her dinner was over, was listening to Miss Perkins' tale with open ears.

"How very odd it is we should all have stones falling down. Our dinner has been spoilt, as I fear you may have discovered, by the fall of something down the kitchen chimney just as the cook was finishing the white soup. The soup was, of course, spoiled, and much of the rest of the dinner too, but we thought it was a brick that fell."

"Not a bit of it," cried Miss Perkins, with excitement. "It is no brick, but one of the most remarkable occurrences that has ever been observed. Verified, too, by so many. Here is *my* piece of stone," she said, diving into her pocket and producing the bit of crystal.

"Why, that is just like the bit in my wife's rockwork," said Mr. Jones, who was on Miss Perkins' other side. "Where did you say you found it?"

"I did not find it—it fell from the sky," said Miss Perkins solemnly, "a meteoric stone—as such, most precious." Mr. Jones said no more but he looked at his wife. The brick or cinder which had fallen into the [Greys'] kitchen lay on the table cloth, side by side [with the other]. Mrs. Jones looked at them and at her husband, and a horrid certainty came over her, that these bits had come from her rockwork. She remembered, now, Tommy's cut arm, and she felt sure that somehow this shower of stones had come from his hand.

"It is rather like bits in our rockwork," she said, faltering, but Miss Perkins said in a decided voice:

"These two pieces have the same origin and I shall take them to my scientific friends who will not be so unbelieving as those we have met here." And so saying, she put the brick with the stone into her pocket.

"Did I hear you say it was like your rockwork, Madam?" said Mr. Gregory, focusing keen grey eyes with their shining spectacles on poor Mrs. Jones. "We can easily discover if any has been taken from your garden."

"Impossible," said Miss Perkins. "How could rocks get from Mrs. Jones' garden down all our chimneys?"

"Quite impossible unless thrown by someone, some *criminal*, I should call him. I shall do my best to discover the author of this deed and shall not fail to prosecute him."

"The old man is growing childish," said Miss Perkins to Mrs. Jones as they left the dining room; but Mrs. Jones complained of having a bad headache and soon went home. Mr. Gregory's words had filled her with terror. What if he should prosecute Tommy, for she felt sure Tommy *had* done it.

The next day, Mr. and Mrs. Jones left for the seaside and not long after, there was a bill "To let" stuck up in their house, so I suppose Master Tommy was taken where he could find new neighbours to torment. Miss Perkins still keeps her meteoric stone in a glass cabinet; and the last time she told the story of its descent, she described how blue and red sparks flashed from the stone and a sulphurous smoke filled the room. Clara generally goes away when the stone is being talked of.

Mr. Gregory examined carefully the rockwork in the Jones' garden and finding no crystal there and the bricks and clinkers disturbed, had no doubt in his own mind as to who was the "criminal." I am not sure that the Jones' did not decide on letting their house on receiving a letter from Mr. Gregory in which he told his suspicions.

At all events, I know that Mrs. Jones has never had another rock-work and I think that they move about a great deal. But whether this is because they want change of air, or because Tommy's neighbours soon find him out, I do not say.

The Monkey on the Moor

T HE CHILDREN HAD ALL GONE to the seaside for the summer. They used to paddle and bathe and find shells. Sometimes they were able to dig such deep holes in the sand with their spades that they could stand up to their knees in the hole, and little Ginia, the youngest, was almost buried in the sand. She thought this great fun and one day she thought she would bury her shoes and socks in the sand; so after she had been paddling, instead of running up and down in the hot white sand to dry her feet as Annie and Harry were doing, this wicked little girl popped her shoes and socks into a hole and covered them well up and then ran off to the sea again. No one had seen what she was doing, and when she came up with her little wet feet to be dried, the shoes and socks could nowhere be found and little Ginia had to be carried all the way home with her bare legs like a little beggar girl.

The next day her mama said she would go into the little fishing town near which they lived, to get a new pair of shoes. Ginia wanted to go too, but her mama said as she had been so mischievous she must stay at home, and Annie and Harry went. They had to go down a very steep road. On one side there was a hedge full of blackberries and Harry wanted to stop, but they knew their mother was in a hurry, so they trotted down the steep stony little road. There were not many shops but there was one which had plenty of sand shoes, and a pair for Ginia was soon bought; and then the children's mama went on to the big shop of the place, where there was a sort of bazaar, a place Harry and Annie liked very much. There they saw dolls and balls, and little dancing bears and wheelbarrows, and they settled together what they would like to have on their next birthdays.

When they were going back, they took another road which led them by the church with the strange old stone cross and the iron gates which shut in a little churchyard. Near these the children soon saw a dark little boy with black hair and eyes and a ragged little coat; but it was not the boy at whom they looked, nor at the little organ which he was carrying, for on the organ they soon saw there was a little brown monkey. He had on a little red cap and coat and had a long curling tail; he seemed very restless and kept jumping up and down. The little boy tried to quiet him and begged for a penny. The children's mama felt sorry for the little boy who looked so

9. Manuscript page of Julia Stephen's *"The Monkey on the Moor."* The note at the top, by Leslie Stephen, reads "I had made some drawings according to a queer trick of mine & Julia thought that they would do for illustrations of some children's stories—alas!" Courtesy of the Bloomsbury Collection at Washington State University Libraries, Pullman, Washington.

ragged and was so far away from his own home, so she took him to a shop and bought him a big roll of bread. He told her he had come from Italy with his father and mother, and now they were both dead, and he had only the organ and his monkey, and he went about from place [to place] getting pennies wherever he could, and sleeping wherever he could find shelter. In the summer he slept under the hedges and in hay fields; but in winter he was so cold, and sometimes when he could find no kind people to give him shelter, he thought he should die with cold. While the children's mama was talking to the poor little boy and pitying him, the children were talking to the monkey and pitying him. They could not get any answers out of him; but they made them up in their own heads, which is often the best way.

The little boy was very grateful for the bread and said he would come to the children's house that evening and play to them and show them the monkey. Annie and Harry were delighted to hear this and made haste to go home and tell Ginia what had happened. As they went, a big jackdaw flew away from the church tower saying, "Jack, Jack," so loud Annie started.

"I think he was talking to the monkey," she said. "I am so sorry for that dear little monkey."

"I am more sorry for the little boy," said her mama. "I think he has no nice bed and no one comes to say goodnight to him and he has to walk all day long and goes to sleep out in the cold and rain. I dare say the little monkey gets much more to eat and much warmer beds than poor little Paul. The monkey can creep into little holes and eat all sorts of nuts and berries which would not feed the boy."

"Oh, but he is chained," said Annie. "He can't go where he likes, as the boy can. He is always tied up and he can't talk to any of his friends. I know he wants to get away and have a game at play." Here they got home and gave Ginia her shoes, and down all went to the beach. Some fishermen were bringing in their nets, and the little silvery fish they did not want they threw out and the children caught them and put them in their buckets. The children climbed about the rocks and found some tiny crabs, but they were kind little children and did not keep the crabs but let them go back to their homes after they had looked at them well.

In the evening they all had great fun in the garden, where they found snails and butterflies and caught bees under tumblers and watched them go into the flowers; but they let all the creatures go again and were very unhappy if by chance they hurt one of them. Though, as Annie said, one must not walk at all if one wanted *never* to hurt insects. There were so many about all the paths and grass that they could not help treading on them sometimes. Just as Nurse was calling them to tea and telling them to make haste as there was some nice hot rolls and honey, they heard someone coming through the garden gate, and as they turned round they saw the little Italian boy with his organ but without his monkey. "Oh, where is the monkey?" the children cried, running up to poor little Paul.

"Alas! He has fled," said the boy, beginning to sob. "I let him loose as I always do for a little to play about and eat his nuts and I went to get a glass of water at the spring by the hill. We had been playing at the big house on the hill and the kind people had given me pennies and Jocko nuts, so I thought we would both have a little rest. I left Jocko to play and drink some of the clear sparkling water, and when I came back Jocko was gone."

"Have you been into the town?" said the children's mama.

"Yes, I have been to all the shops and no one has seen him. I have called him and whistled. Often Jocko runs away and I find he has stolen an orange or a nut from some shop he has seen, but I always get him back—but now he is gone and I have lost my one friend."

Poor Paul began to cry again and the children were almost crying too, but Annie went up and said, "Never mind, the monkey *is* so happy scampering about. I am glad he is free and we will be your friends. Come and have tea." Paul was not quite sure whether to be angry with the little girl for being glad; but her eyes looked so blue and kind and she held out her hand to take him to tea, which he thought would be very nice, so he dried his eyes and went off. The children were full of chatter and pleasure at having this little strange boy. Nurse made him wash well before he came to tea, for she did not like foreigners, she said; but the children did, and they asked him [about] his old home and he told them how he used to live on funny long white things called macaroni and how there were grapes hanging over his father's cottage and big white oxen drew the plow and the sun was so hot—so hot.

"Hotter than here?" said Harry.

"Oh, here it is not hot," said Paul, laughing. "With us the skins grow brown, brown like chestnuts. In the winter, we eat chestnuts and we have yellow maize. Oh, it is much nicer than here."

"But you never bathed in the sea, did you?" said Annie, who liked going far out into the blue sea and was not afraid when a big wave did knock her over.

"Bathe in the sea, no—never. I was not near the sea. I lived among the hills," said Paul, "but the sea here is so cold I would not bathe." Harry was very much pleased at this, for he never liked to go into the sea. He said he was afraid that the waves would come over him; but all the same he used to get very wet, for he used to take off his shoes and stockings and paddle and sometimes even sit down in the sea which made him just as cold as if he had gone right in, and wasn't half the fun.

The children's mama had a little bed made up for little Paul and let him sleep that night in their house, as she thought it would be so sad for him to go and lie under a hedge all alone. He cried when he went to bed, as he said he had always had little Jocko near him and he could not bear to think he should never see the little monkey again; but the children's mama told him they would all help him to find the monkey, and Paul was soon asleep, feeling the nice white sheet and soft pillow very comfortable after the hard beds on the ground he was accustomed to have.

Now don't you want to hear what Jocko was doing all this time? Annie was quite right—the poor little monkey was very tired of going about tied up. He longed to run off and have games with the hares and squirrels. He thought it would be much greater fun to pick the nuts and berries in the woods than always to go along the dusty roads, and he was tired of begging for pennies, which he did not know how to spend. Still he was very fond of little Paul and had never liked to leave him. On that day, though, he thought there seemed to be many kind people near Paul; and when they stopped in the wood for Paul to go and drink the nice cold water in the stream, little Jocko darted off and was out of sight before Paul came back—he did not mean to go right away far, only to have a little fun. When he got out of the wood, he found himself on a wide moor. He peeped out but no people were to be seen. The sun was setting and all the sky was dark, and far away below, there was the bright blue sea in which little Annie had been bathing. On the moor, there were no houses, only big bits of grey stone; and all round the stone and over the moor was a beautiful thick carpet of purple heather mixed with golden gorse. The gorse pricked poor Jocko's legs a little but he found he could easily jump over it onto the grey stones, and every now and then he found a purple bilberry. It was not quite ripe but he did not mind that. As he hopped over a big block of granite, he saw something with a red bushy tail and a sharp nose, looking at him out of a pair of very bright eyes. This was a fox who had come out, he said, to breathe the evening air, but I am afraid he had really come to see if there were any little bunnies who had stayed up late and who would do for his supper. The fox was very much surprised when he saw Jocko. He had never seen a monkey before and he could not make out whether he was a hare—or a hairy little boy. He thought he must be a boy so he spoke very politely, for foxes don't like boys or men.

The monkey was not at all afraid. He had come from over the sea, far, far off, and he had seen a great many foxes and knew they did not hurt monkeys; so he answered the fox's good evening very quickly and asked him where he was going.

Now the fox did not much like this, for he usually found that all animals were afraid of him and so he could make them do what he liked; but this little beast, though he was so small, talked as if he were a wolf at least and seemed to know all about him. "I'm only taking a walk," said the fox.

"So am I," said the monkey. "Let us go together."

The fox did not like this either, for he was very hungry and he was not sure whether his new friend would let him eat the rabbits or kill them either, for he thought to himself, "If this hairy boy likes rabbits for supper, he will eat them himself, and if he likes them as friends, he won't let me eat them, so either way I shall lose my supper." You see, foxes are very clever; they think of things all round and don't just say yes or no when they are asked a question, like sheep or rabbits. The monkey was clever too and he knew what the fox was thinking of.

"I shan't disturb your game if you let me play my own," he said. "I suppose you are really out hunting, though you have not got a red coat on like mine." The fox felt very frightened when he heard this, for he hates the word "hunting" and does not like to see red coats. He now felt sure that the monkey was a new kind of boy and he thought he had better take him right over the moors and into the most wild part and then leave him. He did not think it likely that the monkey would be able to run and burrow as he could. So off the two started on their way. They passed two adders who were slowly dragging themselves over the stones back to their home in the furze bushes. "Nasty things," said the monkey, and gave a little tweak with his sharp white teeth to the long trailing tail of the adder.

"Don't touch them," said the fox in a fright, for the adder turned round and darted out its long quivering tongue. But the monkey had leapt onto a high rock and was looking down laughing, which made the fox again feel sure he was a very clever little man. Then they walked on, and as it grew darker and the sun went down behind the sea, the stars came out and presently a big yellow harvest moon came shining down on them. A bat flew by, slowly creaking his wings, and after him came a big brown owl, heavily flapping. When she saw the fox she stopped, for they were old friends.

"Are you coming to the Quoit?" said the owl.

"Yes, I believe so," said the fox.

"Why, who have you got there?" said the owl, blinking her big bright eyes as she caught sight of Jocko.

"A gentleman I met on the moor who asked me to walk with him," said the fox, feeling very grand.

"An odd sort of a gentleman," said the owl, "for he wears a tail."

"I know you," said the monkey; "I have seen plenty like you."

"Plenty like me?" said the owl. "I don't think you could have seen plenty like me, for there is no other owl here who can spread his wings as far as I can," and she bent forward her head and spread out her wings right round her, while her eyes looked so fierce and she said, "Too whoo, too whoo," so loud that even her old friend the fox felt afraid. The monkey did not.

He stood up on a stone and bent his head just as the owl had done and spread out his arms just like wings and said, "Too whoo, too whoo" just in the same way.

At this the owl was very angry and said to the fox, "I don't think your new friend has very good manners. I advise you not to see much of him—" and taking no more notice of the monkey, she flapped her wings three times and flew off into the blue air, and they could hear her saying, "Too whoo, too whoo" as she went along.

"Old Mrs. Owl is not in a very good temper," said the monkey. "It is a pity she did not stay, I thought we might have had some fun."

"Do you know her," said the fox, "as you call her by her name?"

"I have seen lots like her, as I told her—" said the monkey with a nod, "and I know much better owls than she is. I have seen beautiful round white owls like balls of snow, and big eagle owls which can carry off sheep."

"Hush, hush," said the fox, for at that moment, "Baa, baa," was heard and they came upon a flock of sheep who had crowded down from the hilltop to shelter themselves beside a big block of granite.

"Oh, old sheep, are you there?" said the monkey. "Come give me a ride, Baa Baa," and he jumped on the back of a big sheep and made him gallop up the hill. The sheep was too fat to get very far and the monkey was too kind to tire him out, so he jumped off and went back to the fox, who had been poking his nose everywhere to see if there were any little rabbits or lambs about. But there were no lambs, as it was too late in the year for them, and the bunnies had wisely gone to bed. "Where did the owl say she would see you again?" asked the monkey.

"Oh, at the Quoit," said the fox. "On moonlight nights we often meet there!"

"Does anyone else come too? May I come, Mr. Fox?" said the monkey, giving a tweak to the fox's brush.

"Oh, certainly," said the fox, who all the same was very angry. "You can come as far as I am concerned. I don't know if the others will be glad to see you."

"Oh, everyone is my friend," said the monkey, laughing. "I find my supper on the hedges, so no one guides me—the little rabbits and mice may run as they please, for me. I never disturb them." The fox was very glad to hear this, for he had not felt sure whether the monkey, who was so quick and clever, would not eat *his* supper. The two went on talking and trotting. The fox gave up trying to run away, for the rocks were so big and sharp that he could not run straight, and whenever he tried to get away from the monkey, Jocko was down on him, as he could swing himself over the rocks and he leapt down on the sharpest points of granite without even getting hurt.

The Quoit

At last they got to the very top of the hill. The monkey felt rather cold, for though it was a warm summer night, on the hill came a fresh breeze from the sea.

The moon did not look so big and red now but smaller and paler. There shone many stars, and on the sea red and white lights were dotted about.

"I have come from ships," said the monkey, "I have been in a ship."

"What?" said the fox. "Have you been on that great big tumbling thing that never stays still? Oh, how cold it is and how noisy!"

"Have you been to the sea? I thought you never went near it," said Jocko.

"I never want to go near it," said the fox, "but some of those creatures like you—I thought you were one of them at first, but when you told me you never eat meat I knew you could not be—they came after me one day. They were what they call having good sport. I gave them a fine run, that I did, right over the hill and then to the cliff by the sea. I am light and I ran. The hounds came after, I heard them coming, and quick I darted down the side of the cliff. I thought I could manage it and anything was better than being taken by all those wretches. I got down and just had a splash in the water and off I was, deep, deep into a long hole there was in the sand bank. I heard the hounds crash and splash and one man came down too. They did not escape as well as I did; but I did not look out to see what had happened till it got dark and then I crept away home."

"That must have been a dreadful day," said the monkey.

"Why?" said the fox. "Don't you know that is sport, and people say it is worth living for? But sometimes it does not end so well as that day did, and I never like the sight of a man; I was afraid you were one."

"Why, no," said the monkey. "I have a friend who is one but he does not hunt; he is very kind but very stupid as all men are. Poor things, they have lost their tails—that makes them envy us." The fox was quite pleased to find that the monkey was not a man, and so went on talking in a much more friendly way than he had done at first, and they were very good friends when they reached the Quoit. "There is old Mrs. Owl," said the monkey. "I

10. LESLIE STEPHEN. *Monkey with pipe*. Courtesy of the Woolf Library at Washington State University Libraries, Pullman, Washington.

will give her a fright," and he said, "Too what, too whoo" so loud and so fast that the old owl blinked her eyes and flapped about, wondering where all the other owls could have come from. When she found that it was the monkey, she was very much offended, for owls don't understand jokes. She was seated on a great big piece of rock which lay flat on three pillars of rock. By the side of the owl was a big pig, who looked very proud, and behind the pig was a hare. "What a comfortable place," said the monkey, and up he jumped and pulled a long clay pipe out of his pocket and pretended to smoke just as he used to do to amuse people when he went out with the organ. At the sight of this, the owl flew off, the hare jumped down and then the fox looked rather uncomfortable. Perhaps after all this was a man? Who else ever did such a nasty thing as smoke a pipe?

The pig alone never moved. He knew men very well. He always lived near men, and though they smoked, he knew they couldn't grow tails, so he grunted out to the owl, "Come back, you old stupid—it's only a monkey." And to the hare, "Lily, what are you hiding for? He won't hurt you."

"No," said the fox, who began to feel comfortable again and wanted to show how much he knew, "my friend only eats fruit and grain like the respected Hunks; and though he knows men and has even been on the sea, he never hunts any of us, and I am sure we are all very glad to see him." The owl sailed back when she heard this, but she did not like the pig calling her an old stupid. Just then came a little rat who only saw the hare and was begging to be taken up for shelter among them.

"Go off," said the hare quickly; for he had a kind heart. "Mrs. Owl is just behind." The rat did not wait a minute, but scampered off and was out of sight before the owl knew he had been there.

The monkey, who was still smoking his pipe, was talking to a beautiful white goat with curling horns who was going to his home. "Where is your home?" said the monkey.

"On that other hill over there among the rocks," said the goat. "I live there with a great many more of my family. There is not very much to eat so I come here where there is more, but now I must go back or my family will be frightened."

"May I come and see you?" said the monkey. "I like goats. I often saw them when I lived near the sea, and you look like some of my old friends."

The goat, who was very polite, made a low bow and said, "Come soon, for now the blackberries and nuts are getting ripe and it is a good time for us all," and then he sprang off onto a rock on the other side of the hill and the monkey watched him leaping down the side of the hill. His feet hardly seemed to touch the rocks and soon they saw him begin to mount the other hill on which was his home.

"What are we to do tonight?" said the fox.

"I was just going to speak," said the owl, "but so many low people have been here tonight that really ladies seem quite in the wrong place."

"You can never be in the wrong place, madam," said the monkey. "Such beautiful figures must be right wherever they come."

The owl was pleased at this and said, "I did not know, sir, that you were there."

"Oh, yes," said the monkey, "and I should like to come nearer you, madam, if I may, to see all the shining gold you wear." The wicked little monkey was feeling very cold and thought it would be very nice to get close to the soft down of the owl.

"Pray come as close as you like," she said kindly and opened her wings a little.

"Grun grun," said old Hunks, "we are all so civil tonight that we shall never do anything."

"What have we got to do?" said the fox.

"I had been telling Mr. Hunks when you came up," said the owl, "that near the sea lower down on the moor there is [a] big stone that they say can move. Several people from over the sea, like your new friend, Mr. Fox, are coming to try and move it, and I thought you might like to come. I, being a lady, cannot of course do such a thing."

"That will be very amusing," said the monkey, "let us all go." And down he leapt. The owl flew overhead, directing them by her cry which way they should go; and when they came near the rock, she murmured something about home and flew off. "Why has Madam Owl left us?" said the monkey. "She was nice and warm."

"Ah, yes," said the fox; "but she wanted her supper and so do I. I think she smelt that rat who came up to the stone, for she is very clever, but she does not like people to know that she eats rats."

"I hope the rat will have got off safe," said the hare with a sigh. He could not help feeling afraid, as the fox said he was so hungry, that he might find out the place where his own little leverets were lying asleep.

"Come, come," grunted out Mr. Hunks, "we shall never get to this place if we stay talking. Let us keep our breath for moving the stone." And he trotted heavily down to a jutting-out piece of the cliff on which stood some blocks of rock. On the top of them was another piece not quite flat but it looked as if it would be very difficult to make it move.

A big brown bear had been trying. He now leant back quite tired out. A bright pink flamingo had jumped onto the top; but he was much too light to make the rock stir at all. A big hippopotamus was slowly climbing up the rocks to see what he could do—he was very stupid but very good humoured, and he laughed heartily when he saw the flamingo strutting about on the top.

"A little light thing like that will never move a rock," he said. "Now I am of a good figure and understand such things." So he went on; but Mr. Hunks the pig did not like to hear the hippopotamus talk as if he were the only clever person, so though he could not go as fast, he pushed past the hippopotamus and got his nose well under the stone and asked the bear to sit still and help him by keeping his back against the stone.

"Now I shall get the stone to rock," thought the pig and felt very proud and happy, for a big cow had just come up and was looking on. "That conceited cow," thought the pig, "who makes such a fuss and thinks so much of herself, she will see soon what I can do!"

Poor old pig, he did move the stone; but down it came on his poor nose, for the monkey had sprung up the other side and had been helping to make the rock move; and now, when it was raised, he suddenly let go and down came the stone, just catching the end of poor piggy's snout. He gave a squeal and tumbled back on the hippopotamus, who said, "Mr. Hunks, please get out of my way."

"Out of your way?" said the pig. "It is you [who] are in mine, you stupid old creature. However, I moved the stone, but how it came down on my nose, I can't think."

"It was the monkey who did it," said the cow quietly.

"I'll teach him manners then," said Mr. Hunks, very angry, but when they turned round, where was the monkey? Nowhere to be seen! They looked and called. But no monkey could be seen.

"Perhaps he's gone to his supper," said the fox. "It is very late. I wish we were near a farm; but perhaps some of those gannets might be good."

Chwee, chwee, he heard at his side. He had forgotten a cormorant had come to see the fun. She now flew off to the high rock which stood out of the sea. On it were many gannets, cormorants and seagulls and now the rustle of their wings was heard and they plashed down into the dark blue water, letting Mr. Fox know that he would find no one at home if he took the trouble to call. He took the hint and determined to try if he could follow the hare home; but he had darted off some time before, and the flamingo was strutting up and down on the back of the hippopotamus so his neck was safe. "Goodnight," said the fox, "I have had fun and fasting enough," and off he trotted, and I am afraid he paid a visit to the farmyard on the hill before he went back to his hole on the moor. The other beasts trotted off their different ways but nothing was seen of the monkey.

Jocko had been rather afraid of the pig when he heard him squeal, and he had got tired of all these animals; so he thought he would be off, over the hill, to see the white goat who had looked so friendly. It was a good long way and poor little Jocko was very tired, and almost wished himself back with Paul, who used to carry him so often and used to keep him so warm. He went along the hillside where he had seen the goat go and then down into the valley. There was a nice clear rushing stream which made a pleasant sound as it hurried over the stones to reach the sea. Jocko sat down by it and washed his little tired feet and drank some of the water and picked a late strawberry that he found hiding under the hedge. Then he felt better and jumped up gaily and went up the other hill, where he knew the goats lived. The sky was getting clearer and a pretty pink light seemed spreading over everything. The moon looked very white and tired. She knew that she should soon have to hide her light, for the great gold sun was coming to warm the world. "Baa, baa," the monkey heard, and he knew he was near the home of the goats. There they were, so many of them—more than the monkey could count, for as Paul had never learnt to do sums, Jocko had not either. There were more than twenty strong white goats and a great many pretty little kids, who were just waking up. The old goats were telling them to keep quiet, which Jocko was very glad to hear, for he wanted to rest very much. He soon found his goat friend, who was very kind and seeing how tired he was, found a nice warm corner under the shelter of a rock where the turf grew close and sweet, and near it was a great blackberry bush full of fruit. The monkey picked some of these and then curled himself round in his cosy little corner and was soon fast asleep.

When he woke up, he could not think where he was. Instead of being with little Paul as usual under a hedge, the little organ by his side, he was out on a hillside. He did not know where, and for a few minutes he could not think what had happened. The sun was shining and there was a fresh breeze blowing, which blew through the blackberry bush and even blew down a ripe blackberry to Jocko's feet; this brought him to himself and made him remember where he was and the friendly goats. He jumped out to look for them, for he felt rather lonely. As soon as he got on the top of the bit of rock that sheltered him, he saw his old friend the goat standing and very cheerfully munching some of the short sweet grass which grew between the stones. "I would not let the kids wake you," said the goat, "for I am sure you are tired. Now, would you like to go and find the others? And where they are, you will find some nice fresh bilberries and a stream of water in which you can drink." Jocko was much pleased and soon jumped up the rocks after the goat, though he still felt very tired. When he got to the place where the flock were, he found them all looking very shiny in the morning light. Their silky white coats shone in the sunlight and their curious yellow eyes looked very friendly when poor little Jocko, in his faded red coat, thin on his little brown body, made his appearance.

The little kids were being taught to jump by a very old Billygoat. He had very long horns which curved away sharply and when he tossed his head, they seemed to say, "If you don't do right, you shall feel my horns." But he was really a very kind old fellow and he never hurt any of them. One little kid, who was very mischievous, even came and pulled the goat's beard; but he was quickly scolded by his mother, who told him to go back and jump properly. They all had to learn to jump from one rock to another with their four little hoofs close together and without making any noise. When they could do this well on the level ground, they were taught to leap up and down the hills, going from crag to crag, every day taking a longer jump, and the one who made the widest jump got the prize, which was a lump of salt.

Presently, Jocko heard a great bustle going on. "What is the matter?" he said to his friend.

"Nanny has to go to town," he answered, pointing to a big old mother goat. "She is to give her milk to a little girl who is sick, and she is very proud of going to the town; and when she gets to the house, the children all pet her and bring her sweet herbs to eat and once they made a wreath of flowers for her, so she likes going very much."

"Don't the children try to tie her up?" said Jocko, who thought the children must always want to keep animals, as he had been kept, to beg or earn money in some way.

"Oh, no! They are so kind and bright, but don't you know children?" said the goat. "You look as if you had lived with them or how did you get your coat? And who brought you here from over the sea?" Jocko had been feeling rather ashamed of himself for having left little Paul and now he told the whole story to the goat. "I wonder you left that kind little boy," said the goat; "but it must be nasty to be tied up. I see sometimes that big dogs are; but I think that is because the men are afraid we shall get bitten. We have a man who belongs to us and he is is very kind and he has little children who sometimes come and play with us. Now Nanny is going. Goodbye, Nanny." Here the mother goat came up to them. She looked very proud. Her white coat was finer and longer than any of theirs, Jocko thought, and though she had no long twisted horns, she had a kind, sensible face.

"Who is that little fellow?" she said, seeing Jocko for the first time. And then the friendly goat told her Jocko's story. "He had better go back to the little boy," said Nanny, decidedly. "And he had better go at once with me. The little children to whom I am going are sure to be able to tell us where the little boy with the organ is, for they are *very* clever children."

"Won't they tie me up?" said Jocko anxiously.

"Oh, dear, no," said Nanny, quite indignant. "And we will get them to make little Paul promise not to tie you up again, but then you must promise never to run away again."

"Yes," said Jocko. He was rather sorry to be back but then he felt as if he would never be able to live out on the cold moors with the goats, and he knew little Paul must be very unhappy all alone. So he settled to go off to the town with Nanny.

When he began to run by her side, he found his legs were so stiff he could hardly get along, so he felt very near crying, for what should he do if he could not walk? "You see what it is," said Nanny. "Even that one night out on the moors, and such a hot night as it was, has made you all stiff and cramped. What would become of you in the storms of wind and rain which are coming, and on the cold winter nights when the stars look so big and clear and seem so cold as if their points were little sharp knives? All the brooks are turned into clear white ice, and if there were not all our kind friends near in the farm house, *we* should do very badly even with our thick coats, but you, poor little thing, you would die at once!" Poor Jocko was shaking all over at the thought of himself out on the cold hillside as Nanny described. He was quite ready to go back to little Paul now, but how was he to get to him? Nanny saw how frightened and tired he was and said, "Well, don't cry. I'll manage. You just jump on my back. I am sure you can't be very heavy, poor little fellow, and you will get nice and warm with your feet stuck into my fur; and if you hold on tight, I won't throw you off." Jocko was delighted. He soon jumped on Nanny's back and off they started. Jocko found it rather more difficult to keep on than he had expected; for though Nanny thought she was going very quietly, she could not help jumping over the rocks and going across the hills instead [of] along the high road. However, at last they saw the funny little fishing town stretching out into the sea, the houses all so crowded together, it seemed as if people could not live in them. "The house I am going to is not in the town," said Nanny, "but a little way on one side; it has a nice garden, and the little children will be looking out for me, for I am late." And she sprang forward, almost sending poor Jocko over her head.

They trotted down a little lane and then across a field, then into another lane, where a kind-looking man stood. "Well, old Nanny," he said. "You came nearly as quick as I did in my donkey cart, but who is this you have with you, I wonder?" he said, as he saw Jocko. "However, I must milk you quickly, for the little girl will be waiting." As he talked, he went up

11. LESLIE STEPHEN. *Monkey on goat.* Courtesy of the Woolf Library at Washington State University Libraries, Pullman, Washington.

through a gate into a little sloping garden, the lane full of flowers and rocks; a little fountain stood in one corner and in another was the children's playground. Annie was there on the lookout for Nanny with a cup for the milk from her.

When she saw Jocko riding on the back of the goat, she clapped her hands and flew back to the house, calling, "Paul, Paul, here is your little monkey." Everyone ran when they heard Annie calling out, and little Paul did not say a word, but just ran to the goat and in a moment he had little Jocko in his arms. Though Paul was so happy to see Jocko again, he could hardly help crying, and as for Jocko, he wondered how he could ever have left Paul when he felt how happy he was to see Paul again. He stroked Paul's face and Paul kissed him and kissed the goat, who was standing by waiting to be milked.

The children were all so happy to see Paul with his monkey, but the goat and the monkey had both something to say and they did not know how to say it. "You dear old goat," said Harry, who was not afraid of goats though he would not stroke even a little puppy. "How kind of you to bring Jocko back." Nanny was very glad someone spoke to her, and now the man milked her nice fresh milk into the jug which Annie held and which Nurse came to fetch, for poor little [Ginia], who was ill in bed, wanted [her] milk and they had all quite forgotten [her].

The monkey stroked Nanny too and looked at Paul—he wanted to tell Paul what had happened; but he could not. "Oh, why did you go?" said little Paul. "You must never, never leave me again, Jocko. I must take care that you can't get away." The little monkey gave a sad little look at the goat. He was very glad to get back to Paul but he did not like to think of being tied up again.

The goat understood what the monkey meant but she could not speak to the children. So she only said "Baa" to the monkey and rubbed her nose against little Paul.

Luckily, there was someone who did understand. Little Annie, when she heard what Paul said, knew quite well what the monkey wanted, and said, "No, no, Paul. Now Jocko has come back all by himself, you must trust him and treat him like a friend and never tie him up." Jocko gave a little jump of joy when he heard what Annie said and he stroked her hand and then ran back to little Paul and looked up in his face to show him that he would never run away.

"Well," said Paul, "you shall not be tied up, my Jocko, but never go right away."

"He never will, I know," said Annie—and she was quite right. Jocko used sometimes to go off for an hour [or] two when he got away to the

moors to see his old friends and have a game by the old Quoit; but when
morning came, Paul always found Jocko ready to go about with him and to
take off his cap and beg for pennies. They very often came back to the place
where Annie and Harry lived. It was the place they both liked best; and one
year when Paul had grown bigger, the children's mama told him if he liked to
stay with them and work in the garden, he and Jocko could have a little
room so that they need never sleep under the hedges anymore. Paul was very
glad to do this and so Jocko had a very happy life and was allowed to eat as
many nuts and berries as he liked.

Emlycaunt

I HEAR SOME LITTLE VOICES SAYING, what is Emlycaunt? Who lives there? Is it a place? Can we go there? My dear children, wait a few minutes and you will know as much about Emlycaunt as I do; I don't know if you will ever know more, but there are some little children who say they have been there and that they know all about it. So perhaps you will go there, too.

It was a cold winter's night. Snow had been falling all day. Now it lay thick and soft, covering the roofs with its smooth, white blanket. The air seemed black as the snow fell, yet how white the ground became. The children had watched it and wondered at it till they could see it no more.

"See," said Lily, "that little robin – it can't find its way home," and she ran and opened the hall door, just in time to save the poor little robin from being beaten against it by the wind; its feathers were all soaked and icy, its eyes were dim and the red seemed to have been frozen out of its breast. "Oh, Tommy, it is dead!" cried Lily to her brother.

"No, it isn't," said Tommy. "Let us warm it. Then you will see it will move." Lily got some soft wool and wrapped it round the poor bird; then she breathed on him with her soft warm breath, and the robin began to breathe too, and its round eyes seemed as if they would soon shine again. Tommy ran for some bread and milk and in a few minutes the robin could eat it. I am afraid he would have liked a fat worm better; but the children would never have liked to see a worm eaten up. Though they didn't love worms as much as snails. "Snails are the nicest," said Tommy. "I like their horns."

"I like their shells," said Lily. "I wish we had shells."

"I don't know," said Tommy doubtfully, "I think they would be a bore. They would get broken so soon. I would rather have a tail, I think, and a hairy skin."

"Why, Tommy," said Aunt Joan, "do you want to be a monkey? You could not read about all your dear animals then."

"No," said Tommy. "But I should *be* one. I should like to live where there were only animals."

"I don't think you would," said Aunt Joan. "Would you like to be out in the wild forest of India, and in the night, when you wanted to go to sleep, hear the roar of a tiger who wanted you for his supper?"

12. VANESSA BELL. *Snail.* Courtesy of the Collection of Anna Dorothy Kramarsky, permission of Angelica Garnett.

"Oh, I should live in a house," said Tommy.

"You couldn't have a house if there were no people to build one for you, unless you lived in a beaver's hut," said Aunt Joan; but Tommy thought that there must be some place where the animals were all kind and where though there were no people, there were houses. He sat with his blue eyes blinking at the flames that danced in and out of the big wood fire, and Lily petted her little robin. Aunt Joan was writing her weekly letter to India. The children's Papa and Mama were there and Aunt Joan took care of Tommy and Lily. The next day was to be Tommy's birthday and it had been settled that they were to go to the zoo; but now the snow would be too thick. Aunt Joan said she would take Tommy to the Bazaar, which was quite near, and he should choose whatever present he liked. All night, Tommy dreamt of presents and animals – he thought that he was in a big shop and all the toy animals turned into real ones, and just when he was going to buy a big, brown, hairy bear, which he thought was a toy though it could growl and walk about, it turned round and gave him a hug.

He woke with a start and found that someone *was* hugging him. But it wasn't a big brown bear; but his own little sister Lily, who had crept from her little white bed in the corner and was standing in her nightgown trying to wake Tommy with kisses. When he woke at last, he saw that she had a big parcel in her arms, and in a minute he was undoing all the many knots and papers which were hiding a most beautiful ship. "It's *just* what I wanted," said Tommy. "How could you know?" He forgot that he had said that he wanted a ship at least fifty times. "What shall we call it? Oh, the 'Water Lily,' of course. What fun it will be sailing it, in the Round Pond." The children jumped up at this thought, but there could be no sailing today.

A thick yellow fog seemed to come right up to the windows. Nurse had a bright fire crackling and candles lighted but they had been thinking too much of the ship to notice this before. When they went downstairs, they found that gas lamps were lighted in the street, and in the dining room their big silver lamp tried to make the room look bright, but the fog seemed everywhere and made the children's eyes smart. Tommy could hardly see all the beautiful things that were waiting for him: Aunt Joan had a delightful book full of stories of animals and pictures, and there was a big box with brightly polished Indian toys, bricks of all sizes, red, yellow and green cups and balls, little boxes one within another, and cups, jugs and pots all made by the clever Indians in the bright shining wood – and sent from far over the sea by the children's parents. Tommy found so many delightful things, he could hardly make up his mind to eat his breakfast; but the hot steaming coffee which seemed to overcome the fog with its fragrance was poured out and Aunt Joan said he must eat some of the crisp twisted rolls which Cook had

13. VANESSA BELL. *Ship*. Courtesy of the Bloomsbury Collection at Washington State University Libraries, Pullman, Washington, permission of Angelica Garnett.

made on purpose for him. There was clear golden honey besides, trickling slowly from its waxen comb, and new-laid brown eggs which had been sent for Tommy's birthday by his old nurse in the country. There was plenty of time after breakfast for building, and the children were soon busy making bridges and what they called "morials." The fog was so thick that there could be no thought of the zoo, even if the snow had not still lain outside, and it seemed doubtful whether they would even get to the Bazaar. However, with the bricks and toys, the beautiful book and the "Water Lily," the morning passed quickly. On birthdays, the children always chose their dinners and Tommy had chosen roast turkey and raspberry puffs; then they toasted chestnuts on the hob. Tommy had made up his mind that he should not go to the Bazaar, when all in a moment the fog cleared away and though there was no sun and no blue sky, still the light seemed quite bright to the children and they felt able to talk out aloud, which somehow it had been very difficult to do when it was so dark.

"I think," said Aunt Joan, "you might go to the Bazaar after all, Tommy. I am afraid Lily must not, as her cold isn't well, but we shall not be away long." Lily was sorry not to go but she would not say a word to spoil Tommy's pleasure. "It isn't a good day for choosing a present," said Aunt Joan, "for the Bazaar will be so dark that you will hardly know what you want."

"Oh, I know," said Tommy, nodding his head; "only let us go, Auntie, and I shall soon enough get what I want."

"Very well," said Aunt Joan. "Be quick and put on your little fur coat and cap. It is getting dark and we must make haste."

It was very dark when they got to the Bazaar, and all the things looked strange in the curious yellow light. Tommy was half frightened as they passed through the Chinese part where big golden dragons gleamed out of black screens and curious nodding heads seemed to mock at him. Big black cabinets carved all over with strange beasts which he could hardly make out, filled up the corners and a faint sweet smell came puffing from a little burning cone in a blue plate.

Tommy hurried through this place and came to the toy stall. It was in one of the very darkest places of the whole Bazaar, but Tommy went at once to the corner where he felt sure that he should find what he wanted.

It was a black and white spotted rocking horse. He had often seen it and had longed to have it for his very own. It seemed to him that to have a rocking horse would be next best to having a real horse and that he should never be dull if he could have a ride whenever he wanted.

"Very well," said Aunt Joan, smiling. "I see you have made up your mind. I thought you would have liked a tool chest. Look at this beauty!"

14. VANESSA BELL. *Children playing after breakfast.* Courtesy of the Bloomsbury Collection at Washington State University Libraries, Pullman, Washington, permission of Angelica Garnett.

15. VANESSA BELL. *Chinese doll and poodle.* Courtesy of the Bloomsbury Collection at Washington State University Libraries, Pullman, Washington, permission of Angelica Garnett.

16. VANESSA BELL. *Rocking horse*. Courtesy of the Bloomsbury Collection at Washington State University Libraries, Pullman, Washington, permission of Angelica Garnett.

And she showed him one full of hammers and saws and all the most delightful and dangerous things.

"No, Auntie. This is what I want," said Tommy. "May I have it? May I get on it, now this minute?"

"Yes," said his aunt. "They have to bring me change and I want to look at one of these china pots, so you can take a little ride." Tommy no sooner heard this than, first having patted his new horse tenderly, he jumped on his back. There was very little space for riding, for every corner was full of farm yards, dolls' houses, and carts which made a funny music when they moved.

However, Tommy's horse seemed able to move, for no sooner was Tommy on his back, bounding up and down, than he found himself bounding out of the stall, out of the Bazaar, into the street! The horse did not stop and strange to say, no one tried to stop it. The street was very dark and Tommy felt rather frightened but he thought that somehow the horse would know the way to his home. Tommy had ridden on a real horse, at least on a pony, but the rocking horse went very fast; his feet hardly touched the ground and Tommy felt a little uncomfortable.

However, the ride could not be a long one, he thought, for his home was not far from the Bazaar and at the pace the horse went, they must get there in a minute. How surprised Lily would be to see him riding up to the door on a spotted rocking horse! As he thought of this, he looked right and left to see the door, which they surely must be near, but this was not a street he knew, nor could he see any house. "Stop! Stop!" he cried to the horse, but the horse bounded on along a narrow dark road; if there were houses, Tommy could not see them. The gas lamps seemed all to have gone out. Tommy tried to take his foot out of the stirrup but the horse went so fast he was afraid he should fall. And besides, if he got down now, what should he do? He didn't know where he was, every minute he was getting farther and farther away from his home. As Tommy thought this, he felt a little unhappy; but the horse carried him on so quickly and delightfully that he ceased to be frightened and did not wish to stop. He had forgotten about Lily, about his aunt and about his birthday party; he felt happier every moment. The air too seemed clearer, the thick darkness lay behind him; and in front was a clearer light. No snow could be seen and a fresh sweet breeze which blew on his face seemed to bring with it a scent of hay fields. Winter had gone. The day which had been so cold and dark, now grew bright and warm; the road which had been a dark slippery street, was now a wide country road. There were no houses and no people, but the air was full of buzzing bees. Bright coloured butterflies and swallows darted past; and there was a strange delightful feeling in the air which Tommy had never felt before. He

17. VANESSA BELL. *Tommy on a real horse.* Courtesy of the Bloomsbury Collection at Washington State University Libraries, Pullman, Washington, permission of Angelica Garnett.

did not want to stop the horse now, and this was quite as well, for the horse didn't mean to stop. On and on they went, a bright stream rustled down and a kingfisher flashed across it. The woods were full [of] singing birds and the cuckoo was calling all round. "It is very odd," thought Tommy; "I am *sure* it was winter this morning and that the snow lay thick in our garden, and here the wild roses are out and the birds are singing—besides it ought to be evening and it isn't."

While he wondered how all this *could* be, he saw a strange-looking thing in the distance: it looked like a tower, and on either side of it was built a wall. Where the wall went to, Tommy could not tell, for it seemed to go on and on, and the nearer he got to the tower, the further off the wall stretched. When he reached the tower, the horse stopped, and a gate flew open at the sound of a bell. Who pulled the bell? wondered Tommy. And who opened the gate? The horse walked in and Tommy found they were in a wide green place. It looked very large. Besides the tower, there was no building; but yet the place seemed full of creatures. Wherever Tommy looked he saw some animals and even some toys. Rabbits, little frogs and snails crowded round the horse, and the bees flew, humming and humming, taking no notice of anyone.

The horse stood still; Tommy got down, patting him to thank him for his nice ride and wishing very much that the horse could tell him what this strange place was. "It's Emlycaunt," said the horse, to Tommy's surprise.

"What an odd name," said Tommy. "I never heard of such a place, and who lives here?"

"Emlycaunt is a place full of all the animals the children have been kind to. It would be much fuller if children were kinder—" and the horse sighed.

"What do you mean?" said Tommy.

"You are a kind little boy," said the horse. "When you came to the stall to buy me, you stroked me and did not take hold of my mane as all the other boys have done, but you got up gently and so I was able to come off here. I have been waiting a long time."

"I am glad I came," said Tommy much puzzled. "Why are there so many daddy long legs here?" For wherever he looked he saw the long useless legs of numberless daddies.

"Daddies come here to be safe," said the horse. "Their legs are always in the way—they get into tea cups and lamps, they say, and they are glad to be in a place where there are no tea cups and no lamps."

"Why, there is Jumbo! Dear old Jumbo! How glad I am I came here. If I had been able to go to the zoo, I should not have seen him," cried Tommy.

The rabbits who had been all huddled together now seemed in a great hurry to speak. They did not like to see Tommy walking about and they pressed eagerly up to the horse with their eyes shining and their grey fur standing straight out. "What's the matter, you silly creatures?" said the horse. "Are you afraid of this boy? He won't hurt you or I should not have brought him here."

"Oh, you dear little things," said Tommy. "Do you think I would hurt you?" and he sat down on the grass and stroked the rabbits so softly that they soon became quite friendly and one even jumped onto Tommy's lap. Then a cloud of daddies came flying by and they rode races on the rabbits' backs. Their long legs reached the ground and they looked so funny, their thin wings flapping and their thin bodies shaken from side to side as the rabbits scampered round and round, that Tommy could hardly help laughing; but he thought perhaps the daddies might think it rude and as very thin people are generally very easily offended, he tried to keep quite grave.

One daddy, with the longest legs Tommy had ever seen, came up and made him a low bow, so low that in making it he nearly tumbled over. "I know you," he said. "You are the kind little boy who saved me just when I was going to be burnt in the candle. You caught me and your little sister opened the window and I flew out into the nice cool air. Where is the kind little girl?"

"Lily is at home," said Tommy, who suddenly remembered her.

"How dull she must be! Why didn't you bring her here?" said the daddy.

"I could not," said Tommy, almost beginning to cry as he thought how far off Lily was and how difficult it would be to get back to her.

The horse looked quite vexed. He had thought he was doing such a kind thing in bringing this little boy to Emlycaunt. He never supposed anyone would wish to leave it. He knew *he* should not. "Why can't you stop your stupid old tongue?" he said to the daddy, but the daddy had a feeling heart and the horse, though he meant well, was after all only made of wood.

"Of course he will want to go back," said the daddy. "And I daresay someone will be found to take him. I should think that the General would."

"Who is the General?" said Tommy.

"Why, that big elephant. Though he is so big and clumsy and looks vulgar with his thick legs, he is very kind and he often carries children, so I daresay he would carry you."

"He has often carried me at the zoo," said Tommy, delighted. "I will go and ask him."

The elephant was standing looking at some little frogs who were being taught to leap. "Who are you, little boy?" he said, when Tommy came up, and then, looking nearer, he said, "Why, you are the kind little boy who gave me some nice apples and buns when the other boys gave me ginger nuts, which I don't like, they burn me so."

"I know you, dear old Jumbo," said Tommy. "I was going to see you today and to have a ride on your back but it was so foggy, I couldn't, and somehow I came here. — It is all very odd."

"I have never seen a child here before," said Jumbo, "but I don't think *that* is at all odd. Most children hurt animals and this is the place where animals are happy so, of course, children could not come here."

"Lily never hurts anyone," said Tommy, who remembered Lily more and more as he talked to Jumbo. "I must get back to Lily."

"How will you go?" said Jumbo. "I don't suppose the horse will care to go back."

"Oh no, thank you," said the rocking horse. "I am sorry that the little boy does not want to stay. *I* do. I was very glad to get away from that horrid shop."

"I daresay you will be able to ride home on my back," said Jumbo. "Then you will get your ride, after all. I shall be soon going back to Alice.* Emlycaunt is all very well for things like *that*," and he curled his trunk towards the poor rocking horse, "—he is nothing but a toy—and for silly things like bunnies and daddies, who can't take care of themselves, but there is nothing to be done here and nothing to be seen. I only come for a little holiday." And he made a long brrrrr.

The horse didn't much like being called a toy; but at this moment he saw a very beautiful doll, called Geraldine Eva Georgina, who had once lived in the same shop with him, and he galloped up to her and forgot all about the elephant. Tommy knew Geraldine too, for long ago she had been Lily's doll. Then when Lily was too old to play with her, she was sent one day in a hansom cab with a pot of jelly to little Ethel, who was ill. How could she have got here? Tommy felt that in this wonderful place there was no end to surprises.

"Go and see the place," said Jumbo. "You must not be very long, or it will be quite dark and though they would let me in at the zoo at any time, perhaps you would not be able to find your way home."

Tommy was very glad to do what the elephant said, and a monkey who came cantering up on a donkey advised him to go to the bathing place. "On such a warm day," he said, "we all like to take a swim."

"So should I," thought Tommy, but he remembered that the animals

*See note 11, p. 263.

had no clothes to take off and didn't want towels to dry themselves with, so they could easily take a swim; but it would not be pleasant for him to run about in the sun to dry.

He soon got to the bathing place and was rather afraid to see the big beasts lying about in the reeds, but a friendly pig assured him that it was all right, and asked him to come in. "I am afraid I can't," said Tommy, "I have no towels."

"Towels, what are they?" said the pig. "There is nice warm grass to roll on for those who like, such as our friend Bruin, but I like lying over there," and he pointed to a little sandy shore. "I lie and blink and sleep and get nice and dry."

"I don't think I should like to do that," said Tommy.

"Well," said the pig, "I was always told that children were cleaner than we are. I didn't believe it and now I see it isn't true."

"Never mind him," said the monkey, who saw that Tommy was vexed. "I will show you a nicer place than this. In the wood where the river runs is the best swimming place and you will meet plenty of friends."

"I suppose they are all your friends," said Tommy. "But, you see, mine are children."

"Oh, I thought you were so fond of all of us!" said the monkey. "Why did you come here if you weren't?"

Tommy felt he was getting very red. Was it only last night that he was wishing to be in a place where there were nothing but animals? And now he was in this delightful place, he felt as if he wanted something else. "I didn't know that I was coming here," said he, "but I am very glad to be here and I do love you all; only you see, I love children too, and my aunt and Nurse and oh, ever so many people," and poor Tommy nearly cried as he thought of Lily and Aunt Joan and Ethel and Alice. How could he *ever* think that he should be happy away from them?

"Well, Jumbo will soon take you back. We won't think of it any more," said the monkey, who couldn't bear to see people cry; it was one of the very few things he was not able to do, so he never liked to see other people doing it. "Here we are in the wood."

"What a lovely place," cried Tommy, forgetting his sadness. It was a lovely place. Big oaks and elms shaded a quick rushing river; the branches of the trees were full of birds who sang as if they had never sung before. They were telling each other their histories, how they had got free. Some had been let loose from cages, others had been taken from their nests by cruel boys and then bought by kind ones who set them free. All were singing songs of freedom and joy, two monkeys were swinging on a branch, and through the thicket, Tommy saw the branching antlers of a beautiful red deer; his big brown eyes looked fearless and content, and close to him two rabbits were chattering as only rabbits can. "Just look at the otter going to jump," said the monkey. "He and the beaver are having a race and that silly old bear is to see who wins. He won't put down his pack; he belonged to a circus once and used to go round dancing and carrying things, and he can't forget this and always behaves as if he were still in a circus."

"How did he get here?" said Tommy.

"Oh, he was set free. A gentleman said it was a shame to keep such a fine beast tied to a show," said the monkey, "so he bought him of the circus man and, of course, Bruin soon ran away."

"That wasn't very kind of him when the gentleman had bought him. He should have stayed with his master."

"Ah, but that was the master's point of view," said the monkey, very quickly. "The bear's was quite different." Tommy didn't quite know what a point of view was, and as the monkey spoke rather sharply, he did not like to ask.

Just then a little robin perched on a twig in front of Tommy. It spread out his bright red breast and sang so beautifully, Tommy stopped. Then the robin hopped onto his hand. "Are you the dear little robin who was nearly frozen this morning?" said Tommy.

"Yes," said the monkey. "He has just come, as he was tired of the world and is glad to be in this free place! He is wanting to know about your sister."

"She isn't here," said Tommy. "I wish she were—but why can't the robin talk?"

"He has only two legs," said the monkey. "No two-legged things can talk."

"Why, I can," said Tommy.

"Yes, but you don't belong here," said the monkey, "and you and the fowls are a lower order of creatures with your stupid two legs; you can talk and they can sing but you can't understand each other. It must be a miserable world where you and they live."

"What odd things you say," said Tommy. "There are birds here."

"Yes, those who have been set free," said the monkey, "but birds are such stupid things that, unless they have been caught and put in cages, they don't want to get out of your world, [as] we sensible four-footed people all do."

Tommy felt quite put out but he also felt very hungry and, look where he would, there was nothing to eat. "I will go and ask Jumbo to take me back now," he said, and he walked away towards the place where he had left Jumbo. Jumbo was not there, however.

"Come quickly," said a grey rabbit, "or you will lose the fun."
Tommy never wanted to lose fun, so he followed the rabbit and between two
trees he saw a thick rope stretched on which his friend Jumbo was walking
with uplifted trunk. Little monkeys ran lightly before him. Cockatoos and
opossums clambered above. Tommy was glad he had not missed this sight.
When the elephant had got safely to the end of the rope, he put his trunk
round the stem of the tree and swung himself down.

"Oh, are you there?" he said to Tommy, and he looked very shy, for
elephants are the most bashful of creatures. "I was amusing the little ones
before I went off; we must go quickly now. It is late."

"The sun is shining very brightly," said Tommy.

"It always does here," said the elephant.

"Dear me," said Tommy. "Is it never night? Perhaps I have been here
ever so many nights without knowing it. What will they be thinking? I must
get home as fast as I can," and he climbed up on the elephant's back.

It wasn't very easy to get on, and when he was on, it was not easy to
stay on. A little brown monkey who was standing by them saw that Tommy
looked frightened, and jumped up beside him and held him tight on. "I am
so light, Jumbo won't feel me," he said, "and if you hold on to me, you are
sure to be safe. I never fall."

Tommy felt rather sorry to leave this wonderful place. The gate by
the tower opened wide, and when it shut, Tommy felt as if the sky got suddenly darker and the air colder and as if the sweet fresh scent had gone out
of the breeze, but it was still clear daylight and the hedges and fields were
still full of roses and hay and the larks were still singing. Only, after Emlycaunt, nothing seemed so sweet and bright. The elephant trotted steadily
on. He did not make bounds like the horse but his swinging trot seemed to
take Tommy almost as quickly past all the fresh Spring things which had surprised and delighted him so much on his way to Emlycaunt, but which
seemed less charming, now he was leaving it. "We shall find it dark enough
soon," said the elephant. "It was quite black when I left the zoo. I knew there
would be no fun going on, so I came away."

"Was that really only this morning?" said Tommy. It seemed to him
quite a week since that foggy snowy morning when Lily had awoken him
and he had opened his presents. With them came the thought of the good
breakfast he had found waiting for him and he felt a longing to be home. He
remembered that his cousins were to come to tea, there was to be a grand
cake and crackers, and a conjuror afterwards. Well, all that would be over
now, but he knew Lily would have kept some tea for him.

The sky was getting darker, as the elephant said. The trees seemed to turn brown, then bare, and then vanished. In their place through the gloom, Tommy thought that he could make out the shape of buildings. A smell of smoke, instead of hay, was in the air and the shriek of a distant train replaced the song of the birds. Tommy was glad to hear that, for he knew he must be coming to London, and London meant all the people he loved. And delightful as Emlycaunt and the beasts were, they could not make up for Lily and Aunt Joan. The nearer he came, the more he longed to see them again, and he felt as if he could hardly stay on the elephant's back, that he must run home quicker than anyone could take him. "What a fidget you seem in," said the monkey. "Are you sorry you have left Emlycaunt? You won't find it easy to get back there."

"No, no," said Tommy in a hurry. "I don't want to get back there, I am in a fidget to get home. Emlycaunt is beautiful but I like home best."

"Well, that's an odd taste," said the monkey, "but I suppose you never have anything to do and no one teases you."

Tommy did not answer, for now they were really in streets. Lumps of snow stood at the corners, and in the Square gardens the snow lay thick. The gas lamp[s] glimmered faintly and through open kitchen doors, Tommy saw cooks standing by bright fires, and a fragrant smell of tea and cake came through the dark cold air. "Oh dear," he thought, "have I been away all night? And is it tomorrow? I know the elephant said that there was no night at Emlycaunt and I was a long time there."

"You seem sad," said the monkey.

"Oh no," said Tommy. "Only I was thinking that it must be a long time since I had left home. I see it must be tomorrow."

"What must be tomorrow?" said the monkey. "You are a very odd boy. I can't think why you wanted to leave Emlycaunt. You were much happier there, but I can't take you back, I am afraid."

"Are you going back?" said Tommy. "I thought you were going to the zoo."

"Oh no," said the monkey. "I have had quite enough of the zoo. I don't mean ever to go there again, if I can help it. It is all very well for the elephants. They walk up and down and see the world and they can hurt anyone who teases them; but we monkeys are not free. We are kept in cages and when children come and tease us, we can hardly get our paws [out] to give them a scratch. If we do manage to pull off a little girl's hat, we are punished and our nuts are taken away. I like Emlycaunt where I can run about and tease the bunnies and go up to the tower to see who is coming. I was glad when I saw you, for I thought that you were a monkey, but you are only a boy or you would never go back."

"I am sorry," began Tommy, but he could not go on for he was not really sorry that he was not a monkey. In fact, he did not much like the idea of being taken for a monkey.

"Oh, never mind, it wasn't your fault that you weren't born one," said the monkey. "I daresay one will come some day, but here we are near the zoo and I must jump off. Stop, old Jum," and the monkey sprang off the elephant's back, taking a little swing on his trunk before he darted off.

"Where do you want to go, little boy?" said the elephant. "I am afraid no one would pay to see you at the zoo, so you would be starved, for the keeper would not be able to feed such a very common animal as a boy. You see, there are so many boys in the world."

"I don't want to stay at the zoo at all," said Tommy. "I think I could find my way home now, for I know what street we are in and it is very near our Square. If you will stop, I think I can jump down. Thank you, thank you, dear Jumbo. I hope I shall see you soon." And Tommy scrambled down somehow and found himself on the dirty, slippery London pavement again. "Goodbye, dear Jumbo," he said, going up to the elephant's trunk and giving it a kiss.

"Goodbye," said Jumbo, "I daresay you mean well, but I can't feel kisses," and his big black shape vanished in the growing darkness.

Tommy felt as if he could not run fast enough, now that he saw again the Square railings, the dingy trees and the well remembered pillar post. He recollected how anxious they must be at home about him and longed to know whe[ther(?)] his birthday had been and what they had been doing without him all the long, long time when he had been leading such a strange delightful life. Here he was at last. The hall lamp shone on the steps, which were covered with crisp yellow gravel, and Tommy pulled the bell with a beating heart. The butler, with grave solid face, opened the door. "Well, and it will make even old Bumbles jump to see me back," said Tommy to himself, and he could hardly help laughing as he thought of startling that very respectable old servant.

What was his surprise and disappointment when Bumbles said, "Walk in, Master Tommy, make 'aste. The wind is so bitter cold."

"Why, Bumbles," began Tommy, but at this moment there was the familiar sound of a four-wheel cab which drew up at the door, and out of it stepped Joan.

"Oh, [Tommy], you have been quick," she said. "The people were some time bringing my change and I suppose you thought you would run home to help Lily. I found the shop man would not send your rocking horse today as it was so late, so I took a cab and brought it back, for I was determined you should have it on your birthday."

18. VANESSA BELL. *Monkey hanging from Jumbo's trunk.* Courtesy of the Bloomsbury Collection at Washington State University Libraries, Pullman, Washington, permission of Angelica Garnett.

Tommy hardly heard all this. He put his arms round his aunt. "Dear Aunt, have you been unhappy?"

"Unhappy? Oh, not at all. It was a troublesome parcel, the horse seemed as if it could not keep still. Here's Lily."

"Come up!" cried Lily, running downstairs in her pretty pale blue dress. "Ethel and Alice have just come and we are arranging the tea table. Come, Tommy."

"Lily dear, I didn't mean to be away so long," said the puzzled Tommy.

"You haven't been long at all," said Lily. "At least it hasn't seemed long to me. I had so much to do, I haven't half finished it. The crackers are on the table but the coloured candles are not. But Nurse wants you to come up quickly." As she chattered, they both ran up the carpeted stairs. The air of the house felt so warm and fragrant after the raw cold outside; a big wood fire burnt in the hall, sending out a spicy resinous smell, and Tommy could hear Ethel and Alice's voices ringing as they scampered along the nursery passage. "Where did you go?" said Lily.

"Ah, now I can tell her," thought Tommy. "I went to Emlycaunt, Lily. Such a beautiful place, only I wanted you."

"Emlycaunt?" said Lily. "What a funny name! I don't remember any toy shop of that name, but I suppose it was one of the stalls in the Bazaar. You knew I could not go, Tommy. Aunt Joan said it was too cold for me."

"Oh, it wasn't cold there," said Tommy, "quite hot, like summer. Not a toy shop at all, Lily, but full of bunnies and daddy long legs."

"Good gracious me, what a horrid place!" cried Lily. "What are you talking of? Auntie, where did you get that rocking horse?" she said to her aunt, who was following them. "Tommy says it was quite hot and full of rabbits and daddy long legs."

"We went to Dunn's stall at the Bazaar, of course," said Aunt Joan. "It was very close certainly, and I saw some little grey rabbits, but I certainly didn't see any daddy long legs."

"You weren't there, of course, Auntie," said Tommy. "I am afraid you wondered where I was, but you see—"

"I was rather sorry you ran home in the wet," said Aunt Joan, "especially as I had to have a cab for the horse, but I supposed you were tired of waiting."

"It wasn't that, Auntie, I went to Emlycaunt," said Tommy, determined to be heard. "I saw such lovely hay fields and heaps of roses and heard the cuckoo."

"Dear me," said Aunt Joan, "what a delightful place to have been to, this cold foggy day. How did you get there, Tommy?" she added, laughing.

"On the rocking horse you were going to buy for me, Auntie," said Tommy.

"I *did* buy it, Tommy, and here it is." Sure enough, there was the rocking horse, being carried up by Bumbles and Jones, the boy, who had been busy taking off the covers of paper and cloth in which the horse had been wrapped.

"Oh, you poor dear horse," said Tommy. "How have you got here?" But the horse said nothing. He looked out of his big black painted eyes and never so much as winked.

"It is just tea time, Master Tommy," said Nurse, "and there's the door bell. You must make haste and change your boots, which must be wet through with your having run back from the Bazaar this snowy night. I can't think why you didn't come back in the cab."

"Oh, Nurse," said Tommy, "I didn't come home from the Bazaar at all. I went to such a beautiful place and I came home on the elephant's back."

"I believe you have been dreaming. All this excitement has been too much for you," said Nurse. "It would be better for you if you went to bed and had some rhubarb instead of going down to eat cake and tea." Tommy made great haste to change his boots, he was so afraid Nurse might really put him to bed, and he was not only very hungry but longing to tell Ethel all his adventures.

All the cousins had come and tea was ready. There was a big white cake with Tommy's name on it, and a flag in the middle, and then blue and silver and crimson crackers, shining brightly by everyone's plate. Crisp oatcake and a dish of honey disappeared quickly and a pile of freshly baked rolls of every size and shape soon came to an end. Tommy sat next to Ethel, as he always begged to do on his birthday, and now he had plenty of time to tell her all about his wonderful journey and the strange things he had seen. Ethel listened quite gravely. She did not think he had been asleep or that he wanted rhubarb. Emlycaunt soon became as real a place to her as it was to Tommy. "We will live there when we are married," she said, for they had quite settled they should be married when she knew how to darn. That seemed the most important thing in their lives, for their stockings were always in holes and Ethel reflected it would never do to be married with holes in one's stockings.

As Ethel believed it all, Tommy thought the others might, so he told them; but they all laughed and said they wondered why he had left such a lovely place and that he might at least have brought some roses back. Tommy was getting rather cross when luckily the conjuror came and the children all went to see the puddings which he made in his hat and the eggs

19. VANESSA BELL. *Birthday cake*. Courtesy of the Bloomsbury Collection at Washington State University Libraries, Pullman, Washington, permission of Angelica Garnett.

which he found in his handkerchief and, best of all, when a gold chain was
found in Lily's hair, though she was quite, quite sure she had never put it
there. At last the happy evening came to an end. Tommy had thought that
when he got Lily to himself in the nursery, he would tell her all about his
wonderful journey; but when the time came, they were both so sleepy that
they had hardly been tucked into their cosy beds by kind Aunt Joan before
they were fast asleep.

The next day the fog had all gone, the sun shone brightly. The frost
had come, making starry flowers on the window panes and hardening the
snow. Aunt Joan said she thought that they had better go to the zoo to
make up for Tommy's dull birthday, and though Tommy thought to himself
he had been to a nicer place than the zoo on his birthday, still he was longing to go there to talk to Jumbo again. Suddenly, he remembered that *Jumbo*
had talked at Emlycaunt. It had not struck him as odd there, but it certainly
would be to hear him talking at the zoo. As Tommy thought of this, he remembered that his rocking horse had talked too and there he now stood in
the school room, looking as cheerful and quiet as any spotted rocking horse
ever looked. His mouth was a little open but it certainly did not look as if it
had ever uttered any words; and as for his eyes, they were shiny and black
enough but they neither seemed to recognize Tommy nor to be able even to
see him.

When they got to the zoo, Tommy went straight to the elephant.
"Dear old Jumbo," he whispered, "I am glad to see you again. I told you I
would come soon." But the elephant only lifted his trunk and pushed
Tommy gently away, for he had a number of children on his back and must
take them their ride and be back for the others who were already waiting on
the step. Tommy was very much disappointed but he determined to wait till
the elephant had done taking the children and then have a talk. So he
waited while Lily went off to see the tall giraffes who were stretching out
their tongues in vain.

At last the rides seemed at an end and Tommy again went up to the
elephant, but though Jumbo looked patient and kind, he took no more notice of Tommy than of any of the other children. And when Tommy, putting
his face close to the elephant's trunk, said, "Are you going to Emlycaunt?"
Jumbo only moved his trunk away impatiently as much as to say, "Why do
you stand here if you haven't got a bun?"

Poor Tommy at last went off to the monkeys. He felt very sorry for
them after all his little friend had told him the night before, but they were
all swinging about and chattering, so that all he could do was to give them
nuts and biscuits to make up to them for being in cages. "I am so sorry for
them," he said to Lily.

Lily said, "Why, they seem to have plenty of fun." And so they did as they swung down from the branches and poked their clever fingers in the kind keeper's pockets where they found raisins and figs.

"I am sorry," said Tommy, "because I know they must be longing to go to Emlycaunt and I don't suppose they will ever get there."

"I don't suppose they will," said Aunt Joan, laughing, but Lily said rather impatiently, "*I'm* sick of Emlycaunt." And so perhaps are you?

The Mysterious Voice

IT'S OF NO USE ASKING me to be good. I'm not going to be good," said Jemmy
Stone. "I *like* being naughty—it's no use looking at me like that, Helen.
You can tell Mama if you like. I *shall* poke the fire with my boots and I don't
care if they are burnt nor if they cost a lot. I like being naughty, I do, I do, I
do," he sang out, poking the logs of wood with his feet and watching the
showers of sparks that went up the chimney after each kick. Little Helen
opened her big brown eyes and looked at him with admiration and horror.
She saw it was of no use for her to say any more, so she went out of the
room. Jem did not hear her go out. He was so pleased with his own boldness
that he kept on repeating, "I like to be naughty, I do," after Helen when [she]
was not there to hear him.

"And you shall be naughty if you like, my darling," said a very soft
voice near him. Jem looked round with a start. The voice was not his mother's
nor his aunt's nor indeed was it likely that anyone he had ever seen would
say such a thing to him; and yet it must be someone. Who could it be?

The evening seemed to have become very dark, the logs of wood
sent up no more yellow and blue flames. There was a heavy scent in the air
and Jem felt an odd creepy sensation come over him. He tried to see who it
was who had spoken, but the room was full of shadows, and he could make
out no shape clearly. However, the voice was clear enough whomever it
came from. "So you want to be naughty, Jemmy," it said.

Jem felt relieved. Whoever it was, it knew his name, and no one
very awful would call him "Jemmy." "Yes," he said, getting courageous as he
heard his own voice, "I do like being naughty. Mother always says that good
children are always happy but I know they aren't; when I go out to pay a visit
and sit up right and say 'How dy'e do' and 'Please' and 'Thank you' and people say that I am such a good little boy, I get pains all up my legs and I feel so
dull and miserable; but when I just bang in and out and slam the doors so
that the china plates on the wall shake and tumble, and when I send the cat
into the dairy just when the cream is poured out, then I feel quite happy, so I
am sure it is much best to be naughty!" Jem had almost forgotten that he was
talking to anyone, as he thought of the delightful time of mischief he had
had when he went to see his aunt in the country.

He was therefore rather surprised when the soft voice he had heard before said, "Would you like to be naughty always?"

"Oh, yes," said Jem, "that would be fun, but," suddenly recollecting himself, "shouldn't I get punished?"

"What do you call getting punished?" said the voice.

"Why, having dry bread for tea, going to bed early, double lessons, those sorts of things," said Jem, "and being scolded and kept in."

"Well, would you like to be always naughty if you were sure of never having any of these punishments?"

"Yes, that I should. Oh, what lots I should do!" cried Jem, much excited; "but there's no chance of it," he added sorrowfully as he remembered that punishments always followed his favourite bits of naughtiness, and thought that he was in for one now for having burnt his boots.

"If you really want to be naughty, I promise you that from this day, you may be as naughty as you like, and you will have none of the punishments you have ever had," said the voice which now sounded very grave and distinct, "only you *must* be naughty, you won't find it so easy to be good." Jem felt a little frightened at the way in which these words were said and was preparing to ask more questions, but just then the door bell rang. He heard the hall door open and a cheery sound of voices. In a moment the dining room door was thrown open and Gibbons, the fat butler, came in with the big lamp.

Jem looked round and rubbed his eyes. Where had the voice come from? No one was in the room. All seemed as usual, only he felt unreal; he must have been asleep. Yes, he must have been dreaming, that was it: sitting by the fire, he had dropped asleep, and the delightful promise was nothing but a dream. Jem got up from the fire, feeling rather disappointed: now he was in for a scolding, his boots were in holes, and a strong smell of burnt leather filled the room.

"Why, Master James!" said Gibbons. "You did give me a start. I never saw you in the corner."

"What a smell of burnt leather," said Jem's mother, Mrs. Stone, coming in with her bonnet on. "Something must be on fire." Helen, who had followed her mother into the room, looked anxiously at Jem, who felt sure that his scolding would soon come, and then—tea in the nursery, for he had been told over and over again not to play with fire nor to sit by it unless the guard was on. Helen was afraid too, for she went shyly up to him ready to comfort him; but Mrs. Stone said cheerfully, "I really think that your boots must have been burning, Jem," and stooping down to look at them, "Yes," she said, "they are all in holes." Still her voice had no sound of displeasure in it, and she went on, "Hadn't you better run up and change your boots before tea is ready? I have brought a nice Sally Lunn tea cake which is going to be hot-buttered for you and Helen." Jem felt quite bewildered. Was it no dream after all? He would try what he could do then, so he answered rudely:

"I shan't change my boots but have tea here."

Mrs. Stone nodded, "Very well," and left the room. Jem eat the hot crisp Sally Lunn with an odd feeling of being someone else. His boots were very uncomfortable, and the smell of burnt leather made him feel rather sick; but there was some comfort in the thought that Helen had to smell it too. And he tried to forget that his toes were rather sore and scorched, in the thought of all the delightful things he would be able to do, for now he felt sure that the voice had been real and no dream.

Mr. and Mrs. Stone were going out to dinner that evening, so the children sat alone in the drawing room. Till bedtime Jem had not much chance to make use of his new liberty, for Helen and Harry, his younger brother, always did whatever he wanted. When bedtime came and Nurse called him, Jem felt that he would see what he could do, so he called out: "I'm not coming to bed," and threw himself into his Papa's easy chair, with a story book.

Now Nurse was not a person to be made fun of. Not only did she insist on the children coming to bed the moment they were called, but she never would listen to a word of entreaty from them for even one minute more, and would carry them off remorselessly, whatever they might be doing, the very moment the clock struck. Now, however, she answered quietly, "Very well, Master Jem," and went off without him. Jem felt triumphant but still a little disappointed at this easy victory. Still he *was* triumphant; there he was in his father's easy chair, while Helen and Harry had been taken off to bed like babies!

His story book was a new one, and he was soon deep in it, but he had not thought he should feel so very sleepy—his eyes began to prick and burn, his head seemed as if it were always being jerked forward and although the story was very interesting, it somehow got quite confused. At the end of half an hour he could hardly understand what it was about, and found himself reading the same line over and over again without understanding it a bit, and at the end of an hour he was sound asleep. He woke with a start, hearing voices—his parents had come back from their dinner party. Jem was too confused at finding himself in the brightly lighted drawing room with his mother in evening dress standing before him, to make any explanation. He only said, "I fell asleep." Mr. and Mrs. Stone took no notice, as if it were the most natural thing in the world that he should be sleeping in the drawing room.

They wished him "Good-night," apparently not caring whether he were going to bed or not, and Jem followed them upstairs, feeling rather aggrieved though he could not have explained why.

"At all events," he thought, as he got into his cosy little bed, "I will have a good lie in bed tomorrow," and he stretched himself out in the cool clean sheets, not without a dim sense that he might have been more comfortable if he had gone to bed when Nurse called him.

In spite of having been up so late the night before, Jem woke up early the next morning. The sun shone brightly, the canaries were chirping and Helen and Harry were chattering away, full of plans for the day. They were quite eager to get up when Nurse called them, and Jem heard them splashing about like little fishes in the big bath in the next room. When Jem's turn came, he shouted out, "I'm not going to get up. I shall have another sleep."

"Oh! Come, Jem," cried the children. "It is so late and it is such a fine day. There is frost on the windows. I believe we shall be able to skate."

Jem only answered very crossly, "Shut up! I'm going to sleep." Nurse said nothing and Jem was left to sleep if he could. It isn't very easy to sleep when the sun is shining brightly into the room, birds and children all chirping, and the house is astir, and so Jem found. He pulled the clothes well over him and turned and twisted himself in every sort of way; but instead of going to sleep he got more and more wide awake and what was worse, he began to feel very hungry. The children and nurses were having breakfast, and he could hear them talking and laughing. No one seemed to miss him, and soon there came a smell of hot toast. Helen had been toasting, he felt sure. How good her toast always was, so crisp and hot. And now there was a fragrance of coffee and fried bacon, which made him feel still more hungry and cross—he had never felt so hungry for breakfast before. It was no use thinking of going to sleep, he had better get up, after all. So up he got and dressed himself as quickly as he could.

The gong sounded for the dining room breakfast just as he had finished dressing, and it struck Jem that it would be much nicer to breakfast with his parents than in the nursery. He would go and tell Nurse that he was not coming in to breakfast. He would have much nicer things for breakfast downstairs, for they always had hot rolls for breakfast and sometimes muffins!

Jem just popped his head into the nursery for the sake of showing he could do what he pleased, and said, "I'm not going to breakfast with you." Little Helen had jumped up and made a place for him, but he took no notice of her and said, "I'm going down to breakfast in the dining room."

"Oh, you're up, are you?" said Nurse with a grim smile. "Will you

have some more coffee, Helen dear?" and she went on pouring out coffee
and eating her breakfast as if she were quite accustomed [to] Jem staying in
bed as long as he liked and then having breakfast downstairs.

Down went Jem to the bright breakfast room. The sun shone on
the silver kettle and tea things. Mrs. Stone was making tea, Mr. Stone cutting his newspaper. Jem was not disappointed in the look of things. Not only
were there the usual crisp hot rolls and muffins, but a beautiful white comb
full of clear golden honey lay on a brown dish, and there were new laid eggs,
and fried fish, so that he felt he had done very well for himself in choosing
to breakfast downstairs.

If he had looked forward to astonishing his parents by his appearance, he was disappointed. Mrs. Stone kissed him as usual and when he
muttered something about not having had any breakfast, instead of seeming
surprised and asking questions, she only turned to the butler and said he
had better lay a place for Jem. Gibbons looked rather cross but said nothing;
and Jem sat down and helped himself to hot buttered muffin, no one saying
a word. His mother gave him a cup of coffee and then turned to her letters.
She had a pile by her plate, and as she read them, she every now and then
read a bit aloud to her husband. It seemed to Jem that the letters were very
dull, and he missed the chatter of the nursery. Mr. Stone said very little, and
what he said was about things that Jem could not understand, so that Jem
felt rather depressed and out in the cold. He had never felt shy before with
his parents, but now he felt as if he did not like to speak to them. At last he
said that the honey was very good, but his mother only said, "Yes," looking
at him, Jem thought, not as if she were angry, but as if she did not see him. It
was very uncomfortable, and he was glad when the door flew open and
Helen and Harry rushed in.

Mrs. Stone put by her letters and her face looked all soft and smiling in a minute. Mr. Stone put down his paper as if quite glad to have done
with it and turned to get a bear's hug from Helen. It was the children's quarter of an hour and they all seemed happy that it had come. Only Jem somehow felt out of it today. He could not begin to ask his mother if she had any
nice letters or beg his father to take him to the pantomime, as the other two
did, when he had been sitting with them all the time as if he were grown up,
and no one seemed to remember that he was there.

At last Mrs. Stone got up and said she must go to her housekeeping,
and then Harry said with a sigh, "Oh, it is school time. Are you ready, Jem?"

This was a tremendous moment for Jem. He had always longed to
stay away from school, but Mr. Stone, who was a very punctual man, never
allowed them to delay a minute. He would hear no excuses, and whatever
the weather was and whoever might be staying in the house, the boys were

sent off to their day school the moment the clock pointed to a quarter to
ten. School began at ten o'clock, and as it was ten minutes' walk off, Mr.
Stone insisted on their leaving home at a quarter to ten. This then was the
time for Jem to find out whether he could do *anything* he liked without being
scolded. He felt rather frightened; but called out to Harry, "I shan't come,
you can go without me." Harry was already in the hall, and did not stop to
ask questions or to hear more, but banged the door and ran off. Helen followed her mother, and Mr. Stone, when he had finished his paper, laid it
down and went off to his office, taking no notice of Jem, who fidgeted about,
not quite knowing what to do with himself.

When his father had gone, he began to think that it really was very
delightful to have the day to himself, and that he had better find something
amusing to do as soon as he could. At this moment Gibbons came in to
clear away the breakfast things, followed by the page. A bright thought
came into Jem's head. He had long wanted to do something that would ag-
gravate the excellent but terrible butler, and now was his chance. The page
always took out a tray full of cups, saucers, etc., and Gibbons followed with
the large silver kettle, which he carried with great pride. Jem's plan was to
put his foot out slyly, and trip up the page so as to make him fall against
Gibbons. Jem would much have preferred to trip up Gibbons; but he knew
that that would be quite out of the question, as Gibbons was too stout, and
too wary to allow of such a trick being played on him.

The page had his tray full of china, Gibbons was walking close behind, holding up his beloved silver kettle, when he felt a knock and a crash
as the page fell against him, and it required all his strength and all his dignity to prevent his falling down himself and getting scalded. The cups and
saucers lay smashed in all directions. A boiled egg had broken so that the
yolk made a deep yellow splash on Gibbons' trousers; the tea pot was quietly
pouring out tea on the turkey carpet and the cream flowed in a thick stream,
quickly lapped up by Helen's tabby.

The unlucky page was a mass of milk and honey, both of which he
would have enjoyed very much had they been poured in, instead of over
him! Jem was delighted, he had succeeded better than he could have expected. The crash had been louder, Gibbons' face of fury had been more
amusing than he had thought possible. Gibbons turned angrily on the page
as soon as he had recovered himself a little; but the boy said something
about Master Jem and just then Mrs. Stone and Helen came to ask what
had happened. "Master James, Ma'am," Gibbons began.

"Oh, very well," said Mrs. Stone, "you had better clear up the mess,
Gibbons, and go and change your clothes, John. Your cat seems to enjoy the
cream, Helen," she added and they both left the room without even looking

20. LESLIE STEPHEN. *Cat resting.* Courtesy of the Woolf Library at Washington State University Libraries, Pullman, Washington.

at Jem. It was all very odd. Jem had certainly enjoyed all the mischief he had made; but the pleasure was very soon over, and now he felt very dull, left all alone in the dining room. There was nothing to prevent his going into the drawing room; but he heard the piano, and he knew Helen must be practising, so he would not be able to get much good out of her. After her practise she went to her other lessons with her mother, and then came luncheon time. The morning had gone and a very dull one it had been to Jem – he even thought it might not have been quite so dull if he had been at school. It is true he had carved his name on the dining table and cut the string of the curtains so that when evening came Gibbons would find he could not draw them, but even these forbidden delights seemed dull when there was no one who forbade.

After lunch, Mrs. Stone said she should take Helen to pay some visits with her, and she asked Jem if he would come too. "No," said Jem, "I hate paying visits."

"Then we will go without you," said his mother, and she and Helen were soon off. When they had gone, Jem wished that he were with them. The sun came out again and he longed to be out. He went into the street, and amused himself by throwing stones at the cats and ringing the neighbours' bells and rushing away when the doors were opened. He was just wondering whether he should go still farther and throw a stone at the drawing room window of a very old lady who lived just opposite, when his thoughts were taken off by the sight of an Italian organ boy, with his monkey. Jem knew the monkey well, and had often played with him. He had long wished to own the little animal, and the Italian had not seemed unwilling to part with it; but Mrs. Stone would not allow Jem to buy it. Now, however, Jem thought he could do as he liked. There was nothing to prevent his enjoying the monkey, and he told the boy that he meant to buy it. He had 10/ [shillings], which was what the Italian had always asked; now, however, it seemed that the monkey had become much more valuable. The Italian said he could not think of parting from his little friend for so little as ten shillings. "But it is all I have," said Jem.

"Have you no more truly?" said the Italian.

"That is all, every penny," said Jem, bringing out his purse with his one little gold piece.

"Have you no clothes you could give?" said the boy. "I have a little brother just your size."

"Yes, I have clothes," said Jem but he hesitated a little. Giving away clothes seemed almost too naughty a thing even for him to do.

However, the monkey put his head on one side and looked very comical, and the boy said crossly, "Since you won't buy him you shall not look at him anymore." So Jem made up his mind, remembering that he should not be punished, so what did it matter if he were very naughty? He ran up to the nursery, took down his new velveteen suit and ran back to the monkey boy without having been seen by anyone. The Italian's face gleamed when he saw the good clothes and he trotted off, taking leave of his beloved [monkey] a great deal more quickly and cheerfully than Jem had expected.

Jem soon forgot all about his clothes in the delight of really having the monkey for his very own. He had a good game of play with him and as the monkey was almost as mischievous as Jem, the furniture soon showed signs of his being in the house. He tore the corners of the curtains and carpet, stripped to pieces the nice cane-bottomed writing chair, put his paws in the ink bottle and even smeared them all over the writing table, and amused himself and Jem till, quite tired out, he fell asleep in Jem's arms. Now Jem thought he would carry out a plan which he had long thought of but had never expected to be able to do. He went upstairs very cautiously,

21. LESLIE STEPHEN. *Monkey sitting.* Courtesy of the Woolf Library at Washington State University Libraries, Pullman, Washington.

carrying the monkey, who was still fast asleep; when he got to the nursery he covered the monkey well up in a big flannel, meaning to lay him in the middle of Nurse's big feather bed. Nurse had a horror of all animals. She screamed if she saw a mouse and hated monkeys almost more than mice, calling them horrible reptiles, which always amused the children very much.

Jem thought with delight of her shriek of horror when, just as she was thinking of lying down in her soft comfortable bed, she should find the little brown hairy creature there before her! Jem had to be very careful not to be found out, and it was a long time before he could settle the monkey in bed, for Nurse and Nursemaid both came in and out, every minute. They never looked at the bed, and took no notice of Jem. Still he was afraid every moment he should be found out and, though he might not be punished, he should lose all his fun.

It was Saturday afternoon, and the nurses seemed as if they were moving all the clothes from one room into the other. Jem thought they had never been so slow. At last they seemed to have done and Jem laid the monkey very carefully in the middle of the bed, and covered him well over with clothes, so that he would not be seen.

When Jem got downstairs again he found tea all ready, and Harry had just come in. "How late you are, Harry," said Helen, who was just spreading her bread with treacle. "I thought you would have been back nice and early today."

"Well, work was done early, of course," said Harry, "but then there was a football match and I stayed to see it. It was such fun."

Jem longed to learn what the schoolmaster had said about his not having come, but did not like to ask, and neither Harry nor Helen seemed to give him a thought. Harry went on talking about the football [to] Helen, who was an excellent little sister, having the greatest interest in her brothers' games and work. When she had heard all that Harry had to tell – and Jem thought Harry's day sounded much more amusing than the days he spent at school – Helen said, "Now I must tell where I have been. Mother said I was to go to pay visits with her but I didn't in the least know where we were going, though I knew it would be somewhere nice; and it was, for we went to see Aunt Lizzie."

"Oh!" gasped both boys – Aunt Lizzie was expected back from India, they knew; but they had no idea she had arrived.

"Yes," said Helen. "Mother had been to see her this morning. She arrived quite early in the morning. Mother would not tell me because she wanted it to be a surprise. When we got to that big house in Lancaster Gate I thought Mother must be going to do something more to it, and I couldn't think what, for it all looked so nice and ready when we last went; but there was Auntie in the hall, so I hadn't long to think. She *is* so nice and kind, and she has a black servant all dressed in white muslin with gold bracelets on her hands and feet. Auntie let me help to unpack a box that was full of shawls and muslins. They smelt so nice and stuffy. And she gave me some silver bangles and a funny black doll, and tomorrow we are all to go and see all her things." Helen had to stop for breath here.

"Go on," said Harry, "it sounds so nice. How glad I am that tomorrow is Sunday and there will be no school so I can go too. I wish I had been with you today, Nelly."

"Yes, I did long for you," said Helen. "It is no fun seeing things alone. There were such beautiful pictures of birds, so soft with long tails, all painted on rice."

"On rice, Helen?"

"Well, rice paper, I suppose, only it was very white and thin and soft, so delicate it could hardly be touched. And there were chains which looked like gold, but they were really made of straw. Auntie gave me some for my doll, but I must wear them myself."

"Let's see them," said Jem, and Helen drew out with pride a long chain of dark yellow links.

"I don't think much of that. If all Aunt Lizzie's things are like that, they are not worth much," said Jem, laying hold of the chain. As he did so, the links fell into a thousand pieces.

"Oh, Jem," said Harry, "how could you do that?" Helen said nothing, she picked up all the fragments and did not even look reproachfully at Jem. Jem really felt sorry. He was fond of Helen and had not meant to spoil[?] her chain, but he found no words to tell her that he was sorry, and followed the others silently into the drawing room.

The half hour before late dinner was always the pleasantest time of the day, the children thought. Baby came down and played on the floor, and the children chattered away, not being afraid of their parents, who thought it the nicest time of the day too. Harry poured forth all about his football to his mother while Helen, seated on her father's knee, described the wonders of her aunt's house and showed the beautiful Indian presents. "What is Auntie like?" said Harry. "Is she old or young?"

"Oh, *very* old," answered Helen; "quite, quite old, I should think about a hundred, and very brown, not quite black, you know, but very nearly."

"My dear child," called out Mrs. Stone, "who are you talking of? Not Aunt Lizzie, Papa's sister! Nearly black, and about a hundred—why, she is very little older than Papa and was one of the prettiest girls I have ever seen."

If Mrs. Stone thought she would make the children think their aunt any younger, she was mistaken, for all Helen said was "Oh, I didn't know she was *older* than Papa. She *is* very brown, Mother, but she is kinder than anyone and I shouldn't like her to be a bit different."

"That's right," said her Papa. "I dare say Aunt Lizzie does seem old to you, but to me she will always seem a very mischievous little girl."

Jem longed to ask questions and to join in with all the talk; but he felt as if he could not. Somehow he seemed quite like a stranger and, try as he would, he could not behave as if nothing had happened to him. His father asked him what he had been doing; but as Mr. Stone saw he did not want to tell him, no one asked him any more questions. They all seemed to have forgotten all the naughty things he had done. He was the only one who remembered. When his parents went into dinner, the curtains could not be drawn, and the chair was found to be in pieces, but though Gibbons said "Master James," no one looked at him and his father and mother sat down to dinner without making a remark on the uncurtained windows.

Jem was glad enough to go to bed, when Nurse came to fetch them. He was longing for the time when Nurse would come to bed. Then he should have *his* fun. The others had had theirs but after this uncomfortable evening he should have a good time which they would know nothing about.

Jem was very sleepy after his troubled sleep of the night before, but he determined that nothing should make him go to sleep till Nurse had gone to bed. His little room opened out of the night nursery and as his door was kept open, he could see and hear all that was going on. Nurse had never seemed so slow in getting to bed. Jem's eyes closed at last in spite of himself and he woke with a start, fearing that he had lost the delightful moment. But lights were still burning and he heard voices in the next room, so Nurse had evidently not gone to bed. She was still in the day nursery. It was Saturday night and Nurse had all her clean clothes to sort. Jem had never known they had so many clothes. Surely they must soon all be done. He waited and listened. Nurse was now in the night nursery and he felt certain she would be quickly in bed and he should hear the shriek and have his reward in her fright; but as he listened he still could only hear the word "clothes," and then his door was quietly shut. The light was put out and all was silent. Jem felt thoroughly disappointed. He waited, feeling that he could not sleep, and after some time when all was quiet, he determined to creep out of bed, open his door and peep into the night nursery. It was very cold and he shivered as his little bare feet touched the polished floor. He had hardly opened a crack of his door when he heard "Fire! Murder! Thieves!" called out in a very loud voice. Any other time Jem would have laughed at hearing Nurse call out when she heard him open the door, but now he felt half-frightened himself, though he knew it was only Nurse. The nursery looked so odd with great strange shadows thrown by the flickering fire on the ceiling!

"It's only me, Nurse," he said.

"Do you want anything?" she asked.

"No, thank you," said Jem, who did not know how to tell Nurse that he had only come to find out if she was in bed – and back he crept to his own bed, quite chilled through. It was very odd. Nurse seemed comfortably in bed; but where was the monkey and how had she found him there? It was some time before Jem could get to sleep, and then he was not comfortable. The monkey kept jumping before him in his dreams and begging to be set free. Then the Italian boy seemed to come and take all the clean linen. So Jem went from one troubled dream into another. The monkey at one time turned into Helen and then she looked brown and quite unlike herself. She was dressed all in white muslin with gold chains and she was packing a great black trunk. Jem asked her why she was packing and then he saw that she was crying, and she told him that she was going to India and she should never, never come back, as he was such a wicked boy. This dream was the worst of all. When Jem woke, it still seemed to be going on, he could hardly believe that it was not true. It was day now; but there was no sunshine. Drip drip, he heard the rain on the leads.

The canaries were silent, people were moving about but they seemed so quiet that Jem could hear each drop as it fell with a little cold patter on the window pane. Helen and Harry generally laughed and talked all the time they were getting up; but today they were as silent as the birds. Jem saw by his little clock it was past the time for getting up, and he wondered why Nurse had not called him. Then he remembered that he had not got up when he was called the day before; and perhaps Nurse never meant to call him again! He had always thought it would be delightful to stay in bed as long as he wanted; but now he felt he must get up, so he went into the big bath which he found all ready, and dressed himself as quickly as possible. The day nursery door was shut; and Jem stopped for a moment before going in, for surely he heard Helen crying. His dream came back to him. Everything had been so odd lately, perhaps dreams were going to be true and Helen was going to India! This thought made him open the door very quickly. What he saw made him still more sure that his dream was coming true. Helen was sobbing by her mother's side, and Mrs. Stone was kissing and trying to quiet her. Harry too was crying and Nurse stood by, looking not angry but very grave. No one took any notice of Jem, who ran up to Helen saying, "You're not going to India, are you?" At his voice his mother turned round, and he then saw that she had something lying on her lap.

What was it? Something soft and brown but quite, quite still. Jem looked and looked and knew that he was looking at his poor little monkey, who lay with his little restless eyes quite shut, his little curly tail hanging stiffly down, for he was quite dead. Helen looked up through her tears. "Oh, Jem!" she said and her sobs prevented her saying more. Mrs. Stone laid the little monkey quietly down on the sofa and took Helen away.

She did not look at Jem nor did Nurse, who said to Harry, "I will take the little creature to the gardener to bury it," and carried the monkey off.

Jem, puzzled and miserable, asked Harry what had happened. Harry could hardly speak; but Jem made out that the poor little beast had been smothered, as the nursemaid had laid a pile of clean clothes on him when she went into the night nursery, not seeing in the dark that he was in the bed, and it was only late in the evening, when she took a candle and carried the things away to put them by, that she uncovered the little monkey, who was then quite dead. She had called Nurse, and both had tried to bring him to life, but it was too late. "Oh, Jem, why did you do it?" said Harry, sobbing again.

Jem was generally very sharp with Harry and hated being questioned; but now he felt almost grateful to his little brother for speaking to him. It was so dreadful for no one to take any notice of him. "I didn't mean to, Harry. I covered him up to prevent Nurse seeing him before she went to bed. I only meant to frighten her."

"You covered him up so that he could not breathe," said Harry.

"Well, he's my monkey," said Jem, who did not like Harry to tell him that he had killed his monkey; but he was sorry that he had spoken so, for he saw his mother standing by and her face looked sterner than he had ever seen it.

"Helen is tired out," she said, "and I have put her to lie down again. Nurse is with her. Come downstairs, Harry dear, and have breakfast with us." She never looked at Jem, who stayed behind, not daring to go down, and who had to make what breakfast he could off a little cold coffee and bread and butter, with Kitty the nursemaid, who was running in and out to Helen and Nurse with hot things all the time but did not think it necessary to warm up anything for Jem.

"Oh! Oh! I wish I could be good," said Jem when he found himself again alone. He had gone into his little bedroom and was watching the rain as it fell down, making a dismal little pool on the leads below his window. "Being naughty doesn't seem to be much fun."

"Are you tired of being naughty?" said the voice he had heard once before. "You have only had a day of it, are you tired already?"

"Oh, yes," said Jem, "there's no fun. No one seems to care whether

I am good or naughty and there's no fun in being naughty when no one minds."

"Well," said the voice, "it's very easy to go on being naughty, but it's very difficult to stop; in fact, I don't see how it's to be done."

Jem felt very frightened at this. "I do wish I could be good," he said and his voice sounded as if he really meant what he said.

"Oh, that you'll *never* be," said the voice very cheerfully, "but perhaps if you try very hard you may get punished again," and Jem fancied he heard a funny little laugh.

"I don't *want* to be punished," said Jem. "Why can't I be good and *then* I shan't be punished?"

"I don't think you'll ever be good," said the voice again, "but why don't you go on being naughty? Are not you able to do all you like? I am sure you have done plenty of things in this one day and no one has said a word."

"No, that's just it," said Jem, "and that's what I don't like. I'd rather they scolded or—"

"Or punished," said the voice, which now seemed to sound much kinder. "I thought so. Well, perhaps if you try very hard you may be punished in time." It didn't sound very pleasant but somehow Jem felt happier than he had done when he came into his room. He stayed very quiet all that morning and did all the things he could to show that he wanted to be good, but no one said a word. In the afternoon the sky cleared, and Mrs. Stone said she really thought they might walk across the gardens to see[?] Aunt Lizzie. The death of the poor little monkey had made both Helen and Harry feel so sad that Mrs. Stone was glad to take them somewhere pleasant. The children were delighted to go. Nurse put them in their best things, but when Jem's turn came to be dressed, he had no best things. Nurse did not say a word, but Jem felt very ashamed, as he had to go off in his old week-day clothes to see his new aunt.

Helen and Harry raced along the wet paths of Kensington Gardens, laughing when a gust of wind blew the rain drops from the trees onto their faces. The dead leaves gave out a pleasant fresh smell, and by the time they reached Lancaster Gate the children's cheeks shone like rosy apples. Aunt Lizzie ran down to the hall to meet them with outstretched arms. "There you are, my chicks. I hardly thought you would come this wet day. Who is this little boy and why haven't you brought Jem?" she said, for Helen and Harry looked so bright and rosy and were dressed so prettily she could not think that Jem, whose face looked pale and sad and who was in an old brown suit, *could* be their brother.

"This *is* Jem," said Mrs. Stone gravely, and Aunt Lizzie, seeing something had happened, asked no questions. Jem had hoped that his aunt would not know about him, but he had forgotten about his clothes; and he felt very sad and ashamed as he went upstairs into a room that was more like a big curiosity shop than a London drawing room. Big boxes and tin cases stood, standing half open, with bits of rough yellowish linen peeping out. Great china jars lay on the floor, and odd ebony chairs, carved with strange beasts, were piled up with shawls and bundles of embroidery. "There," said Aunt Lizzie. "Now, Helen, there is plenty for you to do. You may unpack the boxes and arrange the things you find in them just as you like. Harry can help you and there is a box of shells somewhere and plenty of funny things.

"Make this big drawing room look as pretty as you can and fold up all the stuffs properly. I don't suppose there is anything *you* would care to do," she said, looking at Jem. He longed to say he should like to help the others and to promise that he would do no mischief; but the words would not come, and Aunt Lizzie went into the back drawing room where she and her brother and [sister-in-law] were soon deep in talk.

Helen and Harry too were soon absorbed in their delightful work. They felt sorry for Jem; but they did not dare ask him to help, after what their aunt had said. All they could do was to show him all the best things that they found and to ask him where he thought they would look prettiest. He was glad even to be spoken to by them, and he answered them much more kindly than he generally did, and did not once call Helen a silly or Harry a baby. "There seems to be no end to all the delightful things," said Helen with a deep sigh of pleasure.

"There are such funny little black dolls dressed in gold and silver," said Harry.

"Oh, those are the dancing dolls. They must stand on the piano," said Helen; "and here are some big fans. How sweet they smell," and she fanned Harry with the great rough Indian fans made of scented grasses and ornamented with shining beetles' wings.

"Look at these funny ivory balls," said Harry, who had got hold of a Chinese puzzle, one ball inside the other. "How could they get there?"

"And oh, these boxes, what tiny, winy* ones," cried Helen, "red and green. Look, here's another, and the lid fits so well and there's another inside no bigger than a pin's head. Oh, Jem, aren't they delightful?" Another time Jem would have answered curtly and told Helen there could be nothing de-lightful in empty boxes, but now he looked and admired though he did not say much.

Harry now found the shells in a fragrant sandalwood box. They were packed in fine cotton seeds which had such a funny powdery smell that

*Teeny-weeny.—Eds.

the children began to sneeze and laugh and cry and were some minutes trying to see the delicate white nautilus, which had travelled quite safely, and
the shiny green and blue shells which were all mixed up with strange
branches of coral and odd-looking ribbed[?] shells.

"Ah, you have got to the shells, I can hear by your sneezes," said
Aunt Lizzie, coming from the other room. "I am afraid you must make up
your mind to a good deal of choking, Helen, as that box is for you."

Helen got red with delight. "Oh, Auntie, you have given me such
lots of things," she said.

"Well, think of the lots of years I have been away and that I must
make up," said her aunt, laughing. "You haven't come to an end yet. There
are some little boxes that belong to you," and she picked up the very boxes
Helen had been looking at with such delight a moment before. At this moment a native servant came in and Aunt Lizzie spoke to her in a most extraordinary way, the children thought, and the woman went away; but she
was soon back again, to the children's delight, for they wanted to look at her
strange long white covering and her bare feet with thick gold rings on them.

However, when she came back, they had no eyes for her, for what
was that on her shoulder but a beautiful red and grey parrot, who said, "I'm
cold, very cold, where's Jem!" The children were startled at his odd hoarse
voice, and Jem thought that somehow the parrot must have known all
[about] him too, but it went on, "Helen's my darling" and began to sing,
which made them all laugh.

"I taught this parrot your names," said Aunt Lizzie, "but though he
is for Harry, I could never get him to say Harry's name properly. Sabrinah
has come pretty close, haven't you?" she said, turning to the native woman,
who then showed a little bundle of soft wraps that she was carrying, in
which lay a little brown monkey. It looked fatter and happier than Jem's
poor little one, but it had the same bright restless eyes, the same long curly
tail. At the sight of it, the laughter and delight caused by the parrot came
suddenly to an end. Helen began to sob and Jem and Harry felt as if they
should like to cry too.

"Why, my darling!" said Aunt Lizzie. "Are you frightened? – Little
Chow Chow won't hurt you. I got him for Jem as I heard he had always
longed for a monkey; but if you are frightened, he shan't go to your home."

"Oh! no, Auntie, it isn't that," said Helen, still crying, "I love him."
Aunt Lizzie looked at the other children and then at their parents but no
one said anything.

Jem could bear their silent reproaches no longer and cried out,
"Oh! I didn't mean it, I am so sorry, do punish me."

"Certainly," said Aunt Lizzie. "I shall be delighted to punish you, only before I begin, I should like to know why the sight of Chow Chow makes Helen cry and you beg to be punished." Jem got very red but no one said a word and he felt this was part of his punishment, so he looked up bravely and told his aunt all about the poor little monkey.

It cost him a great effort but he felt better when it was done, and Helen had dried her eyes and came and put her little hand in his, and his father and mother both looked at him with [more] tenderness than they had done since that horrid evening which seemed so long ago when he had chosen to be naughty if he need not be punished. Aunt Lizzie looked both sorry and concerned, but she did not want her coming home to be made a time of sadness; so she said cheerfully, "Well, Jem, I am afraid you do want a good deal of punishing and I suppose I ought not to let you have Chow Chow; but that would be punishing myself, for I certainly don't want to keep him. I think every time you see him it will remind you of the worst punishment you have had, which was causing the death of that poor little monkey." Jem was very much relieved to find he might have Chow Chow and he determined to make the little monkey very happy and never to tease him.

They all went home in a cab, for Aunt Lizzie's treasures could not be carried and could not be left. The three children were very happy sorting and sharing all the [treasures.]

[Dinner at Baron Bruin's]

[S]AID] BARON BRUIN, "It is a long time since we have seen any of our neighbours. Suppose we give a dinner party!"

"Very well, love," said the Baroness, "but who shall we ask?"

"Oh, our next neighbours, of course, Mrs. Pig and her son and daughter," said the Baron. "Young Grunter goes to the same school as Bruno and I daresay they have made friends." At this moment, young Baron Bruno came in. When he heard that his father wanted to ask young Grunter, he looked very cross.

"Grunter is very low, sir," he said, for Baron Bruin insisted on his children always calling him sir. "We don't talk much. He is always running his nose in among the roots of the trees for nasty things called truffles, and he eats such very coarse food."

"Miss Grunter too is not at all pleasant," said Bruina, who had just made a most melancholy chord on her harp. "She has no soul for music." When Baroness Bruna heard what her children said, she thought she would venture to speak to[o]. She was much too gentle and frightened of her husband to go against him unless others went too. "I think, my dear," she said, "Mrs. Pig would hardly like to come. You remember what happened when she and the poor Captain dined here last." (Captain Pig had been in the Militia but was now, as we shall hear, no more.)

"Ho, ho," laughed the Bear who had been getting angry and beginning to growl when he heard everyone objecting to his inviting the Pig family. Now he was pleased, as his wife had reminded him of the last party. "Ho, ho. I remember at our last dinner, old Grunter had a little too much of me. I only meant to give him a friendly squeeze, but he was so fat and his neck so short, my hug was a little too much for him; but I don't think Madam Pig will mind coming and I will take care not to hug *her*."

"I should hope not," said the Baroness, who did not like such jokes. "But if we have the Pigs, I don't know who will come to meet them. They have, as Bruno says, such very low ways."

Now Baron Bruin was really angry and he growled out, "I should like to hear anyone say that I have people to dinner whom they can't meet. Everyone *I* ask is only too glad to come, who[m]ever they may meet." The

Baroness was silent at once, and began to write her invitations. She knew what her husband said was quite true, as the Bear was much feared by the whole neighbourhood. So she wrote to Mrs. Pig and asked her and her son and daughter and then asked Lord Falcon and Col. [Isegrim, the] Wolf, Lady Snowy Owl and the young Marquis of King Falcon (who is, as we all know, a member of the Owl family). The Baron became quite good humoured again and told his son how he had found the bees' hive in the old oak tree right in the middle of the forest and how the honey was the best he had ever tasted. "And what have you been learning, Bru?" he said. Young Bruno went [to] a new high school for the higher classes such as bears and lions. A few of the very rich commoners were allowed to come in, such as Captain Pig's son, but they drew the line at wolves and did not allow any of the monkey tribe to come, as they considered them the lowest of animals, being the most like man.

"Well, sir, we did some higher mathematics."

"What's that?" growled the Bear.

"It is something that includes everything," said Bruno, very proud of this sentence.

"And is worth nothing, I'll be bound," growled his father, "as I never learnt it. Don't they teach you scratching and hugging, things that you will want to do every day?"

"Oh, sir, every well-brought-up bear knows how to defend himself," said Bruno. "We are taught definitions too."

"And pray, what are they?" said the Baron.

"Questions such as 'What is man?' sir, and I answered, 'a featherless Biped,'" said Bruno.

"Biped means stupid, I suppose," said the Bear, and laughed at his own joke against men, whom he thought very poorly of.

"Don't be hard on them, poor things," said his wife. "Remember, poor things, they have only two legs and no fur. You can't expect much of them. Now, Bruina, put away your music and go to bed."

Little Bruina went off to bed like a good child. She had a very comfortable bed, all made of sweet smelling dry herbs and mosses. She lived in a little tower of the castle. There was no roof and no panes of glass to the window, only big branches of pine trees sheltered her and she could see the moon as she lay in her bed. The castle had thick walls and many corridors and big halls and towers but no stairs, except the big steps to the dining hall, for bears do not like stairs. They had steps to the dining hall, for they did not like snails and snakes and creeping creatures to come in.

Bruina had a pretty little marmotte to bring her her supper, which was of honey and beans. "We are going to have a dinner party, Ina," she said.

The marmotte gave a little jump, which is what marmottes do when they make a curtsey. They are very polite little beasts and have learnt fine Italian manners. "We are going to have Mrs. Pig," Bruina went on. Little Ina almost forgot her manners and gave a little squeak.

"I like not pigs," she said. "They make such a snurrrrr," and she tried to imitate the pigs' grunt.

"You silly little thing," said Bruina. "They are quite good-natured, only stupid. Is the moss on my bed quite clean, no slugs or earwigs?"

"Ah, no," said Ina. "I gathered it and dried it in the sun and packed it all for your ladyship. Now may you sleep well on it," and she trotted off.

Breakfast at the Gruntery

Mrs. Pig's home was very different from the Bears'. She had a nice cheerful farm. There was a low wall painted white and large stacks [of] yellow straw were to be seen standing all round. There were sunny sloping meadows on which could be seen fat cows; and busy little monkeys were trotting about, pulling down stacks of straw to make fresh beds, for the Grunter family were very particular for pigs, and liked to have fresh beds of straw every day. There was a large garden full of peas, beans, and potatoes — the Pigs did not care for flowers but they liked a nice bowl of green peas as well as anyone. Mrs. Pig's house was a little higher than the garden and yard with straw stacks. There were no towers or long passages but one big square room in the middle and three little square rooms close by. All were painted white and there was no roof and no stairs, not even steps to go up, for the Grunter family were short of breath and did not like any steps at all.

Mrs. Pig was on a nice clean truss of hay with a large bowl of buttermilk and another of mashed peas, beans, and potatoes before her, having her breakfast. Her son and daughter were on either side, each having a bowl full of cabbage and buttermilk, for Mrs. Pig only gave them peas once a week. "Here comes Chips," said young Grunter, "and he's got something. What can it be?" Chips was the monkey who always waited on the Pigs in their house. He had bright brown eyes, which were always looking about, and a long curling tail. He now came jumping in, in a way that gave Mrs. Pig the flutters, she said. Chips had a big letter in his hand with a thick seal.

"What can that be?" said Mrs. Pig, who was very nervous. "I wonder who can have written it?"

"Open and see," said Miss Pigling, who was apt to be pert and who was longing to know what was inside the letter.

As Mrs. Pig was too nervous to break the thick red seal, young

22. LESLIE STEPHEN. *Pig lying down.* Courtesy of the Woolf Library at Washington State University Libraries, Pullman, Washington.

Grunter took the letter. He was proud of being able to read and though his voice was not very clear, he began to read the Baroness' invitation to dinner, for that was the letter Chips had brought. "The Baron and Baroness Bruin request the pleasure of Mrs. Pig and Master and Miss Grunter's company at dinner at 3:30 tomorrow."

"Dear, dear, what an honour," said Mrs. Pig. "But I don't think I can. You remember your poor dear father—what happened to him when he dined there."

"We will take good care not to let the old Baron come near us," said both young pigs. "We had much better go, Mother."

"Yes, yes, let us go," said Grunter. "I know young Bruno and he is, for a thick furred thing like that, very decent to speak to."

"Baroness Bruina plays on the harp," said Miss Pigling, who was sentimental, as well as pert. "How sweet to play the harp. It goes so," and she uttered a most peculiar squeak, like the scratching of a slate pencil.

"I daresay she would teach me. She is not very stupid though she has no complexion," she added, for Miss Pigling was very proud of her bright pink skin. Mrs. Pig never went against her children's wishes, so with a sigh at the remembrance of the Bear's too great civility to her departed Captain, she told Chips to run back and say they would all come to dinner.

When dinner time came, the pigs had a good rub-down in clean straw and set off for the castle. They had to pass through one corner of the

big forest and the young pigs longed to root about for acorns, but they felt
such a proceeding would be thought most vulgar by their Mama, who was
most particular about their manners. The forest was very dark, though it
was a bright sunny day. Little wild strawberries were growing red and ripe in
the shadow of the dark pines and oaks, and the bees made a pleasant hum
as they flew to their home in the middle of the forest, not knowing what the
Baron had been about. At last, Mrs. Pig and her children arrived at the castle. The distance was not great but they were all rather fat and it took them
a long time to walk all together to a particular place. They liked to stop and
turn back whenever they saw an acorn [or] a nut; and besides, the two
young ones were having an argument the whole time as to what would be
the best road for them to take. On the long flight of stone steps which led up
to the dining table, stood twenty little marmosets, with merry little brown
faces. Each held a lighted torch, not that it was yet dark but the Baron
thought it looked grand to have torch bearers. Baroness Bruina came forward as the Pig family advanced, and welcomed them most kindly.

The Baron also came forward with outstretched arms, but Mrs. Pig
gave a little squeak and hopped on one side, showing that she did not forget
that the Baron's hugs were sometimes too warm to be pleasant.

Lady Snowy Owl looked very dignified with her soft feathers all
fluffing out as she turned to Marquis King Falcon and murmured that she
had not expected to meet such company. Lord Falcon looked indignant but
at that moment Col. [Isegrim, the] Wolf, appeared. No one liked him and
the Baron enjoyed seeing the way all his guests moved away from the new-
comer. The Colonel was too much afraid of the Baron not to be on his best
behaviour but he eyed longingly young Grunter's sleek pink skin. Dinner
was then announced and the Pig family found themselves seated at a long
dinner table in a big dining room. A marmoset was behind each chair, and
the Pigs, who were very hungry, eagerly looked about for luscious plates of
food. What was their disappointment to see that the two principal dishes
were honey and sugar cane. Lady Snowy Owl and the Marquis had a dish of
fried mice. The Colonel had a sheep's head and Lord Falcon had an odd-
looking dish which the Pigs did not fancy at all. For them there was, it is
true, a dish of buttermilk with peas which was good as far as it went, but
what a little way that was when one thought of the appetites of three hungry
pigs. However, they ate [it] all up and tried to look pleased.

After the dinner the Bears proposed that there should be some
dancing. The Baron thought he danced the Schottische very well and
begged young Grunter to dance with Baroness Bruina. Poor Grunter had little idea of dancing but he hooked his leg onto the young Baroness' and tried
to hop round and not to squeak,—as he could hardly help doing when she
came down on his toes or his tail, which as a rule curled up quite tight but

23. LESLIE STEPHEN. *Bear standing*. Courtesy of the Woolf Library at Washington State University Libraries, Pullman, Washington.

24. LESLIE STEPHEN. *Wolf.* Courtesy of the Woolf Library at Washington State University Libraries, Pullman, Washington.

in the agitation of the dance had come quite out of curl and hung down in a most melancholy way. Col. Isegrim danced with Miss Pig. He was a very clever dancer and although she was not much better than her brother, the Col[onel] lifted her up and twisted her round in such a wonderful way, she found herself dancing without knowing how. Col. Isegrim kept whispering pleasant things in her ear, and asking her where she lived and if he might call; but Baron Bear, who was good natured though rough, guessed what the Colonel was thinking of and said, "Miss Pig is a good friend of mine, Col[onel], and near her lives General Growler, who has for many years been her guardian." The Colonel looked very much disappointed but tried to smile. He knew Growler very well, the big Mastiff, and he made up his mind he would not go and call on Miss Pig. When the dance was over, the Pigs said goodbye and all the party broke up. The Owls, who had been looking very sleepy, had flown off immediately after dinner; they were not accustomed to such early hours, they said. In fact, they thought it vulgar to eat in daylight. Col. Isegrim had thought he might go part of the way home with Mrs. Pig and if he had, we are afraid that Mrs. Pig would never have got home at all. But when they got to the bottom of the steps, there was General Growler waiting to take care of his friends on their way home.

"So very kind of you, dear General," said Mrs. Pig. "The Colonel is coming with us too."

"Is he?" said General Growler, in a very loud voice, which made Mrs. Pig give another little squeak. "Perhaps as the Colonel and I are old friends, we had better walk on first."

"Oh dear, no," said Isegrim, bowing politely. "I am sure I would not deprive the ladies of the General's society, besides which I have just recollected an engagement I have in another direction." So saying, he gave a low bow and was soon out of [sight]. Mrs. Pig was disappointed at having lost such a smart gentleman as escort and rather cross with Growler for having sent him off.

"Never mind, Mary Pig," said Growler, who always treated her as if she were a pigling. "If you had walked home with Isegrim, you would not have lived to tell the tale. It is not more than a week ago that he ate up several of your family in Berkshire and I did not like his looks today. He seemed hungry."

"So are we all," said the Pigs as they turned into their own white gates and caught sight of the neat trusses of shining straw all ready for them to rest on, while before each was a beautiful trough of foaming buttermilk, heaped up with apples, potatoes, onions and peas, all mashed and mixed together, such a mess as pigs love. Into this they had soon buried their noses, quite forgetting their elegant manners and resolving never to dine with the aristocracy again.

The Black Cat or the Grey Parrot

POPPY SAT AT THE FOOT OF THE STAIRS with the tears rolling down her cheeks. What could be the matter? But there was no one to ask this question, for Poppy's mother had gone into the country for the day and Nurse was up at the top of the house. Jack knew a great deal too well to ask—he stood there with his red, cross face answering nothing when Poppy sobbed out, "Oh, Jack, how could you hurt my little Tray?" Tray was a kind little terrier who was now lying in Poppy's lap and seemed in great pain. Every time he tried to move, he made a sad little noise which made poor Poppy's tears run faster than ever. Tray seemed to know how sorry she was for him, for he put out his little tongue and licked her hands.

"Serve him right!" growled out Jack at last. "He tried to eat my cake and he did get a bit of it."

"You might have had all my cake," said Poppy. "You needn't have minded Tray's having a little bit—it was cruel of you to throw that sharp stone at him. What shall I do! What shall I do!" Jack did not look at all sorry. He was a selfish little boy and did not care if other people were hurt; but he minded it very much when *he* was hurt.

"Don't make such a stupid fuss, Poppy," he said. "The little beast only got what he deserved. I don't believe he is really hurt at all."

"I do wish Mama were at home," said Poppy. "I don't know what to do with Tray's leg."

"Take him to the hospital," said an odd hoarse voice. "Come with me."

Poppy gave a start. Who could be talking? Why, it was the grey parrot, of course. "Polly, what are you putting your finger in the pie for?" said Jack, going up to give the parrot a pinch, but Polly gave him a good nip which made him squeal, on which Polly said:

"Serve him right! Serve him right!"

Poppy had dried her eyes [and] laid Tray carefully down while she tied her bonnet, which had fallen off in her trouble. She had her outdoor things on, for she and Jack had been playing in the garden at the back of their house when Jack had thrown the stone at Tray. It seemed very funny to do what a parrot said, still Poppy knew when their gardener had broken his leg, her Mama had taken him to the hospital; and if Tray's leg were really broken, he must go to the animal's hospital – only she had never heard of one; but then Polly said he knew about [it] and Polly was a great deal older than she. Besides she had often heard her mother say that she was sure Polly knew everything, he looked so wise. Still Poppy could not help sighing and repeating, "I wish Mama were here."

"I don't," said Jack, for he knew if his aunt had been at home, he would have been well punished for his cruelty to poor Tray.

"See if you won't though," said Polly. "See if you won't," and he seemed to laugh as he flew away with Poppy. Poppy trotted along as fast as she could with little Tray carefully covered up in a basket. She took care not to jar him for she knew that any movement must hurt him.

Polly kept flying on a little in front of Poppy which was a good thing, for she didn't at all know where to go. The white street and park looked strange. It was a bright sunshiny day and perhaps it was the sun in [Poppy's] eyes that blinded her, or just the tears that were always coming into them at the thought of her dear dog. However it was, she certainly could not see any of the shops nor the cab stands, nor the Albert Memorial even, which usually shone out a long way off. However, she did not think of all this, for her mind was full of her little pet. Suddenly the parrot stopped and Poppy stopped too. They were standing by a green gate in a high wall, and over the wall Poppy could see tall trees and could hear the cooing of doves.

Polly struck his beak against the door, which was at once opened, not by a man or a maid, but by a soft grey dove with a pretty black hood on. She and Polly seemed great friends, for Polly flew down and flapped his wings and a great deal of billing and cooing went on. [Poppy] could not understand what they said. Polly seemed very excited and talked very fast and loud, but the dove had a soft sweet voice. Presently the dove came to [Poppy] and said, "Please come in and bring your friend." [Poppy] had never heard of a talking dove but she asked no questions. Polly had flown right across the garden and was talking to a big macaw who was sitting on a bit of wood with his head all bound up.

"Captain Grey was here a good many years ago when he hurt his claw. He has the mark still," said the dove as she stepped by Poppy['s] side. [Poppy] wondered at first who Captain Grey could be, but then she remembered that her parrot had a deep mark on one claw, so no doubt he was Captain Grey. How funny we should never know it, she thought. They had now crossed the garden and were at the door of a low white house. The door stood open and the dove went in, telling Poppy to follow.

As they were going upstairs, [they met] a very fat bristling grey hen. "Dear, dear," she said to the dove. "Pray move away. Don't you know that Sir

Juniper Falcon and Sir Golden Owl have been in consultation about his
Royal Highness and are just coming downstairs? Here they are!" As she said
this, Poppy saw a beautiful falcon with bright gleaming eyes and a sharp
curved beak coming downstairs with a very stout wheezy old owl.

The falcon was saying very politely to the owl, "Oh, I could not
think of going downstairs before you, Sir Golden," but when he saw the
dove who was standing as much in the shadow of the stairs as [s]he could,
he forgot his politeness and, saying, "I see there the nurse to whom I want to
speak," hurried down. "Come, Nurse Dove," he said; but the dove, who
seemed very much flustered, said, "I am taking a patient upstairs, Sir Peregrine, and am not allowed to stop," and she flew up the stairs.

The falcon looked very angry but could not follow her as, by this
time, the fat old owl had got to the bottom of the stairs, and Poppy was glad
to follow the dove. She found her waiting at the top and panting a great
deal. "You seem frightened of that falcon," said Poppy, who felt sorry for the
kind little bird.

"Yes," said the dove. "He is very c-clever." Poppy felt sure that the
dove had been going to say "cruel" but she went on, "He is a wonderful sur-
geon. He can cut off a leg in a minute and do other more serious operations.
He is afraid of nothing people do, as he is too fond of showing how clever he
is; but I daresay it isn't true," she added hastily.

"I hope he won't cut off Tray's leg," said Poppy.

"Oh, no! He is sure not to operate on him unless it is quite necessary," said the dove. "All the royal family have him when they are ill. *They*
feel quite safe with him.—But here we are, this is the ward where your friend
will be." Poppy found herself in a long room with large open windows. There
were several little beds and in one lay a hare who had his head all bound up.
A dog was walking on crutches, who looked out of the corner of his eye to
see who was coming in and soon found that it was one of his own kind.
Poppy did not stop to look at all these animals, though she longed to talk to
the hare—she felt so sorry for him. She passed an old bear who was having a
gouty foot tied up. The bear seemed very grumpy and the monkey who was
holding some linen looked very nervous. The dove took Poppy to the farther
end of the room and, quickly pulling out a tall black screen round a little
bed, told Poppy to sit and wait within the screen till she came back. She
would not be long. Poppy felt rather frightened at being left alone in a hospital ward. She had never been in one before and was glad that the screen
closed round her and prevented her being able to see the other patients. She
could hear the old bear growling out that the bandages were too tight and
Dr. Adjutant, whom she had seen standing by, told the monkey to mind
what he was about, in a very cross voice.

When the dove came back, she took poor Tray out of the basket and laid him very softly in the little bed. She did it so gently and quietly, laying her soft grey wing under the poor broken leg, that Tray did not cry out at all. Then [Poppy] heard a rustling, and Dr. Adjutant came from behind the screen. Poppy was rather frightened, for this d[octo]r seemed more likely to kill than cure, she thought. She had hoped that he would not be the one to attend on her Tray.

The doctor's beak was so long and sharp and his head was so bald— only a very few short hairs standing straight up on it. Poppy thought he looked very cross. His legs were so long, he was in a second at Tray's side. He took no notice of Poppy. "Well, well, well, what have we the matter with us? Have we broken our leg?" He lifted his sharp beak a little and laid hold of Tray's leg as he spoke. Poppy could hardly help screaming but Tray did not seem to mind it at all. Presently the doctor said, "We have had a nasty knock, haven't we?"

Poppy thought of Jack but did not like to tell the doctor about his naughtiness. However, as she was beginning to be less afraid of him, she said, "Do you think, Sir, he will ever be well again?"

"Oh, we shall be well," said the doctor. "We shall enjoy our mutton chop," and then half to himself and half to the dove, Poppy heard him say all sorts of funny words, like "*fibia tibia anterior crural muscular.*" It sounded like something out of the "Book of Nonsense" but of course such an old gentleman, or rather such a very old bird, would never think of talking nonsense!

"He isn't a bit like Dr. Charles," thought Poppy to herself. "He never says anything but, 'Dear, dear, dear, we must have a pill.'" All this time Dr. Adjutant was getting ready some linen and bits of wood, the dove helping him; and now he took a pair of scissors and cut away some of poor Tray's hair and then gently washed the wound, after which he put the poor little leg on the sticks and bound it round and round. Poppy was sure it hurt Tray; but the good little dog seemed to know he was being cured and he lay quite still and licked Poppy's hand. "Oh, thank you, Doctor," said she, jumping forward.

The doctor had never looked at her before. "What, what, what?" he said in rather a sharp voice, blinking at her. "Eyes bad, I see. They had better come out. Best without them."

Now Poppy had very large blue eyes and she did not at all like the idea of having them out, so she gave a little jump of fright. "My eyes are quite well, thank you, Sir," she said very politely.

"No, no, they're not," said the doctor, "and you are nervous, I see. All part of the same thing."

The dove looked very uncomfortable. "She is not of the kind we can operate on, Sir," she said. "She is only a friend of the patient's."

"Dear, dear, what a pity," said the doctor. "They would have been a rare treat," and he clacked his bill together with a noise that made Poppy start again.

At this moment she heard a familiar voice saying, "Well, old pill box, still at it, are you?" and from the top of the screen on which he had been perched without her knowledge, flew down the grey parrot. She had never been more glad to see him. He flew onto Dr. Adjutant's shoulder and plucked out one or two of the straight stiff hairs.

The doctor did not like this at all, but he was no match for the parrot. So, saying, "Gently, gently, dear Captain Grey," he made a low bow to Poppy, who could then see his red head and shining neck very well. "I think your friend had better go to sleep now. He will do very well." And off he stalked. The parrot imitated his "Well, well, well" and way of talking, making Poppy laugh.

She was very glad to see the doctor go. "What did he mean about my eyes?" she said to the dove.

"I suppose he thought you must be blind, your eyes are so blue," said the dove with a little shyness. "We none of us have blue eyes if we can see well."

"That wasn't all," said the parrot. "You know, Nurse Dove, our friend the doctor is very fond of eyes for his supper. So he is always making out that people have something wrong with their eyes."

"Hush, hush," said the dove, who was moving the screen softly away and, turning to Poppy, she said, "Perhaps you would like [to] see our house and garden while your friend sleeps. He will be better if he is left quite quiet for a little. Unless you want to go home and would leave him here for the night."

"Oh, no, thank you," said Poppy, very quickly. Then she was afraid that she had been rude. "You are so kind, but I should be so unhappy if dear Tray were away. I should like very much to go about the place with you, and then if you don't think it would do Tray harm, I should like to take him home."

"Very well," said the dove. "When he has slept and had some food, we will put him into the basket. You must not let him try to walk for several days. Now, if you will come, I will show you round."

Just then a monkey came up in a great hurry. "Please, sister," he said to the dove, "will you go across to No. 6? He is making such a noise and won't keep his mustard plaster on." The dove flew off, leaving the parrot to take Poppy round.

"I want to talk to that poor hare who has got his ear bound up," said Poppy, and she went up to the hare's bedside. He lay very still but seemed to be in a great deal of pain. "I wish I could do something for you, poor hare," she said, stroking his soft brown paw. "How did you get so ill?"

"I was shot," said the hare with a deep sigh.

"Shot!" said Poppy. "How dreadful."

"Yes, both my ears were shot and my legs broken. They thought that I was killed; I only wish I had been. Then I should not have to be shot at again."

"Oh, how dreadful," said Poppy, her eyes filling with tears and her cheeks getting white. "Are you a soldier, poor hare, that you were shot; and is there a war in your country?"

The hare looked at her with surprise. "Why," he said, "don't you live in my country?"

"Oh, no," said Poppy. "I have never been there."

"I thought you must have," said the hare, "for I have seen creatures just like you walking about in my woods, and it was someone with two legs like you, only his legs were longer and he was dressed differently, who carried a gun and shot me." Poppy was beginning to say, again, that she did not live in the hare's country; but when he talked of people going about woods with guns, she thought that perhaps the woods and fields she knew were the hare's country. She remembered how some time before, when she was staying with her uncle in the country, she had gone into a beautiful wood full of nuts and blackberries and she had seen a hare and some little hares playing about. Afterwards she had heard [the] "crack crack" of guns and in the evening her uncle had said that they had had very fine sport—and her aunt said she was glad of it, as the larder was empty. All these thoughts had passed very quickly through Poppy's mind but never before had she thought that "fine sport" meant *this*. She asked the hare no more questions. He had shut his eyes and seemed to be in too much pain to speak. Poppy went on, feeling very unhappy.

Then she went towards the bear, who was still looking very cross. "This bandage is too tight," he growled. "I shall never get well in this nasty dull place."

"Where did you come from?" said Poppy.

"Who are you?" said the bear, whose eyes were half shut. "Oh, you are a nice little girl. It is very kind of you to come and see me. I daresay a great many of you would come if they knew that I was here, for I always made you laugh."

"Have you been in the zoo?" said Poppy, who was very glad to find that some of the animals liked little girls.

"No, no," growled the bear. "I would not go to that stupid place, live in a cage and go up and down a pole for buns. *I* am a dancing bear. I have travelled all over the world and there is a big picture done of me called 'Boreas, the dancing bear of the North, dancing before Queen Victoria.' I used to dance on the tips of my toes. No one has ever danced like me. The royal family used to come and speak to me after each performance before them, and I had a diamond snuff box given me by the Emperor of Russia, who is my Emperor."

"Dear me," said Poppy. "How clever you must be. And can you take snuff?"

"Of course I can," said the bear, not very much pleased, "since *you* could do that."

"I hope you will soon be better," said Poppy. "How did you hurt your foot?"

"I never hurt it. I was much too careful of my toes to hurt them. A stupid dog bit me," said the bear, "and I don't believe I shall ever be able to dance again."

"I do hope you will," said [Poppy]. "And I hope I shall see you dance. I have never seen a dancing bear."

"There *is* only one Boreas," said the bear, in a very proud way. "Now, little girl, you can go—" and he waved his paw as if he were the Emperor of all the Russias himself.

"He is not very polite," said Poppy to the parrot.

"All bears are rude," said Polly. "Don't you know how everyone is always saying to that horrid Jack, 'Don't be a bear'?"

Poppy now had a little talk with the dog whom she had seen walking with crutches. "Are you better?" she asked.

"I shall soon be well," said the dog. "Very soon. I think I shall be able to go home tomorrow. I am longing to go home."

"Where is your home?" said Poppy.

"I live with a little boy and we go out together. I know he must want me very much; I know that I want him."

"He must be a kind boy if you love him so much," said Poppy. "I wish Jack were like him. How did you hurt your leg?"

"It was an accident," said the dog.

"Dear me," said Poppy. "What sort of an accident?"

"Haven't I told you enough?" said the dog, hobbling off as quickly as he could.

"Dear me," said Poppy. "How easily they get cross. I didn't mean to ask anything unpleasant."

"The fact is," said the grey parrot, "it was the little boy whom he is so fond of who hurt him, and so he does not like to talk about it. The little boy was playing with a can which held boiling water. His mother had told him not to go near it but he would, and he knocked the can over and it scalded the poor dog."

"How dreadful," said Poppy. "I love the dog for not telling, but how do you know, Polly?"

On which Polly shook his head very busily and said, "I know most things."

They walked into another room, where they found the dove. She was trying to persuade a thin little monkey to keep a mustard plaster on. He had a very bad cough and the doctor had ordered him one. "Now, dear Pico, be quiet," said the dove in her soft cooing voice; but the poor little monkey could not help starting up and giving little squeaks.

"Let me try and amuse him," said Poppy, who was always called "the little mother" at home, she was so helpful and kind. "That is just the way our children go on when they have poultices," and she sat down by the side and, picking up a piece of string, began to make a cat's cradle. The little monkey was so amused at watching her swift little fingers as they worked the string in and out, that he forgot his pain. Then she played at "Is Mr. Fox at home?," making the monkey shut up his little brown hand while she slipped her little fingers in and out.

She amused him so well and so quietly that Nurse Dove said, "You would make a good nurse."

"I mean to be a hospital nurse when I am big," said Poppy. "I am so sorry for sick people."

"That is right," said the dove. "A great many people tell me they want to be nurses, but I find out it is only because they are sorry for themselves, which is quite a different thing."

"She is a good little girl," said the parrot.

"She may be good but she isn't little," said the monkey. "I call her very big. Now I am little," and he showed his skinny little brown arms and legs, which certainly looked very small and shriveled by the side [of] Poppy's smooth firm white ones.

"Would you like to go into the gardens," said the parrot, "and see Field Marshal Macaw and some of the other convalescents?"

"What long words you use today, Polly," said Poppy. "How odd everything is." Everything was so odd, Poppy had almost forgotten *how* odd it was. Only when the parrot began to talk, she remembered how funny it was. "Goodbye, little Pico. I hope you will soon be quite strong and that they will let me come here again."

"I am sure if you want to come, no one can prevent you. You are so big," said the monkey. Poppy laughed, for at home she was always hearing from Nurse that she was such a very little girl and that she must always do what she was told and never think of what she liked. She followed the parrot along a broad passage. As they passed a grand door covered with red velvet with a gold crown on it, they heard a loud roar. Poppy felt very frightened. "What is that?" she said.

"Oh, it is only his Royal Highness, who does not like the dinner Sir Peregrine Falcon has ordered for him, I suppose," said the parrot.

"Who is his Royal Highness?" said [Poppy].

"Why, the king's eldest son, of course," said the parrot.

Poppy was just going to ask who was the king, but she remembered having seen "Lion, King of Beasts" on picture books so she supposed this was the lion's son.

"I never thought you had a Royal Highness," she said.

"I haven't anything to do with him," said Polly. "Surely you must know better than that, as even the baby knows that the eagle is *our* king."

Poppy felt rather ashamed of herself. "What is the prince's name?" she said.

"Leoncel. He came from over the sea only a little time ago and he hurt his foot and had fever, so he came here and is very cross because the doctors won't let him have raw meat."

They heard another roar and Poppy said, "I think we had better go into the garden." She didn't like to say she was afraid of a prince; still she was.

"Oh, you need not be afraid," said Polly. "There is an iron door under that velvet curtain and though he is the king's son, he is kept shut up, for he has a bad temper and does not keep his promises. But here we are at the garden."

Poppy ran down the steps and found herself in a big beautiful garden. There was a broad gravel walk skirting the lawn. Drooping beeches and other trees shaded it, and many bath chairs were being dragged up and down. In one was a goat, who had hurt his foot jumping off wet crags. In another, a fat old pig. "Lazy old thing," said Polly.

"Exercise is all she wants. She does nothing but eat and sleep, and sleep and eat, and the doctors call it gout, but I call it greediness."

The parrot spoke so loud, Poppy thought the pig must have heard. "Have you got gout?" said she very gently.

"Gout?" said the pig. "Are you talking to me, little girl, or to the goat? I daresay he suffers from gout, but as for me I suffer from nerves. I am [a] bundle of nerves. Sir Peregrine said today he wondered how I lived at all, I was so sensitively organized." And the fat pig leant back in her chair and rolled her little eyes and gave a deep sigh, which sounded rather like a grunt. Poppy could hardly help laughing at the thought of a pig with nerves, though she didn't quite know what nerves were. She went on to where the parrot had flown. He was talking to the beautiful macaw. Polly had been quite at his ease with all the other animals who were so much bigger and stronger, Poppy thought; but now he was with one of his own kind, he seemed quite different. As Poppy came up, she heard him say, "This is little Miss Poppy, of whom I have told you."

"What a small brown thing," said the macaw, disdainfully looking at Poppy's brown holland frock. "I wonder you like to go about with a plain miss. Now the duchess who lives with me is something to look at. She has long trains of silk and velvet, and her colours are nearly as bright as mine."

"I daresay she is older," said the parrot, looking uncomfortable.

"She has never been a plain miss anyhow," said the macaw, and he shut his eyes as much as to say he didn't want to talk about such people any more. Poppy was very glad to go on. They came to a nice shady place where, lying on the soft green moss and nibbling at the tender shoots of the young branches, she found two squirrels. They were rather frightened when they saw her, but she soon made friends with them and they told her how they had been caught in traps and showed her their tiny feet all bound round with cool lily leaves.

Poppy heard the sound of fresh leaves rustling and she walked on and found a bright hurrying little river, in [which] several monkeys were swimming. "They are all out-patients," said the parrot. "They have been ill, but now they only come here just to be looked at by the doctor and to get a swim."

"I never knew that monkeys swam," said Poppy.

"Doesn't that horrid Jack swim?" said the parrot.

"Yes," said Poppy, "but he is a boy."

"Well, he is just like a monkey and if he can swim, why shouldn't they?" said Polly. There was a pretty little bridge over one end of the stream, and on it Poppy saw a very grand-looking old bear, followed by a kangaroo, who was carefully holding a parasol over the bear's head. The bear walked very slowly, and the kangaroo had some trouble in making his hops short enough so as not to touch the bear. "How funny they look," said Poppy, laughing. At this moment a loud bell rang and from all sides of the garden came rabbits, hens, kangaroos, antelopes, dogs, and other animals. "What is happening and how well they all run!" said Poppy. "That is the bell to say visitors must be off," said the parrot. "All those you see are visitors like ourselves, come to see their sick friends, and we must be going too." They hurried along, passing a sick hare who was saying goodbye to her leveret and entreating him to keep away from traps and those horrid creatures on two legs called "men."

"I wonder how Tray is getting on?" said Poppy with a sigh. "This is a delightful place and I am very sorry to leave it," and she looked longingly at the little winding paths which seemed full of tall feathery ferns and were scented with the wild roses which grew in the hedges.

"You mustn't wait here," said Polly, "and I daresay Tray will be glad to see you." At the thought of her dear Tray, Poppy quickened her steps, though she longed to talk to a pretty little opossum mouse with big shining eyes and a long curling tail, whom she saw on one of the trees. He swung himself from branch to branch, curling his tail round the branches and leaping across till he got to a big box tree, into the cool darkness of which his tiny fat body was soon lost.

"What a lovely little creature," called out Poppy. "Who is he?"

"He is a possum mouse," said the parrot. "He always lives here because he is very delicate and has to be taken great care of. He is very proud because he is the only one there is in England. Here we are at the house." Poppy followed the parrot up the stairs and along the passage till they came to where they had left poor little Tray. The kind dove had gone back to him and was giving him some soft bread and milk when Poppy came in. Tray was so delighted to see her, he licked her face and hands and made a funny little noise which was the sign that he was very very happy. Poppy kissed him and the little dove, whose soft grey feathers she stroked. "Here is your basket," said the parrot. "For we must get off, it is growing late. We must get home."

How odd that sounded to Poppy. All this time she had not thought about home; but now she wondered what her mother had been thinking and she made up her mind to delay no more, so she lifted Tray into his little basket, putting a bed of cotton wool for his broken leg to lie on. "Goodbye, dear dove," she said. "How kind you have been. How delightful it has been to come here."

"Goodbye," said the dove. "I hope you will come again, for there is a great deal that you have not seen and you are so kind, I am sure you would help those who are very ill."

"Oh, yes, I will be sure to come," said Poppy, and they all went downstairs.

The dove said she would take them through the big dining room — as it was not a longer way than the way they had come and they had not seen it. It was a very big room. There were branches of trees for the birds and nice bins of hay with pails, troughs, buckets, bags, things of all kinds spread with different kinds of food. "What are you doing, Mr. Reineke?" said the dove as they went in. "You have no business to be here. The dinner bell has not rung."

"I came to look at the clock," said a beautiful red fox with a bushy tail and a pair of spectacles.

"I am afraid you came to look for some food," said the dove, "and you know if you eat too much after an operation, you will certainly get fever and your eyes will be as bad as ever again."

"Thank you, sweet nurse," said the fox, coming nearer. "Let me kiss your tender hand."

"No, no," said the dove, jumping quickly behind Poppy, and Poppy remembered she had heard how fond foxes were of eating birds.

Since Polly seemed a little afraid, she asked the fox why he wore spectacles and how his eyes had got hurt. "My eyes were nearly scratched out," said the fox. "And Dr. Adjutant has had the greatest trouble to get them straight at all. I can't see well yet, though I have been here a long time, and it is very dull work living in a hospital when one has been accustomed to run all over the downs."

"How did your eyes get scratched?" said Poppy. "It must have hurt dreadfully," for she remembered one day when she was by the seaside, they had gone out blackberrying and her eyelid had got very much scratched in the brambles; and how it had hurt! So she felt quite sorry for Mr. Reineke.

"Dogs scratched it out," said the fox in a very cross voice.

Poor Tray gave a little start and Poppy covered him with her hand. "Oh, not that kind of dog," said the fox. "Great hounds, brown and white, but it isn't the dogs whom I mind so much. They would not hurt us if it were not for the men, who think themselves so grand dressed up in scarlet with tall white boots; and they ride on such beautiful horses, so that they never tire their own stupid legs but go on riding and riding till the clever dogs have found one of us foxes. It takes a lot of men and horses and hounds to find one fox, they are so stupid. And when they get us, what do they want? They can't eat us, all they want is our tails, which *they* call a brush—as if my tail is a bit like a brush." And the fox stretched out and waved his beautiful curling tail. Poppy felt more and more unhappy as the fox spoke. She had often seen the hunters ride away in their pink coats, and she had heard the hounds baying; but somehow she had never thought before that a poor fox was being driven from his home and hunted about till he was killed and that *that* was what the hunters called sport. She was glad when the fox walked away. The hare had said much the same thing and as Poppy walked away from the hospital, she felt quite sad to think how many of the animals in it had been hurt by men.

"You are tired," said Polly as they walked on home.

"Oh, no," said Poppy. "Only I was thinking how dreadful it was for that poor fox to be hunted."

"Serve him right," said the parrot. "Don't you see how he wanted to snap that kind Nurse Dove? Even I didn't feel very safe and I daresay it was all a story about his eyes being scratched out by dogs. It is much more likely that he was climbing into some hen roost and so got hurt." They walked on quickly. The road seemed shorter and Poppy soon found herself within sight of the street in which her home was.

The hall door was open and Nurse was standing at it. "Oh, Poppy, dear," she said. "There you are. Tea is ready and the little ones are waiting. Where is Jack?"

"I don't know, Nurse," said Poppy. "I am afraid you have been looking for me. Am I very late? I have so much to tell you."

"Oh, no child, I knew you were in the garden, only I could not see you. I knew you were all right, as old Polly was with you; but if Jack hasn't been with you, where can he be? He is nowhere in the house. Why, what is the matter with Tray?"

"Jack hurt Tray with a stone. He broke his leg, Nurse. I don't know what I would have done without Polly."

"Why, what did he do to help you?" said Nurse. "But wherever can that Jack be? I have been into the coal cellar and the dust[bin]. He is sure to be up to some mischief and he can't have gone far, for he is such a coward like all naughty children, he is afraid to cross a road alone."

Polly gave an odd chuckle, with his head on one side. "Far enough," he said.

"Why, what a start you gave me, Polly, to be sure," said Nurse. "Whatever shall I do? It's a comfort your Mama isn't back yet, Poppy, or she would be in a state, though I am sure I wish that unliked, tormenting boy were back among the blacks. But come to your tea, my dear, the others are waiting and I will give another search in the coal hole." Poppy ran up, wondering much about Jack, and longing to tell all her story; but Baby was too little to understand it and Charlie was out with her mother.

Nurse was thinking too much about Jack even to question Poppy as to where she had been. Jack's father and mother were in India among the blacks, as Nurse had said. They had only this one child and they thought that he should be the happiest little boy in the world; so when Jack cried for a thing, it was always given to him; and when he told his nurse that he would not go to his bed his Mama said, "Very well, darling, you shall sit up as long as you like." He was never scolded or punished when he was unkind to people or animals, so he went on till no one loved him; and at last, the doctor told his Mama that Jack must be sent to England, for if he stayed in

India he would have something dreadful happen. Jack's Papa and Mama were very unhappy at parting with their darling boy, but everyone else was delighted when Master Jack was packed off to his aunt, Poppy's Mama.

Everyone was very kind to him, for they loved children and there were plenty of toys and books and paintboxes in Poppy's nursery, but Jack could not read, he did not like learning and his Mama would not have him taught, and he did [not like] playing with toys, only breaking them. So he soon was just as much disliked and was just as unhappy in England as he had been in India. Jack had nothing to do all day long, and that was how it was he hurt poor Tray. And that was why Nurse wished [him] back again among the blacks! Perhaps he has gone to them. Shall we try and find out?

When Poppy left with the grey parrot, Jack amused himself by pulling off the legs of some flies. Then he tried to knock the paint off the doors and then went to the nursery cupboard, where he found a pot of jam to which he helped himself. Nurse and Baby were in the night nursery at the back of the house, so he was not disturbed. What more was there to do? He felt rather uncomfortable after all the jam, and he was lolling back in a chair wondering what mischief he could do next when the nursery door opened very slowly and softly and a black cat walked in. "That's a good job," said Jack. "I didn't know you ever came upstairs, old Zulu. Now I'll have some fun." And he took some peas out of his pocket and was going to shoot at the cat. The cat walked straight up to Jack, not seeming at all afraid, and as she walked she seemed to grow larger and blacker. Her back arched so high and her eyes shone with such a strange red light that Jack began to feel afraid. "Why, I don't believe you *are* Zulu," he said, getting up. He didn't exactly know why he got up, only he felt very little and small as he sat in the chair with this big black cat quietly coming nearer.

"Come," said the cat, in a very curious voice, not at all like a mew or a purr, and not at all like any voice Jack had ever heard. But somehow the word "come" sounded in his ears and who could have said [it] but the black cat? Jack felt very uncomfortable. Of course, he never came when people told him to come, so he was not going to obey a cat; so he went to the other end of the nursery by the window. "That way will do as well as any other," said the cat, who was by his side in a second. Jack stood up on a chair so that the cat might not touch him, and he hoped she would go out of the window, which was wide open. She did get up on the window ledge somehow. "Come," she said again.

"Not very likely that I shall go with you out of a window onto the leads, you stupid thing," said Jack, who though he was frightened, was still rude. But as he spoke, the cat turned round and her shining eyes seemed to make him move in spite of himself, and he found his foot on the window

25. LESLIE STEPHEN. *Cat sitting.* Courtesy of the Woolf Library at Washington State University Libraries, Pullman, Washington.

ledge and then in the gutter which ran round the window outside. And now
he was quite outside. "Oh, I wish Aunt were here," he cried, remembering as
he did so how glad he had been that she was not there when he hurt Tray
and what the parrot had said. Had the parrot known what was going to
happen? How he wished he had never hurt Tray. Here he was on the roof following a black cat, down, down. Far down, he could see the cabs and omnibuses hurrying along. There was the bright red pillar box, which only
looked like a scarlet stick. There was the milkman, whose funny cry sounded
faint. Jack thought of tea but now the cat had turned and Jack had to follow
up a sloping roof. The cat's soft paws trod firmly and lightly, but Jack slipped
and cracked the slates and fell, bruising himself up against a skylight. There
was no time to stop and pity himself—there was no one to pity him. On, on,
he had to go. The black cat seemed to be drawing him on; though how, Jack
could not tell. "Stop," he cried at last, "I can't go on. It will kill me."

"You can't stop," said the cat. "What if you are killed? You are no
good." Jack longed to say that he could stop, but he couldn't. Still more he
longed to say that he was of some good, but still less could he say that. For
once in his life he felt ashamed and had no answer to give. On they went.
Jack felt that if he did not take great care, he should slip; and if he walked
slowly, he might lose sight of the cat, and if he lost sight of her, what should
he do? Roof after roof rose before and behind. All were alike and he knew
none. Up and down, up and down, dark and sooty. Noise seemed all round
him but no streets could be seen. Only roofs and chimneys, chimneys and
roofs. The air was thick and hot, but the cat walked steadily on and Jack,
half choking, followed. At last when Jack could hardly see and hardly
breathe, the cat disappeared suddenly, in a moment. Jack had to follow—
where, how, he could not say, but down he went, swiftly and steadily down
into the darkness. He could see the cat's eyes gleaming and when at last she
stopped and he stopped too, her black fur glowed with a strange light, which
seemed to make the place they were in still darker. As his eyes got used to
the darkness, he could see other strange bright lights which moved curiously
like eyes, but Jack could not see to whom they belonged. "How hot it is,"
he sighed.

At that moment, an icy breath passed over him, making him shiver
and draw his coat close round him. "You had better not complain here," said
the cat and as she spoke, the heat became greater than ever.

Jack felt a sharp sting. "Why, that's a wasp," he called out. He tried
to catch it but it buzzed round his head in the most aggravating way. "I have
been stung," said Jack. He thought the black cat ought to take some care of
him when she had brought him all this way.

"Why shouldn't you be?" said the cat.

"I didn't touch the wasp," said Jack, very cross. "I thought wasps never stung unless they were touched."

"Good wasps don't," said the cat. "But you don't suppose you will find good wasps here any more than good children."

"Are all the wasps bad here?" asked Jack.

"Everything is bad here," said the cat, "or you would not be here. This is the place for you." Jack felt very uncomfortable.

A number of black cats now came up to the first one. Jack longed to get away from the horrid darkness and heat; but where could he go? "Grau grau," the cats called. "We are glad this is a boy at last. How they tease us, throwing stones and setting dogs on to worry us and pouring water on us! Now we can tease him. What has he done?"

"He has not hurt any of us, he has only a pea shooter," said the first black cat, "but he teases everything and can do nothing, so he had to come down here. There was no place for him above. The last thing he did was to break a dog's leg."

"A dog's leg," said the other cats. "Oh, then he is a friend of ours, we won't tease him," and they all came round him, their green eyes blazing out and their tails, which seemed tipped with fire, standing up high. Jack was glad they did not mean to tease him, but all the same, he did not like to feel that he was the friend of these horrid creatures. He would rather have been the friend of dear kind little Tray.

The cats who were dancing round Jack did not see that an ugly grey monkey had crept behind them with a torch with which he quickly touched all their tails—making them jump higher in the air and yell with pain while the monkey quietly hung himself up somewhere out of reach. Much as the cats hated water, they dashed off to a dark pool which Jack had not seen and dipped their smoking tails in. Jack felt afraid that they would be angry with him for not having stopped the monkey, but as they never did kind things to anyone, they never expected kind things to be done to them. As Jack watched them dipping in their tails, he saw a big cruel-looking fish come swimming up with wide open jaws. He was just going to snap at the tail of the cat who had brought Jack down, when Jack pulled the cat back and the fish swam away, disappointed. "What did you do that for?" said the cat.

"That horrid fish would have hurt you dreadfully," said Jack, rather puzzled and disappointed that the cat did not thank him.

"What would that matter to you?" said the cat, looking at him. "I thought you didn't care about other people or I should not have brought you here," and [s]he walked off crossly.

"They are funny beasts," said Jack to himself. "Why, at home I was always being told to save creatures from pain."

"Yes, but you never did. You took pleasure in hurting them or you would not be here," said a voice out of the darkness, making Jack jump. "You can hurt as much as you like here, so you ought to be happy." Jack could not see who spoke; whoever it was, must know all about him, for [though] Jack longed to say that he had not tormented creatures, he could not.

While he was thinking and wondering, he walked on. Dark as it was, an odd light seemed always to come and make the path clear to him, and this light was cold and clear with no brightness nor warmth. A sound of buzzing and humming led Jack to a place where a swarm of gnats and wasps were tormenting a monkey.

Jack felt afraid to help the monkey, whose teeth looked sharp as he tried to snap at his enemies. But a number of robins flew down and pounced on the gnats. Jack saw a black cat coming. "Go away," he said to the robins. "There is a cat coming."

"What business is it of yours?" said the robins, as they flew off.

Jack felt tired and worn out. Was there never to be anything but darkness and quarreling? How he longed to get into the fresh clear air and to hear someone speak kindly; but the farther he went, the farther the darkness seemed to stretch. He passed many animals but none seemed kind. Suddenly he met a rabbit moaning as if in great pain. "What is the matter?" said Jack, but the minute he said it he was sorry, for perhaps the rabbit would only be angry.

"I am very unhappy," said the rabbit.

"Does anything hurt you?" asked Jack.

"I hurt all over," said the rabbit. "This horrid place hurts me. I wish I had never come here."

"So do I," said Jack, glad that at last he found someone who disliked the place.

"Why did you come, then?" said the rabbit.

"I was brought here by the black cat," said Jack.

"But no one comes here unless they like it," said the rabbit. "The cat would not have brought you if he had not thought that this was the place you would be happiest in. What had you done to make him think so?"

Jack did not much like telling about all his naughtiness so, instead of answering the rabbit's question, he said, "Why did you come?"

"Ah!" said the rabbit with a sigh. "I thought I wanted to come. I was cross at home and quarreled there where everyone was happy on the green earth among the crisp green leaves. I thought I should be happier, but I didn't know what it was like. The others seem happy here but I am always longing to get back. I would not mind how much my mother scolded me for eating the wrong leaves or how many lessons I had to do, if only I could see her again and play about in the sandy burrows," and the poor little rabbit moaned so piteously that Jack felt the tears come into his eyes, and a great longing came into his heart to be back at his own home.

"I did hurt a little dog," he said, half crying, "and I did quarrel. Oh, I wish I hadn't. I wish I could go home." Just then a fox came up and the rabbit ran off.

"This is a nice place," said the fox. "No dogs, no men, for you don't count," turning to Jack. "No horses, no traps."

"It's rather dark," said Jack.

"All the better," said the fox. "I like the dark."

"Well, I don't, then," answered Jack.

"You can't have liked the light much or you wouldn't be here," said the fox.

"I was made to come," said Jack.

"Oh, no. No one is wanted here if they get on well up above. No one comes here if they are happy there. You needn't try to make me believe that," said the fox, looking cunningly at Jack. Jack walked off, not caring to tell his story again. "Wherever you were before you came here, you didn't learn manners, that's one certain thing," said the fox, looking at him. When Jack had walked away from the fox, he sat down on a stone. He really felt too tired and unhappy to go any farther.

Just as he was sitting down, he saw that close under the stone crouched a frog. He was afraid he might crush it, so lifted it out of the way. He felt a little more comfortable when he had done it. It seemed to give him a friend to have really helped something. Whether the frog would have thanked him or no, Jack never knew, for a large grey heron came quickly up and, with its long bill, seized and swallowed the poor frog in a second. "You might as well have let that frog alone. The stork would have seen him soon enough and there would have been more sport," said a voice.

"I meant to save him," said Jack. "I didn't see the heron. I thought the stone might crush the frog."

He was trying to make out who had spoken to him and at last saw that he was close to a strange-looking old woman. Her face was shriveled and creased like a dry walnut but she had a pair of black eyes which shone with a cold piercing light, not like any eyes that Jack had ever seen before. In her hands she had shining knitting needles, and a mass of black knitting lay on her lap; but though she knitted on, and the needles clicked and the mass on her lap grew larger, Jack could see no wool. She gave a funny chuckling laugh when he said that he had wanted to help the frog. "Help," she said. "No one wants to help. Why did you come here if you wanted to help? This is the land of hindering, not helping."

"The black cat brought me," said Jack.

"Well, [he] must have thought that you would hinder too or he would never have brought you." She went on, "I am glad you have come. It is a long time since I saw a child."

"Why did you come?" said Jack.

"I didn't like where I was," said the old woman. "Everyone was learning and helping and I was told that I was naughty because I never wanted to learn nor to help; and as I liked being naughty best, I came here where I could do what I please and no one could care, for everyone did the same."

"It must have been a long time ago since you were a little girl," said Jack.

"I don't know anything about time," said the old woman, "but people soon get old here. You will very soon look as old as I do." The old woman looked uglier than ever as she spoke, and she knitted faster and faster. Jack felt dreadfully frightened and unhappy too. Was it true he should soon be like her? Then he looked at her needles. They gave him a little comfort, though they worked so strangely, for surely the old woman was not so cruel as she pretended to be or she would not knit. The clothes could not all be for herself. She seemed to know what he was thinking of, for with a nasty laugh, she said, "Do you wonder why I knit? I am knitting up the selfishness that no one is using, that none of it may be lost. When the heron gobbled up that frog, his selfishness remained behind. There is always plenty to be found here, so my needles are never idle."

Jack could not understand how selfishness could be knitted into clothes. He still hoped that the old woman was really doing something kind — so he said, "*You* are not selfish, for you knit warm clothes for people."

"Does selfishness keep you warm?" said the old woman. "Come and try on the clothes. I daresay they will fit you. Then you will see how comfortable they are." As she spoke, Jack felt a cold wave of air pass near him. The old woman got up and came closer, her needles shone. The thick black clothing of selfishness was being brought near and he heard the old woman's harsh voice say, "These will be just your size. Put them on and you will be comfortable as I am."

"No, no," said Jack, struggling to get away. He felt as if he would bear anything, do anything, if he could only get away from this horrible old woman. His legs seemed turned to stone as he tried to run. He would be glad to find himself near any of the animals. Cruel as they were, they were less dreadful than the old woman. As he strove to get away, a robin stopped for an instant on a stone near, and in the darkness Jack saw the fierce green eyes of a cat just going to make a spring.

With a great effort, Jack jumped forward. For the first time in his life he didn't think of himself. He only thought of saving the robin.

He felt the cat's sharp claws tearing him and he saw her eyes, but they seemed less cruel than those of the old woman; and the warm drops of blood which flowed from him did not seem to pain him as much as the icy breath when the old woman had come near with her cruel clothes. All seemed confused to him and he shut his eyes with a tired worn-out feeling as if he had come to the end of a long journey.

When he opened them, he still felt confused. Where was he? The clear soft air of a summer morning blew through an open window, and stirred the sweetness of the mignonette. "Cheep, cheep," said a bird and Jack saw a canary. Surely it was Poppy's and this was her box of flowers. The sky was pink with the light of the rising sun. The street below seemed silent. But though Jack felt sure in a moment that he should see nothing but darkness and hear the sound of the old woman's voice, he could not help walking towards the door which led to the night nursery.

As he did so, he heard a sweet little voice say, "Have you found him, Nurse?"

And Nurse answered, "No, we have heard nothing. Your poor Mama is worn out with running about all night. We have sent men in all directions but the boy can't be heard of."

"Oh, Nurse," cried Poppy. "And I dreamt he was found. Poor Jack, poor Jack."

Jack had stood still, listening. Was it possible they were in this trouble about him? He ran in quickly, for as he heard Poppy's last words, he could not doubt any longer. "Here I am," he said. "I didn't think you would mind."

"Then my dream has come true," said Poppy, jumping up in delight, though the tears were streaming down her cheeks. "Oh Jack, how glad I am," and she hugged him tight, and for the first time, Jack did not push her away.

"Little vagabond," said Nurse, giving him a push. For now he *had* come back, she could let herself be angry with him. "I must tell your poor Aunt. You would have been no great loss," and off she went.

"Never mind what Nurse says," said Poppy. "She has been just as miserable as she could be. Oh Jack! It is nice to have you back. It was so horrid last night after we had all hunted about without finding you and it got quite dark. Mama said at last that I must go to bed and so I went, but bed was horrid and every minute I kept jumping up to listen."

"I never thought that anyone would miss me," said Jack, feeling very much ashamed. It was true he had been very unhappy all the time he was away, but he had never once thought whether his aunt would be anxious nor whether Poppy would be unhappy without him. "How is Tray, Poppy?" he went on. "I am sorry I hurt him."

"He is nearly well," said Poppy, showing the little dog, who was still in his basket with his leg bound up.

The kind little dog wagged his tail and licked Jack's hand and Jack, who had kept up bravely enough, now fairly began to cry.

"Here's Mama," said Poppy, who was much disturbed at seeing Jack cry, and then came his aunt, looking very white and tired. Jack ran to her and for the first time felt how cruel he had been to them all. He had quite forgotten all their love and had only thought of his own pain and fright when he was away.

"It is a comfort, Jack, to see you back," she said. "I didn't know how I should write the Indian letters today. What dreadful news I should have had to give, if you had not come back! Where have you been and why did you go?"

"I didn't mean to go," said Jack. "The black cat took me. When [Poppy] went off with the parrot, I went to the nursery and eat the jam."

"That you did," said Nurse. "I found the empty pot when I came back and I said to myself, 'When I catch that young vagabond he shall catch it,' and so you shall. Staying away all night and making your poor Aunt so ill. It would have been a good job if you had stayed away altogether."

"Well, you didn't catch him, so he mustn't catch it, Nurse," said Jack's aunt, smiling. "You are just as glad as we are to have him back, but I do want to hear where you have been, Jack, and then we will all go to bed."

"Zulu took me out of the window onto the roof and right away to a dark horrid place."

"Why, Zulu has been in the kitchen all night," said Nurse. "Every time I went in and out, there she sat, blinking her eyes in front of the fire, never going off to her usual corner to sleep, and I said to [Cook], 'That cat, I believe, knows all about it.'"

"And so she did, Nurse," said Jack. "She really did take me, and I saw horrid cats and monkeys and such a dreadful old woman knitting." As Jack thought of the old woman with her unkind laugh and her hard eyes, he shivered.

"You are tired out and chilled," said his aunt. "Don't talk any more. Get into your bed while Nurse makes you some hot coffee." What a wonderful delightful place bed seemed to Jack as he stretched his tired little legs down on the nice clean sheets and buried his head in the soft pillow! He wondered how he had ever disliked going to bed and whether bed had really always been so nice or if there were some change. Nurse soon brought him

some hot coffee and crisp brown toast. As Jack sat up in bed to eat it, he saw
Zulu looking quite quiet and comfortable, lazily blinking her eyes as if she
had never done anything worse in her life than lap milk.

And then came the grey parrot, who said, "Do you feel better,
Jack?"

"Why, that's funny," said Nurse. "I never knew Zulu come upstairs
before and now here's Polly, who seemed fast asleep on his perch when I was
downstairs."

"Polly has come up to see Tray, I am sure," said Poppy. "Do you
know, Jack, that dear Polly took me to such a lovely place where Tray's leg
was mended by an adjutant? It was all so lovely."

"You children must be talking in your sleep, I think," said her
Mama, coming in in a soft white dressing gown. "I am going to lie down too
and mind you, both of you stay quiet in your little beds and don't go wandering off into dreamland again."

"Oh, no, we have not been asleep," both the children cried. "We are
not going to sleep. We are wide awake."

"*I* am, Jack. Aren't you?" added Poppy.

"Yes," said Jack in a sleepy voice. "Wide a—" But what he was going
to say, no one knew for his eyes were fast closed, and as Poppy turned to
look at him, her eyes watered and winked and her soft yellow head drooped
down on her pillow and she was asleep too.

The Wandering Pigs

THREE PIGS LIVED in a very comfortable home near the sea. The cliffs which rose up from the beach were covered with short sweet grass with here and there a tuft of pale pink thrift. In the spring the harebells and yellow poppies bloomed and the bees came humming by. There was a house near and a sheltered garden full of roses and raspberries, in the corner of which stood a row of yellow beehives. The garden was cut out of the side of the cliff and when Aubrey and Conor came up from the beach by the little winding path, they used to stand on the top of the broad stone wall and look down on the yellow roses which grew in a tangled mass on the old apple tree, and Aubrey declared he could smell the honey which was being gathered all day by humming bees.

The pigs could hear the sea splashing up; but even in the roughest weather they never got wet. A bit of overhanging rock sheltered them from the rain and they lived too high on the cliff for the waves to reach them. In the winter they all got close together under the rocks. Chunks, who was the oldest, the fattest, and the most selfish, used to get in the middle, and Grits and little Curly used to lie on either side and so they slept most of the winter. In the summer they trotted about the cliff and lay basking in the sun blinking their little eyes, as they saw the children digging in the sands below or paddling in the clear water. The three pigs had lived together a long time, that is for pigs, who count time quite differently from children. They did not quarrel often for when Chunks wanted more food and the warmest corner, the others only grunted and said, "Greedy boy." (We call greedy boys pigs, perhaps that is why pigs call greedy pigs boys.) One day the sun [shone] so brightly, the waves looked so clear, and the children's voices sounded so merry and so near that Curly, who did not find his two companions very amusing said, "They do have fun down there–how I should like to go down. Look at that little girl with the yellow hair. She is racing into the sea. I can hear the water splash as she dips her head in–how nice and cool it sounds. I am baked up here. Look, Grits, there is the fat little boy called Aubrey–he has got on such a funny collar. See, he is paddling about like a frog. Oh, Conor is drowned. No, he isn't, a wave knocked him over but he is up and laughing–he doesn't mind a bit."

"What *are* you chattering about, Curly?" said Chunks. "We have seen all those silly children a hundred times. It is not worthwhile to wake me out of my comfortable snooze to tell me about *them*. They always do the same things—get wet and cold and then get dry, silly things."

"The men fishing look comfortable," said Grits. "They sit all day in a boat; sometimes they have a fire. I see the smoke curling up and the boat rocks, and the men lie smoking their pipes. It makes me sleepy to look at them."

"*That* sounds nice," said Chunks, stretching himself. "*I* shouldn't mind so much sitting in a boat with nothing to do and being rocked to sleep. There is some sense in that, but I can't see any in just taking off clothes to put them on again and slipping about on the wet rocks as those stupid children do."

"Suppose we do go in a boat," said Curly in a great hurry. He was young and longed for a change. He had never been off the cliff in his life.

"Softly, softly," said Chunks; "you are too young, Curly. You don't think where is the boat and how could we get to it and what should we do. You mustn't be in such a hurry. It is very tiring to be in a hurry."

"There is a boat just below," said Grits, "and we could get to it easily, for it lies in a pool just under our cliff and at low tide we could get into it without any trouble and stay till the tide came in and then we should be rocked just like the men are. Curly might bring our food while I helped you down, Father Chunks." Grits was not as young as Curly; but he was younger than Chunks and much thinner, so he thought it right to call Chunks, Father. Though he was a very quiet and contented pig he had often thought that it would be pleasant to have a little change and get nearer that bright blue sea.

Curly was so happy when he heard they were to go, that he could not help dancing on his hind legs and so very nearly tumbled on Chunks, who at once stopped his fun by saying, "Come and let me bite your tail."

"We had better start," said the good Grits, who did not like Curly to have his tail bitten. "Go and get that juicy lettuce, Curly, and the potatoes. If there is too much for you to carry at once, you can come back again." Curly lost no time in getting all the best of their food, and trotted up and down the hill many times before Chunks thought that they had food enough.

"I suppose we shall be back tonight," said Curly with a grunt which was meant for a sigh, "but it's better than nothing and it will be nice to see those little children in the sea and to watch the fishes swimming around." So off they went. The tide was just coming in but they managed to get into the boat without getting very wet. Chunks was so heavy that the boat rocked

26. LESLIE STEPHEN. *Pig on all fours*. Courtesy of the Woolf Library at Washington State University Libraries, Pullman, Washington.

when he got in and frightened him very much, but there was a bit of rope fastened to the boat and the two other pigs tied it to a rock which stood out of the sea and then they all sat down. The sea came rushing softly in and their boat was soon rocking just like the boats they had so often watched. Chunks, however, declared that it made him sick, so they got him out on the rock which now that the tide had come in was being turned into an island. It wasn't much more lively than being at home; "but it is a change, which is something," said Curly. They could see their home on the cliff but it looked quite different. They had never known how small it was.

Presently the children came racing down the little stony path to the beach, jumping over the little brook which crossed the path. Their white tent was quickly put up and soon the children were splashing and screaming with pleasure in the fresh clear sea. Some of them could swim and dive and the pigs were very much surprised when they saw the bright faces disappear under one wave and come up at the top of another.

Then the merry voices were silent but only for a short time, for now the children were dressed and scrambling over the rocks. "What stupid things children are," said Chunks, "always chattering and moving when they might all be lying in the sun. They go slipping about on damp rocks, tumbling about getting their feet wet and their clothes torn, dabbling their hands in pools all for nothing. They are not looking for their dinners."

"They are only amusing themselves," said Grits. "They are doing that all day long, they don't know any better." He did think children very stupid to find amusement in getting wet and tired; but Curly thought it must be delightful and wished he were not a pig. While the pigs sat on the rock wondering at the children, the fishes who had been swimming round the rock were wondering at *them*.

Who were these sleek pink things so fat and warm lying near the cold blue sea which belonged to the fishes? One great sharp-nosed fish with white hungry teeth knew what they were. He wanted to lay hold of Chunks and pull him over and gobble him up but he could not reach so far—all he could do was to gnaw the rope which held the boat fast, and his strong sharp teeth had soon cut it through. Curly, whose eyes though very small were very sharp, soon saw what the fish was doing. "Jump into the boat," he cried. "A fish is biting our rope and we shall be left on this island." Chunks could hardly get off the rock, he was so fat and sleepy, but Grits helped him down into the boat and Curly was just able to jump in after them before the rope was quite bitten through. It only hung by a thread to the rock and as the boat felt the weight of the three pigs, that thread gave away and the boat whirled round and then bobbed up and down, frightening even Curly. However it soon got quiet and then Chunks said, "Well, it's a good thing we are safe off, it would not have been pleasant to spend the night on those rocks and to get drenched through if a storm came on. Ugh! It makes me shiver to think of it." And his fat sides shook. "Now we shall get home and it will be a long time before I go travelling again."

"Get home?" said Grits. "We are not going home. This isn't the way we came—not that we did come any way, for we only walked to the rock. Now we are far from it—the tide never goes back so far as this. I can hardly see our old home."

"What do you mean?" said Chunks very crossly. "You must be blind, you stupid old Grits," and he raised himself to look out. It was true enough—a soft steady breeze was drifting the boat straight across the bay. In a moment they would be round the point.

The garden with its roses and raspberries looked only a mass of green; the white house on the hill where the children lived seemed a long way off and the children themselves looked like tiny black specks. "Why don't you row back, you empty headed cocoanut?" said Chunks to Curly.

"We have no oars," said Curly. "There were none in the boat—and we don't know how to row if we had them!"

27. LESLIE STEPHEN. *Fish*. Courtesy of the Woolf Library at Washington State University Libraries, Pullman, Washington.

"Don't say we," said Chunks, very angry. "It is all your doing. You made us come in a boat, you made us go on the island"—and he gave poor Curly's tail such a sharp nip that it hung quite out of curl for a long time after.

"Softly, Father Chunks," said Grits. "It was you who wanted to get on the rock—and if it had not been for Curly's sharpness we should all be there still and most likely we should have been drowned."

"And so we shall now," said Chunks, who felt rather ashamed of his bad temper, but would not say so.

"It is such a beautiful calm day," said Grits. "We are not likely to be upset if we sit still; but if you make poor Curly jump and squeal as he did just now, the boat is sure to go over; and I daresay this nice wind will bring us back home again." Grits didn't know much about wind or boats but he knew a great deal about Chunks, who when he heard what Grits said, la[id] himself flat down at the bottom of the boat and was soon feasting on a delicious cabbage.

Curly stood at the prow of the boat, feeling very happy. Now he was really travelling. He could not even see the old home—he felt a little sorry when he thought of little Harry, who used to come every evening to scratch his back and bring him an apple or a lump of sugar, but still it was delightful to feel that they were really off. The waves came brushing up to him with their crisp white crests, the salt spray showering up, but Curly was not afraid. They passed a big black rock standing tall and sharp out of the sea; it was covered with gulls, cormorants, and gannets. As the pigs passed, Curly heard an old seagull say to her little one who was all covered with soft yellow fluff, "Now stand and watch me while I fly and swim and then you will learn how when your feathers come." The seagull went softly up into the air, then came down on the crest of the wave, her gray and white feathers shining like silver in the sun. Then a gannet rose high and straight and like a sail splashed deep through the clear green water, and in a second she was up again with a struggling silvery fish in her strong beak. There was a swift rush of waves near the rock and the little boat rocked about rather uncomfortably. Chunks said he knew they should be drowned and even Curly felt a little frightened. Grits, who had all the time been busy about something, now asked Curly to help him. He had found an old brown sail and mast at the bottom of the boat and he was trying to put it up; from his home on the cliff he had often watched how the sailors, when they wanted to get home, put up their brown sails and the little boats then seemed to sail away—soon out of sight. He thought if he could put up this sail their boat would take them home, but though he and Curly got the sail up with a great deal of trouble, the wind which puffed it out and took them soon past the rocks where the gannets and cormorants were sitting did not take the pigs home. The boat went even further out to sea. They passed a pair of little snowy birds who kept bobbing up and down and chattering to each other as if they found the sea quite as pleasant as the children did.

Then came a crowd of big black tumbling things. What fun they seemed to be having! Their black backs arched above the waves for a second, then down they went and were up the other side of the boat. Curly, who was as usual looking, was rather frightened though it was pleasant, too, to get great splashes of the fresh salt water in his face. One of the black things soon flopped up close to him and said, "Don't be afraid of us, we are sea pigs—though we like better to be called porpoises."

Curly was very much astonished at hearing that these big splashing things were called pigs, and he called out to Grits, "Look! Here are some sea cousins of ours come to make friends." Grits came to the side of the boat and was quite as surprised as Curly.

Several porpoises swam up and they all seemed very friendly. "What made you land pigs come out in a boat?" they said. "We have never seen pigs sailing about before."

The pigs did not much like being called *land* pigs, but they told their story. "Well," said the porpoises, "you are in luck; the wind is blowing you straight across the bay and you will soon find yourselves on a nice sandy shore. You will be able to get out of the boat quite easily, and on the hill above the beach there's a little wood where you can pass the night."

"But, that isn't our home," said Chunks, who had roused up when he heard all the talking.

"What is home?" said the porpoise.

"Well," said Chunks, "I should have thought even a wet creature like you must have known what home was; the place where you live, of course."

"Don't you live on the land, you land pig?" said the porpoise, "and I was telling you how to get to the land."

"Chunks means that the wood you tell us about isn't where we always eat and sleep," said Grits.

"Oh, do you sleep and eat always in the same place?" said the porpoise. "Poor things! All the sea is our home and everyday we find a new and beautiful home, and as long as we live we shall never have come to the end of it. If you were only sea pigs you could swim back to this place where you eat and sleep and which you seem to like so much—but then of course if you *were* sea pigs you wouldn't like it. So it all comes to the same thing," said the porpoise, who was rather fond of talking and had his ideas about most things.

"If we can't swim you can't walk," said Chunks crossly.

"No one would walk if they could swim," said the porpoise. "You poor things walking on the dirty earth with only one little corner which you call home to live in. You don't know what swimming means. We dive down deep and see the pink and silver shells floating about in the gold seaweeds. The sea is never dirty."

"And it's never quiet," said Chunks, who could bear this sort of talk no longer, "and you seem as if you could be never quiet. The earth which you call dirty is a nice quiet comfortable place, not always rolling and tumbling like this salt splashing place."

"Well, goodbye," said the porpoise. "I didn't mean to be unpleasant. I thought everyone must think the sea better than the land, but perhaps some don't." And the porpoise dived down to think the matter over.

The pigs now began to look out for the place where the porpoises said they would [be] able to land. Their boat sailed straight for the pretty bay and they were glad to see the green downs and the little stunted trees turning their heads away from the salt breeze; and then they saw clearly the white sand of the sheltered little cove into which their boat was carrying them safely. Chrr scrr—with a soft little scrunch the boat landed them and the pigs tumbled out. They were rather stiff and they could not at first walk on the fine soft white sand. The beach was all made of tiny shells. They shone in the sun. Under the pigs' little hoofs were all manner of clear blue and opal treasures. The pigs cared for none of them, and crunch crunch they smashed all the delicate little boxes and spirals into a confused mass of glittering colour. There were plenty of children who cared if the pigs did not, and the children kept calling out to each other as they found a perfect shell with delicate gold lines, or a pale pink cowrie, with deep maroon spots. One child with big blue eyes said it seemed a pity to take the shells away from this lovely place to ugly dusty London, but the others said the uglier and dustier London was, the more beautiful things ought to be taken there.

The pigs trotted on, anxious to get off the beach and into the nice wood of which the porpoises had told them, before night came on. They turned into a little cave all tangled with honeysuckle. The lovely Vanessa butterflies dashed backwards and forwards. The sun was going down and the pigs trotted as fast as they could. They passed a clear stream bubbling and rushing over the stones to the sea. A green woodpecker flashed across, crying chee chee. "It is going to rain," said Grits, "let's make haste and get to the wood."

"I am walking as fast as I can and I must stop and have a drink, though it's only cold water and I should be having nice buttermilk at home if it weren't for that stupid Curly," said Chunks. He did not stop very long and they reached the wood just when the sun was making the whole sky seem on fire, and the dark pine trees seemed darker than ever. It was a hot summer evening; no breath stirred the leaves; the shining pine needles crackled drily under the pigs' toes, as they trotted on to find a comfortable place for the night. They came across a few bilberries and some feathery leaves of wild parsley which they were glad to munch. After hunting about for some time, they found a nice soft bed of moss. The trees were so thick that the sky could not be seen through the branches, which gave out a fresh smell of resin. The three pigs were soon tucked comfortably down (for pigs tuck down and children tuck up). Chunks and Grits fell fast asleep in a minute. Curly was too pleased to find himself really away from home to spend the time in sleeping and he sat up and tried to see through the branches. Presently there came a creak of stiff wings and a bat flew swiftly by, singing to himself in a sad little voice. Then there was the soft flap of heavy wings stirring the branches above and Curly knew that an owl was flying overhead. "Too whoo, too whoo," it cried, and "Too whit, too whoo," came the answer. Curly got very sleepy listening to these strange voices out of the darkness. The night was so warm, the sounds were so soothing that though he had made up his mind he would *not* go to sleep, wink, blink went his little eyes and poor Curly tumbled down in a very uncomfortable way and was dreaming and fast asleep about ten minutes after Chunks and Grits had begun to snore.

Crash! Bang! Flash! They were not allowed to sleep long. The woodpecker had told the truth and the storm had begun. The birds flew shrieking out of the wood to see what was the matter as foolish people always do, then back to their homes like wise ones. The rain came pattering hard and then seemed to stop to let them hear the roar of the thunder, while the lightning even shot through the thick files of the pine branches through which no drop of rain could come. The pigs were very much frightened. The noise and the strange bright light made even Curly wish himself back at home. There was an opening in the trees and they could see the rain pouring straight down, making a deep pool; and the blue lightning flashed, making Curly and Grits wink their eyes. Chunks, whom it always took some time to awake, had jumped up when he heard the thunder crashing overhead. "Let me go, let me go, you good for nothing Curly," he said, giving poor Curly's tail a sharp bite.

"What are you biting my tail for?" said Curly. "You don't suppose *I* am making all this noise."

"Let me go, I tell you," said Chunks as another crash and flash came close together. "I won't stay here. I know I shall be killed and I shan't even be bacon."

"Stay where you are," answered Grits.

"You can't get out of the wood. We are very lucky to be safe and dry here. See out there how the rain is pouring and the branches falling about." For the wind had risen and the still summer night had changed, with a wild tempest beating down all the dried branches which should have stayed till the autumn gales.

A little bird half-drowned flew where the pigs were for shelter. It was a little golden-crested wren who lived in a yew tree in the middle of the wood. His pretty yellow tuft was all wet and colourless and his little wings hung dripping so that they could hardly bear him to shelter. "Come here," said good-natured Grits. "Here's a nice warm corner. If you will rub yourself against me your wings will soon get dry."

The little bird was very glad to find such [a] kind friend; but he longed to fly away to his nest. "I am afraid my tree will be struck by the lightning," he said; "it is so old, the oldest tree in the wood." Crack, crash, came a roar worse than any they had heard before, and they saw a tall straight pine which had held its head high and proudly above the rest come crashing down, breaking and maiming the other trees in its way. The little wren was however even more frightened of Chunks, who at this moment gave a loud squeal, threw himself straight down with legs and tail out and said he was going to die. "I think I had better go," said the wren, "this is worse than the storm."

"Oh, no," said Curly, "it is only Chunks' way. Wait a few minutes more, for the storm seems getting less." So it did. The thunder rolled slowly away and the rain, though it fell on, seemed to have lost its fury and the wind had spent its strength.

The little bird would wait no longer. "I ought never to have left them," he said, and he flew away trembling to his wife and children. He found them all safe, their old yew tree standing stiff and strong. His little wife had been dreadfully frightened, but she had made ready a nice supper of the sweet scarlet yewberry and they soon tucked their gold crowns under their brown wings and were fast asleep.

The pigs too had a good sleep after their fright. Chunks had not died and seemed to be a little ashamed of himself. At all events he did not punish Curly anymore. In the morning there was little left to tell them of the storm but the pool of water and the poor pine tree which lay broken down instead of standing erect as it had done.

The pigs took a bath in the pool, a treat which pigs seldom get but which they enjoy quite as much as or even more than other people — certainly more than *some* other people. The sun was making all the wet leaves shine, and the wood smelt sweeter than ever. A little hare was sitting stroking his nose at the edge of the wood. The pigs went up to him and

asked him which road they had better take, and he advised them to go to a
rich turnip field just below in the valley where plenty of good food was to be
had if they did not mind digging for it.

The pigs were very hungry so they trotted down the side of the hill
and soon found themselves in a big green turnip field. The broad leaves of
the turnips held little pools of water but the crisp white roots were fresh and
pleasant to the hungry pigs, who crunched away with great delight. Even
Chunks eat himself into a good temper. "I should like to go and see if the
boat is still on the beach. I don't want to go on that horrid moving sea again;
but we must get home somehow and I suppose there is no other way," he
said. It was very easy to talk of going back but it wasn't so easy to do. The
pigs had never been to school to learn geography and what was perhaps
even worse they had never left their own hillside before, so how could they
know the way to get back? They thought if they went round the bottom of
the hill at the top of which was the wood, they must find themselves near
the sea, but if you ever think that going round a hill will take you to the
same place that going over it will, you will find out your mistake as the pigs
did. They did get to a bay; but it was not their bay. There were no pink and
blue shells, no little children, but plenty of strong fishing boats, with their
brown sails set all sailing straight from the north, and the fishermen in their
blue jerseys smoking and talking—it was quite a different place from any
that the pigs had ever seen. There was a long pier which ran out to sea and
far off, rising straight out of the sea, was a white lighthouse on whose windows the sun was burning fiercely.

On the pier was a monkey painting. Curly, who was never shy,
went up to see what was going on. He was quite surprised to see, on the bit
of board before the monkey, the boats and their brown sails and the blue sea
running into the little harbour. "Dear me, you are very clever," said Curly.

"You are very polite," said the monkey, looking round for a minute.
"Are you an art critic?"

"Oh, yes," said Curly, who did not in the least know what the monkey meant. "I am sure Mr. Fox thinks it beautiful," he said, turning to a fox
who was standing by.

"No, I cannot say that," said the fox. "I was telling friend Guso,
when you came up, that the sea was too blue."

"I don't think the sea can be too blue," said Curly. "The sea is as
blue as the sky."

"I shouldn't think you had ever seen much of the sky, master pig,"
said the fox. "Your eyes are so small and your nose is always so near the
ground."

"Come, none of this," said a bear who came up. "My orders are that everyone must move on or be locked up."

"I wish you would move them on," said the monkey, "their silly chatter prevents my painting."

"No great loss," said the fox, but the bear growled out, "Move on, move on." So off he trotted.

"What made you go and talk to all those people?" said Chunks to Curly. "If you go on chattering like that I shall have to bite your tail."

"Come, come," said Grits, "he did no harm. While you were getting onto the pier and Curly was talking I saw a rat with a pack on his back; and as rats always know everything and go where no one else does, I asked him what the country was like and which way we had better take. He told me that he did not know our home, which was very odd, but that we should find plenty of pleasant places to feed and to sleep in and that today there was going to be a great wrestling match in a field not very far from here – and after the wrestling there would be a great feast. I think we had better go there."

"So we had," said Chunks. He liked the idea of a feast; but he did not like the hot dusty road, with the sun shining down on them, which they had to take.

On their way they met two bears leading a donkey with paniers in which were two little bears. A raven sat on a stone and asked the bears where they were going. "To the wrestling match," they answered. "We cannot stop to talk."

"Who wants you to?" said the raven. The pigs just then came up and she asked them the same question. "I suppose you want to eat at the feast," she said, when they had told her. "You are too fat to wrestle. You would choke if you tried." The pigs did not much like the raven's manners and went on after the bears. As they went they could hear the raven's hoarse voice asking everyone the same question and always answering with something rude.

The way was much longer than Chunks had expected and at last he said that he must rest a little in the shade of a tree. Grits knew there was no use in trying to persuade Chunks. No one ever could when he had made up his mind.

"While you sleep, Grits and I will take a little walk," said Curly, for now they had got off the high road and were on a pleasant breezy common which was shadowed here and there by big trees.

"What a stupid you are," said Chunks, "walking about when you might stay quiet." But Curly and Grits had already trotted off.

"I think I hear voices," said Curly, as they came to a little clump of trees. "Let us go and see who is there." Pigs have no enemies so they are never afraid. The two pigs soon found themselves in strange company. A big elephant was standing under the tree, looking down on a curious black thing which was moving away all on one side.

A monkey was above in the tree. "You nasty ungrateful thing," he said to the creature below, "just to give me a pinch when I was looking at you so carefully and explaining all about you. You might have found out a great deal about yourself if you had behaved properly."

"I daresay he doesn't want to know more about himself. I don't think he ha[s] a good expression," said the owl from above.

"And I don't think you could have told him much," said another monkey from the end of a branch. "For you didn't even know his name. He is a crab and how he got here I can't think, for he lives in the sea." Curly, who had managed to get up a bit of the trunk of the tree, now asked the company if they were near the place where the wrestling match was held. "It won't take any of us long to get there," said the monkey, "but you gentlemen are rather stout and seem to be already out of breath. So I advise you to start at once."

"We are not stout," said Grits, "but we have a friend who is, and if what you say is true, we had better go and rouse him up." So they went back to Chunks.

"Why, I have hardly closed my eyes," he said, "I am sure you can't have been away a minute."

"Remember the feast?" said Grits. "We shall be too late for it if we waste any more time." The thought of this roused old Chunks. They had still some way to go but the path was across the moor on fresh springy turf so they did not get so tired. Then they went downhill and were overtaken by a party of rats and rabbits all packed into a wheelbarrow and driven by a bear and a dog who were trying to race each other down the hill. They did not think much of the rats and rabbits, who were sent tumbling head over heels out of the barrow down the green hillside. Curly ran to pick them up; but they gave him some sharp nips and told him to mind his own business. "Where are you all going?" said Grits to the bear.

"To the wrestling match of course, old grunter," said the bear.

"My name is not Grunter," said Grits.

"I am tired of hearing about this wrestling match," said Chunks. "I wish you would take me in your barrow instead of those stupid low things."

"I would rather not, thank you, old shaky-sides," said the bear who was certainly not polite. "But come along, you low things," he said to the rats. "Jump in or we shall be late." One of the rats, as he did what he was bid, managed to give Chunks a sharp bite in return for having been called a low thing. It wasn't nearly such a sharp bite as Chunks was in the habit of giving to Curly; but the old fellow gave a loud squeal which made everyone laugh. At last they got to the field where the great wrestling match was to be.

They found a crow[d] of animals there, many of which the pigs had never seen before.

"Dear! Dear!" said Chunks. "I hope we shan't be crushed in that crowd. Pray be careful. Oh, dear! Oh, dear! I wish we had never left home."

"I don't," said Curly, who had never felt so happy before as he did now in this strange place. It did look a very strange place though it was only a common grass field. There was a large empty space left in the middle of the field; but round it stood a ring of all sorts of strange beasts. The three pigs managed to find places just in front of a tall giraffe who stretched his long neck scornfully about in the air, curling his tongue round as if he were thinking: how on earth did *I* get here among this *very* low set? Everyone was now gazing at the wrestlers who had come into the middle of the field. They were two monkeys who had on short jackets. Two bears stood by to see that the wrestling went fairly. The two monkeys tried to throw each other, putting their heads down, twisting their little feet and holding firmly with their long thin arms; but they were so well matched that it seemed as if the contest could never be decided. At last the cleverer of the two monkeys managed to hook his foot very carefully into the other monkey's leg and brought him to the ground. Then there was great excitement. The elephant trumpeted, the foxes laughed, and the hares, rabbits, and rats gave shrill screams; the animals who seemed unable to make a noise waved their necks or stamped with their hoofs. The monkey who had been thrown down hopped away, and another monkey came on to wrestle with the conqueror, who was again successful. The pigs liked seeing all this very much, and Curly felt very glad that the boat had drifted away, and had taken them far from their old home. When the wrestling was over, Chunks was very pleased to hear a big bell, which told that the feast was ready in the big tent. Just as it had finished ringing, and the beasts were going in, an old bear came trotting up to ask for tickets. The pigs did not know what was meant. "You can't go to the feast without a ticket," said the bear, "but if there are any left and you have any money you can go and buy tickets."

"We have no money," said the pigs; "when we left home we did not mean to stay away so long and we brought none."

"What did you come here for?" growled the bear. "If you can't pay for food, you can't eat it." Grits asked the bear if he would not let them send him the money when they got home. "Where is your home?" said the bear.

"Across the sea," said Grits, feeling very uncomfortable.

28. LESLIE STEPHEN. *Giraffe*. Courtesy of the Woolf Library at Washington State University Libraries, Pullman, Washington.

"A likely story, as if pigs could swim. I see now you are tramps. You will be locked up," said the bear. A crowd had collected round the pigs. The giraffe twisted his long neck round to see what was the matter but when he found it was all about three pigs, he put out his tongue and said nothing.

The hare whispered, "Can't you run off? That's what I do, and no one catches me." Grits shook his head; they could not run – they were not allowed to eat, and they would now certainly be locked up whatever that might mean. Were ever three pigs so unlucky? Chunks as usual lay down flat – in doing so he touched the bear.

"You rude old fellow," said the bear. "Off with you to prison." But Chunks did not stir.

"Let me go," said Curly. "I made the others come and if I go, surely it will do instead of Chunks."

"You ought all to go," said the bear. "But as the old gentleman seems to be very heavy and will, I daresay, soon be bacon, he shall stay there" – and he gave poor Chunks a kick – "and the others can see how quickly he can get across the sea for his money, for you will stay in prison till he brings it. I suppose you have never been in prison before."

"Of course not," said Curly, who was walking very slowly and sadly by the bear's side. "Pigs never have prisons."

"The sooner they do, the better then," said the bear. "They would learn then not to expect food which they hadn't paid for. Here we are," and he shoved the poor pig into a big dark place, locked a door and was off. Curly could see nothing and tumbled down in the place where the bear had shoved him – full of fright and horror. By degrees he got used to the darkness, which had seemed quite black as he came in from the bright clear sunshine outside. There was a little hole in the roof and though it did not let in much light, nor much air, it was better than being quite in the dark as he had thought at first. He began to move a little but soon found he was touching something warm and soft.

"What is this?" he said.

"What is what, and who are you? And why have you come?" answered the soft thing.

"I am Curly," said the pig, "and have been sent here because I had no money. Who are you?"

"Can't you see, you old stupid, I am one of the wrestlers?"

"Well, I'm very glad to see you," said the pig; "but how did you get here? I thought you were in at the feast."

"That stupid old bear said I had not fairly conquered," said the monkey; "he doesn't know anything about wrestling. A fat heavy old fellow with a ton of skin on. Because he is one of the police he must always be finding fault with someone. We shall have plenty more in here tonight, I daresay; on wrestling days the lock-up is always full. I hope you brought some food with you."

"Not a bit," said Curly with a sigh as he thought of the feast and wondered if Grits would ever be able to get money and set him free.

"Well, you are a silly," said the monkey, "but perhaps you have never been in prison before."

"*Of course* I haven't," said Curly. "You and the bear have both said that to me. You must know very little about us if you think we ever go to prison."

"Well, we do," said the monkey, who didn't seem to mind it at all — "as soon as I saw that old bear coming my way I got hold of a little friend of mine called Jack Hare and sent him to fetch me some nuts and fruits, and he was here and away again before the old bear brought me here — so I found my little store waiting for me."

"I wish I had thought of that," said the pig; "there was a very kind hare who advised us to run away but we can none of us run fast and poor Chunks can't run at all."

"I daresay not," said the monkey; "you are a stupid set. I wonder, if pigs had to be made at all, why they weren't made different. They are not useful and they certainly are not ornamental. It would be a charity to teach you to do something." And the monkey jumped on poor Curly's back, stuck his heels to his sides and, crying out, "Run, run, as fast as you can or I will bite your ears," made poor Curly trot round and round till he could trot no more. "That's not so bad," said the monkey. "You can rest now and I will give you a few of my nuts; not many, for you are too fat already and the thinner you get, the faster you will run." Curly was so hungry, he was thankful for anything; but nuts are dry food. How he longed for pigwash and buttermilk! For the first time he began to wish himself back on the cliff. But after all how much fun they had had, and perhaps more would come; at all events he could go to sleep in the prison if he wanted[?], and that would make the time pass. But this was just what he could not do. No sooner had poor Curly stretched himself out on some clean straw that he found in a corner than the mischievous monkey began to pelt him with sharp nutshells which he somehow always managed to throw on the very spot where they stung most.

"Pray leave off and let me go to sleep," said Curly.

"Why should you go to sleep?" said the monkey.

"I'm so sleepy," said Curly.

"But I'm not," said the monkey, "and I've been wrestling, so you can't be. Why should you be sleepy if I'm not? If you can't tell me that, you can't expect to go to sleep." Poor Curly now really began to feel very unhappy. If he could neither sleep nor eat and had to stay ever so long in the dark with this teasing monkey, he felt he should go mad – and for a pig to think that, means that he is *very* unhappy indeed. "You had better sit up and be sensible," said the monkey, when for the fiftieth time poor Curly had been awoken, just as he was dropping off, by a nutshell on his pink eyelids. "I don't mean to be more disagreeable than I can help, but then you must be pleasant too."

"I am and I wish to be," said poor Curly.

"You don't call it being pleasant company lying there snoring while I sit here wide awake, do you?" said the monkey – and Curly was too honest to say that it was.

"But why don't you go to sleep?" he asked.

"Because I never do in the broad daylight."

"It's not broad daylight here," said Curly, sighing.

"No, but when you have been in prison as often as I have," said the monkey, "you will know that there is no use going to sleep in the day, for what would you do in the night?" Curly thought he could sleep night and day when he was so tired. In fact he nearly went off while the [monkey] was talking; but as he felt another nutshell might be coming, he tried to look bright. "Let's have a good talk," said the monkey; "though you are a pig, you may have something to say for yourself." Poor Curly told the story of their wanderings as well as he could. "Of all stupid creatures, you must be the three stupidest," said the monkey. "Let a fish bite your rope, lose your oars and come to prison without food. You must be lucky or you would never have fallen in with me. I have had a very different life. When I was quite little I lived in a big wood full of cocoanuts which held delicious milk."

"I know," said Curly, "buttermilk."

"No, not buttermilk, you old silly; cocoanut milk, which is much better. My mother used to throw the nuts down from the tree and so break them and she would then feed me with the milk, and with big yellow bananas. One day a party of hunters came through the wood, and one of them shot my poor mother. She was holding me and she never let go of me, though she was so hurt; but we both fell to the ground together. She was killed but I was not a bit hurt, for she had kept me so tight to her. I think the hunters were sorry when they saw they had killed poor Mother, but they are cruel creatures. They spend all their time in killing something. So they didn't think long of her. One of them said that I was a pretty little beast, and that he would take me home, so he put me in a.bag which he carried, and took me off to his tent. We were there several days, and every day the hunters went out, leaving me tied up. I used to hear their guns go crack, crack. Every evening when they came home they brought back dead animals. They killed many more than they or their dogs could eat. Sometimes beautiful birds with orange and blue feathers, sometimes great stags with soft brown eyes; one night they brought a big snake which seemed covered with shining armour. It was dead but I didn't like its look and was glad when it was taken off.

"Then I was put back in the bag and all the hunters rode off to the sea and we got on board a ship. I did have a nasty time always chained up. No trees to swing on, no nice fresh fruit, but the horrid old ship full of people. In the evening my master used to take me on deck, holding my chain while he walked up and down. Then I saw the sea which seemed made of fire. The waves flamed against the side of the ship as if they would burn it; but they never did. When the ship stopped, there was a great fuss and I thought in the bustle that I might get away from my chain and be free; but my master seemed to know what I was thinking about, for he had me fastened to a big box so that I could not get away. I sat all day on the box, for I soon found I should be crushed to death if I did not, the place was so crowded: barrels of sugar, and sacks of rice, and great boxes full of red wood. Little boys were going head over heels and men were selling oranges, cocoanuts and pineapples just like those I used to get at home—only there we picked them fresh. I longed to get one but could not. When my master came by I pulled his coat and put my hand out and, as he wasn't very stupid considering what he is, he knew what I meant, and got me a cocoanut. It wasn't nearly so nice as what I had at home but it was better than nothing.

"Then we went in a train and I kept thinking, and thinking, how I could get away. I thought the country looked very nice after the sea. Big apple trees full of red fruit, I longed to climb them—but I did not know how to get out. My chain was on and I was fastened to part of the carriage where my master had put his gun and sticks. At last I thought of a plan. I knocked my foot against a stick, then I scratched it—then I rubbed the chain up and down till I had made my foot quite sore—then I began to cry and make a great fuss. I felt the train was going slower and I wanted to have my chain off by the time it stopped, so I pulled and pulled and made my leg so bad that my master said, 'Poor little fellow, how he has hurt himself. I will take his chain off and carry him. He won't be able to get away.' It only shows how stupid people are when they have lost their tails. The train stopped very soon after my chain was undone, and in one minute I was off through the window. Everyone was so surprised that they were a minute before they jumped out of the carriage; then I had hopped onto the station roof and had swung myself off the other side, dropping into a garden. I was afraid to stay there and climbed up the tallest tree there was. I saw my master and all the people looking but the train was soon going off again and they had to go.

Afterwards, a man came with a ladder and searched the trees but I had crept into a little hole in a hedge where he never thought of looking and so I was safe and free. I stayed there all night, only creeping out to get some food.

"Oh, what fun I have had. I stir the cream and hear the cat scolded. I take the new laid eggs and traps are set for the foxes, and I eat up the fruit and the boys are whipped. I go from place to place, hiding in hogsheads when it is cold and having fun always. You old pig, you seem fond of travelling. Suppose we set off together when we are let out of prison?"

"Gurrrrr-" was the only answer that came from Curly.

"What do you say?" said the monkey. "I have told you all this long delightful story after your stupid one, and I do believe you are asleep." Curly had tried very hard to keep awake but when the monkey went on, and on, with his long history, poor Curly went fast asleep and if the monkey had not been so much interested in talking about himself, he would have found out long before, that Curly was fast asleep and snoring.

The monkey was just going to wake him but at that moment the door opened, and the old bear was seen coming in. "Where's that pig?" he said very crossly.

"Here I am," said Curly, rubbing his eyes. "What do you want with me?"

"I want nothing *with* you, I want *you*," said the bear still more gruffly.

"Why, what have I done, where am I to go?" said the poor pig, getting frightened.

"You're going back to the feast which you have spoilt for me, you low thing," said the bear.

"I suppose I'm to come too," said the monkey.

"Wait till you're asked, Mr. Jackanapes," said the bear, pulling Curly along and slamming the door in the monkey's face.

"Poor monkey," said Curly.

"You needn't pity him," said the bear, "he's used to it." And then Curly remembered all the monkey had said and thought that perhaps it was as well he was out of mischief.

"Why have I been brought out?" he asked.

"I was told to bring you out but I wasn't told to talk to you," said the bear. "And I don't mean to." The bear was very cross, for he had been scolded. All the animals had been sorry when they saw poor Curly taken off to prison, and they were ready to pay for tickets for all the pigs; but the bear, who didn't want to leave the feast to fetch Curly, would not take the money.

Then the animals went up to the elephant, who was the great judge, and asked him if Curly might not be brought out of prison. The ele-

29. LESLIE STEPHEN. *Bear on all fours.* Courtesy of the Woolf Library at Washington State University Libraries, Pullman, Washington.

phant took a long time to think it over, then he said, "It would never do to send strangers to prison—, but then on the other hand if they were sent to prison it would never do to take them out."

Still it was certain that it would never do to let strangers remain in prison. He was just going to say that though they must not stay in, they must not come out, when the camel stretched out his long neck and said, "Take him out."

"Very true, very true," said the elephant. "Just what I was going to say." Then the hare ran off to the bear, who had just sat down to the feast, and told him he was to set Curly free at once, and that he had better be quick about it as the elephant had said strangers should never be put into prison.

When the bear and Curly got back to the big tent the feast was half over; but Grits had kept a quantity of nice bits for Curly—who was soon well fed and was treated as if he had done something very grand in going to prison. After the feast he was going up to thank the elephant. "Better not," said the camel, who knew the world, "or perhaps he will send you back to prison again; it just depends on where he stops when he begins 'It would never do.' I am the person you ought to thank, for I made him stop at the right place."

"I do thank you," said Curly, "but I am afraid I can't do anything for you."

"I don't suppose you can," said the camel. "People are ready enough to say thank you; but it is very seldom that they do anything."

Chunks and Grits were very glad to have Curly back. They had made friends with a very kind old pig who took them to his comfortable home and gave them a good feed of buttermilk, after which they felt very sleepy. "We will go back to the wood," said Grits.

"Indeed we will do no such thing," said Chunks, "I shall not leave this comfortable home." For now he found himself in a place not much unlike his old home, he did not feel inclined to move.

"I shall be delighted to have you," said the friendly pig, "and there is plenty of room for one, as the friend who used to live with me had to go off yesterday."

"Why did he go?" said Chunks anxiously, for he knew that sometimes when pigs went away they came back bacon.

"Oh," said his new friend, "he only went to the market to find a new home. I hear he has been taken right across the bay to a place on the cliff by the sea. The man who took him said he had lost his pigs. He thought they had got drowned, and that his little boy was so unhappy, he must take a pig back."

"That must be little Harry who used to come and feed us," said Grits. "Your friend has gone to our old home. We were not drowned, only we thought we should like to travel."

"I am sure I never wanted to move," said Chunks; "I wish I had not been so good-natured."

"Never mind," said the friendly pig, "you can stay here now and your two friends can travel as much as they please, for I am afraid there is not room for them." Chunks felt sorry for a minute as he grunted goodbye but when he saw the clean straw and a pail full of pigwash the maid had just brought, he forgot about his friends, and Grits and Curly were very glad to leave him in such a comfortable place. The kind pig told them which road to take to get to a wood where they would be comfortable for the night, and off they trotted. They had a good sound sleep and were ready to start off on their wanderings as soon as the sun rose the next morning. They could get on much faster without Chunks, who was so fat and lazy. Grits was too kindhearted to say or even to think that he was glad that Chunks had stayed behind but Curly was not so particular and he jumped about and curled his tail up quite tight with pleasure at the thought that there was no one to bite it.

They trotted happily along and found themselves in a turnip field after a little time. "This smells good," said Curly. "Let us have some." And he soon dug up some of the round white roots, and by the crunching of his jaws Grits saw that the turnips *were* very good and he pulled one up too. Grits was very prudent and never began to eat a thing till he had seen someone else eating it. This is a very good way.

"Whrrrrr," they heard, and a whirl of brown feathers seemed to brush round them. They had disturbed a covey of partridges. "Never mind," grunted Grits, "we are not men."

"No, I see you are not men," said the mother bird, settling down again. "When I heard the turnip roots go I thought you must be men. They always pull up everything by the roots. Sheep and goats come but they only nibble and hurt nothing, but when men come—crack, crack, go the roots and the poor turnips can grow no more."

"You hate men too," said Grits. "It is very odd, nearly everyone we have met hates men, but in our old home men were very kind to us. We had delicious pailfuls of mash brought to us and clean straw, and we were never hurt."

"That's very odd," said the partridge. "I never heard of men feeding anything unless they wanted to feed themselves. It's a roundabout way of doing it but it's the only way the[y] know, stupid things. I don't suppose anyone *could* eat you," she went on, looking very scornfully at the pigs' hairy skin.

"Now, *we* are most delicious eating; all the same I try and keep my children away from the guns. We have two more months of peace and then the great war begins."

"What war do you mean?" said Curly, looking up from his turnip.

"What war? There is only one war," said the partridge. "The war between the birds and the men. It begins the first of Sept[embe]r and lasts all the winter, but the men never get killed. In the north where it is colder we have cousins called grouse who are killed a month earlier, but no one thinks much of them compared to us. We are known to be best of all."

"You seem to like being killed after all," said Curly.

"Everybody is killed," said the partridge, "only *we* are the best—we are beautiful when alive, delicious when dead. No one can desire more. Come away, children," and they spread their soft brown wings and fluttered off, for the partridge did not care to talk more with such ugly things as pigs who did not even know what they would be when they were dead.

"What an unpleasant creature that is," said Curly, "conceited little pecking thing. I don't wonder men shoot her."

"She was rather rude," said Grits. "All the same I think what she said was true. I believe men generally do feed what they mean to eat. I wonder why poor Crunch went away so suddenly. Just before you came."

"I suppose he went to make room for me," said Curly.

"It wasn't only for that," said Grits. "A strange man came to our master and felt us all and he said, 'This one will be best,' stroking Crunch, and then Master said, 'Very well, I will take your young porker'—that was you, Curly—'if you let me have him and a side of this one.' Crunch went away and you came, but I didn't like the word *side*—and there was something said about ham, and bacon. I never like those words, they make me shake in my ribs."

"Hmm," said Curly, "I don't see that it matters much. Suppose we do turn into bacon, for my part I would just as soon change my name when I am dead as not. Pig is a very pretty name, but I'm not sure that bacon is not prettier and to my thinking it has a savoury sound.

"Anyhow, we are well fed as pigs and we needn't think about bacon."

"Very true," said Grits, but he sighed and didn't get cheerful again for some time.

They walked on a long way, resting sometimes under the hedges. The country was very open, long sweeps of down stretched on and on and sometimes beyond them the pigs could see a faint line of blue which they knew meant the sea. The hedges were full of golden honeysuckle which sent down its sweet breath on the two little pigs as they trotted along, but pigs don't care much for flowers. They were getting rather hot and tired and were glad when they saw a thick clump of trees a little way off. When they got up to the trees they found that the little wood stood at the edge of a dark little lake. The pigs were very thirsty and though they like pigwash better than water, still water was better than nothing.

It was not very easy to get at the water, for big white lilies grew over the lake—the round white flowers with their golden hearts shining out on their broad green leaves. However, the pigs managed to push some of the leaves aside and to get a drink. They frightened a little moor hen who swam off with her little dab chicks.

Then a beautiful white swan sailed out of the shadow, where she had been talking to a kingfisher. "This is a nice cool place," said Grits, "let us find a shady corner and have a snooze."

"Yes," said Curly, "but I should like first to trot a bit in the cool shallow water. I see some delicious-looking mud." Grits was too sleepy even to care for mud and he blinked his little eyes three times and was fast asleep.

It was a nice sleepy afternoon. The soft warm air was full of humming bees who were very happy among the tall golden brown flowers of the bullrush and the purple loose thrift. The swan sailed slowly out to see who Curly was but did not think him worth a quarrel on such a sleepy afternoon. The little fish started away from their hiding places as Curly's little hoofs pattered away. A dragonfly darted past with his glistening wings lighting up the dark corners where the lazy water gnats stretched their long useless legs on the surface of the pool. The soft wet mud was very pleasant to Curly's dry little hoofs. When he was tired of trotting, he followed the dragonfly to the edge of the pool to where a stream ran down from the hills. There he washed his toes and went back to Grits by whose side he was soon sound asleep.

When they woke, the sun was filling the sky with red clouds; even the dark pool seemed on fire. The pigs thought they had better walk on. They were getting hungry. "If we are to see the world," said Curly, "we had better get on. There isn't much to be seen here."

"True," said Grits, "but this is a very pleasant place." After leaving the pool they crossed a lane and got into a wide field. On one side of the field ran a straight white road with strange black lines on it. "Whatever can that be?" said Curly. "Let us go and see." They were near an old mare who was quietly grazing with her little brown foal by her side.

"What are you talking about?" she said.

"We want to know what that white road with black lines is," said Grits. "Perhaps you, Madam, could tell us."

"Any donkey could do that," said the mare with a sniff. "Neddy there knows more than you, though no one thinks him wise," and she pointed to a patient donkey who with one leg tied to a clog was trying to reach some purple thistles who stood stiffly up, holding their heads high in the air.

"Since you don't know, we *will* ask him," said Curly pertly and went off to the donkey. Just as he was beginning to ask—puff, shriek, whirr—a long black thing rushed from the white road. Grits ran away as fast as he could and poor Curly gave a wild jump right into the bed of thistles, who were very cross and pinched him very hard, as now they were broken down, the donkey could eat them. Even kind-hearted Neddy could not help laughing, and the mare and little foal were so much amused that they scampered round the field, kicking up their heels.

At least they said afterwards that they did it for fun, but I think they were frightened too. "What is that dreadful creature?" said Curly when he had got out of the thistles.

"It is a railway," said the donkey. "The engine makes that noise dragging the carriages along."

"It is a good thing I didn't go on the road as I was thinking of doing," said Curly, "though, of course, the engine would have stopped for me. Still it would have been unpleasant to be near such a thing."

"Oh, no, it would not have stopped," said Neddy. "Engines never stop. They go on shrieking and making everything black and filling the air with noise—but they never stop. A dear friend of mine, an ox, was walking on the railroad one day and the train came along. Though he was much bigger than you all and had big horns, the train never stopped and he was cut to pieces." The donkey stopped, he felt very unhappy.

"Well," said the mare, who had heard the story of the ox before, "he would have been cut to pieces anyhow for veal or beef."

"Veal or beef?" said Grits. "What do you mean?"

"Why, what are all you low creatures for?" said the mare. "Oxen are kept to make veal or beef, just as you are kept for bacon."

"There's that horrid word again," said Grits. "Curly, let's go away. I wish we had never left home. We never heard of bacon there."

"Perhaps we should have by this time," said Curly. "Remember Crunch."

"True," said Grits, "but let us go off away from the rail[road] and from people who will talk about bacon." They trotted off as quickly as they could, turning right away from the hard white road with its cruel-looking black lines.

The sky got clearer and paler as the sun went down. The soft short turf on which the pigs walked was full of bright little flowers whose colours came out freshly after the heat of the day.

All at once in the middle of a broad field the pigs saw a great board which was nailed onto two poles.

The board was painted white and on it was written in big black letters "Nyes Nutritious Food for Invalids."

The pigs could not read but a little boy and girl who were standing by the board could. The little girl said, "Tommy, here's the board—'Nyes Nutritious Food.'"

"Yes, there's the board, I see, Lucy, but where's the food?" said Tommy.

"It must be somewhere about," said Lucy and she ran round to the other side of the board.

30. LESLIE STEPHEN. *Pig in profile.* Courtesy of the Woolf Library at Washington State University Libraries, Pullman, Washington.

She had not seen the pigs, and stumbled against Grits. "Oh, perhaps it's this pig," she cried. "Mother has often said she felt as if a nice rasher of bacon would do her good." Curly felt poor Grits' sides tremble as the little girl spoke.

"I don't think Mother would like to cut it off a pig, though," said Tommy. "She meant a bit out of a shop. Besides, pigs always belong to someone and we mustn't take what belongs to other people."

"I suppose not," said Lucy, "but I can't think why 'Nyes Nutritious Food' is put up where there *is* no food. It's too bad and I told Mother I would bring her back something nice." Grits was too kindhearted to bear the thought of the little girl going home without anything to her mother so he poked his snout into her hand. "Oh, look," said Lucy, "this dear pig, I am sure he wants to go home with us," and she stooped down and kissed Grits' hard skin.

"He is a very nice pig," said Tommy, "but we have no food for pigs and I don't think he would care to be cut up. Besides, he must belong to someone."

"I suppose he does," said Lucy; "here is his brother," she added, looking at Curly. "I wonder where their home is and why they don't go to it. Goodbye, little pigs." And the children ran off.

It was getting late. The sky was a clear dark blue and the pigs thought they should be glad of supper and sleep, for it was a long time since they had had any food. The downs grew barer and barer and a nice fresh breeze blew towards them with a salt smell and taste which told them they were getting near the sea. "It smells like home," said Grits. Soon they got to the top of a cliff and saw the sea lying dark and still below. Little villages nestled into the sides of the hills, looking cosy and homelike, but the pigs had heard so much of the wickedness of men, that for the first time they were afraid of them.

They were afraid of falling down the side of the cliff and they crept cautiously along for some time. As they went on, their feet seemed to find their way more easily. A little path which wandered down the hillside became more and more friendly and in the dim darkness they thought they could see some clean fresh straw and a pail of pig's wash. Such a delightful sight made them hurry on, hardly knowing where they were going. A clear bright voice called out of the darkness, "Oh, Father, here are the dear pigs back again. I told you they would never forget us. I am glad I put the pig-wash [out]." The pigs had wandered back to their old home. Even Curly forgot to be sorry that their travels were over when he heard little Harry's kind voice and buried his nose in the delicious tub.

I don't know if they were turned into bacon; but after all, as Curly said, it is well to be useful when one is dead, and bacon has a savoury sound.

Cat's Meat

WHAT A HORRID WET DAY," said Maggie.

"Beastly," said Bob. "I don't believe it will ever be fine again." The two children were pressing their faces against the window of a nursery, high up in one of the big houses of Eaton Square. It was May, but all the same, the Square looked dull enough. The late lilac and horse chestnuts were having their last breath of colour and sweetness dashed out of them by the pitiless rain.

Carriages rolled by, the coachmen with little streams running off their broad shoulders, and the footmen carefully covering their powdered heads and no doubt wondering why their mistresses who *might* stay at home wanted to go out in such weather. A distant scream from the railway reached the children and told that people were rushing about underground. "Watercress, watercress," screamed a little girl, holding up her dripping basket.

"It would be very nice to go about on the streets," said Maggie, "to be out in all weathers and no one to talk about clothes."

"Jolly," said Bob. "When I'm grown up, I'm going to be a crossing sweeper. They have a fine time. They can get into all the puddles, and everyone gives them pennies, and it must be so nice to sweep up those heaps of soft mud and then jump into them."

"I am not sure," said Maggie doubtfully. "I did once step into a big puddle, of course by mistake, but it was so cold and nasty."

"Oh, girls never know what *is* nice," said Bob. "What would *you* be?"

"I'm not *quite* sure," said Maggie again. "Oh yes, I know. I *should* like to be the cat's meat girl. Look, there she comes. All the cats look out for her." Sure enough, the little cat's meat girl came round the corner. She turned into the mews, which the children could just see from their window. An organ was playing there and the little girl, in spite of her basket and the dripping rain, began to beat time with her feet and give little twirls as she went along. The cats were all at their doors and welcomed their provider, so perhaps after all, Maggie had not made a worse choice than Bob, though he did look rather scornful. "I wonder when Mother will come in," said Maggie. "I suppose she is looking after some poor people."

"What a lot of looking after poor people want. I hope they like it," said Bob. "Father and Mother are always looking after poor people. They said we could come down this evening but it's getting dark and they are not in."

"And they are dining out," said Maggie, a little dolefully. "I heard Papa say that they must be sure and be punctual because it was a dinner some way off, and I am sure *it* was all about the poor. Oh, there is the carriage!" The two children rushed downstairs. Maggie need not have complained that her clothes were much thought of, for surely a more untidy little girl never ran down the softly carpeted stairs of a house in Eaton Square! Her hair hung down in loose curls, all the shine gone out of them. Her brown holland pinafore showed signs of use, and her little eager face had those particular black marks on the nose and chin which we can all get if we press our faces against a London window pane for a few minutes.

Lady Middleton, Maggie's mother, saw none of these things. Chilled and tired, she was too glad to see her children to remark anything in their dress. "Oh, darlings," she said, "I am so sorry to be so late. I meant to be in at five and have a cosy tea with you, but there was so much to be done for the poor women and little children that I could not get away sooner! Never mind, you shall give me my tea." Maggie, who though only seven was a helpful little creature, had unfastened her mother's cloak and bonnet, had brought forward an arm chair and now began to make tea. Lady Middleton had a fair, anxious face. The children often said, even when Mother did come home, she seemed as if she had left part of herself somewhere else. The pretty room in which Lady Middleton sat, the nice kettle, puffing and sputtering, the little rolls of butter and hot cakes which stood ready on pretty china plates, all looked the picture of comfort. Maggie found the heavy silver teapot made her little hand shake, but she didn't mind that and she knew just how much sugar and cream her mother liked and soon made her a delicious cup of tea.

"There's your father," said Lady Middleton. "Make him a cup."

"I will," said Bob. "Maggie can hardly hold the teapot. Girls are not much use."

"Gently, my boy," said Sir Robert, coming in. "Slow and steady, remember," for Bob not only filled the cup in his anxiety to show how tea should be poured out, but the saucer and even the tray.

"I hope you are not tired, my love," said Sir Robert, looking at his wife. "I suppose you too have been busy. *I* have had a most interesting day. I spoke at a meeting and think that my words may prove the turning point in the great cause." At this moment the butler came in with a telegram. "Dear me," said Sir Robert. "This is most gratifying. I am requested to conduct a meeting for the improvement of the poorer suburbs of Brickton, which is to take place tomorrow at two o'clock. It is a five hours' journey, but that is of no consequence. You will accompany me, my dear? Feminine influence is most important and I am sure you would wish to help your neglected sisters."

"Oh, of course," said Lady Middleton. "At ten if there is a train."

"Dear me, where is the Bradshaw?" said Sir [Robert], ringing the bell. The butler appeared, followed by the footman, thinking that the bell meant that tea was to be taken away. "No, no," said Sir Robert. "I want the Bradshaw. It should always be here. Why is nothing ever in its place?"

"Here it is, Sir [Robert]," said the butler, giving it to him, and there it had been, just under Sir Robert's nose; only in his anxiety about things a little way off, Sir Robert sometimes overlooked those under his nose. The train was soon found, a telegram sent off, and Sir Robert sat down to the writing table on which lay a pile of letters. Lady Middleton went upstairs to dress for dinner. The children had not understood much of the talk. All that was clear to them was that their mother would be out all that evening and the whole of the next day, and that wasn't a cheerful thought. They had been rather puzzled when their Papa had talked of their Mama's "poorer sisters," for they did not know that they had any aunts. However, aunts at Brickton, wherever that was, could not count for much, and unconsciously the children took a dislike to these unknown relations who were to take their mother away. A loud ring at the bell interrupted their thoughts, and Sir Robert's writing. "Who can it be? A visitor so late? Impossible! I am not at home," said Sir Robert. Whoever it was did not seem to listen to "not at home," for the butler came up very quickly, followed by the children's Grandmama, Mrs. Beetle. The children never called her "Granny"; she had such stiff black curls, and a quick sharp way of speaking and she wore such very thick black silks, no one would ever think of her as "Granny." Besides she liked being treated as a Grandmama and we all know that that is quite different from the way in which we treat a "Granny." "My dear Mrs. Beetle," said Sir Robert, "I am sorry you have come so late. We are just going out to dine in the suburbs."

"Would you have been at home if I had come earlier?" said Mrs. Beetle, whose voice was not very soft. "No, Robert, I know you and Margaret have been out all day, no doubt in some hovel or other. Would you be in tomorrow? No. You will be off on some of your grand schemes. I came tonight and I came late on purpose, for as Margaret is never at home during the day, I thought that I might see her for ten minutes while she was dressing for dinner, for I suppose you *do* dress for dinner. I shall sit with her and I need not detain you here, for I can talk to you through the dressing-room door." The children felt rather sorry for their Papa when they heard this. Grandmama's "talks" were too like "scolds" to be very welcome. As she did not seem to have seen them, they thought they would slip out of the room now and have a few minutes with their mother before Mrs. Beetle came up, but nothing escaped Grandmama's sharp eyes. "Come here, my dears," she said. "*Poor* children."

Her words were affectionate but her voice was rather solemn, and the children felt more inclined to go than to come. "There is nothing wrong with the children," said Sir Robert. "They are quite well and happy."

"They look happy and well cared for," said Mrs. Beetle, eyeing the children in their untidy clothes with strong disapproval. "What have you been doing all day, Robert?"

"Looking out of the window," said Bob slowly.

"I thought so, from your noses," said Mrs. Beetle. "It is no one's duty to look after you and you will go to rack and ruin."

"I must beg, Mrs. Beetle," began Sir Robert, but the children felt that now was their time for escape and off they ran.

"Rack and ruin, I wonder what that is," said Maggie. "I don't like going there."

"Of course not," said Bob. "It means all sorts of bad, and Grandmama always means what she says, so we shall be sure to go there."

These unpleasant thoughts were sent away by the sight of their mother, who turned round as the two children came in, holding out her arms. "You have been a long time, darlings," she said. "But I daresay you have been talking to Papa.—Poor Papa, he is so tired."

"Oh, no," said the children together. "He was busy and then Grandmama came in and she says we are going to rack and ruin. What does that mean, Mama?"

Lady Middleton gave a little start. "I think you can't have heard what she said," she began.

"Oh yes, we did," said Bob, very decidedly. "She said we were untidy and that we were going to rack and ruin."

"You *are* rather untidy," said Lady Middleton, looking at them. "And you know Grandmama always has everything so clean and neat. I am afraid you do look an untidy little pair. What have you been doing?"

"We did our lessons as usual, and when Miss Bruton went, we cleaned the doll's house and as it was too wet to go out, we just stood at the window and watched all the people out in the rain. It was so dull, nothing seemed lively but the rain, so we watched the drops run races."

"Yes," said Mrs. Beetle, coming in and making them jump. "A nice amusement for a big boy and girl to watch the drops run races. You ought to have been at your Latin grammar and sampler."

"We had done our lessons," said Bob, "and Maggie doesn't do samplers, thank goodness."

"Hush, hush," said his mother. "That isn't the way to speak. I am sure it must be bedtime. Run off. I daresay the sun will shine tomorrow and then you will be able to have some good games in the Square. Goodnight, darlings." And the children ran off to bed.

A good game in the Square was not their idea of happiness. Eaton Square is not a very large one. There are more iron railings to be seen than trees, and the few children who walk up and down it are generally very smartly dressed and very carefully watched by nurses and governesses, lest they should spoil their clothes. Bob and Maggie in their brown holland dresses and their longing for wild races, games of hide and seek and football even, felt quite out of place among their smart little neighbours.

The next day the sun shone brightly as if to make up for his laziness the day before. Even the poor lilacs lifted their heads and the puddles dried up. Sir Robert and Lady Middleton hurried off by their early train, just seeing the children at breakfast, a meal which they always had together, but the children did not talk much, for their Papa and Mama always had such quantities of letters to read. After breakfast the daily governess came. She looked very pale and anxious and after teaching the children for about an hour, she said, "I am afraid I can't go on. I wish Lady Middleton had been at home, for I don't like to leave you alone, but my head is so bad I think I must go to bed."

"Oh, poor Miss Bruton," said Maggie. "Of course you must go. I know Mama would want you to go to your home. I am so sorry for you. We will prepare our lessons just the same. Let me help you on with your jacket." Miss Bruton kissed Maggie's kind little face rather anxiously. She did not like leaving the children yet she knew they were often left and there was the nurse "somewhere." The nurse always was "somewhere," but what an odd place somewhere is! All the things and people that can't be found are always somewhere, and Maggie's nurse was never to be found when she was wanted.

"We shall play in the Square," said Bob, "instead of a walk with you this morning, that's all. We often do that in the afternoon."

"Well, be good children," said Miss Bruton, and she went off.

Bob and Maggie took their Latin grammar and read over their list of words very attentively, for at least five minutes. Among the words was "homo hominis, a man, a woman"! "What stuff," said Bob. "How can a man, a woman be the same thing? I always thought Latin stupid. It *must* be stupid if it calls a man the same as a woman." Bob spoke in such a hurry that his own language was not very clear.

Maggie understood him but she didn't take much interest in the question and only said, "It is very hot." It was hot and it was not very easy to sit learning Latin when the sun was blazing into the schoolroom. The window was open and through it came all the sounds of the street, which sounded quite different today to what they had done yesterday through the rain. A thrush sang in the mews and both children went to the window to see if they could catch sight of his cage.

"Let's go out now," said Bob. "It feels so nice and fresh."

"We shall have all the afternoon and evening for our lessons," said Maggie doubtfully. "But don't you think we had better get them done first?"

"Oh, no! Bother!" said Bob. "I've been thinking a great deal. I'm so glad Miss Bruton's head was bad."

"Oh, Bob," cried Maggie.

"Well, I don't mean that I am glad her head was bad, but I'm glad she has gone. I want to talk to you, but I can't talk here." Maggie felt rather frightened but very much interested. She got up and put away her books. Bob, I am sorry to say, kicked his to the other end of the room, but Maggie went and picked them up and both children put on their hats to go out. They met Nurse on the stairs but she did not stop them, and Maggie and Bob were soon through the iron gates of those London gardens in which some children may play and out of which many more are locked. Bob looked very grave and important. "Now, Maggie," he began very solemnly, "I have something to say to you." Maggie felt quite frightened. "It is something quite secret," said Bob. "And that's why I wanted to come out. I thought someone might hear me indoors."

Maggie grew pale. Bob had often got into scrapes throwing the ink over papers of his Papa's or breaking valuable china, but he had never looked so grave before and she felt sure that this time he must have done something very dreadful. "What is it, Bob?" she whispered. "Have you broken the lady's nose?"

The "lady" was a marble bust of a Bacchante which for some unknown reason grateful constituents had presented to the excellent Sir Robert.

"Lady's nose — what *are* you talking of?" said Bob. "I have *done* nothing. I want to do something. I have thought about it all night and I mean to do it at once."

Maggie was trembling with excitement. It must be something grand if Bob had thought about it all night. "Oh, Bob, tell me quick," she said.

"I'm coming to it," said Bob. "You remember yesterday you said you wanted to be a cat's meat girl and I was to be a crossing sweeper? *Now I mean to be them.*" He stopped.

Maggie's eyes were wide open and puzzled. "How can we be anything but what we are? If I'm the cat's meat girl, who'll be me?"

"Well, you are a silly," said Bob. "Of course, you can be a cat's meat girl, but the cat's meat girl can't be you; and I shall be the crossing sweeper, but he won't be me."

Maggie didn't understand it well, even with this clear explanation, but she only said, "How can I be a cat's meat girl when I've no cat's meat?"

"Haven't you some money?" said Bob.

"Yes! I have 2/2 [2 shillings, 2 pence], a crown, and two 3d [three-penny] bits, and a penny," said Maggie.

"And I have five shillings and eleven pence," said Bob. "That's a lot. I'll tell you what we can do. We can buy a basket and cat's meat and a broom and I'll sweep and you will cry 'cat's meat.' Won't that be fun? You can buy a lot of cat's meat for a shilling and sell it at a penny a stickful. I know that's what our coachman pays for Zulu's meat."

"That doesn't seem quite fair," said Maggie. "If I only get twelve bits for a shilling and sell each bit for a penny, then it's all right, but I don't see how I should make any money."

"Well," said Bob, "of all the stupid girls you are the stupidest. Of course, you must make money by selling, or where would be the good? You buy things cheap and sell them dear. That's the way. Haven't you often heard Papa say what a difference there was between buying and selling? Well, now you'll find it out."

Bob seemed very positive as people generally are when they are not very sure of a thing, and Maggie held her tongue for a minute. Soon, however, she began about another difficulty. "Bob dear, how shall we go away from home and what will Mama say?"

"I have thought of how we shall go away. I have thought of *every-thing*," said Bob. "After luncheon, we shall say we are going to play in the garden and that we shan't be in for tea and then after we have been in the Square, we will just run away. We can go down Chelsea. There are lots of crossings and lots of cats and we shall find plenty to do."

"And Mama?" said Maggie.

"Oh, Mama," answered Bob, getting rather red. "Well, you see, Mama won't be back till late. And she'll be tired and will go to bed and we shall soon see her."

"Oh, no, Bob," said Maggie. "Mama will never go to bed when she finds that we have left. She will sit up and hunt and she will cry." Maggie herself began to cry as she spoke.

"Oh, well," said Bob, rather roughly, "if you're going to make a fuss, you had better not come. It was just what you were wanting to do yesterday, and now it's all settled, just like a girl you begin to back out. I'll go by myself."

"Oh no, dear Bob, I *will* go with you," said Maggie. "You know I couldn't stay anywhere without you."

"We shall see a great deal more of Mama then than we do now," said Bob. "Isn't she all day long among the poor, and doesn't she always say that though she wants to be with us, she must first think of others? Well, now we shall be the poor, we shall be others, and so she will come and look after us. Perhaps even she might teach us. You know she has one crossing sweeper in her night school."

"How clever you are, Bob," said Maggie. "I never thought of all that. It would be nice to go to a school where Mama taught, but do you think, Bob, we shall have to go to the suburbs?" Maggie said these words almost in a whisper. The children did not know in the least what "the suburbs" meant, but their father was always talking of going there and they heard fragments of such dreadful stories, all in some way, it seemed, connected with these "suburbs," that the children had got it into their heads that there was some dismal desolate place full of dirt and unhappiness and that this place was called "the suburbs."

"I don't think we need go there," said Bob. "We will try not. First of all, now we must go in and get dinner and pack our bags. You must take your little bag under your cloak. Be sure you put on your cloak. We will put our night clothes [in] and take our purses, and I think we had better take some matches."

"Oh yes, and some soap and our sponges. But what shall we do for a bath and towels, Bob? We can't take them."

"Oh, you must do what the other cat's meat girls do," said Bob. "Of course you won't have everything just like you have at home. There will be no lessons, remember, and we can stay up as late as we like and go wherever we like." This sounded delightful and Maggie forgot all her fears. They ran quickly into the house before the church clock at the end of the Square struck one.

The butler was much surprised to see them back. "I thought you would be sure to come in late today," he said, "as you were all alone, but it's just as well that you are early, as I am going out." The children didn't see what difference they could make to the butler, but Brown always liked to wait on them himself even if they were quite alone; and though he wanted to go off to Richmond that afternoon, he was not going till the children should have had their dinner. A very nice dinner it was. Roast chicken and bread sauce, nice new potatoes looking as if they were almost too young to be cooked, gooseberry tart and Cornish cream.

"I don't suppose we shall have such a dinner as this tomorrow," said Bob, with half a sigh, but he stopped himself, for Brown was just coming in to clear away the things.

"We will go upstairs now," Maggie said, "and," she was going to say, "pack up our things" but Bob stopped her quickly.

"You silly thing," he whispered, pinching her arm. "You nearly let it all out. If Brown had any idea what we were going to do, he would lock the hall door." Maggie said nothing. She didn't like to tell Bob that now the time had really come for leaving their comfortable home, she began to wish that Brown *would* lock the hall door.

The children ran upstairs and met their Nurse just going to her dinner. "Well, you have been quick," she said. "I suppose that old Mr. Brown was in a hurry to get out for his afternoon. Now be good children and don't make a mess, and when I come up, perhaps I can take you out to some shops."

"Oh, thank you, Kate," said Maggie, who loved shopping, and who forgot in a moment all their grand plans.

"Nonsense, Maggie," said Bob. "You know we are going into the Square. We haven't finished that game and I daresay we shall have tea out," he added.

"Have tea out?" said Kate. "Did your Mama say you were to go out? You must change your clothes."

"Oh, only to the Greens'. You know we can always go there," said Bob, feeling rather uncomfortable.

"Very well," said Kate, and hearing her dinner bell, she ran down.

"Oh, Bob," said Maggie. "How could you?"

"How could I what?" said Bob very crossly.

"How could you say we were going to have tea at the Greens'?" said Maggie.

"I didn't say it," said Bob, "and if I did, I don't think *you* ought to find fault. *I* have to do everything. I arrange all the plan and make it all easy for you and I have to tell stories, which is very unpleasant, and you have nothing but the easy work and the fun, you lazy selfish girl."

Poor Maggie's eyes were full of tears. She had not thought of it in that way. Now it did seem to her that she was very ungrateful and selfish, and that she did not help Bob a bit, and yet she was always wanting to help Bob. She determined to get all ready as quickly as she could, so she ran into her room and found her purse there. "Bob," she said, showing him her little coins, "take this and add it to yours. Now what shall I put in my bag?"

"Your nightgown, of course, and sponge and slippers and your little basket and a comb, I should think, and a bit of soap and some stockings."

"Oh and I had better have a pair of shoes in case these get wet." Maggie tried, as she spoke, to stuff her nightgown into her little bag but it was no use.

"You won't want a nightgown," said Bob. "Poor people never have nightgowns."

"Well, that's a comfort," said Maggie, "for I could not get mine in.

The sponge squeezes and will go in easily and so will my comb, but I can't get in my shoes, nor my dear little basket, and I *did* want to take that."

"*I* shall take nothing but matches, which I can put in my pocket," said Bob grandly, "and some pencils and paper. We shall want them to write down our accounts."

"Oh, Bob, you think of everything," said Maggie.

"It's a good job I do," said Bob. "But you're not bad for a girl. Now let us go." The children went downstairs feeling as if they were doing something very strange and wicked. As they passed the cuckoo clock, the little bird hopped out and made them start! "Cuckoo. Cuckoo."

"It's two o'clock already," said Bob. "We had better make haste. Kate is never long over her dinner when she is going out shopping, and Brown will be going off to Richmond. I don't want to meet anyone." They opened the hall door softly and were soon out on the pavement. Carriages rolled past. Hansoms seemed to fly on to Victoria Station. Busy men and women hurried on, all full of their own work. No one noticed the two children, who now that they had the whole world before them, hardly knew which road to take and stood for a moment bewildered on the pavement. Bob soon recovered himself. "Come on," he said. "We'll go straight on. I know we shall soon be in Chelsea. That's a very nice part. There's the river and trees, plenty of crossings and I am sure plenty of cats." On they went, past Sloane Square and, as Bob said, they were soon in Chelsea. They passed the fine old hospital with its garden and stopped for a moment to look through the big iron gates at some old soldiers in their red coats who were sitting in the shade of their chestnut trees. One had a wooden leg and several of them had shining medals on their coats, showing that they had done work in their time.

The children soon came onto the embankment. A fresh breeze blew from the river, refreshing poor Maggie, who was hot and dusty from her hurried walk. "Let us sit on one of those benches," said Bob, and they went into a little garden full of blue irises. It was not like the garden of Eaton Square, for there were no locked gates and little children were dancing and singing in a way that children never do in Eaton Square. "Now, we will settle what we shall do," said Bob, as they sat on a seat near a big lilac bush.

"I daresay there is a broom shop close by, and baskets and brooms are sold at the same shop," said Maggie, proud of her knowledge.

"All right," said Bob. "I don't know where we can get cat's meat but there must be a shop somewhere."

Just then they heard someone crying, "S'meat, s'meat."

"There it is!" cried Maggie, jumping up. "Let's go and ask that man where he bought his."

"No," said Bob. "I don't believe he would tell us, but we will buy some off him for our cat and then we can get a basket and begin to earn money."

"But we haven't got a cat," said Maggie.

"Bother," said Bob, "all the cats are ours now. See if they won't all come to us."

The two children went up to the cat's meat man. He didn't look very nice and certainly the meat looked very nasty. "Please will you give us some meat?" said Bob.

"Why, what for?" said the man, surprised. Though Bob and Maggie were not at all smartly dressed and not particularly tidy, still they did not look like street children.

"For our cat," said Bob, stammering.

"Oh, I suppose you live there," said the man, pointing to one of the tall red brick houses close to the river. "Rum thing you should be sent out to buy cat's meat. How much do you want?"

"How much can we have for a shilling?" said Bob.

"A shilling!" said the man. "You *must* have a lot of cats. Where shall I take the meat to?"

"Oh, we will take it. We don't live near," said Bob, getting very red, and taking out a shilling, he held out his hands for the meat.

The man was still more surprised, but the sight of the shilling made him wish to get it as quick as he could. "How do you mean to carry it?" he said.

"I am going to get a basket," said Bob.

"Well, I never," said the man. "Here's a bit of paper," he added, picking up a piece that the wind blew towards them; and he put the meat on the paper, pocketed the shilling and walked off, for he saw a policeman coming and, as he knew he had given the children very little meat for their money, he went off as quick as he could.

"Well, that's done anyhow," said Bob. "And a shilling gone. We must try and get two shillings for it and we had better go and buy the basket at once." They turned into a long narrow street; but there were no basket shops. Then they crossed the King's Road and into another street. At last a basket shop was found and the basket was bought for 10½d [pence] and a broom for 9d. The woman in the shop looked rather surprised at the children, but some more people came in and she did not question the children, who were glad to get off. "Now," said Bob, "we can begin. You put the cat's meat in your basket and go along calling 'S'meat' and I will stand at this crossing."

Maggie went on as Bob told her, though she felt very uncomfortable. "Cat's meat, cat's meat," she cried, but her voice was not very loud. She was, however, loud enough to be heard by a big black tom who stood at the door of a shop and rubbed his head against her.

The mistress of the shop came out. "Why, is your mother dead?" she said to Maggie.

Poor Maggie felt dreadfully frightened. "Oh, no," she said. "She's only away!"

"Oh, you've come instead of her, I s'pose," said the woman. "Well, I'll take a bit for Tom," and she took out two of the biggest lumps of meat and gave Maggie a half-penny. Maggie knew that she had only five or six bits more, so she stood looking at the half-penny. "Well, what are you waiting for?" said the woman.

"Please aren't you going to give me any more?"

"No, of course not," said the woman. "Get off or I'll send the police after you."

Poor Maggie was so frightened at this, she turned round and ran as fast as her feet could carry her to where Bob stood. He looked very cross and his broom was quite clean. "Have you made anything, Maggie?" he said.

"Oh, Bob," she cried, "the woman said she would send the police after me and asked if Mama were dead, and if she were, how could we know?" And Maggie began to cry really.

Bob looked very puzzled and rather frightened. "What *do* you mean, Maggie? What woman? Did you tell her who you were?"

"Oh no," said Maggie. "She said I must be a new cat's meat girl and was my mother dead, and that frightened me."

"Well, you *are* a stupid," said Bob. "Do you think *our* Mama ever sold cat's meat? You're not a cat's meat woman's child, are you?"

"No, I suppose not," said Maggie, "but when she asked me, I thought she meant our own Mama and then I thought if Mama were to be ill and die, how should we know, Bob?"

"Stuff," said Bob. "What about the police?"

"I asked her for more than a half-penny for two big bits which she took," said Maggie. "And she said she would have the police after me. But never mind, dear Bob, you see she hasn't. Have you made much?"

"Of course not," said Bob. "Can't you see that the crossing is dry? There's nothing to sweep." Sure enough, the hot sun had dried up the rain of the day before and the water carts are not as active in Chelsea as they are in Belgravia, so there was no work for Bob to do. "We had better go to another part," he said and on they walked.

"Do you think we could have some tea?" said Maggie, whose mouth was dry and hot and whose poor little feet were aching.

"I suppose we can get some milk," said Bob, and sure enough in a few minutes they passed a milk shop. "Two glasses of milk, please," said Bob, and he and Maggie were glad to sit down and drink the cool fresh milk. It was not good and creamy like the milk they had at home, nor were the glasses very clean; but they were too thirsty to think of such things and, having paid their pennies, they walked on. "We had better have something to eat, too," said Bob, as they passed a baker's; and they bought some very sweet cake, which they had always longed to taste, covered with sugar and almonds. It was very grand to be able to go in and buy just what you liked; but the cakes weren't quite so good as the children had expected, and they were so sweet that Maggie longed for another cup of milk. She didn't like to say so.

However, Bob said, "Let's have an orange, I'm so thirsty." And Maggie thought this an excellent idea. They got two oranges for Maggie's ½ [d; halfpence] and Maggie felt rather proud at eating fruit bought with their own earnings; besides which they had always heard that it was unwholesome to eat oranges with milk, and what can be more delightful than to eat things which are unwholesome? "Let us try here," said Bob, as they came to a broad open space, where new houses were being built. Heaps of bricks and mortar, mounds of lime, pails of water stood about, and houses a quarter-built, half-built and wholly built, but with no windows, stood all round them. There was plenty of mess and Bob thought he would try what his broom could do to clear it away. He told Maggie to call out "Cat's meat" again. Maggie obeyed, but there were no people living in the houses.

The builders were just stopping work. They looked at her and laughed. "You have come too soon," they said. "There are no people here to buy." Maggie went back to Bob, feeling rather unhappy. Bob had dirtied his broom; but he had not cleaned the road. The mud made by the builders' stuff which had been crushed down by their hand carts, could not be cleared away by Bob's little arms. The two children looked at each other rather unhappily. They had not made a good beginning. "Why, there are two of you," called out a builder, as he went home. "You seem determined to have the first places with the crossing and the cats, but I am afraid you are too early to make anything." And off he went.

The children walked along the empty road. Now the builders had gone and the sun was getting low, things did not seem to them very cheerful and poor Maggie's legs ached more and more.

"Where shall we sleep, Bob? Shall we go home?"

"Of course not," said Bob. "We have had no fun yet. I'll tell you what; we will go to one of those coffee taverns now and get a good hot cup of coffee and a roll. Papa is always talking of them. And then we will find out a place for the night." The children walked on till they came to a coffee tavern which, luckily for Maggie, was not very far off. The big shining kettles gave out a nice smell of boiling coffee and a good-natured-looking woman filled two big cups for them and gave them each a nice fresh roll and a bit of butter. Neither coffee nor roll were as good as what they had every day at home, but Maggie thought she had never tasted anything so delicious. Both the children felt quite refreshed and lively after their meal and Maggie no longer thought it would be nice to go home. "You see what fun it is to go about and get just what we like at any time," said Bob. "Now I have got a good idea. Let us spend the night in one of those empty houses. There are some quite finished except for the windows, and we can creep in. We shall have nothing to pay and we shall be quite safe and comfortable."

"How clever you are, Bob," said Maggie, pressing Bob's arm. "That will be nice. I have always wanted to go into those funny red brick houses. Let us go now."

Bob was very much pleased at Maggie's praise. "Come along," he said, "but you may as well call 'Cat's meat' as you go. If we can make a little money, it will be just as well."

"S'meat, s'meat," called out Maggie, imitating the little girl in Eaton Square, but no one bought any, only a hungry thin black cat came and rubbed himself against her with a maow that went to Maggie's heart. "I *must* give him a bit, dear Bob," she said. "He can't pay but he looks so hungry."

"All right," said Bob, and Maggie stooped down and gave the poor beast one of her little faggots of meat. It soon disappeared in the creature's hungry jaws, but the cat did not disappear. It followed the children, fondling against Maggie's side.

They soon came to the row of red houses. They walked along till they came to one that Maggie thought looked just like a house in Hans Christian Andersen's tales. It had a very high roof and there were quantities of little windows, as yet unglazed, and little corner balconies. "If we can get in there," said Maggie, "it will be fun." Some boards had been put up against the doorway, as there was no door yet to the new house, and the children were able without much trouble to push one board away and creep in. The house did not look quite as nice inside as it did out. There was a great deal of rubbish, and the passage and stairs were not finished, so that it didn't look much like a real house. However, there they were and there they must stay for the night. It was getting dark but they groped their way carefully up the unfinished stairs and into a big room which certainly looked as if it was meant for hide and seek. In one corner was a huge fireplace, big enough for people to sit in it. In another, a funny little gallery which looked as if it were meant for a band. "This *is* nice," said Maggie, racing about. "What fun we shall have here. I wish it were not so dark!"

"Wait a bit," said Bob. "I have got something," and he pulled out of his pocket the match box and with it a bit of candle, which were almost the only things he had brought.

"You dear Bob," said Maggie, delighted. "Now we shall have fun. We can play at hide and seek, puss in the corner, all sorts of games."

"Wait a little, Maggie, don't be in such a hurry," said Bob. "Here are the other things I brought," and he took out his pencils and paper. "We must do our accounts." Bob was always hearing his Papa speak of doing his accounts and though he didn't know quite what use accounts were, as they never seemed to make money more, only less, he thought it would be grand to do them. Maggie looked grave. She did not like sums, but she felt sure Bob was right, so she sat on the floor and held the bit of candle while he added up. "You had 2/8 [2 shillings, 8 pence], hadn't you, Maggie?"

"Yes, and a penny and two three-penny bits," said Maggie, who counted up her money in rather a funny way.

"Well, that's 3/1," said Bob, writing down the figures. "And I had 5/11; that, added to yours, makes 9/ between us. Well, we spent 1/ on cat's meat."

"Oh, but I got a penny back," interrupted Maggie.

"Don't talk," said Bob. "1/ away from 9/ leaves 8/. Then we got the basket and broom. They came to 1/6. That leaves, let me see, that leaves 6/6."

"That seems very little," said Maggie. "I don't think that can be right."

"It *is* though," said Bob. "That's the use of accounts, Father always says, to tell one how quick money goes."

"I suppose there is nothing to tell one how to make it go slow," said Maggie. "That would be the sensiblest, I think."

"Do be quiet, Maggie, and let me go on," said Bob. "Well, 6/6. Then we had milk—2d [pence]; and cakes, they were 4d; and oranges—½[d]. That's 6½d, and then our coffee was 4d, that's 10½d. Well, take 10½d from 6/6. . . . You couldn't do that sum, Maggie?"

"No, I couldn't, but I can count up the money that remains," said Maggie. "And that will be the same."

"No, it won't," said Bob. "You'll see."

Bob did his sum and Maggie counted the money. Sure enough, the sums didn't come the same. Bob said 5/7½ ought to remain, and Maggie, after counting over twice, made 5/8.

"I know what it is, Bob," she said. "It's what I earned. That's the way to do accounts. It's my half-penny. If we can earn something every day, it will be much better than doing stupid sums."

Bob was rather vexed that Maggie had made out the sum without the trouble of doing [it], besides having earned a half-penny; but all he said was, "Well, we had better make a bed somewhere. Let's look about for something soft." It's not very easy to find soft things in new houses; however, there were some trusses of straw, and the children decided to use the little gallery, which was like a fourpost bed, Maggie said, as their bedroom. The boards were not very soft; but they strewed the straw on them and Maggie took out of her bag her sponge and her comb. She *could* comb her hair but what was she to do with the sponge? There was no water. How were they to wash? She had her bit of soap but you can't do much washing with a dry bit of soap. "Never mind," said Bob sleepily, from his corner of the little balcony. "We will wash tomorrow." Maggie did not half like it but she was very sleepy too, and hard though the bed was, she was soon fast asleep.

It seemed to the children that they had only just lain down when bang, clang, whang, went a big bell. They jumped up. What could it be? "Oh, it's the workmen's bell," said Bob.

"I *hope* no workmen will come here," said Maggie.

"It doesn't matter if they do," said Bob. "We have not hurt the house!" However, the workmen all went to the other less finished houses, and Bob and Maggie had time to get up and shake themselves, which was all the dressing they could do, for they had not undressed.

"Let's see if there is any water anywhere. I daresay there is a bathroom," said Maggie. They went up the stairs and found the bathroom but there was no water.

"Never mind; when we have looked well about the house, we will go out and get a wash somewhere," said Bob. They scampered in and out of the strange little rooms, peeked through the casement windows and watched from the top of the house the soft, grey smoke lift up and turn pink as the sun shone more and more brightly, till it seemed to take away all the grey and leave only sunshine. The carts began to roll round and the milkman gave his funny call. "The shops will be open soon now," said Bob, after they had stood for a long time watching all these strange, delightful sights. "We had better go down and see if we can find a fountain where we can wash our faces before we go to a shop."

Down they went. They slipped out of the house carefully and quickly, Bob taking his broom and Maggie her basket. They walked some way before they came to a fountain. They splashed the cold fresh water over their faces with the iron ladle meant for drinking out of. Maggie at last knew that she had brought something useful, for with her bit of soap and her spare pocket handkerchief for a towel, she made herself look a respectable little [girl].

"Now we will go and have breakfast," said Bob. Just then a postman passed with his letter bag.

"Oh, I wonder if he has got a letter for us?" said Maggie.

"Why, what do you mean?" said Bob.

"I know Mama will have written," said Maggie. "She always writes when she is away from us."

"How can she write when she doesn't know where we are?" said Bob. "Of course, she can't know."

"I never thought of that," said Maggie, her tears pouring down. "I made sure we should hear somehow."

"That's because you never think," said Bob. "Now, don't be a stupid, but let's come and have breakfast."

"We *must* write to Mama, Bob," said Maggie.

"If we do, we shall have to go back home," said Bob. "At least you will, for I shall run away. I'm not going to spend any more days in that dull Eaton Square with Papa and Mama always in the suburbs. I'm going to be in a suburb too."

Maggie stopped her tears. "I don't want to go home," she said, "but I *do* want to see Mama."

"You would not see her if you *were* at home," said Bob. "You're much more likely to see her now you are a cat's meat girl." Maggie cheered up at this and they walked along till they came to the coffee house where they had been the night before. It was already full of [people] having their breakfast. The coffee smelt even better than it did the night before, and in a huge pan on the fire, sausages were browning and crackling.

"Why, you're early birds," said the woman, as she filled their cups with hot frothing coffee. "I wonder your mother lets you go out so early. Perhaps you've got none, poor things!" she said. Maggie's eyes filled again.

"Oh yes," said Bob. "We've got a father and mother, Ma'am, but we are trying to earn a little ourselves. I've got a broom and my sister sells cat's meat."

The woman looked surprised, as Bob's way of speaking was not like a crossing sweeper. "Well," she said. "I hope it's all right but—." At this moment a number of workmen came in and called for cups of coffee and the woman had no time to say a word more to the children, who ate up their breakfast as quick as they could.

"It was lucky those men came in," said Bob. "I was afraid that woman would ask our names, and then we would have been given to the police for certain. We must call ourselves some other names. Suppose we say our name is Smith?"

"But it isn't," said Maggie.

"People always give false names when they leave their homes," said Bob. "In all the books I have read, they do so, and even the queen when she goes away calls herself something else. It is called going incog, whatever that may be. So we'll go incog."

"Oh, if the queen does it, it must be all right," said Maggie. "Now what shall we do?"

"Well, you must sell the cat's meat you have," said Bob, "and I'll try and find a wet crossing. What a bore it is, it didn't rain in the night," for the crossings were as dry as a bone.

In vain they looked for a wet one and in vain Maggie called "S'meat, s'meat," in her loudest voice. The cats knew they only got their meals in the evening and they were too sensible to think of even looking round when Maggie passed.

On through the dusty streets the children walked. The sun grew hotter and hotter and poor Maggie began to feel sick and weary. In the distance they saw some trees. "That must be the park," said Maggie. "Let us go there and rest." It was Kensington Gardens and when they got there they found the flower walk full of nurses and nursemaids. The hawthorns were in full flower and the air was heavy with their scent. The tall blue irises and the tiny red peonies made the walk bright with colour. "Let us rest here," said Maggie. "My head aches so." The children sat near a tree and what with the warm, heavy air and their long walk, they both fell fast asleep.

Bob woke first. "I felt someone touch me," he cried. "I am sure I did," and he felt in his pocket, for he had often heard that there were pickpockets in London. Sure enough his purse was gone, no doubt taken by two little ragamuffins whom he could see running away as fast as their legs could carry them. What were the children to do? No use running after the boys. They were too far ahead. If Bob could get a policeman, it would be no use either, as he would be sure to find out who they were and take them home.

"What shall we do?" said Maggie. "All our money is gone," and she began to cry.

"What is the matter, my dear?" said a kind voice and she saw a lady standing by her.

"We have had our money stolen, five shillings and eight pence," said Maggie, sobbing.

"Oh, you naughty child," said the lady. "I thought you were really in trouble. Now I see you are one of those naughty beggar girls who are always pretending that they have had their money stolen." Maggie looked at the lady with big frightened eyes.

Bob, who was bolder, said, "She is not a beggar girl. Our money was stolen. Those boys stole it."

But no boys were in sight and the lady said, "I am sorry to see two children so wicked. If you do not go away, I shall have to send the police to you." And she went away.

Maggie was terrified at her threat and miserable at being told that she was a beggar girl. She took Bob's hand and said, "Run, run." And off they went, determining never to go near that horrid Kensington Gardens again.

It was about two o'clock and they felt very hungry, but how were they to get food when they had no money? "If the worst comes, we can sell our clothes," said Bob. "I have seen plenty of shops with 'Best price given for old clothes' written up, and ours are still very good."

"Let us try and earn some money first," said Maggie. "It will soon be time for the cats and it seems as if this road were rather muddy." So it was, for the water carts had done their work and turned London dust into London mud. But the crossings were full and the sweepers looked angry when Bob and his broom appeared.

"If you don't move on, I'll call the perlice," said a one-legged sweeper, making his wooden leg come down with a *clack* on the pavement.

The two children went on slowly. Then Bob's courage began to give way. Hot, thirsty, dusty, with no money with which to buy a cup of milk, threatened on all sides by the police, were ever two children more unlucky?

"We *must* sell something, Maggie. Let's try your bag first. It isn't much good." Maggie was fond of her bag, her mother had given it to her on her birthday; but she thought it would be selfish to say no, so she agreed and they went into a shop over which hung three golden balls, and in the windows of which there seemed to be all the clothes that had ever been made. Satin dresses rubbed up against scarlet uniforms, sailors' jerseys rested on babies' bonnets.

"You want to sell this bag, my dear, do you?" said a very dirty-looking old man with a hooked nose and long fingernails. "And how much do you want for it?"

"It cost 15/ [shillings], I know," said Maggie.

"Oh no," said the old man. "That must have been a long time ago."

"No, on my birthday only six months ago," said Maggie.

"Well, there must be something wrong with the bag," said the old man. "Why, what has it got in it?" And he opened [it] and saw poor Maggie's little sponge and comb. "Oh no," he said again. "I must know more [about] all this. What's your name?"

"M—, Smith," said Bob, giving Maggie a kick.

"Smith doesn't begin with M," said the old man. "See, on the bag are two letters, MM—I believe you've *stolen* the bag," he said, bringing his face very near Maggie and putting out his long, dirty fingers as if to clutch her.

"Oh, no, it's mine. Never mind if you don't want it, let me have it," cried Maggie in great fright.

"Yes," said Bob, "we'll go."

"Not so fast, young sir," said the man, getting up. "This is matter for the police." Before he could get round the counter to where the children stood, they rushed out of the shop, leaving bag and all, to the old Jew's great delight. He watched them fly down the road, chuckling to himself as he thought of their fright and his own cunning, for now he had got the bag for nothing.

Down the long hot road the children flew. There they turned aside and passed through a cool green Square, which somehow seemed familiar to them but they could not stop to think why. On they flew. They felt sure the police were after them, as they heard footsteps and someone cry, "Stop! Stop!"

"I can't go on," said Maggie, gasping, and she stumbled up against Bob, quite worn out. Bob turned round.

Someone was coming on towards them with flying cap ribbons, and little black curls all out of order. Who was it but their own Grandmama, Mrs. Beetle? And where were they but in the nice old-fashioned Square in Kensington where she lived! "Thank goodness, I've found you." she cried. "Come, come, you dear children. Come to me and have a good meal, poor little darlings," and she half carried Maggie across the quiet little Square, through the old iron gate into her own little garden and into her own square hall with its white and black paving. The children were so surprised, so tired and so frightened, they hardly knew whether to laugh or cry at this strange end to their adventures. They were always afraid of Grandmama, and the thought of being caught by her when they were doing something naughty would have made them shiver at any other time. Now they had an odd feeling of comfort and ease, but they had not much time for thinking. Grandmama had lost all her usual stiff way of speaking. "Run quick to the telegraph office. Don't stand with your mouth open like a chicken in a fit," she cried to her astonished page boy. "Telegraph to Lady Middleton 'Children found, come at once.'"

"Yes'm –!" said the boy, rushing off.

"Stop," said Mrs. Beetle, "I'll write it, for you've no more sense in your head than a pin," and she quickly wrote the words she had said.

Meantime, her maid, who knew her mistress's ways, and who saw what it was the children most wanted, now came in, saying, "If you please, Miss Maggie, if you and Master Robert will come upstairs, you shall have a nice hot bath and then you will be ready for your dinner."

Maggie was soon in the big hot bath, the clean soapy water splashing comfortably against her tired little feet. "Now," said Grandmama, coming in, "you are tired to death, you poor dear, and you shall just pop into that cosy bed while I go and see if your soup is ready." Grandmama was a wise old lady. She saw poor Maggie was worn out with her excitement and fright, and that rest was what she must have.

Maggie was indeed too tired to say a word. How delicious Grandmama's cool white sheets felt and how soft the pillows were! How sweet everything smelt! It seemed years since she had been in a proper bed with sheets and pillows. Could it be only one night? She was half asleep when her grandmother came in with a basin of hot savoury soup of which Maggie drank every drop. Then Mrs. Beetle pulled down the blinds and left the room, saying, "Have a good sleep till Mother comes."

Bob had felt quite fresh after his bath and now that he was dressed and feeling very hungry, he also felt very much ashamed of himself and very uncomfortable, for what a scolding he would get when Grandmama came in!

She did soon come and, with her, Bob's dinner. The dinner, of all others, he liked best, veal cutlets, green peas, raspberry tart and cream. The sight of these good things somehow gave Bob courage. He thought as Maggie had that it was years since he had had a proper dinner. Could it be that he had had one only the day before? Could twenty-four hours hold such quantities of things? Bob never had thought before what a lot of things can happen in twenty-four hours.

Grandmama's room generally looked stiff to the children and Grandmama herself looked prim, they thought; but now the room looked the picture of comfort. There were bunches of roses in big bowls, the window was wide open and the old mulberry tree gave a pleasant shade and rustle. Grandmama, instead of looking prim, looked quite untidy; her cap was not quite straight and her curls were almost out of curl. She moved about, helping Bob, her kind old hands shaking. She asked Bob none of the questions he had dreaded, only piled his plate with good things, and from time to time gazed at the clock and went to the window as if she could not rest herself till the children's mother came. At last came the sound of a hansom, and for the second time, Grandmama ran out, crying as she did so, "Come, Bob, there's Mother."

Bob flew down the little garden and in a minute felt his mother's arms hugging him. "Where's Maggie?" was all she said.

"In bed asleep," said Mrs. Beetle. "Oh, there you are, Robert."

For another hansom dashed up and out jumped Sir Robert. "Yes, I was at the police station and Margaret forwarded your telegram. Oh, my boy, how could you go? Oh, my boy, how could you go?" This was all the reproach Bob had, but he felt very sorry and ashamed; and all the things he had meant to say and all the reasons that had seemed so good when he went away seemed to have vanished. Now he found how much better it was to be at home.

Presently Lady Middleton came in with Maggie, who had been having a good cry, but was now all fresh and happy.

"Tell us all from the beginning," said Sir Robert, and Bob and Maggie told the story I have been telling you.

"Didn't you want to see me, Maggie?" said Lady Margaret, giving her a hug.

"Oh, yes, Mother dear, but we thought if we were really poor children, we *should* see you because you are always with the poor."

"And we thought we would go to the suburbs," said Bob, "for you are always there."

No one could help laughing. "Grandmama is the wonderful one to have found you," said Sir Robert, and it turned out that Grandmama had been hunting for the children all the morning, and even when she got home, she could not rest but went out "just to have another look" and then she saw the two flying little figures. A minute more and they would have turned the corner, but Grandmama somehow always did things just at the [right time].

The Duke's Coal Cellar

IF YOU LIVE IN LONDON, I am sure [you know] Brunswick Square, and if you know the Square, you will know Brunswick House, the biggest house in the whole Square. All the houses are big; but this is, of course, the biggest as the Duke of Brunswick lives in it himself.

It is a white house at one corner of the Square. There is a railing round a bit of dusty, dry grass. There is a carriage drive and there are some lilac bushes so the house looks quite different to all the other houses. There are two white pillars by the big door and two plate glass windows and at those windows are always two white heads which belong to two big footmen with fat silk legs and scarlet breeches.

Little Jim Brown lived in a small room in a small street, not far from the big house in the big Square.

His mother was a washer woman; she was out all day at work and she always locked up the room and turned Jim out, telling him to look sharp and make what he could. After school was over, Jim had to earn as many pennies as he could for he was expected to earn enough to feed himself during the day and to have some coppers over for his mother at night. Jim was a handy little fellow and generally managed to pick up something by cleaning boots, running errands, or holding horses. The one thing he liked doing was to watch the grand footmen at Brunswick Square. Sometimes there was a grand ball given and Jim used to stand and see the ladies jump out of their carriages, if they were young, or hobble out of them, if they were old, onto the steps which were then covered with red cloth, and through into the hall, which Jim saw all shining with light and with banks of roses high up the staircase looking like fairyland, thought Jim. The sounds of music came down to him and he envied the big footmen who saw and heard such beautiful things. One thing Jim longed to do and that was to give the footmen a start; though he envied them he rather despised them for leading such lazy lives. "All day long, looking out of windows," he said to himself. "I should like to give them a rise for nothing!" He was always watching for his chance but it never seemed to come—he wanted to ring the bell of that big house and run away! The footmen would jump up and he would be able to watch their faces of disgust when they found no one was there. He knew of a safe hiding place behind the lilac bushes; but the difficulty was to get up to the door without being seen. The footmen were always there.

One May evening, his chance came. He was walking home, a basket of onions on his arm, when he saw to his delight no white heads at the windows. Now was his time. Up the broad steps he dashed, pulled the bell with all his might; but before he had time to rush away, the hall door was opened—not by the footmen but by the great Duke himself—who was actually opening the door of his own house and letting a gentleman out. Jim was so startled, he did not dare to run. It seemed easier to rush in than rush out. The doorway was wide. The Duke and his friend were talking eagerly and past them rushed little Jim! Through the big hall downstairs—along a passage, on, on, his onions scattering as he fled. He saw an open door in front [of him], it would surely take him to the street. Bells were pealing, voices were calling, the whole house was after him, thought poor Jim, as he rushed through the open door, which landed him, not in the street as he had hoped, but in a big dark place, the Duke's coal cellar! He groped his way into it, creeping to the farthest end amid big blocks of coal, for he had no thought of escape; but sat, panting, down on a big block of coal, thankful to be out of sight and hearing.

He need not have been so frightened. The Duke was much too busy talking to his visitor to notice the little ragged figure that had passed him like a flash. The Duchess was very ill and the visitor was the great doctor, Sir Joseph Jolly. The bells which Jim had heard were for the absent footmen. They had actually left their windows to have a chat with the Doctor's coachman, who was refreshing himself round the corner at the Royal George. The Butler, who had gone for his afternoon nap was roused, and full of anger hastened to the hall and there found the Duke shutting his own hall door! The Butler told the footmen they should leave at once; and the Duke walked slowly upstairs thinking over what the Doctor had told him. No one was thinking of Jim, though he thought that the whole house was after him. If he had only known how busy they all were with their own concerns, he might have walked out quite safely. But this was the last thing he thought of doing. He was not long in quiet, for loud voices and steps were heard approaching. "Thomas, Thomas! Where's that boy?" said a woman's voice.

"Don't know and don't care" was the answer.

"If you don't know, I'll soon [find out]."

At this moment the hall boy came and Jim's heart beat violently as he heard the order given that two scuttles were to be filled at once. He crept far back. He was a very small little boy and the Duke's coal cellar was a very big one and the blocks of coal were big too, so Jim was able to hide behind them and when the hall boy came to fill the scuttles, he never saw the little shaking figure.

After the scuttles were filled, there was a long quiet time and Jim began to feel very tired of his hot, dark hiding place—he was nearly choked with coal dust and longed to get out. He crept cautiously to the door, which the boy had left open. Would it be safe to get out? No, there opposite was the big window of the housekeeper's room. The clean, muslin curtains, the canary hanging up in the window and the tea table at which Mrs. Smith, the housekeeper, sat pouring out cups of tea, all could be plainly seen by Jim. Mr. Brown, the Butler, came in rather late and very fussy. He helped himself to hot buttered tea cake and complained that the butter was salt. Mademoiselle, Her Grace's French maid, in lace apron, fanned herself and declared that it was too hot, either to eat or to drink. Jim wished he had the chance to do either! It was a long time since he had had any food; he thought of the fried onions and tripe they were to have had for supper. Mother was to get the tripe and he had the onions—where were they now? His mouth watered as he thought of them. Presently he heard the Butler say, "I must look after my men. They actually had the impudence to leave the hall, and [there] was the Dook and the Doctor in the vestibule alone, all as if we was commoners —and what do you think I found rolling in the passages? Three big onions. They made my fingers smell. Such goings on must be put a stop to."

"Onions?" said Mrs. Smith. "Well, that's odd. How could they have got there? The vegetable maid has no business upstairs. I must speak to her."

Dear me, thought Jim, much interested. What a lot of speaking for three onions! I wish I could get them back. "Onions, what a horror," said Mademoiselle, shutting her eyes. "Those vulgar smelling things. Bring them not near me."

"They're a good honest smell," said Mrs. Smith, who couldn't bear the French woman, "and are worth a deal more than those nasty French scents which are put on to hide something worse, as everyone knows."

"Come, ladies," said the Butler. "I think we will pass on to something pleasanter than onions. Let me offer you some seed cake, Mamzelle. No? Then some apricot jam. It is our own making, is it not, Mrs. Smith? So it is sure to be good." Apricot jam, seed cake, hot tea. Poor Jim. He watched all disappearing and longed to escape from his dark prison. Surely there would be a chance when the tea was over. He saw Mrs. Smith push back her chair at last, but his hopes of escape were put an end to, for Mr. Brown, getting up, said, "I see Thomas has left the coal cellar door open. I will shut it, although not my place." And Jim had hardly time to creep back before the door was slammed and the key turned and Jim found himself alone in the dark. At first it seemed as if he were quite in the dark but faint glimmers of light presently became clear to him and by degrees he could make out that they came from those round glass panes, which everyone who lives in London knows so well. Poor Jimmy felt very dismal. He had never thought of such a thing as the coal cellar being locked. Somehow or other he had felt sure that he would be able to escape to his mother before supper time, but now he saw no chance of it. There he was, locked in for the night and as he thought of it, Jim could not help beginning to cry. The tears rolled down his cheeks and mixed with the soot which lay thick on them and when Jim tasted them, they were so nasty that he very soon stopped crying, and after all, what was the use? It's poor fun crying when there's no one to hear.

Carriages rolled above him, bells rang, a German band came and was stopped at once by Mr. Brown. Jim could just hear him speaking from the hall door above but no one came for coals, and at last the sounds died away and only a rumble of distant carriages and the calling of cats could be heard, and Jim, tired out, fell into an uncomfortable doze. His bed was not a soft one and though Jim was not accustomed to anything very light and airy as a bedroom, he had never slept in quite such a dark and stuffy place before.

However, sleep he did and woke to find a little streak of light coming from those thick glass windows. His little legs were very stiff and aching and his poor little inside was quite empty. One thing he made up his mind about. That was, the very first time the coal cellar door was opened, he would make his escape. He would not care what happened to him if only he could get out of this dreadful coal cellar. Prison could not be so bad. There at all events you would have food and light. People don't get up very early in Brunswick Square and it was a long time before Jim heard any sounds coming from the big house. The milkman came and went with his funny call, but he left his cans, for no one was up to take them in. At last there was a sound of shutters undoing and windows being opened. Voices were heard. Not many, but still voices and oh, how glad Jim was to hear them. Surely, the first thing to be done was to light the kitchen fire and coals must be wanted. At last, steps came and a sleepy looking girl unlocked the door. She did no more, for Jim's little black face and figure fled past her. Down went the coal scuttle and with a scream the girl fled. "A ghost, a ghost," she cried. The cry was taken up by the kitchen maids, who had just appeared.

"Ghost, thief," cried the hall boy. "Stop thief," and he ran after Jim, who had dashed up the stairs and into the hall. It was empty. The big door stood wide open, for the house maid was scouring the broad white steps. Jim rushed past her but she caught the cry of the hall boy and repeating it, jumped up from her knees and, fearing lest Jim should escape her, she dashed the contents of her pail of soapy water just at the very minute when the poor little fellow thought he was safe. "I've caught him," she called out. "Stop, thief." A policeman passing by heard her cry and saw Jim fall. He picked the boy up and gave him a shake, for though Jim did not look much like a thief and was miserable enough, the policeman thought that a good shake never did a boy any harm.

"What has he been thieving, mum?" he asked the girl.

"I'm sure I don't know. I heard Thomas call 'Stop thief,' so I just soused my pail over the little beggar to stop him. I couldn't catch him. He ran so fast and my hands were soapy." Thomas now appeared.

"Oh, so you've got into the 'ands of the Bobby," he said; "serves you right."

"What has the boy been doing?" asked the policeman, who began to feel sorry for Jim, who was shaking all over. "You call out 'Stop thief,' and as far as I can make out the youngun ain't thieved nothink."

"What business had he in the Dook's 'ouse, I should like to know," said Thomas. "Here's Mary—she will tell you where she saw 'im running from. She thought as how he was a ghosteses, but I knowed better." Mary, who had a little recovered from her fright, was much disappointed to find that her ghost was only a ragged little boy and, as she was a kind-hearted girl, she felt sorry for the shivering child.

"Where did you come from, little boy?" she said.

"Please, mum," said Jim, "I've only been in the coal hole, I couldn't get out and I've been there all night."

"Poor little fellow," said Mary. "How frightened you must have been, and no breakfast."

"The question is how you got into the coal hole," said the policeman. "What was you a doing of?" Jim saw there was no help for it and he told his story. To his great surprise, Thomas, whom he had looked upon as his enemy, became at once friendly and Mary, to whom he looked for help, seemed all at once quite cold.

"I am glad you made those silk legs run," said Thomas, who hated the footmen, but Mary looked grave and said she must go back to the kitchen.

"Well," said the policeman, "you don't seem to have done much harm, youngun, and I don't suppose you'll go for to do it again?"

"Oh, no, sir," said Jim. "I only want to get home."

"Yes, I daresay you've a mother who's been bothering the life out of some of us," said the policeman, "worritting after a little scamp."

"Oh, no," said Jim, "I don't suppose Mother will have worritted much. She's always saying as I'm more trouble than I'm worth."

"Come along home," said the policeman. "You show me where you live and I'll tell your mother all about it, for you're only fit for bed." Jim was only too glad to go off home. It was not a long way, for though Mrs. Brown had two very little rooms in a very little house in a very little alley, it was not far from the great house of the Duke. When they reached the alley, to Jim's astonishment everyone seemed astir. Women were at the doors and everyone was chattering and explaining something.

They were all too eager to see Jim, who went quickly to his mother's door. She lived at the top of a small house and as he came close to her room, he heard her talking and sobbing. "The best of boys, my one comfort, what shall I do without him?" were the words he heard.

What could his mother be talking of? He pushed in quickly before the policeman and, calling out, "Here I am, Mother!" jumped into his mother's arms.

Mrs. Brown, who was busy describing her sorrow at Jim's disappearance, no sooner saw that he was really back than she began to scold him. "What mischief have you been up to, all wet and dirty, coming home like this and giving me such a start?" she said.

"Well, Ma'am," said the [neighbour] to whom she had been talking, "you've been up and down all night keeping the place alive with cries after your Jim and how he was the best of boys and as you would never get on no-how without him, and now you turns against him."

"Yes," said the policeman who had come with Jim, "that's the way with 'em. They kicks up no end of row, whichever way things comes out." Mrs. Brown felt a little ashamed of herself. She was really very glad to have Jim again, only the minute she saw the boy was safe, she began to think how dirty he was and felt angry with him for the trouble he had given her. "Take him to bed, m'm," said the policeman, "that's what he wants and if you turned the hot water cock on him it would be all the better." The room had by this time filled with the neighbours. Jim was questioned as to where he had been and when it was found out that he had spent the night in the Duke's coal cellar, everyone felt that Jim was something of a hero. "Let the poor boy go to bed," said the policeman to the neighbours. "Can't you see that he is cold and tired and hungry?" Mrs. Brown was all the time bustling about, and tired little Jim was soon in bed, which, though not very white, nor very soft, seemed both to Jim after his night among the coals. His mother brought him a good cup of hot coffee and some bread and butter. Jim had never felt so happy and he was soon asleep, though the neighbours and the policemen were still talking about his wonderful night in the Duke's coal cellar.

Essays for Adults

DIANE F. GILLESPIE

*J*ULIA STEPHEN'S OVERVIEW of her aunt's life and accomplishments for the *Dictionary of National Biography* provides facts. *Notes from Sick Rooms* is a handbook of advice based on extensive observation, written for women who find themselves less prepared than they might be to care for the sick and dying. Although it was important that women be included in the *DNB* and that their work be taken seriously, Julia Stephen's aim in these publications was more factual or practical than polemical. Since her close relatives and friends wrote, read, and discussed essays on the controversies of their age, however, her inclination to attempt more argumentative pieces than the brief biography and the pamphlet for nurses is no surprise. Drawing again upon personal experience and observation but reacting to specific provocations, she focused on three topics: the position of women in society, the religious controversies of her era, and the domestic servant problem.

Her three previously unpublished essays are on the last two issues, but Julia Stephen's views on the first are implicit in them and unite what initially seem unrelated concerns. As Noel Annan puts it, Julia agreed with Leslie Stephen and with "the vast majority of their contemporaries—that men and women played different roles in life, roles conditioned by their physiology as well as their education."[1] Still, although she accepted the popular idea of separate public and private realms for men and women, she was one of an increasing number who, as Joan Burstyn says in *Victorian Education and the Ideal of Womanhood*, accepted to some extent "the need for women to professionalise their own sphere," to "be trained to competence" within it.[2] Julia Stephen's *Notes from Sick Rooms* is part of a desire to be more professional; so, in a different way, are her later essays. While she agreed men held the ultimate power both in the family and in the larger society, Julia Stephen

31. STELLA DUCKWORTH's Album. *Julia Stephen writing.* Courtesy of the Henry W. and Albert A. Berg Collection, New York Public Library, and permission of Quentin Bell.

sided with those who insisted women's abilities and activities were as important as men's (VE 40).

Although much variety existed among Victorian women, they were to aspire to a domestic ideal: to organize their households; provide the solace, peace, and companionship their husbands needed when they returned from the conflict-ridden public realm; embody and exercise moral principles in their human relationships and philanthropic activities; and instill these principles in their children (VE 30–33, 39, 41). To deny themselves and serve first family, then nonfamily members, many thought women needed Christianity (VE 109). Most Victorians were certain, in fact, that since morality, or concern for others, depended upon faith, and the entire social structure depended upon morality, a widespread loss of belief would destroy society.[3]

Julia Stephen's religious doubts after Herbert Duckworth's sudden death in 1870, therefore, threatened the linked views of womanhood and society she and so many others espoused. She wrote not only her essay on women and agnosticism but, as we shall see, even her essays on household management in large part to defend her moral principles and the similar concern for others felt by women in positions like hers. When her religious doubts arose, perhaps Julia Stephen had read some essays on agnosticism; we do not know. An essay called "Women and Scepticism" by Leslie Stephen's brother, James Fitzjames Stephen, had appeared in *Fraser's Magazine* already in 1863.[4] More likely she read Leslie Stephen's essays later in the *Fortnightly Review* or *Fraser's*, or in the collection entitled *Essays on Freethinking and Plainspeaking* (1873). Continuing to speak out on the matter, Leslie Stephen published an essay called "An Agnostic's Apology" in 1876, then used the same title for a book (1893). His agnosticism is worth noting in light of Julia's later essay on the subject. To do so is not to suggest he influenced her views on religious faith but rather to indicate their compatibility. Given her reluctance to remarry at all, that she could have married a believer at this stage in her life is difficult to imagine.

As her later comments suggest, Julia Stephen would have considered the departure from orthodoxy in Fitzjames Stephen's "Women and Scepticism" fairly mild. Women are barred from most intellectual pursuits, Leslie's brother says, but they are naturally interested in the current religious controversies. He wants to outline "the sort of position which a pious and reasonable woman, educated as English ladies generally are, would do well to take in relation to such matters in the present day" (WS 679). He would have such a woman say,

> "I cannot see that it has pleased God to reveal out of heaven any set of doctrines which we must all receive; or to institute any scheme of discipline which we must all obey; but he has placed me under circumstances in which I have reason to believe that eighteen hundred years ago transactions took place and doctrines were taught which gradually changed the face of the world. I can worship contentedly according to the forms constructed upon this theory. Perhaps later generations may have more knowledge and more light, and may modify those forms and the views on which they were framed; perhaps they may confirm them and discover new arguments of their truth; but in the meantime I will use them without condemning others; and I hope that worship will be acceptable to the Being whom it is designed to honour, notwithstanding any mixture of error which it may contain" (WS 698).

The results will be "confidence and respect" in addition to affection from skeptical male relatives (WS 698).

Another writer, however, saw increasing numbers of women expressing more serious doubts; she questioned the motives of those who declared themselves agnostics. Well after Fitzjames Stephen's "Women and Scepticism" and Leslie's own essays on religious doubt, Bertha Lathbury's "Agnosticism and Women" appeared in *Nineteenth Century*.[5] Julia and Leslie Stephen had been married two years. In a far less historical and theoretical manner than Leslie's, Lathbury examines what she thinks are the specific consequences of faith and its loss in women's lives. She says that as agnosticism becomes more common among men, women who revere them will adopt their views. These men may not have anticipated the extent to which such women will become dissatisfied with their traditional domestic role. Although some are forced to work, Lathbury says, most women at present have no professions. Looking at young, unmarried women and at wives and mothers, she finds them too busy to question their beliefs. The doubters, she says, are primarily among women without husbands or children who devote themselves to nursing, teaching, or fostering "the well being of those they love" (AW 620).

In order to describe how agnosticism will affect these three activities, Lathbury paints a sentimental portrait of women: they are ruled by emotion, primarily love, not by judgment; they are optimistic, patient, and likely to get personally involved with those they help. At the same time, they are physically weaker than men and their brains "are more easily deranged." Prone to "emulation and jealousy," they cannot rule well, and they make decisions too rapidly. Because Lathbury defines woman as heart, she concludes that agnosticism will have pernicious effects upon that organ: "When the heart is dispirited, or thrown back upon itself, the action that springs from it tends inevitably to fall lifeless to the ground" (AW 620–21).

The woman who becomes an agnostic will have to tend the old, the sick, and the poor, Lathbury warns, without hope of an afterlife, any belief in virtue through suffering, or any sense that a spiritual force determines events. Focusing upon progress and guided not by emotion but by reason, as agnostics are, the skeptical woman will even see euthanasia as sensible in the face of "dimmed intellect or terrible disease" and she will not want to support "the hopeless lunatic or incurable pauper" with her taxes (AW 620–21).

If the agnostic woman teaches, to what end does she do so, "if this life is all" (AW 622)? Lathbury is concerned with the education of the working classes, whom she wants to accept their lot. Why help the poor to realize that nothing exists for them but the sufferings of this world? she asks. Why make them discontented by teaching them what they, realistically speaking, can never have or achieve? Even if a majority of the lower classes were taught to read, write, and count, save money, keep clean, avoid public houses, and seek more valuable leisure-time activities, what good would their improved lives be with no hope of future lives? And what other comfort is available to most of the poor (AW 623–25)?

The final interest Lathbury discusses is women's patient concern for "those who have chosen to pursue an evil path." What does the agnostic woman do in such cases, she asks, without prayer to give her hope, endurance, courage, even happiness, and to enable her to impart those same virtues to those who most need them? The agnostic woman cannot comfort the remorseful and dying with promises of virtue gained through suffering and of a better life to come (AW 625).

Lathbury predicts that women, rather than passively endure the loss of such hope, will seek to substitute the professions; even their present opponents will support their attempts to "fill the void" that their loss of faith has created. Most women, however, will remain "the centre of home life" and, Lathbury asks ingenuously, how can they function there cheerfully without faith (AW 626)? She urges, therefore, that women examine the sources of their power for good in the world, evaluate their motives for agnosticism if that is their position, and consider the consequences upon others of their views. If women are agnostics out of honest conviction, Lathbury objects less than if they merely want "to be in the front ranks of progress, and in the tide of intellectual fashion; to rise above the 'prejudices' that spring from our instincts rather than our reason; and above all to be in sympathy with the men they admire" (AW 626–27).[6] Even those with honest convictions should consider what they can offer "in compensation" for loss of hope. "Physical, mental, moral culture," she declares, is not enough for the individual who must die or for humankind as a whole: "If such is the only truth possible for mankind, in very mercy let us pause long before we help others to attain to it" (AW 627).

Julia Stephen probably wrote her response immediately, wishing to reply to someone who questioned the motives of agnostic women like herself and predicted dire results if their numbers increased. Although she must have felt personally attacked by this article and forced to define her own motives, the tone of her rebuttal is thoughtful and objective. Her essay speaks for itself, but it is worth noting that her main objections are to Bertha Lathbury's assertions that without faith women have no incentive for moral behavior; that agnosticism makes women unfit for nursing, teaching, or philanthropy; and that many agnostic women are simply courting the admiration of agnostic men. To counter Lathbury's inclination to believe agnostic women have no incentive for nursing if they cannot believe in an afterlife for their patients, it is also worth noting that Julia Stephen uses a weapon her opponent, ironically, does not. She quotes scripture. People must work while it is day, she says, "for the night cometh in which no man can work" (John 9:4). What happens after death, we do not know; we do know that we have some time on earth and had better use it effectively.

For faith as a motivation, Julia Stephen substitutes the work ethic. Although she did not go so far as to work for pay, she did not adopt that portion of the feminine ideal of her time which dictated that women embody their husbands' financial success by being "idle and nonproductive" (VE 135). As Richard Altick says of the Victorians,

> Work, in a secular context, was the counterpart of faith in a religious one, and its efficacy too was regarded as infallible doctrine. "Industry" and "work" were holy words in the contemporary lexicon, and the moral imperative they embodied was identified with that of faith and elevated into a virtual eleventh commandment by Carlyle: "For there is a perennial nobleness, and even sacredness, in Work . . . The latest Gospel in this world is Know thy work and do it. . . . Admirable was that of the old Monks, 'Laborare est Orare, Work is Worship.'" Utilitarians and Evangelicals alike subscribed to the ethic of work.[7]

Although she calls it "hackneyed," Julia Stephen quotes the same motto. To her, work well done was the foundation of morality.

Work, however, must benefit others. "The Evangelicals' sense of moral responsibility was one thing, sometimes the only thing," Altick says, "which most Victorian agnostics salvaged from the wreckage of a faith they could no longer accept. The very loss of that faith in many cases intensified the promptings of the conscience."[8] Leslie Stephen thought morality essential for the survival of the community, even of the human race.[9] But he was sure that it "springs simply from the felt need of human beings living in society," not from religion.[10] When he lost his faith he declared, "I now believe in nothing, to put it shortly; but I do not the less believe in morality."[11] Julia Stephen claims for the agnostic all of the true Christian virtues: "purity of life, sincerity of action, obedience to law, love of our fellow creatures." So armed, she challenges Lathbury's charges against agnostic women and their usefulness in society.

Her children's stories, like her essays, spring in part from a desire to inculcate basic virtues. She encourages concern for others not by promising children divine rewards or by threatening divine retribution but, as in her story "The Mysterious Voice," by promising participation in or threatening exclusion from the community. Her daughters learned their lesson. In Virginia Woolf's *The Voyage Out*, Helen Ambrose, who resembles Vanessa Bell more than Julia Stephen, reads about "the Reality of Matter, or the Nature of Good" and worries about her children's nurse teaching them to pray in her absence. "'So far, owing to great care on my part, they think of God as a kind of walrus,'" she says and exclaims, "'I would rather my children told lies,'" than grow up conventionally religious.[12] Virginia and Vanessa found philosophical rather than traditional Christian support for what they defined as moral behavior; however unconventionally they defined it, they valued highly their special community of family and friends.

Fortunate in her own marriage to someone who shared her scepticism, Julia Stephen maintains that any division between husband and wife on the matter of religion is not good, but, she adds, a schism between a believer and an agnostic is no worse than any other. Nor is it likely that agnostic women will rush en masse into the professions suddenly opened to them. Although women's work is different from men's, she declares, it is equally significant. In morality, moreover, there are no separate spheres; the motives of men and women should be judged alike. A woman especially ought to trust the motives of her own sex. Women do not just adopt the views of the men they admire, she insists; with the same "courage and sincerity" as men, women make up their own minds about religion.

Whether Julia Stephen really felt that she had made her arguments "feebly," as she says at the beginning of the last paragraph of her essay, or whether she had some other reason for not publishing her comments, we probably will never know. Her essay shows anything but a feeble mind at work. It is true that Julia's rejection of the traditional Christian faith and her assertions about women's intelligence and moral strength did not cause her to question the economic and gender-based hierarchies of Victorian society. Nevertheless, the role played by the women of her social class, those whom Virginia Woolf was later to call "the daughters of educated men,"[13] was to Julia Stephen a responsible, indispensable, dignified, and challenging one. She worked as hard at her nursing and philanthropy as any driven professional man of her time, harder perhaps than the husband who was part of her concern even during what might have been her hours of rest.

Another part of her profession as upper-middle-class wife and mother was her large household. Given her commitment to work well done on behalf of others, it is no wonder that the Victorian controversy over domestic servants should have interested Julia Stephen and prompted the other essays

32. STELLA DUCKWORTH's Album. *Julia Stephen.* Courtesy of the Henry W. and Albert A. Berg Collection, New York Public Library, and permission of Quentin Bell.

she wrote late in her life. The controversy resulted, in part, from the fact that the size of the middle class doubled in the twenty years between 1851 and 1871. The new administrators of businesses or factories wanted "servants as the symbol of and the reward for their success."[14] Even though many of these families could only afford a single servant, the demand increased markedly. By 1891, "the servant class was among the largest groups of the working population: 1,386,167 females and 58,527 males were indoor servants in private homes out of a population of twenty-nine million in England and Wales. Of these, 107,167 girls and 6,891 boys in service were aged between *ten* and fifteen years."[15] Affected by the factory era, both employers and employees "began to think in terms of a commercial exchange of services for money" (DR 30). Yet many employers also thought of the personal loyalties and long-lasting bonds between employers and servants they associated, not always accurately, with past eras.[16]

Although some came from foreign countries, most of the domestic servants in the wealthier areas of London, like Kensington where the Stephens lived, were girls from rural areas (RFVS 28, 115). They sought domestic service in spite of several disadvantages. Among these were accommodations that were the worst in the house (RFVS 115, DR 51–54). But because these rooms were still more spacious and private than the rural cottages or London tenements which usually were the alternatives (DR 68, NFS 17), servants were more likely to complain about their food. While probably not worse than the usual working class fare, it was often far inferior to what their employers ate (DR 55, 68). Some employees devised ways to gain more free time, but generally their hours were "always long and arduous," often "fifteen to eighteen hours per day" with only a half day off on Sunday, one day off per month, and maybe a fortnight off every year (DR 68, RFVS 96).

One reason for this onerous schedule was that, as Virginia Woolf noted in an essay entitled "Great Men's Houses," Victorian homes were inefficient. Writing from the vantage point of an age increasingly blessed with "bath, h. and c., gas fires in the bedrooms, all modern conveniences and indoor sanitation,"[17] Woolf uses the Carlyles' house in 5 Cheyne Row as her example of the previous era:

> The high old house without water, without electric light, without gas fires, full of books and coal smoke and four-poster beds and mahogany cupboards, where two of the most nervous and exacting people of their time lived, year in year out, was served by one unfortunate maid. All through the mid-Victorian age the house was necessarily a battlefield where daily, summer and winter, mistress and maid fought against dirt and cold for cleanliness and warmth. The stairs, carved as they are and wide and dignified, seem worn by the feet of harassed women carrying tin cans (GMH 24).

These cans were filled with water which "had to be pumped by hand from a well in the kitchen," boiled in kettles, "then carried up three flights of stairs" and emptied into a yellow tub for Mr. Carlyle's bath (GMH 23–24).

Servants had other complaints: the demand that they behave deferentially and dress in prescribed ways (DR 25), the lack of provision for sickness, old age, and illegitimate pregnancies resulting from sexual contact not only with male servants but with near relatives of their mistresses. In these circumstances, and in cases of drunkenness and theft, employers often dismissed servants without the references that would assure re-employment. Without any network of family or friends to assist in a crisis, about a third of the servant population, one historian estimates, became part of the "disreputable poor" (DR 98–99).

Another third of the domestic servants, however, bettered themselves. For this reason, large numbers of rural people, especially women who initially had few other employment options, continued to come to the cities. Service paid fairly good wages considering that food and lodging, however inadequate, were provided. Employers and guests added gifts and tips of various kinds; shopkeepers sometimes gave servants kickbacks. Many could save enough money to help support the families they had left behind, make good marriages, or eventually set up small, independent businesses of their own. Others moved up within service to the more powerful positions of cook or housekeeper (DR 57, 83). A final third of the servant population stayed on in the lower ranks of service, went back to the country to marry or otherwise to live, or moved into the urban working class (DR 98).

In the nineteenth century young girls going into service were taught by books like *Advice to Young Women Going to Service* and periodicals like *Servants' Magazine* that God instituted the social hierarchy. Biblical texts, like the one Julia Stephen herself quotes for a different reason in her defense of agnostic women, reinforced diligent service and subservience: "'Whatever thy hand findeth to do, do it with all thy might – Ecclesiastes ix. 10'" as well as "'Servants, be obedient to them that are your masters . . . as unto Christ – Ephesians vi. 5, 6'" (NFS 12). Nevertheless, near the end of the century, young girls felt "a growing reluctance to enter service. . . . They resented the drudgery, the reddened hands and arms which were their lot as domestics, preferring instead to seek employment in shops, offices and factories." They had new options, and those who did go into service kept changing jobs in search of better ones (RFVS 24). With public education also expanding to keep children in school longer, the servant population declined as demand continued to increase (DR 115–16).

While historians perhaps can see the overall picture of Victorian domestic service more clearly than anyone living at the time, Victorian periodicals contained many insightful and some fairly heated discussions of the pros and cons of domestic service as well as employer-employee relationships and household management in general. Leslie Stephen; his sister-in-law, Anne Thackeray Ritchie; and his sister, Caroline Stephen, all contributed. Leslie's unsigned article entitled "Housekeeping" appeared in 1874 in *Cornhill Magazine* which he edited from 1871 until 1882.[18] He recognizes that social changes are affecting household management and agrees with the reformers that homes ought to be run more rationally and efficiently. Servants increasingly object to their jobs, and employers, often lacking interest in their employees, want less responsibility for them (H 72–73). Agreeing "that the relation between master and servant is being radically transformed," Leslie Stephen thinks that "the real object of reformers should be to take care how the transformation may sweep away as little as possible of what is good in the old relation" (H 76). He does not propose to accomplish this task himself, merely to define the problem. Since people will continue to employ servants for some time to come, reformers should focus upon the practical ways employers and employees can get to know each other as human beings and the means by which "mutual good feeling may still be cultivated under changed circumstances, and a friendliness, degrading to nobody, be substituted for the old relations of patronage and respect" (H 78).

Anne Thackeray Ritchie immediately tried to do, in part, what her brother-in-law recommended. She looked into a recent Blue Book report to the House of Commons and tried to find the human significance in the statistics about some 650 young girls who went as maids-of-all-work in the cities after training at various kinds of schools for the poor in the early 1870s.[19] She quotes the good-humored comments of one little maid in an attempt to make the abstract concrete. Then she talks of the need expressed by one of the Blue Book investigators for "'mothering'" in the pauper schools (MBB 286). The report itself, she says, shows a motherly concern that is admirable in the face of truly difficult problems resulting from the children's previous physical and mental deprivations (MBB 287–88). Maintaining that women are the ones most qualified to write such reports for the legislature, she approves the recommendations in this one: the government should keep track of girls from the pauper schools and set up homes where they may go for "help and advice." Her own recommendation is less specific: "a multiplying, renovating charity, or pity and goodwill" (H 295–96).

Five years later, by focusing on the mistress and her servants, Caroline Stephen responded in more detail to the call for practical ways to cultivate satisfying human relationships. Like Leslie Stephen she recognizes related changes in the public and private realms but, she insists, the basic domestic problems and principles of governance remain. For the good of both employers and employees, she says, "the mistress of a household has, before all things, to rule."[20] Ruling, however, must be carefully defined. Although the relationship between mistress and servants is difficult, she disapproves of the current "commercial ideal" according to which the employer has no obligation for the employed beyond providing room and board and paying for services properly rendered. Caroline Stephen advocates, instead, a "domestic ideal" like Anny Ritchie's: mistresses should consider themselves mothers of sorts to everyone in their households and exercise "care and gentle watchfulness" over young female servants as well as over their own children (MS 1054). Sympathy and kindness, open friendliness and respect do not preclude "the exercise of . . . lawful authority," clear commands, or sound rebukes (MS 1056). The motherly mistress who acknowledges her servants' "true value as human beings", Caroline Stephen thinks, will improve the morality of her charges; she may even "learn something of patience, cheerfulness, self-denial, and kindness" from her employees (MS 1057–58). The motherly mistress, recognizing that family concerns are an area of "common interest," will learn something about the servant's family and help her to benefit those she loves. Regretting that other similar areas of interest do not exist, Caroline Stephen recommends that the daughters in a family learn housekeeping from the servants, and that servants participate in their mistresses' philanthropy (MS 1062–63). The essay ends with a description of an ideal Julia Stephen would have found appealing:

> The best loved, the best served, the most deeply reverenced mistresses I have known have been some mothers of families who counted not their time their own, whose care and affections were not limited to their own children or their own households, but whose lives were spent in daily ministering to the wants and the sorrows of all who were in need. They never shrank from trouble or from inconvenience if they could be of use, nor from rebuking wrong-doing when it came before them, but their joy was to spread joy around them; their children and servants gradually grew up into the privilege of sharing in their labours of love, their very names bring tears to the eyes of many whose hearts they never knew that they had won, and their memories remain as an inheritance of light and of hope for succeeding generations (MS 1063).

Did Julia Stephen attain any such stature so far as her servants were concerned? It is difficult to tell. As Noel Annan points out, "She prided herself that until just before her death no servant ever gave notice except to get married" (LS 104), a situation increasingly rare in Victorian society (DR 74). Not much is known about Julia's servants except that there were seven at 22 Hyde Park Gate and at least three of them, the cook and two maids, accompanied the family every summer to St. Ives.[21] While married to Herbert Duckworth, Julia had employed a Swiss maid named Suzette and kept her on until she died some time following 1888, the year she had an operation for cancer. A children's nurse named Leyden was with Julia equally long.[22]

Sophie Farrell, the cook, however, seems to have been the most powerful servant in the house. She indulged the Stephen children by putting extra food
into a basket lowered on a string from their window when she was "in a good
mood," and cut the string when she was upset.[23] After Julia's death, she remained with the family. Quentin Bell describes her as "inflexible in her ad-
herence to a tradition of decent extravagance" which resulted in bills beyond
what Leslie could bear. Vanessa, then in charge of household matters, got
into trouble unless the accounts were doctored to make them more accept-
able.[24] Given Mrs. Ramsay's reluctance in *To the Lighthouse* to tell her husband about certain expenditures,[25] similar difficulties probably existed under
Julia's household management.

A late memoir written by Virginia Woolf suggests that her mother and
the servants did have some difficulties. Woolf remembers that the servants' sitting room in the basement was "at the back; very low and very dark,"
decorated with a painting of Mr. and Mrs. Pattle that had been "relegated
to the room because it was so big, so cracked, so bad. . . ." Woolf concludes
that "the basement was a dark insanitary place for seven maids to live in"
and recalls that one of them once dared to tell her mother, "'It's like Hell.'"
Julia Stephen reacted with "the frozen dignity of the Victorian matron; and
said (perhaps): 'Leave the room'; and she (unfortunate girl) vanished behind
the red plush curtain" (MOB 116–17). Vanessa Bell also recalls the dark basement where the servants worked. They must have had eyes like cats, she
says, in order to produce clean plates and cooked food.[26] Woolf also remembers the way the house at 22 Hyde Park Gate was arranged in four stories
with her father's "great study" and the servants' bedrooms at the top where
there were no more carpets and pictures on the landing. She recalls that
"Once when a pipe burst and some young man visitor . . . volunteered help
and rushed upstairs with a bucket, he penetrated to the servants' bedrooms,
and my mother, I noted, seemed a little 'provoked,' a little perhaps ashamed,
that he had seen what must have been their rather shabby rooms" (MOB
118–19).

Julia's servants form part of the background in Woolf's fictional portrait of her mother in *To the Lighthouse*. A Swiss maid named Ellen brings
in the dinner. Mrs. Ramsay ladles the soup herself, asks the maid to take it
away, then observes Mr. Ramsay's chagrin when Mr. Carmichael asks for
another serving. The maid brings in the main course just as Minta Doyle
and Paul Rayley arrive, and Mrs. Ramsay helps the girl to place the large
dish on the table. In the background is a cook who has spent three days con-
cocting the Boeuf en Daube from a French recipe belonging to Mrs. Ramsay's
grandmother, but Mrs. Ramsay, who serves it to her guests, gets all the credit
for the "triumph." Mr. Bankes is especially impressed: "How did she manage

these things in the depths of the country? he asked her. She was a wonderful woman" (TTL 151–52). Mrs. Ramsay helps her guests to additional portions, they help themselves to fruit from the centerpiece, then family and guests go their separate ways. Presumably the servants clean up.

The final draft of the novel gives the servants slightly less prominence than an earlier draft in which the cook has a name (Mildred) and worries over getting the Boeuf en Daube exactly right, especially when dinner is delayed.[27] A maid named Janet brings in "a large earthenware pot" and a Swiss girl brings in "more dishes" (TTLHD 162). Mrs. Ramsay and her family and friends may pay little attention to the help, but at least once in both the early and final versions of the novel we see the mistress of the house from an employee's point of view. In an early draft of the "Time Passes" section, "old Maggie," a charwoman, recalls "Mrs. Ramsay in and out of the kitchen, but liked well enough by the maids" (TTLHD 182). The "but" suggests that such interference would ordinarily have been resented by the servants. Or it may suggest that, while the cook resented supervision, the maids did not. Perhaps the ambiguity caused Woolf to delete the passage. In the final version it is Mrs. McNab, lurching and leering through the deserted house, who remembers its occupants. The old charwoman in both drafts remembers Mrs. Ramsay's thoughtful request that the cook give her a plate of milk soup after the long walk from town.

In Julia Stephen's stories, many of the children live in relatively affluent, even aristocratic worlds in which nurses, butlers, governesses, and other servants supervise and teach, cook and serve meals, answer doors, carry messages, fetch coal, light fires and lamps, do laundry, and scrub steps. The children take servants for granted and often they are the butts of jokes for naughty boys. In "Tommy and His Neighbours," for instance, the boy is a trial to everyone, including the servants in his own house. He also scalds the cook in a nearby home and ruins her soup. In "The Mysterious Voice" Jem trips the page, who drops his tray of china and bumps the infuriated butler. Then, trying to scare the nurse, Jem puts a monkey in her bed. The stories do not countenance such behavior but, perhaps inadvertently, they reveal some of the realities of domestic service. In other stories, however, the relationship between children and servants is concern, even affection, on both sides. Maggie in "Cat's Meat" sympathizes with her governess who has a headache. In "Emlycaunt" the cook makes special treats for Tommy on his birthday, including fresh eggs sent for him by his old nurse who now lives in the country. Yet there is always a clear perception of social hierarchies, even in animal stories like "The Wandering Pigs" and "Dinner at Baron Bruin's." In the latter, Bruina has a marmotte to wait upon her, and marmosets serve the guests at the din-

33. STELLA DUCKWORTH'S Album. *Julia, Leslie, and Virginia Stephen.* 1892. Courtesy of the Henry W. and Albert A. Berg Collection, New York Public Library, and permission of Quentin Bell.

ner party. Monkeys make beds of fresh straw for the pig family members and Chips, another monkey, carries their messages.

Julia Stephen undoubtedly knew her husband's views on the servant question and probably had discussed the issue with her friend Anny Ritchie. Indeed, several of the arguments in Julia's essays suggest knowledge of these earlier discussions as well as of an interchange published in *Cornhill Magazine* in the same year as Leslie's and Anny's comments, 1874. In "On the Side of the Maids," someone identified only as "E. L. L." sums up the general dissatisfaction: "The masters resent the endeavour of servants to better their condition; the servants resent the endeavour of masters to keep them in the old inferior grooves."[28] Employers want slave-like subservience without any of the responsibilities accompanying slave ownership. E. L. L. lists the standard servants' complaints and adds others: uncomfortable accommodations, inferior food, few holidays, little free time, confinement to the house, rules forbidding contact with people outside, dull incessant work with nothing educational or pleasurable involved, and no protection against or provision for illness or old age. Servants must repress all emotions and behave deferentially, even though their employers may address them with "harsh language" (ELL 302–4). Although they deem people wise if they do the same in any other walk of life, employers are personally insulted if servants move on to better positions. Finally, those who model their spending behavior on their employers' are criticized by them. E. L. L. concludes that many mistresses are hypocrites. They claim equality with men, but ruin their case by treating their servants as inferiors. Servants deserve as much respect as women who teach school, keep shops, or make hats. Thought of as "a distinct profession" like these others, domestic service will cease to be degrading (ELL 305–6).

In "On the Side of the Mistresses," "A Suffering Mistress" dismisses E. L. L. as an ignorant bachelor who lives in a lodging house and is waited upon by a laundress. Insisting that only "a mistress can know the sufferings of a mistress," she challenges E. L. L.'s conclusion that employers no longer see their employees as human beings.[29] First of all, she says, he idealizes the past and blames mistresses for the inevitable problems of overcrowded urban life. Secondly, she claims that servants are not really so dissatisfied as he thinks, especially with their accommodations (ASM 460–62). If mistresses occasionally speak harshly to their maids, she insists, they certainly feel "some sense of shame" when they do so. To compare them to slave holders is pure hyperbole. Servants do have outside contacts, she says; they are free to walk and correspond with male acquaintances, although it is true that only a fiance can be allowed to visit. Female friends are not permitted in the house because some are not respectable and all are distractions during working hours (ASM 464). Look at the maids, this mistress says; their faces are "pretty and cheerful and smiling" (ASM 465). If some mistresses deny them education, it is because they are women, not because they are maids; these mistresses also prohibit education for their own daughters. "A Suffering Mistress" says that, while she would not welcome a servant with an annoying penchant for piano practice, she would encourage one with a quieter talent, like a gift for foreign languages (ASM 466).

If coldness and jealousy exist between employers and employees, she concludes, the entire English class system is at fault, not the mistresses and maids. Young women are not available for domestic service, not because they reject it but because the demand has increased so markedly and because more occupations are open to women now than in the past. Although the work is equally hard in other jobs and the accommodations are worse, women are attracted to them not so much for the wages as for the "freedom to go out anywhere and everywhere and in what company it may please them" (ASM 466–67). For these reasons, not because they long for education and the rose-covered cottages of home, domestic servants are scarce and can demand higher wages.

Although Julia Stephen probably knew this exchange in *Cornhill Magazine*, she seems to have written her responses specifically to a later series of articles on the servant question in *Nineteenth Century*. The most recent one, "The Dislike to Domestic Service" by Clementina Black, was a reply to previous articles in the same publication: Elizabeth Lewis's "A Reformation of Domestic Service" and George Layard's "The Doom of the Domestic Cook." These two essays express the viewpoint of the employers. Lewis, after contrasting the present to the past and defending the dignity of manual labor, lists the problems of keeping servants: meeting their demands for free time, providing them with accommodation, preventing them from disseminating information about their employers' private lives, and protecting one's person and possessions from them and their companions. Like the servants, many of the women who employ them want more freedom from conventional duties and worries. Evening meals and unreliable cooks are paramount among their aggravations. Lewis recommends "a culinary depot in every street, from which the meals could be sent out after the fashion of every foreign town where *restaurateurs* and *trattori* abound."[30] Such a system would result in better meals, relieve the timid employer from daily wrangles with her cook, and give servants greater independence and more time to themselves. Layard notes that the arrangement is common practice in large business and educational institutions.[31] He presents statistics to prove how economical the "culinary depot" would be and concludes that only "our insular prejudice against radical change of any kind" stands in the way.[32]

While her predecessors deal with the servant question from the employer's point of view, Black tries to explain the dislike young women feel for domestic service. In most jobs, employees exchange hours of labor for pay but, apart from those hours, have no contact with their employers. Servants have no such independent existences. Cut off from family and friends, they are among people whose company they have not chosen and whose good opinion they have to retain whatever their treatment. Such "total personal subservience" is "intolerable and degrading," and women with far worse jobs look down upon servants.[33]

Exiled from their proper circle, Black continues, servants must behave according to a strict set of rules, repressing their natural desires for contact with their equals, for variety, and for freedom. Ungratified in the ordinary ways, these desires find illegitimate outlets. Black points to the numbers of servants in homes and refuges for unwed mothers who then cannot find employment because of stains on their characters. She concludes that, were she a working-class mother, she would choose factory work over domestic service for her daughters: "The work would probably be harder, the material comforts less, and the manners rougher, but the girls would be working among their own class and living in their own home; and their health, their happiness, their companionships, would be under their mother's eye." If servants, like "dressmakers and charwomen," could work for their employers and then go home, domestic service might be more attractive (DDS 456).

Julia Stephen's essays on the subject, probably two of three tries at the same essay, advocate, like Caroline Stephen's article, not the new commercial ideal but an older, matriarchal, domestic one. In "The Servant Question" Julia disputes Clementina Black's claims that mothers and daughters are turning against domestic service. Then, like E. L. L. but for different reasons, she challenges the claim that domestic service is inevitably degrading. She turns to and dismisses the other complaints: "dependence," "dullness," "absence from their homes." Sending maids away to sleep, ordering food in, and other similar recommendations are simply abnegations of responsibility on the parts of those who employ servants. The alternatives are systems in which the maids live in large hotels, and mistresses have no authority over them so long as they put in their hours and do their work. England, she says, should retain the "strong bond between server and served" and resist change simply for the sake of change.

Julia Stephen's matriarchal view of the world, then, complemented Leslie Stephen's patriarchal one. As a woman she was to mother not only her immediate family but also others, including those who served her, who needed nursing or teaching, sympathy or cheering. With this commitment and her own work habits, she had trouble comprehending the claims that religious doubt obliterated morality or that even menial tasks were degrading to the worker. Virginia Woolf recalls, with some resentment, how her mother imposed her ethical code of work and self-sacrifice, particularly where Leslie Stephen's health was concerned, upon her children. Her over-protective attitude towards Leslie and others who needed her ultimately deprived her children of their mother: "—she wore herself out and died at forty-nine," Woolf says, "while he lived on, and found it very difficult, so healthy was he, to die of cancer at the age of seventy-two" (MOB 133).

On the edge of the eastern part of Highgate Cemetery in London are their graves. The simple stones have not worn well and are almost obliterated by heavy vines. Julia and Leslie Stephen did not anticipate an afterlife apart from the fruits of their work on earth. Julia may have counted on being remembered by those whose lives she touched. But she probably would have been skeptical of any kind of immortality to be achieved through her daughters' reputations and, most of all, through any writing of her own. She would be surprised, no doubt, by this volume and amused or appalled by the continuing reevaluation of women's roles in society and the parts the women of her family play in this reappraisal. Yet ironically, as her essays show, she is part of the change. Jolted by tragedy out of complacency and into a role at once self-assertive and self-defeating, Julia Stephen, for all her traditional notions, lived with dilemmas still familiar to many women.

Julia Margaret Cameron

CAMERON, JULIA MARGARET (1815-1879), photographer, born at Calcutta on 11 June 1815, was the third daughter of James Pattle of the Bengal civil service. In 1838 she married Charles Hay Cameron, then member of the law commission in Calcutta. Her other sisters married General Colin Mackenzie, Henry Thoby Prinsep, Dr. Jackson, M.D., Henry Vincent Bayley, judge of the supreme court of Calcutta, and nephew of Henry Vincent Bayley, Earl Somers, and John Warrender Dalrymple of the Bengal civil service. Miss Pattle was well known in Calcutta society for her brilliant conversation. She showed her philanthropy in 1846, when, through her energy and influence, she was able to raise a considerable sum for the relief of the sufferers in the Irish famine. Mrs. Cameron came to England with her husband and family in 1848. They resided in London, and afterwards went to Putney, and in 1860 settled at Freshwater in the Isle of Wight, where they were the neighbours and friends of Lord Tennyson. In 1875 they went to Ceylon; they visited England in 1878, and returned to Ceylon, where she died on 26 Jan. 1879.

Mrs. Cameron was known and beloved by a large circle of friends. She corresponded with Wordsworth; she was well known to Carlyle, who said, on receiving one of her yearly valentines, "This comes from Mrs. Cameron or the devil." Sir Henry Taylor, a valued friend, says of her in his "Autobiography" (ii. 48): "If her husband was of a high intellectual order, and as such naturally fell to her lot, the friends that fell to her were not less so. Foremost of them all were Sir John Herschel and Lord Hardinge. . . . Sir Edward Ryan, who had been the early friend of her husband, was not less devoted to her in the last days of his long life than he had been from the times in which they first met. . . . It was indeed impossible that we should not grow fond of her—impossible for us, and not less so for the many whom her genial, ardent, and generous nature has captivated ever since." A characteristic story of one of her many acts of persevering benevolence is told in the same volume (pp. 185-8). Her influence on all classes was marked and admirable. She was unusually outspoken, but her genuine sympathy and goodness of heart saved her from ever alienating a friend.

At the age of fifty she took up photography, which in her hands became truly artistic, instead of possessing merely mechanical excellence. She gained gold, silver, and bronze medals in America, Austria, Germany, and England. She has left admirable portraits of many distinguished persons. Among her sitters were the Crown Prince and Princess of Prussia, Charles Darwin, Lord Tennyson, Mr. Browning, Herr Joachim, and Sir John Herschel, who had been her friend from her early girlhood. Mrs. Cameron wrote many poems, some of which appeared in "Macmillan's Magazine." Her only separate publication was a translation of Bürger's "Leonora," published in 1847.

[Personal knowledge.] J.P.S.

[JULIA PRINSEP STEPHEN]

Biographical sketch of her maternal aunt written by Julia Duckworth Stephen for the *Dictionary of National Biography*, eds. Sir Leslie Stephen and Sir Sidney Lee (London: Oxford University Press, 1917).

Notes from Sick Rooms

Preface

MY EXPERIENCE both as nurse and as patient has been too limited to jus-
tify me in adding to the existing stock of notes upon nursing, were it
not that I have taken pains to note down things which have come under my
actual observation, either as giving relief, or causing discomfort to the sufferer. I must leave much that is obvious unsaid, and I am aware that I say
much which seems too obvious to require saying.

My excuse must be that I have wished to keep strictly to what I
have learnt, or unlearnt, in sick rooms. I do not pretend to lay down any
large rules as to nursing, but I wish to point out how some of the many disagreeable circumstances attendant upon illness may be diminished or removed. I have been able to watch the nursing of experienced hospital
nurses, and I have been with those who had the highest characters for efficiency, and with those who were neither trained nor efficient, but who yet
had something to teach.

I have also had the actual nursing of some cases, and have suffered
too much from my own shortcomings not to wish to turn them to account
for others.

Notes from Sick Rooms was originally published in 1883 by Smith, Elder, & Co., London. Subheads have been inserted in the present text, whereas they originally appeared as running heads.

Notes From Sick Rooms

I HAVE OFTEN WONDERED why it is considered a proof of virtue in anyone to become a nurse. The ordinary relations between the sick and the well are far easier and pleasanter than between the well and the well.

There are no doubt people to whom the sight of physical suffering is so distasteful as to turn a sick room into a real Chamber of Horrors for them. That such unlucky persons should ever have authority in a sick room ought to be an impossibility; but if by some unlucky chance they ever have, we should surely reserve our pity for the unfortunate invalids in their charge.

Illness has, or ought to have, much of the levelling power of death. We forget, or at all events cease to dwell on, the unfavourable sides to a character when death has claimed its owner, and in illness we can afford to ignore the details which in health make familiar intercourse difficult.

The ways in which our friends dress, bring up their children, or spend their money, are apt to cause disagreement more or less marked between us when there is no thought of suffering or loss; but the moment we are threatened by either, how slight such matters seem! We can contemplate without irritation the vivid fringe of hair when the head which it disfigures is aching and fevered; and we feel equal to allowing the spoilt children to put their feet in the "crystal butter-boat," like the never-to-be-forgotten little boy of our childhood, if it will give any pleasure to the over indulgent mother who is racked with pain.

A nurse's life is certainly not a dull one, and the more skilful the nurse the less dull she will be. The more she cultivates the *art* of nursing, the more enjoyment she will get, and the same may be said of the patient. The art of being ill is no easy one to learn, but it is practised to perfection by many of the greatest sufferers.

The greatest sufferer is by no means the worst patient, and to give relief, even if it be only temporary, to such patients is perhaps a greater pleasure than can be found in the performance of any other duty.

Nursing Instinct

It ought to be quite immaterial to a nurse whom she is nursing. I have often heard it urged against trained nurses that they look upon their patients as *cases*. If to look on patients as a case is to feel indifference towards them, then the charge is indeed a reproof; but assuming that the nurse is not indifferent, how should she look on her patient but as a case; and further, why should she?

The genuine love of her "case" and not of the individual patient seems to me the sign of the true nursing instinct.

It would be hard if those who were specially charming, or whose antecedents interested, were alone to be tenderly nursed. Every nurse, whether trained or amateur, should look on her patient as a "case," nursing with the same undeviating tenderness and watchful care the entire stranger, the unsympathetic friend, or the one who is nearest and dearest.

In most cases of illness nursed at home, even if there be a trained nurse, there is generally some member of the family watching and helping— more often hindering the work of the sick room.

Much may be done by such helpers to make the lives of both pa-tient and nurse easier and brighter; but unless such outsiders help with skill and tact, as well as with zeal, their presence in the sick room is dreaded in-stead of desired.

To avoid confusion I have used the word "nurse," but many of the little hints which I have noted down are for such watchers. One imperative duty of all those in attendance on the sick is that they should be cheerful; not an elaborate, forced cheerfulness, but a quiet brightness which makes their presence a cheer and not an oppression. It may seem difficult to follow this advice, but it is not. Cheerfulness is a habit, and no one should venture to attend the sick who wears a gloomy face. The atmosphere of the sick room should be cheerful and peaceful. Domestic disturbances, money mat-ters, worries, and discussions of all kinds should be kept away.

Lying

There can be no half dealing in such matters; hints and whispers are worse than the whole truth. There is no limit to a sick person's imagination, and this is a fact which is too often ignored, even by the tenderest friends. The answers, "Oh, it is nothing," "Don't worry you[r]self," when suspicion is once aroused, are enough to fret the unfortunate patient into a fever. She will tor-ture herself with suspicion of every possible calamity, and at last, when she has nerved herself to insist on being told, her unconscious tormentor dis-closes the fact that one of the pipes has burst!

If trouble should come, and it is important that the invalid should be kept in ignorance, her watchers must make peace with their consciences as best they can; and if questions are asked, they must "lie freely."

Crumbs

Among the number of small evils which haunt illness, the greatest, in the misery which it can cause, though the smallest in size, is crumbs. The origin of most things has been decided on, but the origin of crumbs in bed has never excited sufficient attention among the scientific world, though it is a problem which has tormented many a weary sufferer. I will forbear to give my own explanation, which would be neither scientific nor orthodox, and will merely beg that their evil existence may be recognised and, as far as human nature allows, guarded against. The torment of crumbs should be stamped out of the sick bed as if it were the Colorado beetle in a potato field. Anyone who has been ill will at once take her precautions, feeble though they will prove. She will have a napkin under her chin, stretch her neck out of bed, eat in the most uncomfortable way, and watch that no crumbs get into the folds of her nightdress or jacket. When she lies back in bed, in the vain hope that she may have baffled the enemy, he is before her: a sharp crumb is buried in her back, and grains of sand seem sticking to her toes. If the patient is able to get up and have her bed made, when she returns to it she will find the crumbs are waiting for her. The housemaid will protest that the sheets were shaken, and the nurse that she swept out the crumbs, but there they are, and there they will remain unless the nurse determines to conquer them. To do this she must first believe in them, and there are few assertions that are met with such incredulity as the one—I have crumbs in my bed. After every meal the nurse should put her hand into the bed and feel for the crumbs. When the bed is made, the nurse and housemaid must not content themselves with shaking or sweeping. The tiny crumbs stick in the sheets, and the nurse must patiently take each crumb out; if there are many very small ones, she must even wet her fingers, and get the crumbs to stick to them. The patient's night-clothes must be searched; crumbs lurk in each tiny fold or frill. They go up the sleeve of the nightgown, and if the patient is in bed when the search is going on, her arms should hang out of bed, so that the crumbs which are certain to be there may be induced to fall down. When crumbs are banished—that is to say, temporarily, for with each meal they return, and for this the nurse must make up her mind—she must see that there are no rucks in the bed-sheets. A very good way of avoiding these is to pin the lower sheet firmly down on the mattress with nursery pins, first stretching the sheet smoothly and straightly over the mattress. Many people are not aware of the importance of putting on a sheet *straight*, but if it is not, it will certainly drag, and if pinned it will probably tear. The blankets should be put on lightly, one by one, not two or three at a time. There is an appreciable difference in the way in which coverings are laid upon people. Each covering should be laid on straight and smooth; no pulling straight should be done afterwards. If the patient is in bed when her bed is made, the lower sheet should be half rolled up and laid on the edge; the patient should then be lifted over the roll on to the fresh sheet, half of which has been spread over half of the bed. The old sheet can easily be pulled away, and when the new one is unrolled it can at once be tucked in and pinned if required. The upper sheet is rolled or folded breadth-ways and laid under the blankets, beginning at the feet; it is then quickly drawn up and the old one removed, the blankets not being disturbed. All blankets and quilts should be so arranged as not to drag and not to slip; any extra covering which is required only over the feet should not drag down to be pulled off by each movement of the patient, or by a careless passer by; it should be supported on a towel-horse unless there is a good footboard to the bed. If there is not a good footboard, it is well to improvise one by putting a plain deal board at the end of the bed between the mattress and the bars, as the legs of a towel-horse or a chair are very liable to be kicked by passers by, and the bed gets shaken, a thing much to be avoided.

If an eider-down quilt is wanted, it should be pinned with American safety pins on to the top covering.

Bed

A sick bed is apt to become close and unpleasant, but the nurse may refresh it without chilling the patient if she raises the top sheet, with the coverings resting on it, three or four times, thus fanning the bed and causing the patient no fatigue or chill. An invalid can air her own bed in this way if she can raise her knees; she need then only lift the outer edge of the sheet up with her hand and raise one knee up and down; but this of course requires some strength, and the bed will be more effectually aired by some one standing by the side of it.

Some people think that the whole comfort of a bed depends on its pillows, and I am not sure that they are not right. Certainly a hard or a pappy pillow will make an otherwise comfortable bed a most unresting one. Everyone has their own way of arranging their pillows: some like them smooth and straight, while others twist and turn them till it seems as if no head could find rest. The nurse must find out which way her patient prefers before attempting to arrange the pillows. I have often seen a sick person tormented by the over zealous nurse seizing the pillow and altering what certainly seemed a most uncomfortable arrangement, but one which was in fact exactly suited to the patient's needs, and only attained after many struggles. The nurse must be always ready to turn the pillow when wanted; she can do this without fatiguing the patient by placing one hand at the back of the sick person's head, while with the other she quickly turns the pillow and slips it back into its place. I say hand advisedly. The palm hollowed inwards a little should be used. Nurses very often make use of two fingers, which, when well pressed in at the back of the head, make the turning of pillows a very torturing process. Where no second pillow is at hand, and the patient wishes to have her head higher, she can make a comfortable change for herself by doubling the corner of the pillow back or under her cheek; but no nurse can attempt such an arrangement, as it may be such an uncomfortable one, that it is only by the patient's own hand and cheek that the proper curve can be made.

Waterproof

If a waterproof sheet is necessary, the best way to make the bed is as follows: —The bed having been made as usual, with a good blanket under the lower sheet, the waterproof should be laid on it, over the waterproof a blanket, and again over the blanket a sheet; these should not be tucked in. When the waterproof is no longer wanted, the top sheet, blanket, and waterproof can all be drawn away from under the patient, who will find herself on a clean, freshly-made bed.

The shorter time that a waterproof can be kept under a patient the better; the smell and heat cause much discomfort, and with a good under-blanket the mattress will seldom come to grief. Nurses are very apt to exaggerate the necessity for a waterproof, and are unwilling to believe in the restlessness and discomfort created by one. Economy is a great virtue in a nurse, for all illness, however slight, involves expense; but the virtue may be carried to excess.

There are, I believe, many people who would rather suffer a great deal of discomfort than swell their washing bill; and if the nurse should find this to be the case, she must do all she can, while keeping the patient sweet and fresh, to save expense. Nothing can do a sick person more harm than to worry over accounts and expenses, and if the patient should be one of those notable housewives to whom any exceeding of a certain sum is absolute misery, her peculiarity in this as in all other respects during illness should be respected. If, however, the nurse has not got to deal with such a patient, but may secure the *luxuries* of cleanliness, I would counsel her to have as much clean linen and as many clean clothes as she can lay hands on.

It is, as far as I have been able to judge, an invariable rule among nurses that when only one clean sheet is used, the clean one should be placed on the top, and the one that was on the top should be placed below.

The obvious reason for doing this is, that the top sheet is the one that is seen, and therefore should have a glossy freshness. The obvious reason against it is that the bottom sheet is the most felt, and therefore, in the interest of the patient's comfort, I would beg that whenever one clean sheet only is put on, it may be the one on which the patient has to lie. I am quite aware that the top sheet is only *tumbled*, not soiled; but it is that very tumbling, that want of smoothness and freshness, that makes a long stay in bed so trying. And if, as we take for granted, the top sheet *is* only tumbled, the doctor can surely be allowed the sight of it. Unless the patient be a Mrs. Skelton, she will prefer to have her comfort consulted rather than her appearance.

Handkerchiefs

If crumbs are the most tenacious inhabitants of a bed, handkerchiefs may be considered as the most transitory; they disappear mysteriously, although they have been invariably placed under the pillow. To obviate a little the perpetual game of hunt the handkerchief, it is well that the patient should be provided with two handkerchiefs—one placed under each end of the pillow. If the invalid should wear a bed jacket, it should be furnished with pockets. With regard to jackets, I would advise that they should be made with large armholes and sleeves, sufficiently large to allow of the night-gown sleeve passing under with ease. There should be no thick frilling or trimming at the throat; although in the hand such jackets look pretty and becoming, they are hot and uncomfortable to wear, and as the frills soon turn in and get untidy, in a short time they do not even look well.

Washing

There is no part of nursing more troublesome, more necessary, or more to be deplored, than washing. We know that there are many people who have a perfect mania for washing. Speaking to such invalids, I would entreat them to repress their desire for soap and water as if it were for gin; to be content with a small wash every day, and not to torment themselves with the idea that, unless they are washed all over every day in the most scrupulous manner, they must be dirty. The nurse, however, has not come to root up her patient's theories, but to carry them out as far as may be in ac[c]ordance with the patient's well-doing. This is often not very easy; but a very thorough washing may be done without risk of chill, and with comparatively little fatigue, if the nurse manages well.

All that is required for washing should be ready at hand—hot and cold water, a bath-thermometer, and plenty of warm towels; an old flannel dressing-gown; a spare blanket should also be at hand. Before attempting to uncover her patient, the nurse must be certain that she has all she can possibly want; there should be no moving to and fro, no coming into the room, and no delays when the work of washing has once begun.

The patient must of course be washed piecemeal; the uncovered part must be covered with a loose flannel which has been warmed, and the washing and drying must be done under this flannel whenever it is practicable.

Each part should be well dried, and covered with something that will not slip off—if the clothes cannot at once be put on—before the rest of the washing is begun. A little vinegar, eau de cologne, or rose water, makes washing more refreshing, and eau de cologne prevents a chill. The towels, which should all be well warmed, should not be scorching. The skin is very sensitive after washing, and the towel should be of an equable warmth, with no very hot bits, and should be given gently; the sudden giving of a towel and flapping the air against the patient's wet skin produces an icy chill, a fact of which nurses are too often unconscious. If there are two attendants while washing is going on, one should busy herself with the towels, moving them in front of the fire, so that every part is well warmed while none is scorching. If the nurse is singlehanded, she should have her towels warming at a little distance from the fire some time before washing begins, and should turn them when she begins. If, by a chance, she finds any part of a towel has become too hot—and she should always pass her hand rapidly over the towels before using them—a quick shake out while the patient remains covered would make the towel of a comfortable temperature.

When there is no fire a hot foot-warmer, round which the towels can be wrapped, does almost as well.

Bath

In giving a bath the same course must be pursued in a great measure; but if the patient has to be carried into the bath, the nurse must be very careful to lower her gently into the bath. In bathing a helpless patient it will be found almost imperative to have two attendants. The patient's feet should be allowed to feel the water first, and the water should be moved by the hand of the nurse, while the patient is being placed in the bath, so that it laps up to the patient's body, and that she avoids all shock. Being lifted into a bath causes great nervousness, far greater than the bystanders can credit; and the nurse should make her patient's mind as much at rest as she can, not only by telling her the exact temperature of the water, but by letting her feel it with her fingers before she is put in. When lifted out, a large warm sheet should be ready with which at once the patient is covered; she must then be carried to a sofa, on which must be spread a warm blanket; on this the patient lies, and in it she is wrapped; the sheet which has taken off the first wet is removed from under the blanket, and the patient is dried thoroughly with warm towels. A patient bathed in this way should feel little fatigue; but the bathing and drying must be done in silence. The useless remarks in which attendants indulge are absolutely injurious to sick people. The "All right," "Oh, here it is," "Wait a moment," irritate and take away all the refreshment which the bath would have given.

The nurse must be very careful not to hurt by rubbing or by soaping any scratch or sore place that a patient may have. The hurt may seem insignificant, but nothing is small in illness, and a little scratch well soaped will set up a very considerable "raw," and effectually prevent a nervous patient from sleeping. The nurse should be careful to keep her hands smooth and her nails short; the lovely filbert nails which are the pride of many are very literal "thorns in the flesh" of the unlucky patient, who derives no consolation from the assurance given by the nurse, "You can't feel a pin, ma'am, for my fingers are there."

When the hands are washed, the basin should be held below the hand, so that the water may drip down, not run up the sleeve, as is often the case. If by chance the sleeve should get wet, a piece of cotton wool should be placed between the wetted part and the arm, and the wet spot should be well sprinkled with eau de Cologne. If the bed should be slightly wetted, eau de Cologne sprinkled on it will prevent a chill; but if there is much wet, and it is impossible to change the sheet, a hot iron should be passed up and down the wet part, which will soon dry. In doing this extreme care must be taken not only that the patient should not be burnt, but that she should herself feel assured that such precautions have been taken that she cannot be burnt.

It is a great refreshment to sick people to have their feet washed, and no part of the body can be washed more safely and with less fatigue to the patient. A warm flannel must be put under the foot, which should hang a little over the side of the bed, the foot-tub or basin must be just below, and the foot can thus be soaped and sponged easily and effectually.

Each foot must be washed separately, and, as the sponge is removed, must be wrapped in a warm flannel and dried with warm towels. In cases of advanced chest disease, the patient will probably be very much afraid of having her feet washed; but if the nurse can persuade her to have them done, she will reap even greater advantage than other patients, for in such diseases a thick dry skin forms over the foot, causing intolerable heat and irritation. When actual washing is not required, refreshment will be found in rubbing eau de Cologne over the feet and between the toes.

Hair

In doing the invalid's hair, the nurse would do well to use at first only a comb with large teeth, or, if she has not got one, only to use the large teeth of an ordinary comb. She should hold the hair near the roots with one hand, so that the patient should not suffer if a tangled part has to be combed out. The hair should be lightly touched, the head being kept steady, not pulled from one side to the other, as is often done.

The nurse should be careful to see *where* her brush goes. It is an absurd but unpleasant fact, that an invalid's eyebrows often get quite as much of the brush as her hair. The nurse should always clear the brush of loose hairs before using it. Few things are more aggravating than to have a long hair brought slowly over the face each time the brush comes round.

Hairs are not so bad as crumbs, but they are very tormenting bed-fellows, and there is little excuse for any nurse who, after brushing the patient's hair, allows any stray hairs to remain on the night dress or bed-clothes.

When the bed-pan is required the nurse should not oblige the patient to raise herself twice; she should slip the pan at once into the proper position, and when she removes it she can at the same time straighten down the patient's clothes.

If the invalid should be very weak and nervous, a small waterproof and towel can be kept under the bed-pan; these can be placed at the same time as the pan itself. Burnt vinegar is the most pleasant of scented disinfectants. An old jam-pot with vinegar in it, into which one or two live coals are dropped, is the safest way of using it. The scent of the vinegar, unless the patient objects to it, is far more healthy than ruban de Bruges, or pastilles. Sanitas is an admirable purifier. When used in a little squirt, it will soon remove all unpleasantness; it is most refreshing on the clothes and inside the bed. Boracic acid is an admirable deodoriser; if some of the crystals dissolved in water are placed in the utensil before it is used, no unpleasantness will be perceived, and, as it is colourless and without smell, it is preferable to either Condy or carbolic acid.

Air

Such great authorities have written on ventilation, that I need only say that there is no danger in having a thorough draught through a sick room each day, provided that the patient is not only thoroughly well wrapped up while the windows are open, but for some time after they are shut, and that the coverings are only removed by degrees.

Candle smoke is one of the most unpleasant smells in a sick room, and it is so constantly breathed by invalids, even when they have careful and considerate nurses, that I will venture to assert emphatically that there is only one way in which the smoke can be destroyed with absolute certainty —that is, by dabbing the wick with a spill, paper cutter, or any flat light thing that may be at hand.[1] The wick can be raised the moment the flame is out, and the candle will not be spoiled. Blowing a candle out upwards, or blowing it out while it is held up the chimney, are good ways, but not infallible. An extinguisher is the worst of all, as it imprisons the smoke, which either discharges itself by degrees, thus lengthening out the torment, or remains in the extinguisher till the candle is again wanted, and then escapes, and the last state is without doubt worse than the first. Night-lights should be dabbed out too, for they have a most unpleasant smell; they should never be put in the fire; there is no smell more offensive than that of grease burning.

Light

Many invalids object to a light in the room at night. When this is the case, the nurse should dispense, if possible, with one. It is more often possible than nurses are willing to think. Candles and matches must, of course, be at hand, and it is well to have a light in the next room or passage; but if a patient wishes her room to be dark, the nurse should endeavour to make it so.

When a light is required, it should be skilfully shaded. By skilful shading I mean not only that the light itself should be shaded, but that its

---

1. Since writing the above, a friend has sent me a delightful pair of snuffers, the only ones I have ever seen that quench the flame without producing smoke: they are flat instead of box-shaped, and neither cut nor crush the wick, while they effectually prevent any smell.

reflection must be hidden as much as possible from the eyes of the sick person.

I have seen a candle shade carefully arranged by a kind and skilful nurse so as completely to hide the actual candle, but she ignored the fact that the light was reflected by a mirror just behind it. A night-light is often put in a basin for safety and shade, but a beautiful globe of light will be reflected on the ceiling, the light of the little lamp being increased tenfold by the glazed china. Daylight has to be shaded with equal care. If the blinds and curtains are drawn, the nurse must see that there is no crack left open. A slant gleam of light is more trying than the broad shaft which would come if the curtains were not closed.

Wherever lights are placed the nurse must be careful that they are not near anything which can suggest the idea of danger to the patient's mind. One of the many terrors which haunt the helpless is that of being burnt in their beds. Distances do not appear the same to those up and those in bed. What may be obviously safe to a person standing up, looks perilously close to one in bed; and the nurse must not argue the point, but must either move the light, or, if that cannot be, she must *prove* to the patient's own satisfaction that there is no danger.

One of the many mistakes into which nurses fall is that of persuading patients, or at least trying to persuade them (for we know how seldom people well or ill *are* persuaded). A sick person will often give in from sheer fatigue; but she remains unconvinced, and her mind is not at rest; she goes over and over her reasons and the nurse's; and worries herself over a thing of small importance, because she does not like to reopen the discussion. I would impress on all nurses strongly that, as far as lies in their power, they should keep their patient's mind at rest. They cannot control the disturbing influences which find their way into the sick room, nor can they overcome all the varied miseries which beset the sick brain; but some of these miseries they can soothe, and they can and should always be careful not to cause any themselves.

Fancies

Invalids' fancies seem, and often are, absurd; but arguing will not dissipate them; it will only increase them, as the patient will hide what she feels, and so increase her mental discomfort—a sure way of augmenting her physical suffering. One of the many rewards that come to a careful and considerate nurse is that the patient's fancies are not absurd. If the invalid knows that her nurse has undertaken to see that a thing is right, she will have an easy mind about it, and will not worry the nurse with useless questions and suggestions.

There are, of course, patients who, without meaning to be exacting, are so delicately organised, or whose senses have become so acute through suffering, that they can detect a draught or a smell where even careful and discerning nurses can find neither. The nurse must, therefore, not deny that the evil exists; a door or a window may have been opened without her knowledge, and the current of air may be felt by the sick though not by the well. Something may have been dropped on the kitchen fire, or there may be some minute escape of gas which is imperceptible to all but the invalid. The nurse must remove these evils should they exist, and thoroughly investigate the evil real or fancied. Cold cannot be taken through the imagination; but a nervous dread of chill can make a sick person thoroughly wretched, and one of the chief duties of a nurse is to make her patient thoroughly comfortable in mind and body.

If the patient be well enough to be left for any time she should always have a bell, and any small thing that she is likely to want in a hurry, close by her. The nurse should never leave her patient hastily, but wait to be certain that all the things are there, and that the invalid has said all she wants. The mind moves slowly to expression in illness, and the feeling that the words are impatiently waited for takes away the power to utter them.

A nurse, especially if she be an amateur, will find it useful to keep a written record of the events of the sick room – the hours at which food and medicine are taken, and variation of temperature or symptoms, the amount of sleep that the patient has had, &c. The monotony of a sick room is very great. Anyone who tries to remember in their order the small events which made up the invalid's day will be astonished to find how perplexed she is when any doubt is thrown on her statement. The doctor is very glad to have the diary of a careful watcher. Such symptoms as flushings, restlessness, excitement, and the hours at which they occur, are important features in illness, but at the time of the doctor's visit the nurse is nevertheless very apt to forget them, unless they have been noted down.

Visits

It is a truism that one's friends are one's greatest enemies, but in illness it is a very painful fact; and the number of ways which kind people find of tormenting each other would be amusing were it not so painful. Most invalids have some hour when they may be visited, but it is in vain that they impress this fact on their friends. Day after day the unwelcome announcement is made that so and so knows she is too early but she will wait. The invalid hurries through her meal or her dressing, or whatever she may be about, and so is quite unfit to enjoy her friend's visit when it is paid.

Visitors have an uncomfortable habit of apologising for their visits. The invalid has, no doubt, much she wishes to say and to hear, and the time for the visit is short; it is therefore extremely irritating to have it made shorter by visitors who keep on assuring her that they won't stay a minute, and they don't mean to talk, &c. There is a delusion under which most visitors to an invalid labour—that all illness affects either the brain or the hearing. It is impossible otherwise to account for the patronising cheerfulness and the peculiar distinctness of utterance which such visitors affect. We are reminded irresistibly of the excellent Mrs. Peckaby, who spoke broken English in order to make herself understood by M. Baptiste.

Visitors should come straight into the sick room; there should be no delay and whispering outside after they have been announced; they should not begin to talk till they are well within eye and ear range of the sick person. The habit of coming half in, of beginning to speak while still at the door, and still worse speaking while holding the door open (this practice is the almost invariable one of servants bringing a message, and should be checked by the nurse), all show that the visitors had far better keep away till their friends are well. If the patient is asleep and a visitor comes in, she should go away instantly, not stand and gaze till the invalid wakes, as she invariably does, with a start.

The patient's bed should never be sat upon nor held. Such remarks may seem uncalled for, but very little experience in a sick room will convince anyone that they are not. Hurried visits are much to be discouraged. An invalid would often prefer not to see her greatest friend than to feel that the visit is such a gasp; no pleasant talk can be heard, no refreshing sight of each other enjoyed.

The nurse must take it upon herself to turn away visitors. If it is difficult and disagreeable to her to do it, she must remember that it is far more difficult and unpleasant for the patient herself, who probably would not have the courage to tell her friends to go, though she will be very thankful if her nurse does.

Noises

All movements in the sick room should be quiet. I do not mean in the matter of banging doors and creaking footsteps, for people who are so noisy have no business in a sick room.

Nurses or visitors to a sick room should be quiet and steady in all their movements; they should not start up from their seat, however hurriedly they may be required; the rustle of clothes, the dropping of things off a lap, and the search for them afterwards, make the invalid regret that she caused such disturbance.

When evening draws on, the nurse should see that she has all the things in readiness that her patient can possibly require. She should not only have the food and medicines which are to be taken during the night, but she should see that the kettle is full, that she has matches, wood, and coal, a spare candle or two, plenty of water, and that materials for making poultices are at hand. It is a common experience how often illness takes a turn or a new form in the night; and the nurse should be provided with all ordinary remedies so as to be able to lose no time in applying them. Nothing should have to be sent for late. There should be no bustle or noise in the sick room. As night approaches the room should become gradually still. The fire must be arranged early, for no noise is more exasperating than the scraping up of cinders, or the raking out of coals. In short, the room should be so gently hushed that the patient should feel able to drop off to sleep at any moment, and not lose her one chance of rest, perhaps, from the sense that there is something disturbing still to be done. A night nurse should sit near the fire so as to keep her hands warm, as much for her patient's sake as her own. The touch of a cold hand will rouse a person thoroughly; and though the patient may be awake, the nurse's object is to soothe her off to sleep as soon as may be. A pair of housemaid's gloves ought to lie by the coals, which can then be put on the fire without risk of disturbing the patient or of soiling the nurse's hands.

Feeding

If food has to be given at night, the heating of it or other preparation should, if possible, take place in the next room to the patient's. If this cannot be, the nurse should be very quiet about it, and, when prepared, she should not offer it to her patient, except in cases of excessive weakness, unless she is quite sure that her patient is really awake.

It is one of the vagaries of illness that a sick person, who has been unable to sleep all night, will drop off the moment after she has asked for her meal. There would seem to be something in the knowledge that something is being actually prepared for their relief, which rests the mind and makes the sufferer go to sleep. When this is the case, however troublesome it may be, the nurse must make up her mind to let the food remain untouched, and to prepare fresh the next time it is asked for. The food should be given in a regular, monotonous way, so that the patient is as little roused as possible.

A spirit lamp is invaluable for heating food or boiling water; it should be placed on a marble stand or table, if possible, as the spirit is constantly upset, and though the flame is soon extinguished and not very harmful, the flame rouses and alarms the invalid.

If the patient likes being read to at night, the reader's voice must be clear and loud enough for each word to be heard without effort. If the patient should fall asleep while the reading is going on, the reader must on no account stop, but must go on reading for some time in the same tone, and then gradually allow her voice to die away.

When an illness has gone on for some time the sick person becomes very weary of the things which surround her. She has looked at all the pictures which hang on the walls, and at the patterns which ornament or disfigure the paper, till she can bear them no longer. The nurse cannot, of course, alter all these things, but she can give a certain change to the aspect of the room. A looking-glass so placed that it can reflect the sky and trees, or, if the sufferer is in London, some portion of the street, will be a refreshment to the eyes which have for long not pierced beyond the narrow boundary of the sick room.

Plants and flowers should be placed so as to show their best shape and colour to the invalid's eye, and in such a position as to be seen by her easily without any exertion. Many people are worried by the sight of a thing placed crookedly, and a nervous patient will dread the appearance of anything placed near the edge of the table. She will go through in imagination the crash which will follow if the book or vase is swept down by a passer-by.

When a message has to be given or a note written, the nurse or friend should endeavour to carry out the sick person's wishes as quickly as possible. The most patient of invalids cannot overcome a feeling of disappointment if told that what they have begged may be done at once, has been put off, or will be done in good time. In the dulness of an invalid's life small trifles become important; and although the note which had to be sent may have been of no great moment, the invalid has probably been counting on the answer, and may very likely another time make an effort to write herself rather than be kept in suspense.

Dressing

When the patient can be dressed and put on a sofa, the nurse must gather the patient's sleeves up in her hand, so that the arm may pass in without difficulty.

All clothes should be warmed before being put on, and all should be put on straight, not dragged straight afterwards. The first getting up is made miserable to the convalescent by her clothes; every movement rucks them up, and she is not yet strong enough to stand up and give them a shake down.

The nurse must always be ready to pull down the patient's clothes, and she must begin with the flannel, or whatever garment the patient wears next her skin, and work outwards, not, as is almost invariably done, begin by the petticoat, and so leave off where she should have begun. Care must be taken not to pull the clothes down too tight, or they will drag at the throat, which is most uncomfortable.

I have tried in the foregoing pages to note down some of the ordinary duties of a nurse; I have tried to point out how many little details there are in the every-day work of the sick room which can hardly be called nursing, and yet which, if badly performed or neglected, materially affect the patient's comfort, perhaps even retard her recovery.

Cooking

I now wish to add a few words about various remedies and the ways of making use of them in various forms of illness. I am quite aware that I must leave much unsaid that ought to be said, but I wish only to give my own experience, and to tell of remedies that I have found useful, or useless, in such cases of illness as I have had the opportunity of watching. As all nurses should know something of cooking, and be ready to prepare food for their patient, I will begin with the invalid's food. The nurse must of course see all the food before it is given to her patient, even when she does not give it herself. Beef-tea often comes from the kitchen with a fair coating of grease. The nurse can remove this by floating little bits of whitey-brown paper on the surface, which will blot up the grease in a very few seconds. As the cup will probably smell greasy and look messy, the nurse should pour the hot beef-tea into a clean hot cup which she should have ready. If the beef-tea should be thick, the nurse should strain it through a piece of muslin which she has wetted in cold water. After doing this, she will have to warm up the beef-tea on her spirit lamp.

Food

One or two extra cups, glasses, and spoons, a bowl, and clean cloth should always be at hand. The best feeding cups are of glass, which are easily cleaned with a baby's bottle brush. A certain variety may be made in beef-tea, of which patients are certain to weary, by mixing veal with the beef.

The best beef-tea is made of two or three pounds of freshly killed beefsteak, with an equal quantity of veal. The meat must be cut up into dice, all fat and skin being removed, and placed in a jar with a little salt, and enough water to cover the meat. This jar, which must have either a lid or a thick cloth tied over the top, is then placed in a saucepan of water on the fire and left to stew. In three hours a cup of strong beef-tea is procured; but it is better to let the whole quantity be made and allowed to get cold; the fat can then be cleared off, and the beef-tea, which is then jelly, can be warmed as it is required. If a large quantity is made at once, it must be well boiled up every day or it will turn sour. The nurse and patient must remember that the strongest beef-tea does not produce a stiff jelly. Unless a little of the shin of beef or knuckle of veal is put in, a jelly of any consistency cannot be got. This must be done if the invalid likes sometimes to have jelly instead of soup, and the beef-tea must be well reduced or the jelly will be insipid.

Reducing simply means letting the beef-tea boil away; you reduce the quantity but not the quality. This explanation seems superfluous, but I have known a good nurse "reduce" beef-tea by adding water to it. The nurse must remember that when gravy or broth is much reduced it does not require salt. A patient suffering from soreness of the mouth will often complain that too much salt has been put in the beef-tea, and will be silenced by the answer that there is none. If the patient is suffering in this way, her food must not be much reduced, for the increased strength produces increased saltness. If the invalid has to be fed, the meat must be cut up most carefully, the patient's tastes being scrupulously observed. The mouthfuls given must be of medium size; people often imagine that little scraps will tempt a patient, but the fact is that very tiny mouthfuls weary the patient of her food long before she has eaten all she should. The nurse must never touch the patient's food with her hands, and must have perfectly clean hands before she begins to feed the invalid; she should never blow anything that is hot.

When helping the patient to eat or drink, the nurse should support the head with her hand and tilt the cup or glass gently, but sufficiently. It is most aggravating to be able only to sip when you want a refreshing draught.

Beef-tea may be thickened with Groult's tapioca, sufficient being put in to make the soup of a pleasant consistency; the tapioca must be stirred in while the soup is boiling. Arrowroot can be put in soup in the same way, and is useful when the bowels are relaxed. Macaroni boiled in gravy is nourishing, and can be taken with meat when vegetables are either not allowed or not liked. The macaroni must be well stirred while cooking in the gravy, or it will not be soft, although it may have been cooking a long time.

If vegetables are taken, they should be removed from the room at once, as any green vegetables have an unpleasant smell.

Remedies

In cases of nausea, cold food will be found far more palatable than hot; cold quenelles or cold fowls, boiled or roast, with thick cold white sauce or a beef-tea jelly, can be taken when any hot food would create disgust. In cases of violent sickness, Brand's essence of beef or strong meat jelly can be taken in very small quantities alternately with lumps of ice. Whey is also very useful in sickness, as it can be retained when nothing else can. Unappetising as it looks, people suffering from deadly sickness will keep it down, and it is very nourishing.

For any affection of the bladder the patient will frequently be ordered a milk diet.

The nurse must see the milkman herself and impress on him the importance of sweet fresh milk from one cow being always brought. When brought she must empty the milk into a flat pan, such as is used for rising cream in a dairy; this pan must be placed in a cool place, and must be well scalded each time it is emptied.

The nurse must skim the milk carefully herself, for in such cases the patient must have no cream. The tumbler of milk must be stood in some warm water before it is given to the patient, so that the milk may be of the warmth of new milk. This milk cure is much used and is most valuable, but the nurse must remember that a milk diet is not heating, and that the patient must be kept warm, and great care taken that she should never have a chill while she is undergoing it. The illness itself will conduce to chilliness, and the lowness of diet makes it imperative that the patient should be warmly covered, and that the room be kept of an even temperature.

Air and water cushions are of great use to those who have been long in a sick bed. Water cushions are more comfortable and healthier, but they are colder, than air. Each should have flannel and linen cases. A water cushion should be filled with warm water, not hot, but decidedly warm; otherwise it is a most chilling thing. The same rule applies to a water bed. The water in a water bed should be replenished every three weeks; care must be taken to fill both bed and cushions *too* full of air and water. They can easily be reduced when the patient is on them, but cannot be filled, and no one but the patient can tell the exact fulness which is comfortable.

Enemas are constantly given by nurses, but they may be made such a torment to the sufferer that simple as the process is I will write as if the use of them were unknown. When the water is of the right temperature and mixed with the soap, oil, arrowroot, or whatever may have been ordered, the nurse should fill the enema and then empty it once or twice; she should then hold the pipe and tube under the water, while with her hand she firmly squeezes every particle of air out of the enema. She must then withdraw the pressure and let the enema fill gently, touching the bulb to feel that it is well filled, and keeping both tubes and the pipe under water. When the pipe is oiled and placed, the nurse must squeeze the enema steadily, always keeping the other end of the tube under water, so that as the enema is emptied it fills. In this way the patient will have received no wind.

If the patient has suffered much from severe straining, hot flannels applied to the part will be found comforting. At first the flannels must not be applied very hot, as the skin is very tender, but by degrees they may be as hot as the nurse can make them.

When there is illness, whatever the time of year, the nurse should always be allowed easy access to a fire. Hot water, hot flannels, and poultices may be required suddenly in almost every case, and the relief they give is in proportion as they can be applied quickly. A severe headache is often lessened, if not removed, by putting the hands and feet into very hot water. It is a great relief to have the head sponged with almost boiling water; a mustard leaf at the back of the neck is of use in cases of severe nervous headache. When the patient is weary and restless, it will be found soothing to sponge her back and limbs with hot water. Sleep may even be induced, and the nurse can go on sponging while the patient is dozing, never relaxing in the monotonous movement; but she must in such a case have a second person at hand to renew the hot water. If an invalid complains of sudden violent pain in the back or side, the nurse should at once apply poultices and hot fomentations even before the doctor comes. Such pain often means the beginning of internal inflammation, and the hot applications must be used without delay.

The water in which flannels are wrung out for fomenting must be so hot that the nurse cannot bear to put her hands in it; she should, therefore, always have two good sticks about fourteen or eighteen inches long, and several pieces of flannel with hems at each end, into which the sticks can easily pass. The flannels are dipped into water, the nurse holding the sticks, and when the flannel is well soaked she wrings it round the sticks, twisting each way till it is dry enough to apply, when the sticks are quickly slipped out. In this way the flannels are very hot, thoroughly wrung out, and the nurse is not hurt.

Linseed poultices are generally made too hard and dry, and consequently soon become cold and heavy. The nurse should have a basin near

the fire into which she puts her linseed, pouring on it boiling water and stirring with a wooden spoon till it is as smooth as cream. The piece of muslin
(which is better not quite new) must be at hand, and the linseed poured into
it, and the ends turned up over the poultice. A flannel should be laid over
the poultice, and sometimes oil silk is used over the flannel, but this makes
the poultice heavier. When the poultice is removed, the nurse should wipe,
or rather dab, the part with a warm towel, and place a piece of medicated
wool where the poultice has been.

 Medicated wool, as it is called, is most valuable in cases of rheumatism; it must always be placed near the fire before it is used. When it is
warm, it will puff out to double its original size; care must therefore be taken
not to put it too close to the fire, or it will be in flames in a second. If lini-
ments are to be used warm, the best way is to place the bottle in hot water.
The heating of the liniment causes the stopper to rise, and the bottle is easily upset and its contents lighted if it has been placed by the fire, causing a
most alarming aspect of conflagration, although the flame is soon extinguished. In placing the bottle in hot water the label will often come off;
different coloured threads should therefore be tied around the necks of the
bottles so that the nurse should not make any mistake as to what she uses.
Wool sprinkled with laudanum is comforting in cases of acute rheumatism.

 Hot bran, or salt bags, give great relief. The bags should be made of
flannel and shaped according to the part they are to cover. The bag should
not be filled too full. If salt is used it can be heated in the kitchen oven, as it
retains the heat. If bran, it must be warmed in a saucepan on a fire in a
neighbouring room, as it becomes cold very quickly. While heating the bran
the nurse must stir it, and then pour it carefully into the bag, watching that
no spark has fallen in. This must be done with the most anxious care, for a
tiny spark may easily escape observation, and the bran may be put into the
bag with apparently no more smoke than is caused by the heat. Yet after
some time the patient finds that her poultice becomes hotter and hotter,
and finally discovers that her clothes are smoking, and that they are slowly
burning away. In rheumatism of the joints the part affected must be covered
with wool, and the wool covered with oil silk. The wool must be constantly
renewed, and when taken away it will generally be found to be wringing wet
with cold perspiration. Rheumatism often causes intense irritation of the
skin, although no eruption or even redness is visible. Boracic acid melted in
water will often relieve this, although ointments and soaps have been tried
in vain. Most illnesses affect with less or greater importance the water that
the patient passes; the nurse should, therefore, have a clean covered utensil
in which to keep it, and should never omit to show it to the doctor.

 When strapping is required the nurse should be particularly careful only to moisten the ends of the plaster. If, as is often thoughtlessly done, the whole plaster is wetted, it had better be thrown away, as it will do more harm than good. The greatest care should be taken that the lint, or whatever is next the inflamed part, should protect it well from the plaster. The plaster must be pressed on gently, though firmly, as the surrounding parts of an inflamed spot are sure to be tender. If there should be any tendency to soreness of skin, the tender part should be washed with brandy and water, so that the skin may harden; it should always be most carefully dried. If soreness should actually exist, or there be anything in the shape of a bed sore, great comfort will be derived by a small pad being used. This is merely a bolster of wool covered with linen or washing silk, the ends of which are sewn together, so that it resembles a giant corn plaster. The hole must be the size of the sore, the bolster resting only on healthy skin. It is kept in its place by straps of plaster placed crossways, the ends of which are warmed so that they adhere to the skin. This kind of pad is extremely useful in the case of boils.

When bandages are required they should be made of very tightly rolled stuff. Common towels, if they are smooth, may often be used. They must be rolled tightly and smoothly, and pinned, so that when they are required they are fit for use. The nurse should hold the roll of linen in her left hand, the end which she has undone being in her right, so that as she unrolls she tightens. She must fasten her bandage, if a large one, with safety pins (the American are the best); if a small one, it will be wound round and across till the limb or joint is well strapped, and can then be sewn.

In cases of advanced cancer, the attendant must remember that the bones are apt to become very brittle. In moving such sufferers the greatest tenderness must be observed. Even with great care a limb will often be broken; and although, where disease has conquered the body so completely, the pain of a fractured limb is small, still the inconvenience and discomfort of a broken limb add to the miseries of the already tormented life.

In moving sufferers the nurse should be very careful to have the night dress smooth under her arm. A tiny fold of linen may seem perfectly harmless; but if the patient's back is examined after such a tiny fold has been pressed in by the nurse's arm it will be found to be red and indented; the tenderness of the flesh in illness, and the especial sensitiveness in particular cases, cannot be overestimated.

Nerves

When there is great nervous excitement, the nurse may be able to soothe her patient by holding her hand and talking to her quietly without apparent

motive or effort, but keeping her object in view, and becoming gradually
silent if she sees that her patient is not becoming soothed.

Nervous people often awake with a sudden start, feeling as if they
had been struck violently. It is long before they can become calm, and the
startings recur with more or less violence each time they drop asleep. A good
remedy for this, if it can be taken, is a breakfast cup of milk in which a table-
spoonful of brandy is stirred. This should be taken before the patient settles
herself to sleep, and after it has been continued a few nights, the chances are
that the nervous startings will have ceased.

Another painful form of nervousness is a convulsive twitch, which
patients suffering from nervous exhaustion will often give when wide awake,
and which produces a sort of shudder and horror. The nurse may calm
much of this nervous condition by gently rubbing the limbs. Rubbing, if
skilfully done, will often compose the sufferer and induce sleep. All such
rubbings must be done deliberately and with certainty. There must be no
niggling. The patient must know exactly when and where the nurse's hand
will come; she must not rub with jerks and starts, but slowly and smoothly
pass the hand up and down. Rubbing is a real art, and, in many cases, a professional rubber will be found to give relief when all other remedies have
failed; but all nurses should be able to rub, and to use their fingers, softly
and tenderly manipulating the patient. A severe neuralgic headache may be
driven away by the slow touch of sympathetic fingers.

The quiet and calm which should make the foundation of a sick-
room life are nowhere more necessary than when the patient becomes
hysterical.

It is not easy, even with the best intentions, for a nurse to remain
perfectly calm with an hysterical patient, and in the effort to do so she often
affects either an unnatural gravity or cheerfulness, both of which increase
the attack. The nurse should never speak to a person in hysterics, nor look
at her. What has to be done in the way of giving salts, cold water, sal vola-
tile, &c., should be done as silently and as naturally as possible. The few
words that may have to be said, must be as few and as commonplace as possible. There must be no gaiety and no reproof.

If the nurse feels that there is any danger of her becoming upset
herself, she should at once leave the room. A second away, a whiff of salts,
will steady her nerves; but if she gives way in the least, her patient's attack
will be much more prolonged; and as there is little that can really be done,
it will be better that the nurse should remain out of the room. This applies
especially to amateur nurses; trained nurses are not liable to be easily affected.

In cases of sore throat, especially if there be any tendency to diph-
theria, the nurse must be particularly watchful. The doctor will probably

paint the throat with a few drops of muriate of iron mixed with water; but the nurse must not wait for the doctor's visit; she must look down the patient's throat every hour, and if there is the least sign of the fatal white film forming, she must remove it at once with the throat-brush. After having used the brush, she must wash it with the greatest care. The film which has been removed from the throat will stick firmly on to the hairs of the brush, and it must be completely cleared away before the brush is finally rinsed out. Lumps of ice should be given frequently; in such a case the ice acts as a tonic on the throat, and it is an immense boon to the sufferer, whose throat, when in that condition, is most painful.

In cases of severe retching, ice will again be found most useful, and all food should be iced. A lump of ice placed on the nape of the neck will stop the severe straining of sickness. In such cases, when the patient feels inclined to retch, the nurse may stop it by giving her iced water, in which some ozonised water has been mixed, to wash her mouth out with.

Sickness induces great thirst, and, as drinking anything will again produce sickness, the nurse must moisten her patient's lips and even her tongue with lemon juice and water. A patient suffering from nausea should not be allowed to see or smell food, and all handkerchiefs or towels used should be clean. Even when the actual sickness has stopped, it may be brought on again by the sight or smell of anything.

Conclusion

If the patient should die, the nurse must remember that though her help may still be needed her place is not by the death-bed unless it is requested. She should make her presence felt as little as possible. If she has done her work well in all ways she will find that all turn to her; but she should be perfectly quiet, and forbear to make any remarks or suggestions. Unless she sees that the relations are unwilling to do so, she should make no attempt to close the eyes of the dead nor to tie up the chin.

If all such last duties *are* left to her, she must make her preparations as silently and unobtrusively as possible.

These remarks may seem uncalled for, but experience has taught me that not only the trained but the amateur nurse requires to be reminded that in the presence of death all bustle is unseemly.

To those who have watched and suffered with the sufferer there is nothing but rest at first in the knowledge that death has come, but the feeling of peace is destroyed by the terrible and unreal garb we are in the habit of using for our dead. If instead of the pinked-out band of hard white linen a soft silk handkerchief were placed round the head – if the warm coloured dressing-gown which has been associated with the living might clothe the dead, the last hour would not leave on us the painful impression that it does.

When the requisite washing has been tenderly done, and the fresh white clothes have been put on, the head, bound up by a silk handkerchief, should be laid on a low pillow, not put perfectly flat; the covering, whatever is wished, should be laid over the body, and then the relations, if they have remained away, return, not indeed to find all that they loved, but not to be shocked by a terrible picture which will haunt them long and destroy the memory of what they held most dear.

[Agnostic Women]

IN A KINDLY but condemnatory article in a recent *Nineteenth Century*, Mrs. Lathbury pronounces the doom of all women who call themselves Agnostics.[1] From the moment they discover that there are things beyond their credence and that they cannot therefore belong to any known sect, they shut the door on hope, love, work except of the driest and most unsatisfying kind. Mrs. Lathbury speaks as one having authority and therefore I, a woman—though I know no such Pariahs—feel bound to discover who they are and above all *why* they are. She does not at all wish women to adhere slavishly to a faith because they have been educated in it. Freedom of thought she considers as necessary to woman as to man, and she desires that they should have the courage of their opinions, but she considers that these women who become Agnostics are not forced to that conclusion by their own reason, but because they have subjugated themselves to the intellect of some man and become Agnostics from reverence, love, admiration, whatever the feeling may be which they have for an Agnostic.

Men, however, are not pleased by this devotion. We are told in the first paragraph that men, though themselves Agnostics, "prefer to hope that women will be slow to drive logic to its ultimate end, that they will [still] cling with womanly inconsistency to all that is refining and soothing in the old creeds." This assumption we must let pass. Who can fathom the depth of a man's heart? We certainly cannot. While desiring that his son should be a free thinker, may he not for some occult purpose wish his daughter to remain a papist? Women are said to be complex creatures, but what can be said of men, at least of Agnostic men? To return, however, to these devoted women; to what class and age do they belong? Not, as we might have guessed, to the young and enthusiastic. These have lawn tennis and such diversions and do not trouble their heads with creeds. Not the wives and mothers either for they are cumbered with much serving and cannot pause in their daily work to reconsider their belief[s]. The Agnostic woman is found in the vast army of those who, having no near ties or home duties to bind them, are free to choose their own lives, to follow their own yearnings, and these choose, not from logic, not from conviction, but from abstract reverence for some leader, to become Agnostics, and in doing so give up all that would make life worth having.

Are there indeed such women and is such their fate? It is difficult, without much more proof than could ever be obtained, for us to believe that there are numbers of women who, . . . being blinded by the personal influence of one particular man, still give up what has been a part of their lives and what is still perhaps a part of the lives of those they hold most dear for the sake of being the disciples of an unwilling master.

We would rather think that women who give up the faith in which they have been educated do so from a feeling that it no longer satisfies them. They cannot with truth any longer profess belief in their old creed. They can find no new one which fills up the gap, and therefore they are content to confess not their belief but their ignorance. Whether it is to be deplored that women should ever waver from the creed in which they have been brought up is another matter and admits of too much argument for me to venture into it; but I doubt if the question arose, as I believe it has occasionally arisen, of a protestant girl being educated from infancy among aliens and professing their creed, whether the Christian relations whatever their sect would not be considered justified if they sought, as soon as they were in a position to do so, to use every means in their power to turn the girl from the Jewish, Musselman, or whatever other faith she had till then held and believed in to that which they professed. The reasons which cause women to become Agnostics are no doubt as various as those which cause them to become wives, and sometimes as frivolous as those which make them one year consent to be walking balloons, the next to be bound like a bundle of sticks. Assuming that there are a number of female Agnostics and that they would naturally nurse, teach, or devote their lives to the care of the poor, we have to discover why these channels of usefulness are shut out from them because they profess no definite creed.

We believe that those who have experience in nursing among sick and poor will say that doctrine is out of place in the sick room; but Mrs. Lathbury thinks that no Agnostic will enter a sick room as a nurse. There can be no incentive to help those suffering here if we are not certain of their fate hereafter. Is there then no significance in the words, "Whatsoever thine hand findeth to do, do it with all thy might, for the night cometh in which no man can work"?[2] Truly the night cometh, for all, and whether as some believe the night is a prelude to the glorious day of Heaven or the deepest night of Hell (for these beliefs are obviously inseparable) or whether annihilation or transmigration be our doom, we have still our day on earth. It is that day in which we have to work with all our might, whatsoever our hand findeth to do, or night will overtake us while it is yet day, the night of deep est death, of sloth, of hardness of heart, of wasted opportunity. We think no woman who has the charity and the power to become a sick nurse will waver because she cannot assure herself that those whom she has helped here will have a bright hereafter; nor can we see how she has unfitted herself for such work. In struggling with physical pain the mind is seldom clear enough to enable the most inquiring soul to question the problems she could [resolve?] in health. The devout Christian needs no assurance from without. Did his creed fail him when he stood in most need of it, would the assurances of his nurse avail? If the sufferer be one whose life has been so dark that the altruistic nurse is compelled to believe that the gates of Hell are opening for him, will she, while tenderly soothing his bodily agony, torture him with a description of the terrors which will soon encompass him, the joys which he may never taste, thinking that in doing so an expression of sorrow for his past sins may be wrested from him and that it will avail to change those terrors into joys, that soul which loved darkness into one which loves light? Can such nurses, if such there be for we have not known them, be chosen for the care of their patients?

Bunyan we know was no Agnostic. His faith was a living thing. Heaven and Hell were to him vivid realities. He was profoundly convinced that the unregenerate would be burnt with the fire that never quencheth, stung by the worm that dieth not. Yet he says emphatically, "I am no admirer of death bed repentance for I think verily it is seldom good for anything."[3]

We believe that protestants sometimes reproach the white capped *soeur de charité* for her zeal in proselytizing even in the sick room; but on all sides it is agreed that she is a skilful, tender nurse; yet if she thinks at all of the faith of her patient, it is with a shudder, and the praise which is most often bestowed on her is that she does not speak of her creed. Yet an Agnostic is utterly condemned because she cannot speak of *hers*. Among those who have been prominent leaders of nurses and nursing we can remember no outward profession of faith being given or required.

Laborare est orare[4] is a hackneyed motto for nursing institutions. If it means anything it means that we, having chosen the work of nursing, give to it the best that we have—our lives. We are not thinking that we shall gain a glorious immortality, that we shall be crowned as saints because we have helped our fellow creatures, but they are our work. We are bound to these sufferers by the tie of sisterhood and while life lasts we will help, soothe, and, if we can, love them. Pity has no creed, suffering no limits. And shall we, who are not helpers but sufferers, refuse to be helped in our turn by those who differ from us in doctrine but who are one in heart?

Philanthropy would seem to be governed by much the same spirit

as nursing, and we do not think the differences of creed in those who have
really the welfare of the poor at heart affect their success. Mrs. Lathbury
thinks that Agnosticism may cause the poor to leave off drink and take [to]
coffee houses and reading rooms instead of the public house; but though
they may thus be induced to lead orderly and moral lives, what gain will
there be since they will have no certain assurance of a future life? We doubt
if there exists an Agnostic man or woman who looks forward to their agency
helping to produce such an Utopia. It is difficult to understand how the
pressure of a few individuals can effect such a startling change, one which
years of constant endeavour on the part of many noble men and women of
all creeds and all sects have not been able to effect. Were any creed to claim
such a result justly, we should feel tempted to say, "Is it not written, 'by their
fruits ye shall know them'?"5 And it would be difficult to believe that such
fruits could be gathered from any but the tree of life.

But putting aside such dreams we are reluctant to believe that there
is to charity a limited creed. Kindness, sympathy, and help are given by
women of all sects and denominations to the poor of all sects and denominations. The evangelical lady with her tract on the scarlet woman does not
insist (though she ought if consistent) that the rosary must be burnt before
she can heat the beef tea. Nor does the high church young lady, though her
zeal may sometimes out run her knowledge, require the little heathen infant
to be baptized before she tends its dying mother. Why then should the Agnostic find her help rejected as useless because she cannot profess any given
creed? She will, no more than the others, force her opinions on those whom
she is helping and the very negativeness of her position may possibly help
her to sympathise with the various and widely divergent characters with
whom she has to deal.

With regard to the other career chosen by women, that of teaching,
there can surely arise no difficulty. An orthodox father or mother would
always, we should think, inquire well into the creed of the person to whose
care they entrusted their child. No one anxious for a Parisian accent would
entrust the teaching of French to a native of Yorkshire. No one desirous that
their child should be brought up repeating the Athanasian creed would en-
gage a governess who was Turk, Heretic, or Infidel. Such people as are themselves Agnostics will desire such teachers for their children and no others.
The supply will cease if there be no demand, and if there are no Agnostic
parents, we may be pretty sure there will be no such teachers.

Mrs. Lathbury deplores the home influence or rather want of influence of the female Agnostic. She therefore, we suppose, concedes that there
may be a certain number of wives and mothers who have, to quote her
words, "driven logic to its ultimate conclusion." Any schism in a household

is to be deplored, and if we are to suppose that any woman has given up the faith of her husband for any other or, as in an Agnostic's case for no other, we may imagine discord and difficulty arising, but if it should be greater in the last mentioned case than in any other, we cannot discover.

The prayers and devoutness of life of a mother or sister have, we fear, seldom turned a man from the error of his ways. But we can believe that a long and patient continuance in well doing when joined to intense love and sympathy may cause a father or son to pause in their career of indulgence or vice and gradually make their lives more in accordance with the lives of those who love them in spite of their sins. Who would deny that in every creed in every sect there are such mothers, wives, and sisters. Because some cannot truthfully assure the sinner that the flames of Hell will devour him or the glories of Heaven surround him according as he continue in sin or repent, have they no influence to restrain and purify?

If the sinner be reformed through such vivid word painting, can we believe the reformation will be more sincere, more lasting than if he, by slow conviction and hard struggles, step by step overcame the enemy, incited to his fight by no thought of future advantage, no fear of future torture but from the conviction slowly dawning on him that he had higher instincts and better work to do than he had before been conscious of? Judgment comes to us while we live. The distant flames of Hell can surely not cause the agony which remorse brings on us. The sorrow we have caused those who love us best, the misused opportunities of our lives, the wasted energies line up against us and torture us more than the words of the preacher.

Mrs. Lathbury states that the Agnostic rate payer will refuse to pay her rates. She may indeed do so. We fear that the rates would fare badly were they optional, and though as a rule the man is supposed to be the ratepayer as his misdeeds are not in our province we will concede sorrowfully that women have a strong disinclination to pay rates and taxes. But is this reluctance confined to Agnostics? We fear not, and at first we have some wonder as to why they should be singled out for this reproach, but we find it is only the "pauper lunatic" rate which they decline to pay, for according to Agnostics such unfortunates should be put an end to, not supported.

This view of Agnosticism is completely new to us, and we think Mrs. Lathbury can hardly have remembered it when further on she says, as a plea against Agnosticism, that we cannot expect it "to be always confined to really conscientious people." A really conscientious citizen [must ever?], while the law remains in force, consent to pay his taxes. That all Agnostics are really conscientious is a statement which we can have no means of verifying, but granting that they are, we must not accuse them of failing in their legal obligations. Whether it be a benefit to themselves or to others that

pauper lunatics should be allowed to have their miserable existences prolonged though they cannot be improved, we would not venture to say. No
one who has witnessed physical or mental suffering in its hopeless stage can,
we think, repress the longing that it may soon be ended. Such feelings are
surely not only confined to Agnostics. Who has not heard the devout
mother express her hope that the Lord will soon remove her idiot child?
Who has not heard the pious ejaculation that "It was a happy release"? The
law does not allow of any undue termination of even the most terrible and
hopeless diseases, and we are bound to obey the law, but do we never evade
it and see it evaded with thankfulness? If we go into a hospital for painful
and incurable diseases, do we not bless the drugs which make the unfortunate patient pass from one heavy sleep to another, a short interval of pain
being all that can be called life intervening? These drugs no doubt in many
cases shorten the life as well as the sufferings, but would we have them with-
held? The materialism which Mrs. Lathbury apparently reproaches the Agnostic with should tend to prolong life, and to beautify it. The stronghold of
the Christian is the Christian life in its highest type. Purity of life, sincerity
of action, obedience to law, love of our fellow creatures, all those qualities
which ennoble life are the stronghold of the Agnostic. How far Christians
and Agnostics fall short of their ideal we may not inquire. But we would
venture to suggest that those who have not the power to follow the reason-
ing of Christianity should not therefore be denied all spiritual life.

Women are not all blind followers of men. They have power to
think as well, and they will not weaken their power of helping and loving by
fearlessly owning their ignorance when they should be convinced of it. Mrs.
Lathbury thinks that when women have become Agnostics, men, out of
pity for the way in which they have been cut off from all their natural occupations, will then open to them all professions. This is hardly such an
Utopia as Agnosticism opens to the poorer classes, still to many women it
would be Utopia. But we fear that again such dreams are vain. Will com-
petitive examinations cease? Will women surmount all these obstacles of
their sex which have hitherto happily restrained them? And, should Agnosticism place women in the Cabinet and in the houses of the stock exchange,
what will it mean for men? Will their chivalry have no reward? We can see
no hope for them when this millenium for women arrives.

We have tried feebly enough to show that, while women wish to
work and have power to help others, no difference of creed should cause
their help to be rejected. We now ask that the motives of women should be
trusted, and we think we do not ask too much. Women do not stand on the
same ground as men with regard to work, though we are far from allowing
that our work is lower or less important than theirs, but we ought and do

claim the same equality of morals. We will not concede that when a man chooses or rejects a faith from conviction, a woman does so from a desire to please. In moral courage the lives of women afford brilliant examples. They have perhaps seldom as much at stake as men, and therefore to be courageous is not so difficult, but in the acceptance or rejection of a creed let the woman be judged as the man. In this, if in this alone, man and woman have equal rights and, while crediting men with courage and sincerity, do not let us deny these qualities to each other.

[The Servant Question]

A NUMBER OF ARTICLES have appeared lately dealing with the life of domestic servants and of the difficulties which beset their lives and those of their employers from the present system.[1] We are told that the life of a servant is so subservient,[2] her duties performed under the present rules of service are so much disliked that mothers would prefer to send their daughters into factories than to service, and that the life of a factory girl is to be preferred to that of a domestic servant. It is difficult to reconcile this statement with the undoubted fact that each day shows us papers [with] columns of advertisements from servants seeking places. A still stronger proof, which is constantly brought before us, [is] when we are asked by those who must know best what domestic service is, having been themselves servants, to get places for their children. That our former servant should come with sister or child to claim the help of her old mistress in the placing of them, must be a frequent and a pleasant experience to us all, and it affords, we conceive, a conclusive proof that all mothers do not consider the factory a better field of service than the home.

The word "servant" seems to constitute the degradation, and yet to serve is no bad office, and the service which is as valuable and useful as that of our domestic servant should be no degradation. The word "domestic" is, when we come to think of it, the word in which the sting, if there be a sting, lies for no one would cast a slur on the word[s] "public servant." Pity seems to be required for our cook or parlour maid but none for their brothers, the soldiers and sailors whose service, however worse paid, worse fed, and with stricter rules, is dignified by the word[s] "public servant."

While we are to compassionate our domestic servants for their lives of menial duties, we are on all sides ourselves undertaking far harder work. In most families now there is one sister who is a hospital nurse. She is certainly neither to be pitied nor applauded for having chosen her very arduous life. She wished to serve and found it easier to do so under strict rules and with clearly defined duties than to fulfil the ordinary and manifold duties of home life which we each of us have at our hand[s] and which, conflicting as they often are, are less easily to be carried out than if they could be marked for us with a chalk on a black board to be sponged out when

248

completed. The duties of a hospital nurse are, however, much harder, more anxious, and less varied than those of the ordinary domestic servant. The rules under which a nurse must live are strict, the duties required of her are the most menial, and her salary is that of a cook in a small household.

It is not, therefore, for their work that we must pity our servants, but we are told it is for their dependence, their . . . dullness, their absence from their homes. These are the things which they feel and which make service so detested. The question of dependence is too large a one to be dealt with, but a woman who earns her bread in an honourable calling can hardly be considered as dependent in any sense but the one in which we happily all share, that we cannot do without our fellow creatures. In the varied life which falls to a servant we wonder that dullness can find a place. It is true in small households leave for constant outings cannot be given, but if this be a drawback, which we doubt, it is compensated by the fellow feeling that exists between the employers and employed, and we believe that few servants are happier and [more] contented than those in very small households where the work is very constant but where it is shared by the mistress and her children.

A far more serious charge than that of dullness is brought against our present system of domestic service in the statement that homes and refuges are chiefly filled with girls from the servant class. Even this, we think, may prove a less grave indictment against the position of a servant than it at first appears. Homes and refuges are as a rule supported by ladies. It is therefore natural that the servants whom these ladies or their friends have employed should turn to them for help, and it is a testimony in favour rather than against the relation betwixt mistress and maid that the maid when in trouble should claim and should receive help from those whom she has served. The poor factory girl has too often no such friend, and if she is also without a home hides her sorrow in the workhouse.

The assumption that our servant girls would be saved from the inevitable difficulties of their lives by sleeping outside the home in which they work is strange, but to judge from the articles written on the subject, the argument in favour of the sleeping out, I gather, is said to be that the servant could then return each night to her home from which she is otherwise entirely cut off. It is unnecessary to dwell on the evils to a girl of having to walk night after night from her work. If a census were taken of the homes of London servants, we fancy that very few would be found to be within easy range of the houses in which they work. A very great proportion of young servants, such as kitchen and scullery maids, are imported from the country, to say nothing of the numberless foreign servants to be found in London. Where are these girls to spend the night? It is clear that to them to live out of their mistresses' home[s] will not mean to live in their mothers'. We must suppose that some establishment will be provided where all will be received with a competent matron at its head, but unless the matron had power over the hours of the girls and over the associates whom they might introduce, where would be their safety? If she had, where would be their freedom?

It is curious that at the moment when the "housing of the poor" is absorbing the attention of many, when block buildings even of the most approved stamp are looked at with doubt, when workhouse children are boarded out in homes rather than kept together en masse, that we should wish to oust from our own hearths those women who of all others should receive from us most care and for whose welfare we are responsible, however much we may desire to shift the responsibility onto other shoulders.

It is urged that charwomen and needlewomen do not sleep in the homes at which they work. Charwomen are as a rule married women no longer young, and they have homes to which they return at night. The position of a needlewoman is rather different from that of a servant, but she too has probably a home of her own where she does most of her work. The life of the needlewoman's apprentice is more like that of a day servant and is open to the same objections. It is needless to dwell on them; but the fact that many young girls have to walk home night after night from their work is one which all must agree in thinking a deplorable one, and we cannot calmly anticipate adding to their numbers.

If we assume that in some way this difficulty is overcome, and that our maids have all homes near their work, it would be well before we send them hence to find out the conditions of these homes. The "home" of a Londoner generally means a lodging, and in most cases an overfull lodging. The parents of our servant are probably in some business. Whatever the work may be, which they have done during the day, we may be pretty sure, however well off the mother is, that the evening is no leisure time to her. Nor does she see why her daughter should not help her in the mending, washing, etc. in which she is engaged. There may be small brothers and sisters, and the sister will naturally put them to bed. Bedtime is at varying hours in their class, and children go to bed just when it is handy to put them there. All these duties are not hardships, but they do not represent rest or the leisure for which servants are said to crave.

We have difficulty in realizing that servants, more than any other people, are longing for leisure. The desire for amusement, for companionship, for rest, belongs to us all, but the desire for "leave to do nothing" seems to be the boon which under different names is the property of the highest and lowest natures. The poet in his easy chair with blue curls of smoke circling round him enjoys, we suppose, in its highest expression, and the pig lying in its succulent litters in its lowest. But the greater number of us, neither poets nor pigs, chiefly desire employment and rest, and the servant, when her day of varied work and companionship is at an end, wishes, we believe, most of all for her bed. Here another disadvantage is apparent between her home and her mistress's. Although servants' rooms are not sufficiently considered in many homes, it is seldom that there is such a want of ventilation and comfort as is found in a lodging, and the chances are that the tired girl's bed is shared by her little brothers and sisters.

The out-of-door system, if we may call it so, which seems to us so full of discomfort and danger to servants, has at first sight a tempting aspect to the mistress when she thinks of herself only as a caterer. It is impossible not to feel sympathy with the writer who some weeks ago expressed the joy and relief it would be to her if each day a varied menu were set before her, and no doubt as to the success of her dinner would enter her anxious mind. There is a delightful story of a little girl who was found crying by her mother, and when asked why said, "I am thinking of how many times I shall have to wash and dress if I live to be as old as you." There is no escape we fear from the sorrow of that little girl, but washing, like "ordering" dinner, may have its good side. The restaurant system which is advocated sounds very pleasant, and though London restaurants are not supposed to have a particularly good cuisine, we may assume that from the new order a new race of cooks will spring who will not require the same reminders and hints that we are weary of giving to the present race. The nearest approach to this state of things is, we suppose, the life in a university town where the college kitchen helps the don's wife through her dinner parties. Even here, we fancy, perfection is not attained. There is a certain sameness in the dinners and . . . , good as the chefs of some colleges are, their menus are not as varied or as economical as might be desired.

Even if the dinners were . . . good enough, varied enough, and cheap enough under the new regime, yet another practical difficulty remains. What regular machinery is there which can supply the irregular calls which sickness makes on our home kitchen? Will the trained machinery which supplies our table be ever able to take the place of our friendly cook who tries first one thing, then another, sending up little dishes just when they are wanted and tries with the zeal of a friend to help us back to health? We confess that we expect, as little as we wish, to see this perfection reached. And on the maid's side, how is she to be looked after when she falls ill? The answer, "Send her to the hospital," may not be applicable, and the comforts of home and the personal attention of her mistress to which the maid has a right can hardly be hers when she is lodged away with a number of others of whom her mistress knows nothing. There must be a responsibility on the shoulders of householders. There must be a tie between mistress and maid. The more fully this responsibility is recognized [and] the closer this tie becomes, the easier it will be to bear.

The comfort of an English home has been a proverb. And this comfort is due in a great measure to our servants and the fact that they are not only working to make the home comfortable but [are] part of that comfort themselves. When we all live in towering flats, darkening our streets and choking up the little air there is to use, and turn our servants out to sleep, we shall find ourselves not in Arcadia but in a Parisian *appartement*. Those who have experience of this life tell us that household difficulties in England are simple indeed to those which beset the mistress of those delightful looking, white-capped *bonnes*. The reason is not far to seek. The *bonnes* all sleep out, not indeed under another roof but in another quarter of the big hotel which contains many families and in one part of which all the servants are congregated. When the day's work is done, the servants are locked out and go where they please. The mistress has no control. The *concierge* is bribed by gifts from the servants. Often the bribe is the food pilfered from their employers' table[s], and the servants are then free to spend their nights where they will. So long as they are back for their work and do that properly, the mistress who has shifted her responsibilities on to the shoulders of a hall porter has no right to inquire. Let us pause before we bring even a semblance of such an institution as French servant life into our English households.

The youngest and oldest of our civilizations may serve as warning and monument. America, which teaches us so much, is as much or more ahead of us as Italy is behind, but the American woman, with all her power and all her charm, will tell us that it is in vain that she looks for comfort and faithful service from the hired servant who has been so strangely misnamed her "Help."[3] We who have the old tradition in common with Italy that there is a strong bond between server and served, have made a far less good use of it, and the happy, easy relationship which exists as a rule between the heads of a household and their dependents in Italy is far too rare here; but the relation does still exist, and while our interests are united we can best help them by making the union stronger, not by separation. That the tradition is an old one need not mean that it is worn out, nor is the new always the good. As the late Master of Trinity said, "Even the youngest of us may sometimes make a mistake."

[Domestic Arrangements of the Ordinary English Home]

AMONG ALL THE CHANGES and upheavals which late years have brought about, the domestic arrangements of the ordinary English home have remained untouched. A certain undercurrent of grumbling may always be heard as to the way in which our homes are managed; but the actual methods have till now not been assailed. The most advanced of women still has kept her cook and her parlour maid, and the rule of home as applied to our own hearths has not yet come to mean the revolution of home.

A revolution is, however, at hand even in the pantry and kitchen, if we may believe the writers of various interesting articles which have appeared this year. We are told that domestic service is becoming more and more hateful to the class which has hitherto filled its ranks, that no servants are to be found. No mothers will allow their daughters to take service. The life of a factory girl is considered by them far preferable to that of a domestic servant. If this be indeed the case, we may as well trouble ourselves no more with the servant question. For if no servants can be found, the question of arranging their lives and ours with them ceases to be a matter for our concern. But in the face of the fact that numbers of young women are applying for places, we must not too hastily draft the race of domestic servants into the regions of the extinct.

Without having statistics at our command it is difficult to refute a statement as to the decline in the number of domestic servants, but judging as we most of us have to do from the homes with which we are acquainted, it would seem to us that the actual number of women servants now employed is as great as it has been at any time. It must be an unusual experience, we think, which leads the writer to conclude that most mothers would prefer the factory for [t]he[i]r daughters to domestic service. Old servants, and to many of us the name means old friend, are, we venture to think, more frequently found bringing their children up for service than for the factory—and the friends whom the old servant has made while in service are those whose help she first claims when sending her child out in the world. We are told that the word "servant" is objected to; it is degrading that one human being should serve another. This cannot of course be taken as a real state of things. Service is the condition of our being, and the mistake seems

253

to lie in the assumption that the service which a domestic servant has to perform is in itself degrading. That any useful service can be degrading if performed with zeal and efficiency we find it difficult to believe, or that household duties can ever be considered degrading.

The subservience of domestic servants must lower them, it is urged, and subservience is no doubt lowering by whatever class it is practised, but the class of servants may, we think, be considered as free from it as any other. It is a curious fact that while domestic service is held up to reprobation, we see on all sides young women entering into it in its hardest form, that of hospital nurse. The wages are not the temptation. The freedom is not, for there is none. The strictest observance of rules is one of the first duties of the hospital nurse, and while her work is both manual and mental, she is not treated as a heroine nor as a slave. She has chosen her lot of enforced work and of rigid rule, because she found that to serve was the highest expression of her nature and that to her it was easier to live under strict rule with clearly defined duties, than to live as we most of us have to do, fulfilling as best we can conflicting duties with too often the uneasy sense that the service which life has required of us has been scamped or left undone.

It is agreed on all sides that work is no misfortune, and, as we have pointed out, when the work which we choose to call menial and which in our daily life we find it convenient to relegate to others, is chosen by those whose choice is free, it is clear that domestic work carries with it no stigma. It is the lives which our servants lead, not the work they do, which then reduces them to despair. They are so horribly dull, no change, no leisure, no freedom, and above all their dependence. The woman who earns her bread in domestic service cannot be said, except in a very restricted sense, to be dependent. So long as her services are worth the wage she receives, the thought of dependence need not trouble her, and we should be much surprised if it ever did. She is dependent, as we all are, on those with whom she lives. As surely as we know anything we are convinced that dependence on each other is the most unvarying as it is the happiest law of life.

Dullness is the condition of dull people, and it would seem as hopeless to aim at destroying it in the life of a servant as in that of a Queen. A life of varied employment, of varied companionship, such as that of the ordinary domestic servant, should not be dull. And to judge from the cheerful buzz and merry talk which has risen to us from many kitchens, is the life found to be so deadly by those who are passing it? There is an element of respectable dullness in the vision of the family butler. We will at once confess that to ourselves he is intimately associated with the abstract idea of a bishop. But we believe that in the concrete the bishop and the butler both unbend and are able to enjoy a joke. But, in the case of the butler, we feel that his dullness is part of himself; for in the smaller household where we find the parlour maid, no trace of dullness exists, and it is in these smaller households where the work is hardest, where of necessity there are fewest outings, and where there are fewest chances of relaxations that we find as a rule the servants are most contented.

NOTES

Editorial Note

1. *Notes from Sick Rooms*, originally published by Smith Elder in 1883. Julia Stephen also wrote a letter to the *Pall Mall Gazette* which appeared on October 4, 1879. In it she reproaches St. George's workhouse in Fulham "for giving in to the temperance movement and cutting off the half-pint of beer" allowed inmates. See Noel Annan, *Leslie Stephen: The Godless Victorian* (New York: Random, 1984), pp. 102, 370. According to John Bicknell (letter, February 12, 1987), the Guardians of the workhouse replied on October 15, prompting Julia to write a second letter on October 17.

2. Virginia Woolf, "Leslie Stephen," *Collected Essays*, 4 vols. (New York: Harcourt Brace Jovanovich, 1967), 4:77.

3. Frederick W. Maitland quotes Virginia Woolf's comments in *The Life and Letters of Leslie Stephen* (London: Duckworth, 1906), p. 474.

4. The manuscript with Leslie Stephen's comment is in Manuscripts, Archives, and Special Collections, Washington State University Libraries, Pullman, Washington.

5. More recently, Anthony d'Offay proposed a similar publication, or else a new story, by Angelica Garnett, written to correspond with some of the drawings. Deciding against both alternatives, he dismantled the casually assembled volume and in 1984 sold seven of the drawings to five separate individuals. Manuscripts, Archives, and Special Collections of the Washington State University Libraries purchased the typescript of "Emlycaunt" Vanessa used as well as nine of her drawings in 1986. The remainder, so far as we know, are still at the d'Offay Gallery in London.

6. A good collection of representations of Julia Stephen is in the National Portrait Gallery Archives in London, although duplicates and variations of some of the Cameron photographs are scattered far and wide. Many of the photographs have been reproduced in books on photography and on Cameron. One is *Victorian Photographs of Famous Men and Fair Women by Julia Margaret Cameron*, edited by Tristram Powell (Boston: David R. Godine, 1973). The volume, first published in 1926, contains introductions by Virginia Woolf and Roger Fry. A *Victorian Album: Julia Margaret Cameron and Her Circle* (New York: Da Capo, 1975) contains over a dozen of the photographs of Julia taken by her aunt in the mid-1860s.

7. The painting currently is in the Brighton Royal Pavilion Art Gallery. Among

257

the other representations of Julia Stephen as a girl are a sketch by G. F. Watts, reproduced in Vol. III of M. S. Watts' *George Frederick Watts: The Annals of an Artist's Life*, 3 vols. (New York: George H. Doran; London: Hodder and Stoughton, n. d.), and the marble head by Marochetti in the garden at Charleston farmhouse, Sussex, where Vanessa Bell lived.

       8. Julia Stephen is identified as the model by Penelope Fitzgerald, who incorrectly dates the painting as 1874, in *Edward Burne-Jones: A Biography* (London: Michael Joseph, 1975), p. 179, and in *The Paintings, Graphic and Decorative Work of Sir Edward Burne-Jones 1833–98* (The Arts Council of Great Britain, 1975), p. 54. For a perceptive discussion of the painting see Julia Cartwright, "Sir Edward Burne-Jones, Bart.," *Art Annuals* (1894–99), p. 21.

       9. Quoted in Leslie Stephen, *The Mausoleum Book*, ed. Alan Bell (Oxford: Clarendon, 1977), p. 35.

       10. William Rothenstein, *Men and Memories: Recollections 1872–1938*, ed. Mary Lago (Columbia: University of Missouri Press, 1978), p. 60. In the first volume of the three-volume, unedited edition (London: Faber and Faber, 1931, 1932, 1939), Rothenstein recalls finding the drawing thirty-five years later: "Although it did but scant justice to Mrs. Stephen's great charm and rare beauty, it was not quite so bad, perhaps, as they thought it" (I, 98). The sketch, in fact, is Plate I in *The Portrait Drawings of William Rothenstein 1889–1925* (London: Chapman and Hall, 1926), a volume that also includes a drawing of Sir Leslie Stephen done on his death bed in 1903 at the request of Trinity Hall, Cambridge. See volume 2 of the three-volume edition of *Men and Memories*, p. 53.

       11. *The Letters of Virginia Woolf*, ed. Nigel Nicolson and Joanne Trautmann, 6 vols. (New York: Harcourt Brace Jovanovich, 1975–80), 3:7. The National Portrait Gallery dates the Rothenstein drawing of Leslie Stephen reproduced in this edition also as c. 1903.

       12. Stella Duckworth's album is in the Berg Collection of the New York Public Library. The album also contains a photograph of Julia Stephen reading with Vanessa, Virginia, Thoby, and Adrian, reproduced in Lyndall Gordon's *Virginia Woolf: A Writer's Life* (New York: Norton, 1984).

The Elusive Julia Stephen

       1. Among the ever increasing sources of information on the Victorian woman are Martha Vicinus' two editions of essays, *Suffer and Be Still: Women in the Victorian Age* and *A Widening Sphere: Changing Roles of Victorian Women* (Bloomington: Indiana University Press, 1972, 1977); Janet Murray's collection, *Strong Minded Women and Other Lost Voices from Nineteenth-Century England* (New York: Pantheon, 1982); and Joan N. Burstyn's *Victorian Education and the Ideal of Womanhood* (Totowa, N.J.: Barnes and Noble; London: Croom Helm, 1980).

       2. Virginia Woolf, *To the Lighthouse* (New York: Harcourt Brace Jovanovich, 1976). All references will be abbreviated TTL and documented in the text.

       3. For reference to an additional publication, see note 1 under "Editorial Note," above. *Notes from Sick Rooms* was originally published by Smith Elder in 1883.

       4. There seems to have been some plan to publish the stories. See Alex Zwerdling, "Julia Stephen, Mrs. Ramsay, and the Sense of Vocation," *Virginia Woolf Miscellany* 22 (Spring 1984), 4. In *Virginia Woolf and the Real World* (Berkeley: University of California Press, 1986) Zwerdling cites his source as "two of Leslie Stephen's letters to Julia (5 February and 18 July 1885)" in which "he refers to negotiations with Routledge—ultimately unsuccessful—for publishing 'our little work'" (pp. 190, 342 n. 15; John Bicknell first found this reference).

5. In addition to her stories and essays, much of the correspondence between Julia and Leslie has survived. Portions of it will be published in *Selected Letters of Leslie Stephen* (London: Macmillan) edited by John Bicknell. Evelyn Haller is at work on an article about Julia Stephen's letters to the biographer, Sidney Lee. Alan Bell has edited *Sir Leslie Stephen's Mausoleum Book* (Oxford: Clarendon, 1977). All references to the latter are abbreviated MB and documented in the text.

6. Both memoirs have been published in *Moments of Being: Unpublished Autobiographical Writings* and *Moments of Being*, 2nd ed., edited by Jeanne Schulkind (New York: Harcourt Brace Jovanovich, 1976, 1985). The second edition adds a recently discovered section to "A Sketch of the Past," one of the memoirs relevant to this study. Therefore all references, abbreviated MOB and documented in the text, are to that edition. Elements of Julia Stephen appear in other of Woolf's characters as well, and some of Mrs. Ramsay's traits do not correspond to Woolf's mother's. Julia Stephen often is more professional in attitude than is Mrs. Ramsay, as Alex Zwerdling points out in *Virginia Woolf . . .* , pp. 187–91. When *To the Lighthouse* appeared, Vanessa Bell wrote to her sister, "you have given a portrait of mother which is more like her to me than anything I could ever have conceived as possible. . . . You have made one feel the extraordinary beauty of her character" (L III 572). Woolf was pleased (D III 35) but expressed some amazement that a child could understand her or see her objectively. Vanessa, Woolf suspects, also formed part of the characterization of Mrs. Ramsay (L III 383).

Woolf also refers to her mother in her diaries and letters. References to *The Diary of Virginia Woolf*, ed. Anne Olivier Bell, 5 vols. (New York: Harcourt Brace Jovanovich, 1974, 1978, 1980, 1982, 1984) and to *The Letters of Virginia Woolf*, ed. Nigel Nicolson and Joanne Trautmann, 6 vols. (New York: Harcourt Brace Jovanovich, 1975, 1976, 1977, 1978, 1979, 1980) are abbreviated D and L respectively and documented in the text.

7. Many of these books are in Manuscripts, Archives, and Special Collections of the Washington State University Libraries, Pullman, Washington. In subsequent notes, the abbreviation is MASC, WSU.

8. See pages xvii–xxii for a chronological summary of these facts and the bibliography for the biographies which provide partial outlines of Julia Stephen's life. These sources are not always complete or consistent. My concern is to present enough information to "place" Julia Stephen's writings for her new, twentieth-century readers.

9. Virginia Woolf, *A Room of One's Own* (New York: Harcourt Brace Jovanovich, 1957; first published, 1929), p. 79.

10. See, for example, Jane Marcus, "Liberty, Sorority, Misogyny," in *The Representation of Women in Fiction*, ed. Carolyn Heilbrun and Margaret Higonnet (Baltimore and London: The Johns Hopkins University Press, 1983), pp. 60–97. See also Marcus' "Virginia Woolf and Her Violin: Mothering, Madness and Music"; Martine Stemerick, "Virginia Woolf and Julia Stephen: The Distaff Side of History"; and Evelyn Haller, "The Anti-Madonna in the Work and Thought of Virginia Woolf," all three in *Virginia Woolf: Centennial Essays*, ed. Elaine K. Ginsberg and Laura Moss Gottlieb (Troy, N.Y.: Whitston, 1983), pp. 27–49, 52–80, 93–109. Martine Stemerick's dissertation, "From Stephen to Woolf: Victorian Family and Modern Rebellion" (University of Texas at Austin, 1982) is also, I understand, relevant. Currently, however, it is unavailable from University Microfilms. Finally, see Sara Ruddick, "Learning to Live with the Angel in the House," *Women's Studies* 4 (1977), pp. 181–200.

11. See, for example, Virginia R. Hyman,. "Reflections in the Looking Glass: Leslie Stephen and Virginia Woolf," *Journal of Modern Literature* 10, 2 (June 1983), 197–216; S. P. Rosenbaum, "An Educated Man's Daughter: Leslie Stephen, Virginia Woolf and the Bloomsbury Group," in *Virginia Woolf: New Critical Essays*, ed. Patricia Clements and Isobel Grundy (London: Vision;

New York: Barnes and Noble, 1983), pp. 32–56; and Katherine C. Hill, "Virginia Woolf and Leslie Stephen: History and Literary Revolution," *PMLA* 96 (1981): 351–62.

12. Vanessa Bell, *Notes on Virginia's Childhood*, ed. Richard F. Shaubeck, Jr. (New York: Frank Hallman, 1974). Unpaginated.

13. Virginia Woolf, *To the Lighthouse: The Original Holograph Draft*, ed. Susan Dick (Toronto: University of Toronto Press, 1982), p. 104. Virginia Woolf, it is appropriate to note, wrote a children's story herself, published in *TLS* in 1965, in 1966 as "Nurse Lugton's Golden Thimble" by the Hogarth Press, and as "Nurse Lugton's Curtain" in *The Complete Shorter Fiction of Virginia Woolf*, ed. Susan Dick (London: Hogarth, 1985), pp. 154–55. In the story, as Nurse Lugton snores, the animals in the fabric she was sewing into a curtain come to life and gambol about.

14. Quentin Bell, *Virginia Woolf: A Biography*, 2 vols. (New York: Harcourt Brace Jovanovich, 1972), 1:17.

15. Anne Thackeray Ritchie, *Five Old Friends and a Young Prince* (London: Smith, Elder and Co., 1876), includes contemporary versions of "The Sleeping Beauty in the Wood," "Cinderella," "Beauty and the Beast," "Little Red Riding Hood," and "Jack the Giant Killer." The book is in MASC, WSU.

Julia Stephen kept a lot of Herbert Duckworth's books as well, and Virginia Woolf eventually inherited them through her father. Like Jacob's in *Jacob's Room*, they are various, reflecting the education and interests of "the perfect type of public school man" (MB 35): Virgil and Ovid, Addison and Steele, Kipling, Cowley, Collins, Herrick, Thomas Moore, a book on English universities, one on the Highlands, a New Testament, a novel by Barrie, and a travel book by Kinglake.

16. Anne Thackeray Ritchie's *Miss Angel and Fulham Lawn* is volume 8 of *The Works of Miss Thackeray* (London: Smith, Elder, 1876). Winifred Gérin, in *Anne Thackeray Ritchie: A Biography* (Oxford: Oxford University Press, 1981), pp. 174–76, describes the origins of *Miss Angel* (1875) but sheds no definite light on Julia Stephen's involvement with it. Gérin does note, however, that "there are passages in the book, treating of Angelica's heartbreak and of the consolation she sought and found in her art alone, that make revealing reading when seen in the context of Anne Thackeray's own life at the time" when her love for Richmond Ritchie seemed impossible (p. 175). Perhaps Julia's own bereavement and consolations also helped Anne Thackeray understand Angelica Kauffmann's. Julia also received from Anny her essays on Mrs. Barbauld, Miss Edgeworth, Mrs. Opie, and Miss Austen collected into *A Book of Sibyls* (London: Smith Elder, 1883), now in MASC, WSU. The book, in part a study of influences, forecasts Virginia Woolf's observations that women writers look back to their female predecessors.

17. Gérin, p. 177. See Leslie Stephen's descriptions of Anny in MB 12–15, 23–25.

18. Gérin, p. 187.

19. Sir Aubrey DeVere, *Mary Tudor: An Historical Drama in Two Parts and Sonnets* (London: Basil Montagu Pickering, 1875), p. 374. In MASC, WSU. Julia Margaret Cameron photographed DeVere in 1865 and included his portrait in an album she gave to her sister Maria Jackson, Julia's mother. The album also contains fourteen photographs of Julia Stephen. See *A Victorian Album: Julia Margaret Cameron and Her Circle*, ed. Graham Ovenden (New York: Da Capo, 1975).

20. Isa Blagdon, *Poems* (Edinburgh: William Blackwood, 1873). In MASC, WSU.

21. Blagdon, pp. 110–11.

22. Coventry Patmore, *Amelia, Tamerton Church-Tower, etc. with Prefatory Study on English Metrical Law* (London: George Bell, 1878), pp. 206–7. In MASC, WSU.

23. Frederick William Maitland, *The Life and Letters of Leslie Stephen* (London: Duckworth, 1906), p. 313.

24. Maitland, p. 314. The poem Leslie Stephen criticizes is in Patmore's *The Unknown Eros* (1877). My thanks to John Bicknell for this information.

25. Virginia Woolf also had a copy of *The Poetry of Pathos and Delight: From the Works of Coventry Patmore* (1896) inscribed "L. M. Rudd from V. S. Maxwell" but marked with her little square bookplate containing the initials, AVS, and the date, 1905. In MASC, WSU.

26. James Russell Lowell to Mrs. Leslie Stephen; August 11, 1889; in *Letters of James Russell Lowell*, ed. Charles Eliot Norton, 2 vols. (New York: Harper, 1894), 2:375. The originals of Lowell's letters to Julia Stephen are in the Berg Collection, New York Public Library.

27. James Russell Lowell to Mrs. Leslie Stephen; February 20, 1888; in *Letters of James Russell Lowell*, 2:348.

28. Martin Duberman, *James Russell Lowell* (Boston: Houghton Mifflin, 1966), pp. 350–51.

29. James Russell Lowell, *My Study Windows* (Boston: Houghton Mifflin, 1882) includes "On a Certain Condescension in Foreigners" in which Lowell declares that "It will take England a great while to get over her airs of patronage toward us, or even passably to conceal them." Julia seems to have been an exception in his mind. Lowell also inscribed copies for her of *Among My Books* and *Among My Books: Second Series* (Boston: Houghton Mifflin, 1882), essays mostly on British literary figures. His *Heartsease and Rue* (Boston: Houghton Mifflin, 1888), containing poems under the headings of Friendship, Sentiment, Fancy, Humor and Satire, and Epigrams, is inscribed "To Julia Stephen with the author's love." All of these books are in MASC, WSU.

30. Henry James to Grace Norton; January 4, 1879; in *Henry James: Letters*, ed. Leon Edel, 4 vols. (Cambridge: Harvard University Press, 1974, 1975, 1980, 1984), 2:209.

31. Henry James to Alice James; February 17, 1878; in *Henry James: Letters*, 2:157.

32. Lowell's "Verses Intended to go with a Posset Dish to My Dear Little God-Daughter, 1882" was copied by Leslie Stephen inside the front of Volume 1 of *Letters of James Russell Lowell*, ed. Charles Eliot Norton (London: Osgood, McIlvaine, 1894). Leslie also transcribed the poem into another copy of the same book for Gerald Duckworth. Both copies are in MASC, WSU. The poem is reprinted in Maitland, *The Life and Letters of Leslie Stephen*, pp. 318–19.

Leonard Woolf was less impressed by the Pattle beauty in general and by his late mother-in-law's in particular. Looking at the Cameron photographs, he admitted that she and her ancestors were "extraordinarily beautiful, but it was a beauty which was or tended to become rather insipid. It was, I think, too feminine, and not sufficiently female, and there was about it something which was even slightly irritating." He was glad Virginia and Vanessa combined "the more masculine Stephen good looks" with the beauty inherited from their mother. *Sowing: An Autobiography of the Years 1880 to 1904* (New York: Harcourt Brace Jovanovich, 1960), p. 185.

33. George Meredith to Vanessa Bell; February 23, 1904; in *The Letters of George Meredith*, ed. C. L. Cline, 3 vols. (Oxford: Clarendon, 1970), 3:1491.

34. George Meredith, *Diana of the Crossways* (London: Chapman and Hall, 1885). In MASC, WSU.

35. George Meredith to Julia Stephen, *The Letters of George Meredith*, 2:743.

36. George Meredith to Julia Stephen, *The Letters of George Meredith*, 2:964. Beatrice Webb, best known as a Fabian socialist, also signed the appeal. In *My Apprenticeship* (New York: Longmans, 1926), however, she admits that she made a "false step . . . thereby arousing the hostility of ardent women brain-workers, and, in the eyes of the general public, undermining my

reputation as an impartial investigator of women's questions." The main cause of her antifeminism at that time, she says, was "the fact that I had never myself suffered the disabilities assumed to arise from my sex" (pp. 341–43). In quite different ways, neither had Julia Stephen. Neither had Mrs. Humphry Ward who, although relatively independent in her thinking and active in public affairs, also supported the petition.

In 1886 Henry James, perhaps thinking he would have a sympathetic reader, inscribed a copy of *The Bostonians* to Julia Stephen. According to Sotheby's sale listing of April 27–28, 1970, Virginia Woolf inherited the book, but it is not among those at the Harry Ransom Humanities Research Center, University of Texas, Austin, or at MASC, WSU.

37. Susan Merrill Squier, *Virginia Woolf and London: The Sexual Politics of the City* (Chapel Hill: University of North Carolina Press, 1985), pp. 27–28.

38. Quentin Bell, "Introduction" to *The Diary of Virginia Woolf*, vol. 1 (1915–19), ed. Anne Olivier Bell (New York: Harcourt Brace Jovanovich, 1977), p. xix. Compare Virginia Woolf's description, MOB, pp. 116–19.

39. Vanessa Bell, *Notes on Virginia's Childhood*, unpaginated.

40. Quentin Bell, *Virginia Woolf*, 1:26.

41. Annan, *Leslie Stephen*, pp. 110f. See also Note 11, above.

42. Constance Hunting, "Introduction" to Mrs. Leslie Stephen's *Notes from Sick Rooms* (Orono, Me.: Puckerbrush, 1980), p. 9. All references are abbreviated NFSR and documented in the text. Cf. MOB, p. 131.

43. Marcus, "Virginia Woolf and Her Violin," p. 29.

44. Henry James to Theodora Sedgwick; March 30, 1895; *Henry James: Letters*, 4:8.

Stories for Children

1. Jakob Ludwig Karl Grimm (1785–1863) and Wilhelm Karl Grimm (1786–1859) collected and wrote down traditional tales in Germany between 1812 and 1818. The first English translation of *Kinder- und Hausmärchen* was published by C. Baldwyn in 1823, translated by Edgar Taylor as *German Popular Tales* and illustrated by George Cruikshank. Virginia Woolf has "Mrs. Ramsay" read a Grimm fairytale to James in *To the Lighthouse* (1927); see Diane Gillespie's general Introduction to the present volume.

2. Hans Christian Andersen (1805–75): his *Eventyr og Historier* [*Fairy Tales*], first published in 1835, was translated into English in 1846 by Mary Howitt, Caroline Peachey, and Charles Boner in separate editions.

3. Harriet Martineau (1802–76): the Playfellow series included *The Settlers at Home*, *The Peasant and the Prince*, *Feats on the Fiord*, and *The Crofton Boys*. "Published in 1841 by this social reformer and political economist, the books in the series are today considered to be among the first real adventure stories written for children." (Elva S. Smith, *The History of Children's Literature*, rev. and enl. by Margaret Hodges and Susan Steinfirst [Chicago: American Library Association, 1980; hereafter cited as "Smith"], p. 154.) Subjects included school, travel, and history.

4. Captain Frederick Marryat (1792–1848): his first and most popular tale for children was *Masterman Ready* (1841). Others include *The Settlers in Canada* (1844), *The Mission, or, Scenes in Africa* (1845) and *The Children of the New Forest* (1847). *The Mission* leans heavily on animal description. See also Virginia Woolf's memorial essay "The Captain's Death Bed" (1935), which discusses *Jacob Faithful* and *Peter Simple*, two of Marryat's adventure tales for adults.

5. Lewis Carroll, pseud. of Charles Lutwidge Dodgson (1832–98): most famous as the author of *Alice's Adventures in Wonderland* (1865) and *Through the Looking-Glass, and What Alice Found There* (1872), Carroll also wrote the nonsense epic *The Hunting of the Snark* (1876) and another entertaining piece of story literature, *Sylvie and Bruno* (1889, 1893), as well as poems and puzzle-pieces for children. For a brief but spirited defense of the Alice books as "a stepping-off place" for children's books published thereafter, see Smith, p. 164. F. J. Harvey Darton, *Children's Books in England*, 3rd edition, rev. by Brian Alderson (Cambridge: Cambridge University Press, 1982; hereafter cited as "Darton"), p. 260, calls *Wonderland* "the spiritual volcano of children's books, . . . a revolution in its sphere." Virginia Woolf's essay "Lewis Carroll" (1939) is biographical.

6. Carroll's dates place him halfway, chronologically, between Julia's mother (whose famous sister, Julia Margaret Cameron, practiced photography at the same time as Carroll, though with more skill) and Julia herself. Since the books that Julia read as a child and adolescent were not retained by Leslie Stephen, probably because unavailable to him, it is impossible to precisely document that reading. Deductions about the subject in this essay are based on likelihood and facts concerning the pervasive cultural milieu of the nineteenth century.

7. The word "one" is used deliberately: as with Carroll's books, Julia Stephen's stories can be enjoyed by adults as well as children.

8. Though an American exemplum, the heroine of *Elsie Dinsmore* (1867) by Martha Finlay (1828–1902), and a score of other books with Elsie at the center, is probably the most famous of the lachrymose, pious female child-figures found in Victorian literature. I am not suggesting that Finlay directly "influenced" Julia Stephen but that this type of character rose naturally from the autocratic, male-dominated domestic scene as perceived in the late 1800s. Elsie is simply an extreme.

9. Rudyard Kipling (1865–1936); Kenneth Grahame (1859–1931); Beatrix Potter (1866–1943); Hugh Lofting (1886–1947).

10. "Mrs. Molesworth" (1842–1921).

11. The Zoological Gardens founded in 1828 at Regent's Park was the home of Jumbo, one of the largest African elephants in the world. When sold in 1882 to P. T. Barnum for 2,000 pounds, he was the darling of Britain. The other elephant, Alice, mentioned in "Emlycaunt," though popularly supposed to be Jumbo's "mate," never mated with him. (Historian Ann Saunders calls him "moody.") Not long after reaching America, Jumbo collided with a train and was killed; the train was also hurt. (See Ann Saunders, *Regent's Park* [N.Y.: Augustus M. Kelley, 1969], p. 156; and E. V. Lucas, *A Wanderer in London* [N.Y.: Macmillan, 1907], pp. 242–44.)

12. See Alex Zwerdling, *Virginia Woolf and the Real World* (Berkeley: University of California Press, 1986), pp. 190, 342. John Bicknell located the letters.

13. E.g., *Chatterbox*, 1866–1948; *The Children's Prize*, 1863–1931; *The Leisure Hour*, 1852–1905; *Little Folks*, 1871–1933; *Young Folks' Paper*, 1871–97. (See Darton, passim.)

14. As indicated by the text, it is not my own purpose to affix a label to each story beforehand, but examples personally arrived at include: "buoyant"–"Emlycaunt"; "Gothic"–"The Black Cat or the Grey Parrot"; "sociable"–"Dinner at Baron Bruin's."

Essays for Adults

1. Noel Annan, *Leslie Stephen: The Godless Victorian* (New York: Random House, 1984), p. 110. All subsequent references are abbreviated LS and documented in the text.

2. Joan N. Burstyn, *Victorian Education and the Ideal of Womanhood* (London: Croom

Helm; Totowa, N.J.: Barnes and Noble, 1980), pp. 21, 27. All subsequent references are abbreviated VE and documented in the text.

3. Walter Houghton, *The Victorian Frame of Mind, 1830–1870* (New Haven: Yale University Press, 1964), p. 58.

4. Noel Annan identifies an essay entitled "Women and Scepticism," *Fraser's Magazine* 68 (December 1863), 679–99, as Leslie Stephen's. See *Leslie Stephen*, p. 370. Annan provides a detailed consideration of Stephen's views in the chapter "Agnosticism," pp. 235–66. John Bicknell, however, identifies the "Women and Scepticism" essay as James Fitzjames Stephen's; so does James A. Colaiaco, *James Fitzjames Stephen and the Crisis of Victorian Thought* (London: Macmillan, 1983), pp. 183–84, 247. Both Bicknell and Colaiaco follow Leslie Stephen's attribution in his biography of his brother. All subsequent references to "Women and Scepticism" are abbreviated WS and documented in the text.

5. Bertha Lathbury, "Agnosticism and Women," *Nineteenth Century* 7 (April 1880), 619–27. All subsequent references will be abbreviated AW and documented in the text.

6. For a record of independent thinking on religious matters, see Beatrice Webb, *My Apprenticeship* (New York: Longmans, 1926), chapter 2, "In Search of a Creed." Later in her account, Webb worries that agnosticism is too rational, that it does not appeal sufficiently to the emotional side of her nature (pp. 98, 100).

7. Richard Altick, *Victorian People and Ideas* (New York: W. W. Norton, 1973), pp. 168–69.

8. Ibid., pp. 201–2.

9. See Annan's chapter "The Moral Society," pp. 267–99, for a description of Leslie Stephen's combination of ethics with Darwinian evolutionary theory and John Stuart Mill's Utilitarianism.

10. Leslie Stephen, "An Agnostic's Apology" (1876), reprinted in *Leslie Stephen: Selected Writings in British Intellectual History*, ed. Noel Annan (Chicago and London: University of Chicago Press, 1979), p. 252.

11. F. W. Maitland, *The Life and Letters of Leslie Stephen* (London: Duckworth, 1906), pp. 144–45. See also Annan, pp. 264–65. It would be instructive to compare in detail Leslie and Julia Stephen's views of morality along the lines suggested by Carol Gilligan's book, *In a Different Voice: Psychological Theory and Women's Development* (Cambridge: Harvard University Press, 1982). Gilligan shows how women's moral development differs from men's: women move, if they develop at all, from a concern for others to more assertion of their own rights and more recognition of their own responsibilities; if men develop they move from declarations of independence to recognition of the value of relationships with others. My thanks to Evelyn Haller for calling this book to my attention.

12. Virginia Woolf, *The Voyage Out* (London: Penguin, 1970; first published by Hogarth in 1915), pp. 29, 22–23. Helen Ambrose is reading the philosopher G. E. Moore. See J. K. Johnstone, *The Bloomsbury Group: A Study of E. M. Forster, Lytton Strachey, Virginia Woolf, and Their Circle* (New York: Noonday, 1963), p. 20.

13. Virginia Woolf, *Three Guineas* (New York: Harcourt Brace Jovanovich, 1966), p. 14.

14. Theresa M. McBride, *The Domestic Revolution: The Modernisation of Household Service in England and France 1820–1920* (New York: Holmes and Meier, 1976), p. 19. All subsequent references are abbreviated DR and documented in the text.

15. Frank Dawes, *Not in Front of the Servants: A True Portrait of English Upstairs/Downstairs Life* (New York: Taplinger, 1974), p. 9. All subsequent references are abbreviated NFS and documented in the text.

16. McBride, p. 16; Pamela Horn, *The Rise and Fall of the Victorian Servant* (Dublin: Gill and Macmillan; New York: St. Martin's, 1975), p. 109. All subsequent references are abbreviated RFVS and documented in the text.

17. Virginia Woolf, "Great Men's Houses," *The London Scene: Five Essays by Virginia Woolf* (New York: Frank Hallman, 1975), p. 26. All subsequent references will be abbreviated GMH and documented in the text.

18. "Housekeeping," *Cornhill Magazine* 29 (1874): 69–77, is identified as Leslie Stephen's by S. O. A. Ullmann in "A Checklist of Works by Leslie Stephen," *Men, Books, and Mountains: Essays by Leslie Stephen*, ed. S. O. A. Ullmann (Westport, Conn.: Greenwood, 1956), p. 240. All subsequent references are abbreviated H and documented in the text.

19. Anne Thackeray Ritchie, "Maids-of-all-Work and Blue Books," *Cornhill Magazine* 30 (1874): 281–96. All subsequent references are abbreviated MBB and documented in the text.

20. Caroline E. Stephen, "Mistresses and Servants," *Nineteenth Century* 6 (1879): 1051. All subsequent references are abbreviated MS and documented in the text.

21. Quentin Bell, *Virginia Woolf: A Biography*, 2 vols. (New York: Harcourt Brace Jovanovich, 1972), 1:31.

22. Leslie Stephen, *Mausoleum Book*, ed. Alan Bell (Oxford: Clarendon, 1977), p. 81.

23. Quentin Bell, 1:34. See Virginia Woolf, "A Sketch of the Past," *Moments of Being*, 2nd edition, ed. Jeanne Schulkind (New York: Harcourt Brace Jovanovich, 1985), pp. 132–33. All subsequent references are abbreviated MOB and documented in the text. George Spater and Ian Parsons reproduce a snapshot of Sophie Farrell in *A Marriage of True Minds: An Intimate Portrait of Leonard and Virginia Woolf* (New York: Harcourt Brace Jovanovich, 1977), p. 17.

24. Quentin Bell, 1:63.

25. Virginia Woolf, *To the Lighthouse* (New York: Harcourt Brace Jovanovich, 1955; first published 1927), p. 62. All subsequent references will be abbreviated TTL and documented in the text.

26. Vanessa Bell, "Life at Hyde Park Gate 1897–1904," unpublished memoir which I saw through the kindness of Angelica Garnett.

27. Virginia Woolf, *To the Lighthouse: The Original Holograph Draft*, ed. Susan Dick (Toronto and Buffalo: University of Toronto Press, 1982), p. 129. All subsequent references are abbreviated TTLHD and documented in the text.

28. E. L. L., "On the Side of the Maids," *Cornhill Magazine* 29 (1874): 298. All subsequent references are abbreviated ELL and documented in the text. John Bicknell (letter, February 12, 1987) identifies E. L. L. as Eliza Lynn Linton.

29. A Suffering Mistress, "On the Side of the Mistresses," *Cornhill Magazine* 29 (1874): 459–60. All subsequent references are abbreviated ASM and documented in the text.

30. Elizabeth Alicia M. Lewis, "A Reformation of Domestic Service," *Nineteenth Century* 33 (January 1893): 135.

31. George Layard, "The Doom of the Domestic Cook," *Nineteenth Century* 33 (February 1893): 310. See Clementina Black's *A New Way of Housekeeping* (London: W. Collins, 1918) for a detailed discussion not only of a "culinary depot" but also of a full household management center. "Home should be the place of family companionship, of intercourse, rest, and hobbies," she says, "not the workshop of its women" (p. 98).

32. Layard, 317.

33. Clementina Black, "The Dislike to Domestic Service," *Nineteenth Century* 33 (March

1893): 454–55. All subsequent references are abbreviated DDS and documented in the text. Black uses Fanny Burney's experiences as an attendant upon Queen Charlotte to prove the domestic servant's subservience. Burney's *Diary* reveals that "the waiting maid . . . regarded her position as one of distinction, and professed an almost religious regard for her mistress. Yet," Black adds, "is there any reader of her vivid narrative to whom the position does not seem intolerable?" (454). In another brief attempt to begin her own essay on this subject, not included in this edition, Julia Stephen also uses Burney as an example of "absurd humility" in her attitude towards her mistress, but Stephen does so only to register her doubt that "any servant of the present day is likely to suffer from subservience." Probably Julia Stephen is not just echoing Black's reference to Burney. She certainly had access to her husband's seven volumes of the *Diary and Letters of Madam d'Arblay*, edited by Burney's niece and published by Hurst and Blackett in 1854, as well as his five volumes of *Cecilia, or Memoirs of an Heiress*, 5th edition, 1786. Leslie Stephen wrote at the bottom of the page describing a scene in which Cecilia is polite and deferential to Mrs. Delvile, "One begins to understand how Miss Burney could be a ladies maid to the Queen." Virginia Woolf inherited these books from her father and they are now in Manuscripts, Archives, and Special Collections, Washington State University Libraries. Yet Burney also wrote, "I have always and uniformly had a horror of a life of attendance and dependence," initially found being summoned by a bell a "mortifying mark of servitude," and disliked being ordered about by Mrs. Schwellenberg, the Queen's old servant. See *The Famous Miss Burney: The Diaries and Letters of Fanny Burney*, ed. Barbara G. Schrank and David J. Supino (New York: Minerva, 1976), pp. 160–67, 171, 175.

[Agnostic Women]

1. Bertha Lathbury, "Agnosticism and Women," *Nineteenth Century* 7 (April 1880), 619–27. Both Mrs. Lathbury and Julia Stephen capitalize "Agnosticism" in all its forms throughout.

2. Julia Stephen has combined two Biblical passages here. In the King James version they read, "Whatsoever thy hand findeth to do, do it with thy might; for there is no work, nor device, nor knowledge, nor wisdom, in the grave, whither thou goest" (Ecclesiastes 9:10) and "I must work the works of him that sent me, while it is day; the night cometh, when no man can work" (John 9:4).

3. The Biblical allusion is to a refrain in the Book of Mark: "Where their worm dieth not, and the fire is not quenched" (Mark 9:44, 46, 48). John Bunyan's comment is in "The Life and Death of Mr. Badman: Presented to the World in A Familiar Dialogue Between Mr. Wiseman and Mr. Attentive" (1666) (London: Dent, and N.Y.: Dutton, 1963), p. 296. Mr. Wiseman says, "I must confess I am no admirer of sick-bed repentance, for I think verily it is seldom good for anything."

4. To work is to pray.

5. "Every tree that bringeth not forth good fruit is hewn down, and cast into the fire. Wherefore by their fruits ye shall know them. Not every one that saith unto me, Lord, Lord, shall enter into the Kingdom of heaven; but he that doeth the will of my Father which is in heaven" (Matthew 7:19–21).

[The Servant Question]

1. In an article in *Nineteenth Century* 33 (March 1893), 454–56, Clementina Black makes several of the points that Julia Stephen takes up. Black, in turn, responds to two previous

articles in the same periodical: Elizabeth Alicia M. Lewis, "A Reformation of Domestic Service," 33 (January 1893), 127–38, and George Somes Layard, "The Doom of the Domestic Cook," 33 (February 1893), 309–19.

2. Clementina Black uses Fanny Burney's experiences as attendant upon Queen Charlotte as proof. See note 33 under "Essays for Adults," above.

3. I have reconstructed the two sentences at the beginning of this paragraph from a pastiche of partly canceled, partly retained sentences and phrases by choosing the legible over the illegible.

SELECTED BIBLIOGRAPHY

Annan, Noel. *Leslie Stephen: The Godless Victorian*. New York: Random House, 1984.

Bell, Alan. "Introduction." *Sir Leslie Stephen's Mausoleum Book*. Ed. Alan Bell, ix–xxxiii. Oxford: Clarendon, 1977.

Bell, Quentin. *Virginia Woolf: A Biography*. 2 vols. New York: Harcourt Brace Jovanovich, 1972.

Bell, Vanessa. *Notes on Virginia's Childhood*. Ed. Richard F. Shaubeck, Jr. New York: Frank Hallman, 1974.

Boyd, Elizabeth French. *Bloomsbury Heritage: Their Mothers and Their Aunts*. London: Hamish Hamilton, 1976.

Duberman, Martin. *James Russell Lowell*. Boston: Houghton Mifflin, 1966.

Gérin, Winifred. *Anne Thackeray Ritchie: A Biography*. Oxford: Oxford University Press, 1981.

Gordon, Lyndall. *Virginia Woolf: A Writer's Life*. New York and London: Norton, 1984.

Haller, Evelyn. "The Anti-Madonna in the Work and Thought of Virginia Woolf." In *Virginia Woolf: Centennial Essays*. Ed. Elaine K. Ginsberg and Laura Moss Gottlieb, 93–109. Troy, N.Y.: Whitston, 1983.

Hunting, Constance. "Introduction." Mrs. Leslie Stephen. *Notes from Sickrooms*. Ed. Constance Hunting, 5–12. Orono, Me.: Puckerbrush Press, 1980.

James, Henry. *Henry James: Letters*. Ed. Leon Edel. Cambridge: Harvard University Press, 1975, 1984. Vols. 2 and 4.

Kushen, Betty. "The Failure of Symbiosis: 'I run to a book as a child to its mother.'" *Virginia Woolf and the Nature of Communion*, 9–44. West Orange, N.J.: Raynor, 1983.

Lilienfeld, Jane. "'The Deceptiveness of Beauty': Mother Love and Mother Hate in *To the Lighthouse*." *Twentieth Century Literature* 23, 3 (October 1977): 345–76.

269

Love, Jean O. *Virginia Woolf: Sources of Madness and Art.* Berkeley: University of California Press, 1977.

Lowell, James Russell. *Letters of James Russell Lowell.* Ed. Charles Eliot Norton. New York: Harper, 1894. Vol. 2.

Maitland, Frederick William. *The Life and Letters of Leslie Stephen.* London: Duckworth, 1906.

Marcus, Jane. "Liberty, Sorority, Misogyny." In *The Representation of Women in Fiction.* Ed. Carolyn Heilbrun and Margaret Higonnet, 60–97. Baltimore: Johns Hopkins University Press, 1983.

————. "Virginia Woolf and Her Violin: Mothering, Madness, and Music." In *Virginia Woolf: Centennial Essays.* Ed. Elaine K. Ginsberg and Laura Moss Gottlieb, 27–49. Troy, N.Y.: Whitston, 1983.

Meredith, George. *The Letters of George Meredith.* Ed. C. L. Cline. Oxford: Clarendon, 1970. Vols. 2 and 3.

Ovenden, Graham, ed. *A Victorian Album: Julia Margaret Cameron and Her Circle.* New York: Da Capo, 1975.

Poole, Roger. *The Unknown Virginia Woolf.* Cambridge: Cambridge University Press, 1978.

Rose, Phyllis. *Woman of Letters: A Life of Virginia Woolf.* New York: Oxford University Press, 1978.

Rosenbaum, S. P. *Victorian Bloomsbury, The Early Literary History of the Bloomsbury Group.* Vol. 1. London: Macmillan, 1987.

Rosenman, Ellen Bayuk. *The Invisible Presence: Virginia Woolf and the Mother-Daughter Relationship.* Baton Rouge: Louisiana State University Press, 1986.

Rothenstein, William. *Men and Memories: Recollections, 1872–1938.* Ed. Mary Lago. Columbia: University of Missouri Press, 1978.

Ruddick, Sara. "Learning to Live with the Angel in the House." *Women's Studies* 4 (1977): 181–200.

Spalding, Frances. *Vanessa Bell.* London: Weidenfeld and Nicolson, 1983.

Spilka, Mark. *Virginia Woolf's Quarrel with Grieving.* Lincoln: University of Nebraska Press, 1980.

Squier, Susan Merrill. *Virginia Woolf and London: The Sexual Politics of the City.* Chapel Hill: University of North Carolina Press, 1985.

Stemerick, Martine. *From Clapham to Bloomsbury: Virginia Woolf's Feminist Rebellion.* London: Harvester Press, forthcoming.

————. "From Stephen to Woolf: Victorian Family and Modern Rebellion." Ph.D. Dissertation. University of Texas at Austin, 1982.

————. "Virginia Woolf and Julia Stephen: The Distaff Side of History." In *Virginia Woolf: Centennial Essays.* Ed. Elaine K. Ginsberg and Laura Moss Gottlieb, 51–80. Troy, N.Y.: Whitston, 1983.

Stephen, Leslie. *Mausoleum Book*. Ed. Alan Bell. Oxford: Clarendon, 1977.

––––––. *Selected Letters of Leslie Stephen*. Ed. John Bicknell. London: Macmillan, forthcoming.

Woolf, Virginia. *The Diary of Virginia Woolf*. Ed. Anne Olivier Bell. 5 vols. New York: Harcourt Brace Jovanovich, 1974, 1978, 1980, 1982, 1984.

––––––. *The Letters of Virginia Woolf*. Ed. Nigel Nicolson and Joanne Trautmann. 6 vols. New York: Harcourt Brace Jovanovich 1975, 1976, 1977, 1978, 1979, 1980.

––––––. "Reminiscences" and "A Sketch of the Past." *Moments of Being*. 2nd ed. Ed. Jeanne Schulkind. London: Hogarth, 1985.

––––––. *To the Lighthouse*. New York: Harcourt Brace Jovanovich, 1955.

Woolf, Leonard. *Sowing: An Autobiography of the Years 1880 to 1904*. New York: Harcourt Brace Jovanovich, 1960.

Zwerdling, Alex. "Julia Stephen, Mrs. Ramsay, and the Sense of Vocation." *Virginia Woolf Miscellany* 22 (Spring 1984): 4.

––––––. *Virginia Woolf and the Real World*. Berkeley: University of California Press, 1986.

INDEX